TRAIN MAN

ZERO OPTION

"*Zero Option* delivers . . . [Deutermann] keeps his story moving briskly."

—*Proceedings*

"Exciting, moving . . . a top-notch topical thriller."

—*Publishers Weekly*

"[Deutermann] returns in top form with this gripping tale . . . intensely plausible entertainment."

—*Kirkus Reviews*

SWEEPERS

"An explosive drama . . . Deutermann fans like myself will be thrilled to see that he keeps getting better."

—Nelson DeMille

"Deutermann's inside knowledge of the Navy and Pentagon politics, coupled with his likeable protagonists, make this a gripping new addition to his line of naval mysteries."

—*Publishers Weekly*

"A fine page-turner."

—*Library Journal*

OFFICIAL PRIVILEGE

"A tight story line . . . An attractive combination of murder mystery and naval politics."

—*The New York Times Book Review*

"P.T. Deutermann has become one of our best thriller writers . . . A keenly entertaining, fascinating mystery."

—*Observer* (Florida)

"Superb plotting and characterization are here, as is suspense and a clear awareness of the dangers and dalliances that can thrive in official Washington . . . *Official Privilege* is more than just a whodunit and a Navy story; it is a suspenseful indictment of power politics."

—*Florida Times-Union*

THE EDGE OF HONOR

"One heck of an exciting voyage . . . P.T. Deutermann ships a reader onto the bridge in that special place—where men go down to the sea in ships. He adds a first-rate suspense novel as bargain."

—*Tampa Tribune and Times*

"*The Edge of Honor* is the rare book that addresses the complexities of war at the front and also at home. The author captures the Vietnam period and its confusion perfectly. Particularly interesting—and horrifying—is the culture depicted on the Hood, a real-life ship around which the novel is set."

—*The Baltimore Sun*

"*The Edge of Honor* . . . is headed up the bestseller list."
—*The Atlanta Journal-Constitution*

"Utterly convincing . . . Unlike many technothriller writers, he has as good a grasp of what makes people tick as of what makes a modern warship function. Deutermann's clear mission is to picture Navy life in a depth we have not seen before, and he succeeds brilliantly. His craftsmanship is amazing."

—*The San Diego Union-Tribune*

ST. MARTIN'S PAPERBACKS TITLES
BY P. T. DEUTERMANN

Hunting Season

Train Man

Zero Option

Sweepers

Official Privilege

The Edge of Honor

Scorpion in the Sea

DARKSIDE

P. T. Deutermann

St. Martin's Paperbacks

DARKSIDE

Copyright © 2002 by P. T. Deutermann.
Excerpt from *The Firefly* copyright © 2003 by P. T. Deutermann.

Cover photo © Robert Karpa/Masterfile

Library of Congress Catalog Card Number: 2002068393

ISBN: 0-312-98636-X

Printed in the United States of America

St. Martin's Press hardcover edition / December 2002
St. Martin's Paperbacks edition / October 2003

St. Martin's Paperbacks are published by St. Martin's Press, 175 Fifth Avenue, New York, NY 10010.

10 9 8 7 6 5 4 3 2 1

This book is dedicated to the Brigade of Midshipmen at Annapolis, who inevitably rise to the standard of personal and professional ethics set for them by the example of their superior officers.

Acknowledgments

It's been almost forty years since I graduated from the Naval Academy, so I needed a lot of help to get abreast of the many institutional changes. My special thanks to Pamela Warnken, formerly of the Academy's public information office, for fielding countless E-mails and getting me to the right people for answers. My thanks also to the superintendent at the time of my research, Vice Admiral John Ryan, USN, for arranging my initial tour of the contemporary facilities. The academy hosts 1.5 million guests each year, and I certainly appreciated the degree of access extended to me in preparation for this story. Thanks to Don Schwartz for expert advice on firearms, and to "Doc" Bellows of Schurr Sails for help with yachting details. I also received a great deal of useful insight from both academic faculty members and officers of the Academy's executive department. They might not recognize what they told me once they read the book, but, as always, I pick and choose what I need to best enhance the story. Any resulting errors in Academy procedure or organization are, happily for them, all mine.

Solo

He floated at the top of the dive for what seemed like forever. Perfect takeoff, his legs delivering just exactly the right
amount of spring, his arms balanced level with his chest and
slightly behind, fingers webbed together, hands slightly
cupped, eyes wide open, grinning nemesis back on the
ledge, helpless to hurt him anymore. For what seemed an
eternity, he hung suspended, and then, instinctively, as gravity beckoned, he tucked, arcing down through the calm
morning air, his body aligning itself perfectly with the gathering slipstream, the darkened windows beginning to blur, a
reflexive keening noise rising in his throat as he saw the diamond pattern of the plaza below coming into incredibly
sharp focus as he held his breath and his perfectly vertical
position in midair, no imbalance this time, no wobble in his
legs or hips, statue-straight, rigid, accelerating, his best dive
ever, the diamond pattern dissolving into individual seg-
ments of polished granite, bits of mica gleaming wonderfully clear, beckoning him to join them in their crystalline
perfection, his eyes tearing from the rushing air. Time to go.
Close your eyes, time to close your eyes. Inhale for the entry, your most perfect—

1

The ashen-faced cook was close to hyperventilating. He was sitting at the first table inside the mess hall, hands clamped down on spread knees, eyes bulging wide open, staring straight ahead, as if not wanting to see the red stains all over his whites.

"Hey, man, it's okay," Jim Hall said. "Just take it slow. Breathe. No, slower. Deep breaths. Slower. Yeah. That's it. Take a minute. It's gonna be okay."

The cook, a pudgy white guy in his forties, didn't respond, but he began to get his breathing under control. Jim looked at his shoes. He, too, did not want to dwell on the cook's gore-spattered uniform. He imagined he could smell it, and felt his stomach do a small flop. Finally, the cook looked up at him.

" 'Okay'? *Okay?* Hell it will," he croaked. "It was like . . . like he was trying to fly."

"Say what?"

"The guy? It looked like he was trying to fly. I saw him. One split second. Arms wide, like one of those high divers, you know? His eyes were closed, though. Like he knew."

Well, no shit, Jim thought. Of course he knew. Doing a swan dive from six stories onto flagstone? Yeah, the dude probably knew.

"Young guy?" Jim asked. He'd seen the body. It was actually a reasonable question.

"Yeah, probably a plebe. I mean, like, a really young face."

Jim nodded. He tried again to shut out the image of the wreckage out there in the plaza between the mess hall and the eighth wing. Wait till the breakfast formation gets a load of that. He felt his stomach twitch. People had no idea.

He made a couple of notes, waiting to see if the cook had anything more to add. Then he heard one of the EMTs outside call in the DOA code. Got that right, he thought. The semirigid cook now had beads of sweat all along his forehead, and his lips were turning a little blue. Jim stepped over to the double doors and called the EMTs to come over. One pushed through the doors of what was formally called King Hall, the Naval Academy's hangarlike mess hall. The cook looked like he was about to flop and twitch on them.

Jim motioned with his chin. The medic took one look and went right to work. Then a short, scowling Navy captain came through the doors and signaled that he wanted to talk to Jim. And here we go, Jim thought, closing his notebook. Here we go.

As he headed back through the doors, he wished the NCIS agents would hurry the hell up. He definitely did not want to deal with Capt. D. Telfer Robbins, the commandant of midshipmen, all by himself, no way in hell. And he really didn't want to see any more of that mess out there in the plaza.

He scanned the small crowd outside. As the Naval Academy's civilian security officer, he was nominally in charge of the scene until the Naval Criminal Investigative Service people showed up. There were the Academy's own police, a couple of Annapolis cops, and some shocked-looking naval officers. The impatient captain was waiting for him next to his official sedan, rising up and down on the balls of his feet, a cell phone in his hand and anger bright in his eyes. Jim resisted the urge to page the NCIS office again, just as the 6:30 reveille bells began to ring throughout the eight wings of Bancroft Hall. He was pretty sure he knew exactly what the commandant was going to say to him.

2

Everett Markham, full professor of international law and diplomacy in the Political Science Department, Division of Humanities and Social Studies, United States Naval Academy, banged his head on an open cupboard door and dropped his coffee mug, all in one graceful move. He swore as he batted the offending door shut, rubbed his head, and groped around the darkened kitchen floor for the mug, which, fortunately, had been empty. He couldn't find it.

This is what it's like to turn fifty, he thought. Need coffee in the morning just to get stereo vision, and every supposedly inanimate object in the house knows it and lies in wait for you. Or, you could turn on the damned light, he said to himself. But that would hurt my caffeine-deprived eyes. He realized he was doing this a lot these days, talking to himself, even holding some fairly detailed conversations in his head on the most absolutely inane topics. He gave up, turned on the kitchen lights, opened one and then the other eye, and spied the mug lurking next to the center island. He managed to plug in the tiny Krups coffeemaker without executing himself, rubbed the back of his head again, and went out to the front porch to see where the village idiot had thrown his *Washington Post* this time.

Ev Markham was a widower. He lived alone in a large two-story house overlooking the head of Sayers Creek, which was an inlet of the Severn River just upstream of the

Naval Academy. The house had belonged to his parents, and he'd grown up in Annapolis, in the shadow of the Academy. Like more than a few such kids, Ev had been mesmerized from an early age by the proud ranks of midshipmen bedecked in blue and gold, the midweek parades, the boom of the saluting guns, the thunderous Army-Navy game pep rallies, choral recitals in the cathedral-like chapel at Christmastime, and those big mysterious gray ships anchored from time to time out in the bay. His father, who had served in the Navy during World War II, had been a doctor with good political connections in both the capital and in the Yard, and he'd eased the way for an appointment for Ev, who had graduated from the Academy himself in 1973.

He retrieved the plastic-wrapped newspaper out of an injured camellia bush, frowned at the broken branches, summoned visions of retribution, and then went back into the house. Maybe if he put up a piece of piano wire across the sidewalk, say about neck-high, Einstein might slow down long enough to put the paper somewhere near the front porch. But then he remembered that the paperboy was no longer a boy on a bike, but an elderly Korean gentleman driving a little Japanese pickup truck. And besides, there never had been sidewalks. He plodded back to the kitchen, poured a mug of coffee—into the cup this time—and went out onto the back porch, which overlooked two hundred feet of lawn and trees descending to the creek. Two sincerely ambitious Yuppies were straining at their oars as they sculled out from the other side in their fancy singles. The water was perfectly still, and they cut through the foot-high mist like competing phantoms under power.

His lawyer and best friend, Worth Battle, harped incessantly on the subject of Ev's living alone in a house so full of family memories. Worth also kept trying to set him up with lady friends, but, with the possible exception of one really nice lawyer, none of them had raised even a spark of interest. He smiled at the thought of going through life with a name like Worth Battle. Back when they had been plebe-year roommates at the Naval Academy, Ev had appreciated all the hell his roomie caught for having such a name, because it deflected a lot of fire from himself. As early as plebe summer, they had speculated that one day Worth would have to become a lawyer, if only to get even.

The problem was, Ev loved the old house. He lived in it mortgage-free, and now, with five wooded acres directly overlooking Sayers Creek and within healthy walking distance of the Academy and the state capitol, it was worth a small fortune. But more than that, he'd grown up here. It was the only home he'd ever had. It was also the only home his daughter, Julie, had ever known, and during the past four years, it had allowed him to see much more of her than did most parents of midshipmen. It was a place she could bring her friends and classmates, a place where they could act like normal college kids once in awhile instead of spit-and-polish tin sailors. But since his wife, Joanne, had died, he'd seen less of Julie than he'd have liked. And when she graduated in a few weeks, he'd see nothing of her except for the occasional Christmas leave, as she dropped into that same naval aviation pipe he'd been in for so long. The irony did not escape him. Pretty soon, there'd be nothing but memories here. Good ones and not so good ones. Then he might actually have to decide.

The phone rang. It was Julie. Midshipman First Class Julie Markham, United States Naval Academy, he reminded himself. Soon to be Ensign Julie Markham, United States Naval Reserve.

"Dad!" she said breathlessly, scattering his ruminations with her energy. "Have you heard?"

"Heard what, Jules?" he asked patiently. Julie seemed to go through life at full burner lately, as commissioning day approached.

"A plebe. Fell. Or jumped. Off the eighth wing's roof. Into the road between King Hall and Mitscher Hall. Megagross. Like, fire-hose city."

"Thanks for sharing, Julie," he said, quickly blanking out the gory image. He'd seen the aftermath of a plane captain falling eighty-four feet from the flight deck of a carrier onto the pier below, courtesy of a jet engine turnup. "What do you mean, fell or jumped?"

"Oh, you know. Dark Side is saying that of course he fell; the word in the Brigade is that he jumped."

"You're going to have to lose that 'Dark Side' business once you get out there in the fleet, Julie. Your senior officers won't appreciate that stuff."

"And they do something about it, from what I've been told, which is, of course, why they're called the Dark Side."

"Yeah, but think about this: You go naval air, you're looking at almost a ten-year obligated service. By then, you'll be up for light commander. How do you make the transition to O-four if you've been calling everyone who's an O-four or above the Dark Side?"

"Oh, Da-ad," she said. "Ten years? That's eons from now. Hey, I gotta run—it's two-minute chow call."

"Rock and roll," he said, but she was already gone. He hung up the phone. It was almost amusing, he thought, how pervasively the fleet junior officer culture infected the Brigade, especially the seniors, or firsties. After the naval aviation Tailhook scandals of the early nineties, many junior aviators felt they had been made scapegoats for incidents to which a nonzero number of very senior officers had also been party. Some of these senior officers had been only too willing to offer up an unlimited number of JO careers if that meant they could save theirs from the ensuing feminazi witch-hunts. The JOs had secretly begun calling any officer over the rank of lieutenant "the Dark Side," with a cultural nod to Darth Vader of the *Star Wars* films. When this term filtered up to the senior officers, there were immediate and heavy-handed back-channel thunderations, which, of course, only served to cement the appellation.

He finished his coffee and went upstairs to get ready for work. His first class today was at ten o'clock, so there was plenty of time. One of the bennies of being a full prof. But maybe too much time, because as he entered the bedroom, he was struck again by how quiet the damned house was. It didn't even have the decency to creak and groan, like any self-respecting fifty-year-old house should. He felt the familiar flush of desperate loneliness that seemed all too ready to overwhelm him at moments like this. He took a deep breath and willed it away.

She was gone.

That's all, just gone. Just gone. And there was nothing he could do. He had gone through his entire life asserting control over himself and his circumstances. But when that state trooper had come to the door, stone-faced, rain-soaked hat in hand, Ev had known in an instant that those days of even keels and steady, visible purpose had just been hit by a large torpedo. Just like Joanne. Who was just—gone.

They had had the life they'd had. All the memories were banked, the good ones gaining ground, the not so good ones fading like old newsprint, visible if you really wanted to see it, but disappearing if you were willing to leave it in a drawer somewhere for long enough.

You do this one day at a time, he told himself. Just like the twelve-steppers down at AA. You concentrate on what you're going to say at the ten o'clock seminar. You focus on doing the next thing—shower, shave, get dressed. He swallowed hard as he stood there in the bedroom. He knew all the standard nostrums by heart, could hear all his friends reciting them so sincerely and earnestly. Meaning well. Trying to help. Breathing silent sighs of relief that it hadn't happened to them.

He couldn't help wanting to remind some of them.

He looked at himself in the full-length mirror hanging on the bathroom door. Just over six feet, black hair—well, mostly black—a narrow, lean face with intense brown eyes, a crooked nose, courtesy of an unruly canopy, and more lines than had been there the last time he'd looked. He'd managed to keep himself fit and trim, which, given the physical fitness culture of the Academy, was unremarkable. But the lines were deeper and the shadows under his eyes more pronounced. Funny how living alone changed things, and how the body kept score.

He sighed. Damned house was ambushing him again.

Maybe Worth was right. The day after Julie threw her hat in the air at graduation was going to be emotional for them both. The day after that, once she had driven away to Pensacola and her new life, was going to be a genuine bitch.

"But right now," he said out loud, "it's shower time."

That's right, it's me. Aren't you glad? Sure you are. I've just been walking down the passageway, yelling at the chow-callers to keep their eyes in the boat, and, just maybe, they won't attract my attention. They don't want to attract my attention, because today I'm Psycho-Shark, man-killer, man-eater.

I love to look at all the pretty plebes, the live ones. Standing rigidly at attention next to the upperclassmen's rooms, clamoring like the sheep they are, counting down the minutes until morning meal formation. As if the superior beings inside the rooms didn't know what time it was. "Sir! There are now three minutes until morning meal formation! The menu for this morning is . . ." *Seriously dumb!*

There was one who didn't get the word about me. I gave him the Look. Let my eyes go blank, opened my mouth just a little, showed all my teeth, slowed my stride fractionally, made it look like I was turning in his direction, just like a big tiger shark, perusing prey, easing past the target, then the sly turn, the effortless dip and bank of pectorals. I love it when their voices pitch up a note or two as they continue to shout out the required formula while pretending—no, hoping, praying—I'm not coming back to them.

They know, the plebes. They know about me, even if a lot of my so-called classmates don't. It's the nature of prey to recognize a predator, you see. And I am, by God, a predator. A top predator, in every sense. They get a come-around to my room, they don't sleep the night before. Especially the girls.

There's one girl they call Bee-bee, the fat girl. Bee-bee for Butterball. All quivering chins and heaving bosoms under that flushed face. Trying desperately not to acknowledge that I'm walking past. I can smell the sweat on her from twenty feet away—we can do that, you know. We have a truly excellent sense of smell. All those tiny, exquisitely tuned dermal receptors. It's a chemical thing. Just kidding, of course. But sharks can do that, so I assume the profile as much as I can. For Bee-bee, I change my sequence. Just a little. Slow down, turn my head, oh so casually in her direction, stare down at her—belt buckle, yes, and listen to her squeak. What does she think I'm looking at, her crotch? Not with that fat roll hanging over her belt, I'm not.

But you know what? I can smell her fear. She's not going to make it here. The Dark Side hates fat midshipmen. As well they should. Fat people are lazy, unmotivated. Natural prey, by definition. As I've always said, the girls can stay, but only if you remain sleek and strong.

I prowl every day. My grand passage to formation. I leave my room with just less than two minutes to get down the ladder to the zero deck and out onto the formation yard. I have it timed, you see. Right to the second. After almost four years of this bullshit, any competent firstie does. That's how I make it look so effortless, arriving at the edge of the formation just as the bells ring, always supremely casual, totally nonchalant, just like a big shark rising from somewhere down in the deep gloom, appearing miraculously alongside and slightly below a school of underclassmen. Well, what the hell, it is morning meal formation. You know, chow time? Heh-heh.

And I love it when the guys on the team call me the Shark! Let's face it, when it comes to men's freestyle, I AM the team. Six three in my dripping feet, 210 pounds of spring steel, and shaped like a humanoid manta ray, only I'm faster, much faster. I'm the monster of the freestyle. Fast enough that I actually have time to look sideways and lay dead eyes on anyone who can keep up with me. It's so cool: I give him the Look, show those teeth, watch him stub his stroke for a second or two, or screw up his breathing when he realizes I'm not breathing and I'm still staring right at him. And then I'm gone, accelerating without seeming to change anything. I've heard the norms talking, in the locker

room head afterward. "*Fucker just stopped taking air, man.
Looked at me like I was meat, like he was gonna slip under
the lane divider and, like, fucking bite, man. Freaked my ass
out.*"

It's my teeth. I can't help it. I have really big teeth. One
time before a meet, I borrowed some black nail polish from
one of my Goth moths and painted my teeth to look like
points. Final heat, there was this guy, thought he was pretty
good, grinned at me when he realized he could stay with
Navy's monster right through the final turn. Then I gave him
the Look, and a second later, exactly one stroke later, I
showed the teeth. Poor baby did a guppy mouth. Tried to
swallow the pool. Made him heavy, I suppose. Shit happens.
He was lucky his timer saw him go down. I never saw him, of
course. I was too busy winning. I did see the bubble, now
that I think of it. Big one, too.

The best part of formation time is when the plebes, all finished with their chow calls, come chopping down the center
of the passageway, hands rigid at their sides, eyes in the
boat, yes, sir, knowing within a few seconds what time it is,
but having to give way to the upperclassmen, because that's
how it works here at Canoe U. They had sixty, now fifty seconds to get down the stairwell—that's ladder to you, plebe-
dweeb—and into ranks. We don't obstruct them on purpose,
although it does happen. And, of course, you bump into me
and you get an automatic come-around. On the other hand,
if they aren't in formation by the time the formation bell
rings, they're down on the demerit pad anyway. Can't win, if
you're a plebe, can you? No, you can't. That's the beauty of
the system. Make it hopeless, see what they do, see who
gives up, who doesn't, and then help the strong ones figure it
out. To recognize the system, and, better yet, how to beat the
system.

That's how I've done it, only I was doing it long before I
got to this place. Beating the system. Every place I've been,
since I was a little kid, there's always been a system. Whether
in Juvie Hall, the foster homes, the parochial school, there's
always been a system. If you truly want to rule, all you have

to do is first recognize the system, then beat it by appearing to play by its rules while taking what you want. And you know what? The people who run the system are usually so damned dumb, they can't see you doing it. This place is no different in that regard. They've got all these chickenshit rules, so you focus on those rules. Shine your shoes, polish your brass, keep your room sharp, bounce that dime off the bedspread, man. Study what they tell you to study, excel at all things athletic, stand tall, speak loud, keep your hair short, your body pumped, your abs ripped, and, man, you will be a star. Just like me. Oh, you might not have many friends, but, hell, I didn't come here for friends. I came here to get those wings of gold and that great big Mameluke sword.

See, you don't need friends to select Marine aviation; you only need a certain percentage of your class to stand lower than you do. It's like if you and I were being chased by a big bad bear—I don't have to outrun the bear. I only have to outrun you. So my classmates don't like me. Big deal. But they sure as hell know who I am. And the Dark Side, especially the Marines? Hell, they love me. Set me up at attention in a set of tropical whites, take my picture while I'm bellowing out an order, I'm Poster Boy.

Well, it's going on class time. Just a couple more weeks and we get to flee this place. I finally get to join my mighty Corps, and, of course, learn all about a new system. They'll have one. And being Marines, it'll be a pretty simple system. Not simple as in dumb, but simple as in clear, pure, strong. But I'll play it and beat it, too. Piece of cake. Easy as slurping down the weekly shit-on-a-shingle breakfast in King Hall. Hope they hose off the plaza over there before noon meal. I saw a fire truck, but there's been no fire that I know about. Something messy on the plaza, I hear. Or was it someone? A plebe, maybe? Hope so—there're too many of them.

Just before noon, Ev Markham stood on the front steps outside Sampson Hall, wishing he could have a cigarette. He'd quit smoking when he'd left carrier aviation, but the desire for just one had never been truly extinguished. It was a perfect spring day in Annapolis, with clear blue skies and a vigorous sea breeze coming in off the bay. The trees were in bloom, the lawns were coming green again after the wintry depredations of dark ages, and the Severn River was positively sparkling. The wedge of Chesapeake Bay he could see from Sampson was a vast sheet of silver punctuated by fishing boats and the seemingly motionless silhouette of a black-hulled tanker pushing its way up to Baltimore. It was no wonder the visiting West Point cadets, whose fortresslike academy up on the Hudson was still ice-bound in the early spring, called their rivals' school in Annapolis "the Country Club."

The last midshipmen were exiting the granite-covered academic building, hustling back to Bancroft for noon meal formation, throwing a chorus of obligatory "Morning, sir" at him as they trotted by. He was a popular-enough professor, and it didn't hurt that he taught a subject that was considered non-life-threatening, as compared to, say, advanced organic chemistry. He was finishing his imaginary cigarette and admiring the big houses on the cliffs across the Severn River when Dolly Benson, the Political Science Department's secretary, stuck her head out one of the massive bronze doors and called him in for an urgent phone call from his daughter. Surprised, he followed her back to the departmental offices. A call from his daughter at this time of day, with noon meal formation bells about to ring, was unusual. The Naval Academy was a place of rigid routines. Any break in that routine usually meant trouble.

"Yeah, Julie. What's up?"

"Dad, I think I've got a problem. My company officer came to our room and told me to get into Class-A's and report to the commandant's office."

"Whoa. Why?"

"I have no idea. I don't think Lieutenant Tarrens does, either. He just said to get up there ASAP. What should I do?"

"Get up there ASAP. And you have no idea of what this is about? Academic? Conduct?"

"No, Dad," Julie said in a mildly exasperated voice. Rightfully so, too. Julie stood in the top 20 percent of her class academically and had never had a significant conduct demerits problem.

"Well, then, go find out. If you haven't done anything wrong, just go see the Man. He doesn't bite."

"That something you know, Dad?" she asked, but her normal bantering tone wasn't there. He realized Julie was scared. He also knew that Captain Robbins, the commandant of midshipmen and a recent flag officer selectee, was not exactly a warm and fuzzy kind of guy.

"Listen, Jules: The commandant is all about business. Whatever it is, he'll be professional about it. However, if you think you're being accused of something, stop talking and call me right away. On my cell number. And before thirteen hundred, okay? I've got a department staff meeting then. Now hustle your bustle."

"I guess. Shit. I'm going to miss lunch."

He could hear the formation bells ringing out in the halls. "I believe you already have. Get going. And call me back."

He hung up and stood there for a moment. He was grateful that the departmental office complex was empty. Everyone else, including Dolly now, had gone somewhere, either for lunch or to work out. There were individual offices for the department chair, who was a Navy captain, and for each full professor. There was also a conference room, and some smaller shared offices for newer faculty and visitors. There were no students hanging around, either. Unlike students at a civilian college, midshipmen had their time strictly regulated: They were in Bancroft Hall, out on the athletic fields, or in class in one of the academic buildings. Midshipmen rarely spent time lingering around the departmental offices.

He walked over to his own office to make sure his cell phone was on, wondering what the hell this was all about. The commandant of midshipmen's office was in Bancroft Hall itself. He and his deputy, Captain Rogers, directly oversaw every aspect of the midshipmen's daily life through a chain of command comprised of commissioned officers who were designated battalion and company officers. The four thousand midshipmen were assigned to six battalions of five companies each. Having been a midshipman, Ev knew that a summons to the commandant's office was trouble, plain and simple. With her high academic standing and her athletic achievements as a competitive swimmer, Julie was one of the stars of her class, so this wasn't likely to be about a conduct offense. Another large-scale cheating episode, perhaps? God, he hoped not. The Academy didn't need another one of those, especially after all the ongoing controversy over the ethics and honor courses.

Forty-five minutes later, his suspicions were confirmed. Julie called in on his regular number. She asked in a wooden, stilted voice if he could come over to Bancroft Hall.

"Certainly," he said, not liking her tone of voice. "But what's going on?"

"Can't talk," she said, lowering her voice. "I'll meet you in the rotunda. We can talk there."

"Five minutes," he said, and hung up. He left a note for Dolly that he had been called away on an urgent personal matter and would be late for the departmental meeting. Then he grabbed his suit coat and hustled out the door.

Julie was waiting for him in the spacious main entrance to Bancroft Hall, the eight-wing, five-storied marble and granite Beaux Arts dormitory complex that was home to the nearly four thousand midshipmen composing the Brigade. She was standing to one side of the ornate marble-floored entrance, looking small beneath the massive naval murals lining the cavernous rotunda. He felt a small pang in his heart when he looked at his daughter: Julie looked so much like her mother—medium height, dark-haired, pretty, and bright-eyed, except that right now she wasn't so bright-eyed. Her face was rigid with what looked to him like massive embarrassment. Fifty feet above her head was a twenty-foot-wide color mural depicting battleships under air attack in World War II. It somehow seemed appropriate.

He went to her and saw that she was struggling to contain tears. A couple of passing midshipmen, youngsters, with a single anchor insignia on their shirt collars and arms laden with books, glanced at him in his civilian suit and tie but kept going. Being sophomores, they wouldn't necessarily know he was faculty, so he looked like what he was: a visiting father, here to talk to his daughter. A freestanding wooden privacy partition masked the side hallways leading back into the Brigade hallways. He saw a lieutenant he did not recognize standing next to the executive corridor partition, watching them. Probably someone from the Executive Department. Given the weird acoustics of the rotunda, he was close enough to eavesdrop.

"Want to go somewhere?" he asked softly, eyeing the watching officer.

"Can't," she said through clamped jaws. "They say I have to meet some people from NCIS in a few minutes."

That stopped him. NCIS: Naval Criminal Investigative Service. Emphasis on the word *Criminal.* "NCIS? What the hell, Julie?"

She looked right at him, keeping her back to the lieutenant and her voice low. "That plebe who jumped this morning? They're saying it had something to do with me. The commandant just put me through some kind of interrogation. It's almost like they think *I'm* responsible. You know, for what he did."

"Good Lord. Did you even know him?"

"Only sort of," she said. "I mean, he's a plebe. Was a plebe, I guess." She turned and glared pointedly at the lieutenant. The young officer finally stepped back behind the partition to give them some privacy. That was his Julie: not one to take crap from anybody.

"Why do they think that?"

She shrugged. "They say there's something that ties him to me."

"Like . . ."

"The dant wouldn't say. It was like 'We'll ask the questions; you answer.' "

He started to say something but stopped. The word had gone through the entire Academy like quicksilver before first-period classes. A plebe named William Brian Dell was dead, the victim of a fall from the roof of the eighth wing. And now there was something that tied the victim to Julie?

"I don't know what's been going on since the incident," she said. "But they sent for me just before I called you. The dant just sat there. Captain Rogers did the talking. Asked if I knew him. I did remember him from plebe summer detail. His name was Dell. Like the computer company? He was in our batt. Had him come around a few times, but then, I don't know, I quit running him. He seemed to be flailing. I didn't think he'd last."

Julie had been a member of the prestigious plebe summer detail, a small cadre of rising seniors who ran the seven-week summer indoctrination program for the incoming class of plebes. The objective of plebe summer was to turn civilians into midshipmen. It was an exhausting regimen, during which the plebes got a taste of what was coming when the full Brigade returned from its summer cruise. But only a taste—the reality was worse. Up at West Point, they called their version of it "Beast Barracks."

"So what—you were helping him?"

She turned away for a moment. "When I called you this morning, I didn't know it was Dell. Who jumped, I mean. Anyway, they started in asking if I knew Midshipman Fourth Class Dell. I told them, yes, I did. Then they told me he was the one who fell. They keep saying 'fell.' "

"They probably don't know yet, Julie. They're going to have to do an investigation."

"They seemed pretty insistent that he fell, like they'd heard the scuttlebutt going around and were laying down the party line. You know, play down any suicide angle. But then—"

She stopped. The lieutenant was back.

"So they're bringing in NCIS?" he asked. "Are they accusing you of something?"

"I don't know. That's what's pissing me off. And the dant wasn't exactly being friendly. You know, what's happened has to be someone's fault, because of course it's going to embarrass the Academy. But NCIS? Should I have a lawyer or something?"

Ev hesitated. Whenever a Navy service member was seriously injured or killed while on active duty, it was standard procedure for his command to initiate a so-called line-of-duty investigation. NCIS normally would not be brought in unless the authority convening the investigation thought that the incident was the result of criminal or suspicious acts.

"And they won't tell you what this so-called tie is between you and Dell?"

"No. I asked. They said that was privileged information for the moment."

Ev didn't like the sound of that. The lieutenant was signaling something to Julie. As Ev turned to see what was going on, the commandant himself appeared and headed toward them. Ev felt Julie stiffen to attention by his side.

Jim Hall perched on the edge of the conference room table, a Styrofoam cup of coffee in one hand. He was trying not to stare at the female NCIS agent's legs, but it was difficult— she was sitting rather carelessly in the armchair at the head of the conference table while she read the report from the ER, and the view was expansive. Her partner, a young-looking black guy, who was sitting in one of the side chairs, saw Jim peeking and grinned at him. What the hell, Jim thought. She has great legs, even if she is a cop. Correction: special agent. As in Special Agent Branner. No first name, apparently. Branner was the head of the Academy's local NCIS office. She shook her head and looked up.

"Panties? This kid was wearing *panties*?" she said. Her voice was throaty, as if she might have been a smoker at one time.

"So it would seem," Jim said. "There was a Naval Academy laundry mark. We scanned the lists and found out the underwear belongs to a firstie, one Midshipman Julie Markham. That's the one you're interviewing in a few minutes."

Branner looked over with raised eyebrows at her partner, Special Agent Walter Thompson, who shrugged elaborately. Branner was a handsome woman in her thirties. If a bit of a hard case, Jim thought. Attractive face, bright red hair, wide-shouldered, athletic upper body, slim-hipped, and, of course, those racing wheels decked out in some shiny beige stockings. But an all-business set to her expression. He'd met this kind before, in the Marine Corps, women who knew they were attractive but, by God, were not going to allow that to interfere with their male counterparts taking them seriously. Except there she was, flashing the world like a pro. She looked back down at the report. If she was aware that he was looking her over, she gave no indication. And attractive women are always aware, he reminded himself.

"And the DOA? This Midshipman Dell?" she asked, flipping through the three pages of the report as if the answer would leap out at her. "What do you have on him?"

It was Jim's turn to shrug. "Plebe. We've sent for his admissions file, but they have to retrieve it from some records warehouse over in Baltimore. Full name is William Brian Dell. His roommate wasn't too much help this morning—still pretty shook-up. His company officer, one Lieutenant Gates, will be up here shortly, along with Dell's squad leader, the roommate, and his company commander."

"Parents?"

"Parents live in Norfolk. His father is retired Navy enlisted. His stepmother has severe emphysema, confined to home care. Oxygen-bottle on wheels situation. Dell was his father's child by a first wife. She has not been located. The father and stepmother were notified in person at ten-thirty this morning by a CACO."

"Shit."

"Yeah, have a nice day. Somewhat rougher for the kid, of course."

"No take on suicide or accident?" she asked.

"That's all yours to investigate, Special Agent," Jim said. "Although the dant probably has some preferences on that matter."

She gave him a quick look to see if he was being facetious about her being a special agent. She apparently decided he was not, but she did rearrange her skirt. Slowly, though. Lady knows exactly what she's doing, he decided. "But of course the dant wouldn't think of indulging in any undue command influence over your investigation," Jim continued.

"Much," she said, and they all smiled. Everyone knew that a ruling of accident rather than suicide would be better for the Academy's image. Marginally better, but better. Midshipmen at Annapolis did not go around committing suicide, and certainly not on Capt. D. Telfer Robbins's watch.

Branner slid the report over to Thompson and got up to refill her coffee cup. Jim had scanned the report, which contained a brief medical description of Dell's injuries and a preliminary cause of death determination: massive trauma due to sudden impact with lots and lots of concrete. No surprises there. Initial toxicology screen negative for alcohol or drugs. Further analysis pending autopsy. DOA. No effort made to resuscitate. Got that right, Jim thought, remembering the strangely diminished, almost two-dimensional corpse, out of which an amazing volume of fluids had leaked.

The commandant had made it clear out in front of the mess hall that he wanted this matter to be labeled an accident until proven otherwise, and that no one, and he did mean no one, was to speak to the media except the Academy's own Public Affairs spokespersons. Jim had pointed out that there were civilian police and EMTs already involved, but Robbins simply told him to take care of that problem himself. Jim dutifully instructed Lieutenant Gates, the plebe's company officer, who had been throwing up in the bushes, to seal Dell's room and to make arrangements for the roommate to move in with someone else for the time being. He had then spoken quietly to the EMTs, relaying the commandant's request for discretion. He hadn't bothered with the Annapolis cops, who would have been insulted. The EMTs had taken the body over to the Anne Arundel County morgue for the required autopsy.

Branner returned to the table, ran her fingers through her hair, and sat down with her knees primly together this time. Jim was almost disappointed.

"By rights, he should have gone to Bethesda," she said. "This is a federal case."

Jim shrugged again. "I should think an autopsy is an autopsy," he said. "The city cops and EMTs got there first, so that's the gutting table he went to. You want to object, get him moved?"

Branner shook her head. "Not now. It's just that we'd control the reporting better if he were in Navy channels. But, what the hell, they know what killed him."

"So it would seem. You guys ready for Midshipman Markham?" Jim asked.

Branner nodded. "Midshipmen in panties," she muttered.

"Actually, this one ought to be wearing panties," Jim said. Just like you always should, he thought.

Branner just looked at him. "Okay, Mr. Hall." She sighed. "Let's talk to Midshipman Markham."

"Professor Markham, good morning," Captain Robbins said. He didn't offer to shake hands, and his expression wasn't promising. The commandant of midshipmen was a short, intense-looking officer with graying hair. He appeared to be all edges: taut face, prominent beaked nose, and Marine-style buzz cut. His service dress blue uniform, with its four shining rings of gold on the sleeves, was pressed into straight lines wherever possible. His mouth was a thin sliver of determination. Ev had met the captain, soon to be a one-star admiral, but had never had occasion to speak to him one-on-one until this morning. The academic department and executive departments were, by design, worlds apart. Robbins was a surface ship officer and had a reputation for being a stickler for detail, a strict disciplinarian, a workaholic, a physical fitness nut, and a walking, talking personality-free zone. In short, the ideal commandant. But Ev wondered if the chronically choleric captain might not also suffer from short-man's disease.

"My daughter just told me she's to be interviewed by NCIS, Captain," Ev said. He wasn't sure whether or not to address Robbins as captain or admiral, but since he was still wearing four stripes, he settled on captain. "She need a lawyer here?"

Robbins's eyebrows rose. "A lawyer? I should think not, Professor. NCIS is here because of the unexplained death of an active-duty midshipman on a federal reservation. They have exclusive jurisdiction to investigate. Standard procedure, within the overall context of a JAGMAN investigation. If it makes you feel better, Midshipman Markham is just one of several people being interviewed."

Julie was looking straight ahead, her arms still at her sides. "She has the sense that someone thinks she's involved with this incident," Ev said, realizing that they were talking as if Julie wasn't standing there, listening to every word.

"'Someone'?" Robbins said contemptuously. He glanced around the rotunda as if in search of the world-famous "someone." A few midshipmen had slowed down to see what was going on when the commandant appeared in the rotunda area. His quick glance sent them scurrying. When Ev didn't say anything, Robbins continued. "The county medical examiner called with an initial report," he said, lowering his voice. "No one's accusing anyone of anything at this moment, Professor Markham. But there may be issues here." He looked at his watch. A tall civilian had appeared from behind the partition. He looked to Ev like a Marine masquerading as a civilian. He signaled to Julie.

Issues, Ev thought. It had become the latest buzzword when people couldn't or wouldn't be specific. He nodded thoughtfully. "Well, Julie," he said to his daughter, "if you get the sense that someone—excuse me, *anyone*—in authority is even thinking about holding you responsible for what happened this morning, you stop talking and call me."

"It's not going to be like that," Robbins protested, but Ev raised a hand. With the height disparity between them, an observer might have thought Ev was going to swat the captain. "Captain, I had to deal with NCIS before, back when I was on active duty. I'm sure you have, too. I submit that you have no idea of how it's going to be, especially since you can have no direct influence over their line of questioning, correct?"

"Well, of course, Professor Markham," Robbins said, visibly angry now. He was trying to be polite but barely making it. "We just need to find out what happened, and why, if that's possible. A young man's dead, sir. His parents are going to want to know why."

"I understand, Captain Robbins," Ev said, matching the commandant's formal civility. "But this parent wants to make sure there's no rush to judgment for purposes, say, of getting this unfortunate incident rapidly behind us."

Robbins stiffened at that. Ev was speaking in code, but it was a code they both understood. The Academy was highly sensitive to bad news, and the administration had become very adept at damage control in recent years. From the look in Captain Robbins's eye, Ev realized he might have pushed things too hard. The commandant was the number-two executive at the Academy, reporting only to Rear Admiral McDonald, the superintendent. A civilian professor, tenured though he might be, was well down the food chain from the commandant of midshipmen. But Ev sensed he needed to put the administration on immediate notice: Any attempt to railroad Julie was going to light some fuses.

"Midshipman Markham," Robbins said, turning to Julie. "Please go with Mr. Hall there. He will escort you to my conference room, where you'll meet with the NCIS people."

"Aye, aye, sir," Julie said, and headed for the rangy civilian standing next to the partition. Ev waited for her to disappear into the executive hallway before turning back to the commandant. "The word in the Brigade is that the plebe jumped," he said.

"The 'word' in the Brigade is more properly called *scuttlebutt* and is almost always bullshit, Professor," Robbins said. Ev noticed that Robbins was beginning to do what the mids irreverently called the "Dant's Dance," popping up and down on the balls of his feet whenever he became impatient.

It probably didn't help that he had to crane his neck to look up at Ev. "Look, we'd appreciate it if you would back off for the moment and let the system work. I guarantee you that your daughter will be treated fairly. She has an excellent reputation in her class. Again: Our objective here is to find out what happened and why. That's all."

Ev started to reply, but the way Robbins had said "That's all" sounded very much like a dismissal. It was not an unreasonable request. Julie was an adult, twenty-one, and about to be a commissioned officer. Even as a parent, Ev had no legal standing here; thus, discretion was probably the better part of valor at this juncture. If he got too far up the commandant's nose, it would be Julie who'd take the heat for it. He nodded and left the rotunda. The commandant, still rocking up on his toes, watched him go for a moment before heading for the partition that separated the public Academy from the very private one.

It would take Ev five minutes to walk from Bancroft Hall back to Sampson Hall, home of the Division of Humanities and Social Sciences. It was 1:30, so the mids were all in class by now. Except for tourists, he had Stribling Walk to himself. The central Yard was a beautiful parklike setting, with its many marble monuments to famous people or incidents of naval history. The brick walk began at the imposing circular colonnade in front of Bancroft Hall and ended one thousand feet away at the equally imposing marble facade of the Mahan Hall complex. There were statues, cenotaphs, an obelisk, heavily oxidized bronze busts, and cannons littering a landscape of brick walks and bright green grass, all presided over by stately old trees. The towering dome of the Academy chapel rose twenty stories through the trees to his left, and the glimmering surface of the Severn River shone between the academic buildings to his right. Stubby gray Yard Patrol boats, YPs, used for seamanship training, blatted their horns out along the quay wall. He had to step around some open trenches, signs of the Academy's notorious "diggers and fillers" at work on their seemingly perpetual endeavors.

An NCIS investigation, he thought, mentally shaking his head. Overseen by the Academy's administration. Hell, maybe the FBI would even get into it, depending on what those mysterious "issues" were. There were already too many bureaucracies getting involved in this incident. And once the media engaged, Ev knew the administration would begin to circle the wagons, if they weren't doing so already. He was determined to make damn sure they didn't leave Julie outside the circle. He stopped halfway down Stribling Walk, thumbed his cell phone open, and called Worth Battle, Esquire.

"Rivers, Linden, Battle and Hall," a smooth female voice answered. Ev loved the title of the firm: It had such a reassuring resonance.

"Hi, Felicity," he replied.

"Oh, hi, Professor Markham," she said.

"Is himself around?"

"Let me check," she said, putting him on hold to the sound of Mozart. Ev sat down on one of the benches that lined the walk and waited. Worth came on the line.

"Doctor," he said.

"Counselor," Ev responded in the familiar litany. "We may need a lawyer."

"We?"

"Julie and I."

"Are we on a cell phone by any chance?"

"Yes."

"Call me on a landline. Say thirty minutes."

Ev went on back to Sampson Hall, which flanked Mahan at the end of Stribling Walk. He headed directly for his office, putting a finger to his lips when Dolly tried to tell him the meeting was still going on. He shut the door as quietly as he could and sat down at his desk. There were no messages. He worried about Julie, sitting in the commandant's conference room with two thugs from the NCIS.

Thugs—that's too strong a word, he reflected. NCIS agents weren't thugs, but his experiences with NIS, the current organization's predecessor, had not impressed him. Maybe things were different now that they had a new title and civilian leadership. He just wished it wasn't his only daughter they were interrogating. Okay, interviewing. He sighed and checked the clock, anxious to talk to Worth. To his surprise, the intercom line on his phone rang.

"Mr. Battle, sir," Dolly said. He punched the flashing button on his elderly Navy desk phone.

"Okay, what's going on?" Worth asked without preamble.

Ev described what had happened that morning, then told him that Julie was now closeted with NCIS agents over in the commandant's office.

"Right. And nobody will say what put the spotlight on Julie?"

"Nope. I talked to the dant himself. He wasn't exactly forthcoming. The word in the Yard is that the kid was a jumper, but the official party line is accident until proven otherwise. Supposedly, everyone's still in the fact-finding mode. There are, apparently, 'issues.'"

"Did Julie know this kid? As in, Anything going on?"

"Not like that. Yes, she did know him. She was on last year's summer detail, and she'd had him come around a couple of times during the year. But no to your second question. Worth, she's a firstie. This kid was a plebe, and, according to her, something of a weak sister. Firsties don't get emotionally involved with plebes, except when they're yelling at them."

"That's not something you could probably prove, Your Eminence. But, okay, I'll stipulate. For now. Look, you remember Liz DeWinter? I introduced you two at that dinner party I did on my boat?"

"Of course." He did indeed. Liz DeWinter, a classy thirty-something who was also a lawyer. And twice divorced, he reminded himself. She had been vague about exactly what kind of law she did—something political, having to do with the fact that Annapolis was the capital of Maryland.

"You ever call her, by the way?" Worth asked.

"Well, no, I didn't. She was very nice and eminently streetable, Worth, but . . ."

"Yeah, 'but.' Always the 'but.' Well, look, she's a criminal defense lawyer. Under all that linen, legs, and lace, she's a gunfighter. Does mainly political corruption cases, of which we always seem to have one or two going here in the capital of the great state of Maryland, my Maryland."

"So I've read. I mean about the corruption. Sounds a little high-powered for what's going on here. I mean—"

"You just stepped off your rock of expertise, Doctor, if I may be so bold," said Worth, interrupting him. "If you think Julie's in trouble, high power is what you want right out of the gate. Especially if the Dark Side over there in Bancroft Hall is going shields-up, Mr. Sulu."

Ev smiled at Worth's wild blend of metaphors and Hollywood allusions. But then he thought about what Worth was saying, which was precisely what he'd been worried about earlier.

"Look, I'll call Liz for you," Worth offered. "You know, a referral. Then she'll owe me lunch."

"Can I afford this?" Ev asked.

"Can you afford *not* to? Yes, Liz is expensive, but you've got the money, right?"

Worth was right about the money. Joanne had been killed one rainy night by a drunk driver, an elderly but still practicing surgeon, no less, at the top of the towering Chesapeake Bay Bridge. He'd passed her in a drunken weave on the westbound bridge at high speed and lost control on the wet, steel surface. Caroming off both guardrails, he'd come back at her, head on, and knocked her car completely off the bridge. The state troopers had found her car's license plate in the road debris. It had taken divers two days to find the car, intact but windowless, so she'd probably survived the bridge impact, but not the drop into the bay from nearly two hundred feet in the air. Or maybe she had, considering the fact that her air bag had been deployed but the shoulder belt unlatched. Joanne wouldn't start the car without her seat belt.

Even worse, her body had never been recovered. While Ev and Julie were still reeling from this news, Worth had stepped right in, threatened the doctor's insurance company with a $20 million personal injury lawsuit, and obtained a substantial seven-figure settlement in less than a week, plus a public admission by the drunk-driving doctor that he was an alcoholic. So, yes, he had the money. He would have preferred to have his wife.

"Okay, Worth," Ev said, still thinking about what had happened to Joanne. "And, not for the first time, many thanks."

"Semper fry," Worth said, and hung up.

Ev made an almost-perfect landing with his scull alongside the pontoon dock, then nearly tipped himself into the creek extracting himself. He ended up sitting on the hemp mat with skinned knees and elbows, holding on to the slim craft with one heel. He looked around as discreetly as he could to see if any of his rowing neighbors on the creek had been watching, but no one appeared to be about except Mrs. Murphy next door, who waved and smiled. He smiled weakly, waved back, and pulled the scull up onto the dock, secured it on its rack, and went up the path to the house, cooling rapidly as the sweat evaporated from his skin. He'd gone all the way up to the Route 50 bridge in a burst of sustained effort he hadn't attempted since his days rowing crew for the Academy. He would pay for that run tonight, he realized, but this business with Julie had stressed him out, and heavy-duty exercise was his best cure for that.

He got a shower and checked messages. Nothing from Julie, but there was one from Liz DeWinter. She'd given him her home number. Brother Worth coming through, he thought. Battle had become a big-time legal eagle in the capital, and Ev knew he was lucky to have him as an attorney. He went out to the back porch to start up a charcoal fire, got himself a glass of wine, and then called Liz. Just when he thought he was going to get voice mail, she picked up.

"Hi, Liz, this Ev Markham. Is this a convenient time to talk?"

"It is indeed, Ev. How are you?"

"Worried."

"Yeah, Worth filled me in. Have you heard any more from your daughter?"

"No, I haven't, but I expect she'll call tonight. You know how it is over in Bancroft Hall—they keep those kids running all day and half the night."

"So I've heard. But she hasn't been accused of anything that you know of, right?"

"That's correct."

"What's her connection to the plebe who died?"

"Don't know," he replied. "I'm waiting to find out what that is, assuming she's found out by now."

"Okay. Let's assume I do get into this. She would be the client, right?"

"I think so. She's legally an adult. I sure as hell know nothing about all this, except for what Julie is telling me, so I can't imagine I'll need representation. But I'd feel better if Julie had access to legal counsel, if not outright representation."

"Understood. Usually government bureaucracies, like the Academy or the state government, which is my area of expertise, act differently if they know there's a lawyer in the game for the other side."

He considered that. "The Navy's pretty conservative," he said. "If Julie gets a lawyer right away, will it make her look like she's done something that now needs defending?"

"If you detect that, you simply mention my name and tell them that I'm *your* attorney and that you've told me there's something going on. That way, you're just an individual who put a call in to his lawyer. Trust me, the bureaucrats will get the message."

"And Julie? What does she say?"

"As little as possible. How old is your daughter?"

"She's twenty-one. Which means that technically, even as her father, I've got no standing in this."

"Which makes you feel just wonderful."

"Exactly. I just beat my brains out on the Severn in my scull to decompress."

"I know that feeling: I go to the pool for laps when I get that way."

He remembered her more clearly now, especially when she mentioned the swimming. She was no more than five two, if that, but sleek, with short dark hair, intense blue eyes, and a full-breasted, voluptuous body that he'd noticed all the way across the lounge before they'd been introduced on Worth's yacht. "Now I'm trying to decide between drinking or taking some Chinese herbs before I stiffen up in this chair," he said.

"No contest there," she said. "Those Chinese are all Communists, so go for the vino. When your daughter checks in, have her call me if it isn't past eleven. If I'm going to be her lawyer, she has to ask me directly."

"I'll tell her. And thanks for getting on this so quickly. And, of course, I'll be paying the bills. Is there a retainer?"

"Yes, but let's see what we've got first. Who knows, they may just be playing it straight and interviewing anybody who might have known the dead guy."

"I guess that's what they should be doing," he said. He thanked her again, hung up, and went to throw a fish he'd bought earlier on the grill. The porch was settling into shadows as evening fell. The property was heavily wooded, and he could only see the homes on either side because of their lights. The creek behind the house, which was an estuary of the Severn River and not a real stream, was nearly two hundred feet wide. Its surface was calm and black except where lights from houses across the way reflected on it. Someone's dog was barking excitedly on the other side.

The lady lawyer was probably right: This would blow over once they ruled it a suicide, and that would be that.

You hope, a voice echoed in his head.

Conscious of thinking in circles, he checked to make sure his fish wasn't burning. C'mon Julie, he thought. Call me.

Jim Hall tossed the remains of a greaseburger extravaganza into the pier Dumpster as he walked through the darkness toward his boat. He lived aboard a thirty-six-foot Pearson ketch. His father had owned a large boat-repair yard in Pensacola, and he'd spent his childhood in the yard, learning everything there was to know about steel, aluminum, and wooden hull repairs, diesel and gasoline marine engines, and the byzantine economics of the boat business, from small runabouts all the way up to large commercial fishing boats. He'd restored the ketch after buying it at an insurance auction for one-tenth its initial price. He'd been living here in the Bayside Marina ever since his original assignment as the CO of the Academy's Marine detachment, which meant he'd been a resident of Crabtown for going on six years now.

He let himself through the wire gate at the head of the pier and made his way down the gangway to the floating portion of the pier. His boat, at nearly forty feet, took up almost one entire side of the pier, its graceful bow looming over the sun-bleached planks and bobbing inflatable fenders. He automatically inspected the mooring lines as he walked down its shining white length. He was proud of his work on the *Chantal,* which had been named for the hurricane that had brought the boat to him, literally. He was equally proud of the fact that he owned her outright, unlike his three neighbors on the other side of the pier, who were never more than one or two bad days on Wall Street away from being *ex*-owners. He disarmed the alarm system, using the keypad at the top of the gangway, and then let himself in through the railing gate. As soon as he stepped aboard, there came a throaty squawk from inside the main lounge. Guard parrot on the job, he thought.

Jim changed into jeans and sweatshirt, turned on the air conditioning to refresh the air down below, and then took a small scotch up the companionway to the awning-covered cockpit and plopped himself down in the large captain's chair. Jupiter, his double yellow-headed Amazon parrot, was perched on the left shoulder of his bird vest, where he began his preening ritual. Jim had to keep his glass on the upwind side to avoid the silent rain of fuzz, down, and other feathery debris that always accompanied the nightly preening session.

"You're a dirty damned bird," he muttered.

"Dirty damned bird," Jupiter croaked, unmoved by epithets.

The evening was cool and clear, and the water was relatively quiet. Someone was having a small party two piers over, and he could hear the background music, but the liveaboards in this marina were pretty considerate about not making too much noise on weeknights.

It had been an all-around ugly day. Unsure of the police protocol, he'd not stayed for the NCIS interviews, nor had the two agents—no, *special* agents—asked him to. He was the Academy security officer, but they were the investigating agency. They had made that "exclusive jurisdiction" point several times to anyone who would listen, especially Flasher Babe, who was apparently very sensitive about her bureaucratic prerogatives. The local Annapolis cops backed out with what to Jim felt like unseemly haste, but he supposed they had enough on their plates without getting entangled in what was sure to become yet another Naval Academy media success.

He had secured the impact zone, his term for it, as best he could for the NCIS Crime Scene Unit, and also the boy's room on the fourth floor of the eighth wing. Only later in the morning had he thought to secure all access up to the wing's rooftop gallery. Agent Branner had been upset about that, forcing him to remind the two ace investigators that they hadn't directed him to secure anything. The grumbling subsided after their CSU came up virtually empty at the end of the day. There were no evidentiary questions to be explored down on the plaza, where the boy had actually landed, the cause of death being copiously obvious, even after the efforts of a medical decontamination unit. The plebe's room had apparently produced no evidence of a crime.

The choleric Captain Robbins had spent the afternoon in a marathon meeting with his executive staff. Jim had tried to duck out, but Robbins wanted everybody present for duty. The Academy's Public Affairs officers, knowing what was coming, had spent a lot of time preparing everyone for the inevitable media onslaught. The commandant himself had crafted the approved spin: The investigation team assumed it was an accident but was going to also look into the possibility of suicide. Given what he had seen of the plebe's remains after impact, Jim thought that was going to be a tough call.

He shook his head. Suicide didn't compute. Here was an eighteen-year-old kid who had successfully navigated the annual service academy admissions wars, and now he was a smashed pumpkin in a drawer over at the Anne Arundel County morgue. There were over ten thousand applicants each year for *each* of the academies, twelve hundred of whom were finally appointed after a grueling year and a half spent dealing with the competitive admissions process. Granted, plebe year at the academies was a rough road, as he knew from personal experience. But to have achieved sustained success for twelve years of primary and secondary school in academics, extracurricular activities, student government offices, athletics, and then the Academy appointment process, and then to jump off the roof? The Academy typically graduated 76 percent of an entering class, which meant that three hundred or so mids fell to attrition out of every entering class. Usually, they either failed academically or decided that the program was too hard and opted out on their own. But suicide?

He'd been intrigued by the one interviewee, the bright-looking female first class midshipman—what was her name? Mark something. Markingham? Admittedly, he hadn't paid that much attention to her name. But she was going to be one important way into the investigation, given that the deceased had been wearing her underwear. On the other hand, he thought, if this was something more than a suicide or accident, and you were a bad guy and wanted to implicate somebody in a crime, that was one sure way to do it. But that meant murder, and Jim simply could not envision any motive for murder within the Brigade of Midshipmen. The possible exception would be a boy-girl thing, and even that was remote. Midshipmen did date other midshipmen, but usually within their own year group. It was sufficiently unusual that even the mids called it "dark-siding." And plebes weren't given time to think about dating.

Jupiter shook his feathers out, producing a veritable cloud of parrot dust. Jim waved his hand in front of his face and was rewarded by a love nip to his left ear.

"What's your act, bird?" he asked, looking up sideways at the bird's beady-eyed face. Jupiter ignored him and began to gnaw on one of his claws, gripping harder with the other one. Jim was glad for the padded bird vest. Jupiter could really grab if he wanted to, as some of Jim's lady friends had found out. Jupiter wasn't a bad parrot; he was simply Jim's parrot.

He finished his scotch, grateful for its ability to overcome the queasy-greasy feeling in his stomach. Tomorrow will probably be worse, he thought. Tomorrow the press will be into it. He suddenly felt very tired.

"C'mon, bird," he said, getting up out of the chair. "It's tree time in the city." He swept the bird off his shoulder and onto his right hand, then held the parrot over a sand-filled trash can, where Jupiter did the right thing. "Good bird," he said.

"Good bird," Jupiter acknowledged, and they went below.

At nine o'clock that evening, Ev was in his study, correcting some student papers, when he heard Julie bang through the kitchen screen door and call for him.

"In here, Julie," he called back, placing the papers in a folder and closing it. She came in a moment later, dressed in full sweats. Her face was bright red, almost the color of the reflective vest she wore over her hooded shirt. She dropped the headless eight iron she carried to ward off unruly dogs and flopped down in one of the big leather chairs. Both she and the chair let out an enormous exhalation.

"Want a beer?" he asked brightly, and she managed a smile.

"Whole point was to work off the last one," she gasped. "But I'm definitely going to walk back. Slowly, too."

"Okay, so give: What went down with the NCIS people?"

She took another minute to regulate her breathing. Every night except Sundays and Wednesdays, firsties in good academic standing were allowed to leave Bancroft Hall after dinner for what was called "town liberty," but they had to be back in by midnight. Given the academic load, Julie rarely took town liberty during the week.

"I didn't want to use the hall phones," she said. "Everyone's eavesdropping at the pay phones, and the cell phones—"

"Are radios. Right, I know that. Now, what happened?"

"There were two of them," she said. "A man and a woman. They started out being real polite. Then they went into one of those good cop/bad cop routines. I mean, how dumb is that? It was so cop show."

"What was the connection?"

She told him.

He blinked. Panties? "WTF? Over."

"Roger that, Father Time. They traced them back through my laundry number. I mean, c'mon, Dad, how embarrassing is that!"

"Certainly different," he said, getting up from his chair. "And they assumed that you and this plebe were closer than the regs envision?"

"They weren't exactly sharing. They flat out asked if Dell and I had been intimate. Answer: negative, of course. I wouldn't be caught dead dark-siding a plebe, even if it were legal, which of course it isn't. No firstie would."

"But he *was* found wearing your underwear, and dead, to boot. Logical question: How did he get your skivvies, and why on earth would a normal guy wear women's underwear?"

"You're assuming Dell was normal," she snapped. "Ipso facto, he wasn't."

"Is there some way a plebe could raid your skivvy drawer?"

"He'd have to be pretty brazen, but, yes, our rooms aren't locked during the academic day. You know, for surprise room inspections."

"So he could have knocked on the door, stepped in, and sounded off. Anyone in the passageway seeing him do it would assume that he was coming around. If no one happened to be in the room, once the door closed, he could take anything he wanted?"

"I suppose," she said. "Except this plebe, well, I don't think he'd have the balls to do that."

"So you did know him?"

She shrugged defensively. "Sort of. Like, I helped a lot of plebes during plebe summer, Dad. That's what we were there for, to get them through it, and to keep them from bolting out the front gate on parents' weekend."

He paced around the room, while Julie remained sprawled in her chair. "And they wanted to know if you remembered Dell, right?"

"That was the gist of their questions: Did I *know* Midshipman Dell? When was the last time I'd seen him? Did I have *any* sort of relationship with him? Had I contacted him via E-mail? Did I have him come around often?"

"And you told them what, exactly?"

"That I'd trained him, plus a thousand other worms, during plebe summer. That I'd had Dell come around a couple of times earlier in the year. I actually had to explain what a come-around was. That woman was pretty ignorant."

"Or playing dumb," he said.

"Whatever. I guess I *saw* Dell from time to time. Just like I saw every other plebe in our battalion. But I didn't really know him. He was just another plebe, you know? Unless they're really screwed up—you know, notorious—all plebes look alike."

"You said they did a bad cop/good cop routine. Over what?"

"The black guy played good cop. He was encouraging me to think real hard, remember every detail. Sincere. Concerned. Encouraging. The woman—" Julie shivered. "She was a piece of work. Good-looking, but so full of herself. Acted like she thought she was on TV or something. Kept reminding me they'd be checking my answers out with lots of other mids, so make sure I didn't hold anything back. That I was under oath, and that they'd be reporting everything to the commandant. Like that. It was *so* transparent."

"Unless they're partners, in which case they may have rehearsed all those moves," he said. "But I guess I can understand their interest."

"Dad, there's nothing to tell. He was just another plebe. Really! There are over a thousand of them."

"Okay, okay," he said, sitting back down so he could face her. "Were they, in fact, interviewing other mids?"

"I saw his company officer, the Twenty-fourth Company's commander, and another plebe in the commandant's waiting room. You should have seen the looks I got."

Julie was a pretty girl, so naturally other mids might make assumptions, Ev realized. Except he knew from his own personal experience that the plebe-firstie taboo was pretty strong. Plebes were lower than whale shit, and no firstie would demean him- or herself—by getting into any kind of relationship with such a lower-tier life-form other than to run the hell out of them. On the other hand, Ev had graduated before there had been women midshipmen at the Naval Academy, so maybe the dynamic had changed more than he knew.

"How'd they leave it?" he asked.

" 'Thank you for your time, Midshipman Markham. We'll be in touch if we have further questions, Midshipman Markham. Don't talk about this interview to anyone, Midshipman Markham.' Oh, and the kicker: The woman gets up, shakes my hand, and then goes, 'We're finished with you. For now.' "

Ev frowned. "You think you're not done?"

"I was waiting for her to say, 'Don't leave town, Midshipman Markham.' I put out rumor fires for the rest of the day within my own company. Hosed a control system quiz this afternoon. Then, of course, we had the obligatory company all-hands, touchy-feely to 'talk out' the Dell incident. Lieutenant Tarrens playing at grief counselor. That kind of wimp-ass, liberal shit really bites, you know? And there've been lots of grave pronouncements from the commandant's office. Heavy-duty cautions about discussing the incident: 'Remember, there are grieving parents involved here. Don't make it worse.' Like that."

"That last bit is reasonable enough," he said. "A midshipman is dead, after all. His parents didn't send him here to die."

"Okay, but you know what? There're lots of channels open if a plebe is having that much trouble. Everyone gets training on how to detect a suicidal situation, and every plebe is told a million times he can take a time-out if the plebe year shit gets too heavy. Where were his own company firsties? And how about *his* squad leader? The youngsters who're supposed to be mentoring? That's who they ought to be grilling, not me."

"Except for that one odd feature," he reminded her.

She flushed. "Okay, so I can't explain that," she said, getting up to go get something to drink. "But it wasn't like I was wearing *his* underwear."

He followed her into the kitchen. She was bent over, rooting impatiently around in the refrigerator for something to drink. Joanne had done the same thing in precisely the same way. Julie was even shaped like Joanne. He was struck by how much his daughter was like her mother. More so, now that Joanne was gone, he realized. He told her about calling Liz DeWinter.

"Really?" she said, straightening up with a jug of skim milk in her hand. "You think I need a *lawyer*?"

"Maybe," he replied. "And so does Liz. Especially right now, when everyone's staking out their positions. If nothing else, it will make them be more careful, say, if there's more to this incident than we know."

" 'Liz'? Do you know this woman from before?" she asked a bit too casually. He hesitated a fraction of a second before replying. Julie was still sensitive about the possibility that another woman might replace her mother. She could mouth all the right words about his getting on with life and so forth, but all the same, Ev knew he had to be careful. "Worth Battle recommended her, after I called him. I'd met her once at one of his boat parties. He thinks she's pretty good."

"But won't they find it suspicious? That I called for a lawyer? Since I truly wasn't involved?"

"You didn't call for a lawyer. I did. Which is why you'll let me break that news to them, okay? You're twenty-one, about to be commissioned, so the administration will deal directly with you. But I want you to call Liz. Now, in fact. You can stay for another few minutes. Let her tell you what to say if anything else comes down."

"And she's a *criminal* defense lawyer?"

"Well, you were talking to the Naval *Criminal* Investigative Service today, Julie."

"Got yourself a point, there, Judge," she said, going for some more milk. "Sure, I'll talk to her. Hell, yes. Then I've got to get back. Have an econ test tomorrow. God! Two more weeks."

Well, it's 2:30 in the morning and I'm back. Undetected, of course. I think I told you that I was going to be running the tunnels tonight. Left at 12:10, out the eighth wing's basement door, the one the mokes use to remove the daily trash. Dressed myself out in full sweats, the ones with the West Point Army logo, courtesy of a swim match bet against the Whoops a year ago. Had to wear the hood up so my shiny head didn't show. Did the usual recon: a slow jog, down to-

ward the seawall. Everyone thinks I shave my head for the swimming, but, hell, I'm the Shark! Don't need any edge. No, I shaved it for the resident Marines. Let 'em know I'm gung ho. I jog like I swim, with power and precision. Always have some Marine trail cadence echoing in my mind as I pick 'em up and put 'em down. Marine cadence: Le-oh-ft— le-oh-ft—le-oh-ft, right, le-oh-ft. Army cadence: Left, left, left . . . When I need to really breathe, I let my mouth hang open, baring my teeth. The Shark. Hungry. Top predator on the prowl. Cruising. I sometimes hope I'll run into someone out on those marble terraces at night, give 'em a mouthful of white teeth inside a darkened hood.

But not tonight. I'd called my little Johnnie vampire over on campus. You don't know her, but you'd like her, I think. Well, maybe not. She's just a little bit bent. Heavy into magic mushroom just now, and not the kind they serve in the mess hall. Made the cell call right after evening meal. Did it right in front of two plebes I had sweating bullets while plastered against the wall in their room. Made a little torment drill out of it, talking so they could hear, purring out some highly suggestive sweet nothings about her underwear. They couldn't hear her, but they sure as hell could hear me. A little phone sex routine, just to bother them, kept it going even after she'd hung up. But not before she set things up for after midnight, her room, of course, candles, some of that dismal shrieking shit they call Goth music, and with maybe a few friends to watch. . . . Goths love to watch. And so many of them are so stone-ugly that watching is all they'll ever get.

Anyhow, the Yard's a ghost town at that hour. Mother Bancroft at darkened-ship except, if you look closely, you can see the occasional flicker of flashlights where some poor bastards were sweating out a 2.0 average. I don't have that problem, of course. I study. Well, actually, there's a little bit more to it than that. It's what I study that makes the difference. I always get the Gouge. I am a master of the Gouge. Three, four times a day, I'm out there on the Academy intranet, sifting for fast-moving intelligence about the next day's quiz, or past patterns of questions. And: news flash! I actually study the material assigned by the profs. What a concept, huh? See, I've figured out which profs telegraph their test questions in their homework assignments. And which ones are too lazy to create a whole new quiz or exam, which means they go back to previous exams. All of which have to be approved. Via the faculty intranet. Where I have learned to lurk.

But you know, the system here is pretty straight-ahead. You work like hell to get the good grades going early on, and then ride the expectations train, with a little help from some selective hacking. After awhile, the profs expect me to do well, and then grade accordingly. That's how I have a 3.69 cume after almost four years. I do get help from the profs, of course. It's just that they don't always know they're helping me. . . .

So, where was I? Oh yeah, jogging down the road along Santee Basin, listening to the Academy sailboats bouncing around on a light evening chop coming in from the bay, their halyards clinking in time on their masts. Isn't that poetic? Easing on down to Dewey Field, which always smells like fresh-cut grass and dead fish. Then the obligatory recce run: jogging around the perimeter, scoping things out. They've got all those big light towers out there, but the rich people across the river bitched about the lights being left on all night, so now they shut 'em down, which is perfectly cool for us night runners.

But of course I wasn't out there for any exercise. I was on the lookout for the Jimmylegs. Funny-ass name. Apparently in days gone by, really gone by, the Academy's civilian police wore white lace-up leggings on the bottoms of their trou. Now, of course, they drive around in small pickup trucks, one, sometimes two to a truck, patrolling the entire Yard and the housing areas. Looking for A-rabs, probably. That's why I start out a tunnel run with a little topside jog, because the cops wouldn't care about a lone jogger, assuming they could even see me out here in the darkness along the river. Us mid coolies are supposed to be locked up for the night, of course, but sometimes guys come out to decompress from a bad day, and there have been lots of those over the past years, haven't there? This whole place is mostly a succession of bad days. You know what they say: This place sucks so bad, there's a permanent low pressure system over Annapolis.

Like today. Some plebe offed himself. Now that was news all right. No Gouge today on the LAN. Everybody with verbal E-diarrhea, sending shitloads of E-mail, bogging down the system. And the officers: oh, yeah. The officers were all stone-faced. Big trouble on the Dark Side. Made me smile, watching them today. Made me show my big teeth. And there are rumors. Man, are there some interesting rumors. Serious scuttlebutt moving down the wires. But you probably know all about that by now.

So here's the drill! I jog around until I see the headlights, then step over to stand next to a light standard, right on the seawall. Gray on black. Invisible when the security truck comes around Rickover Hall and goes down Holloway Road. Drive right on by without a pause. Gotta improve that situational awareness, guys, A-rabs in the bushes, get you killed someday if you don't. Every Marine knows that. Anyway, once the truck goes by, I hop the seawall. Last night, I had a nice high tide, which is cool—we sharks like deep water. I untied the rope from around my waist, hooked it up, and then climbed down onto that grating that covers the big storm drain. Which you've probably never seen, because it's usually underwater. The seawall stones are slippery and smell of dead fish and crabs. Yuk-os. If all those Save the Bay tree-huggers are doing such a great job, how come the bay always smells of dead fish?

Do you know the drain I'm talking about? No, of course you don't. It's made of concrete, and it's, like, five feet in diameter. I have to stoop over to make it. There's always a little bit of water running down the center. Condensation from all those steam tunnels up ahead—you know, the ones that crisscross under the Yard. I do my usual knee-capping running drill. It's fifteen hundred feet, almost exactly. I know the tunnels, you see. Really know them. You'd be amazed at what's down there. The graffiti, for instance. Guys have been *going down there for a long time. Playing games. Wonderful games, some of them.*

Last night, my objective was what I call "Broadway," that big tunnel that runs under Stribling. The storm drain's dark, but Broadway has lights. You get a nice burn in your thighs, bent over like that, high-stepping up a slope that goes three football fields. But, hell, I'm, like, tough as nails; I could run that particular tunnel all night. It takes 210 steps before you hit the flap doors. You have to count—it's pitch-black until you open the flap doors.

Everything's different when you're underground, you know. Well, you're a norm. Semi-norm? Maybe you don't. But I do. For one thing, the air doesn't move much. It's always warmer than you expect, especially around the steam lines. A peculiar smell, steam. Actually, it's all the old lagging that smells. Steam's just hot water. You get a hint of it in the storm drain, but once you get into Broadway, it's really strong.

Broadway is the main drag of the tunnel system. Ten feet square. Overhead lights in those little metal cages. Filled with steam pipes, telephone lines, electric power cable bundles, compressed-air lines, and even the sewer and water mains servicing Bancroft Hall. They have these underground concrete chambers that branch off of Broadway all along its route, where they have these huge chillers for air conditioning. Cross passageways that branch out to all the main academic buildings, the administration building next to the chapel, and the chapel itself. A whole world down there. My world.

Did you know I've been running those tunnels since the middle of youngster year? I have. A teammate on the swim team—guy was a serious sex hound—showed me something that not too many people know about: Ever since the Academy moved the power plant out of the Yard, every one of those utility lines eventually runs out into dear old Crabtown. Now, of course, as a firstie, I get town libs, but, hell, that's no fun. And besides, my time is the deep night-

time. Begins at midnight, because that's when my little vampires come alive over in town. What a guy won't do for true love, huh? Goth love. Now that's a game to die for, right? So to speak.

3

There was a phone message from Liz DeWinter waiting when Ev got back to his office from his Tuesday-morning seminar. He'd left the kitchen the previous night to give Julie some privacy when she had talked to Liz, so he'd been expecting this call. He answered a couple of questions for a waiting firstie, then closed the door to return Liz's call. From out in the Yard came the boom of the saluting cannon, signaling the arrival of a visiting foreign admiral. He reached a secretary, who put him through to Liz.

"Morning, Ev," she said. "I talked to Julie last night. Any further developments?"

"Not that I've heard," he said.

"Good. Oh, I need to fax you a client-representation form."

"Why don't I come out into town to get it, if that's okay? I don't want to use the office fax for that."

"Of course. Walk up Maryland Avenue to State Circle, turn left, go down Beale Street and look for number one oh seven. Two-story Georgian with black iron railings. I've got to get over to court right now, so I'll just leave the paperwork with Mary Angeles, our legal secretary."

He hesitated before asking her a question but then decided to go ahead. "Did she—I mean, did you get the impression that there was something going on? Like between her and that plebe?"

When she didn't answer right away, he wondered if he'd suddenly strayed into attorney-client privilege territory. "No," Liz replied, "I got zero indication of any personal relationship. She sounded mostly baffled by all the attention. Except of course for that bizarre underwear business."

"Yeah, that's weird, isn't it? Julie's such a straight-arrow girl. Wearing academic stars, top swimmer, popular without working at it, and, as best I can tell, accepted by her classmates as one of them and not some damn complaining girl."

"Good for her," Liz said. "But of course, you're a parent."

"You mean she could have taken a walk on the wild side and I'd be clueless?"

"Clueless, yes. Synonymous with *parent* among the college-parent set."

"Well," he said slowly, "I guess that's always possible. Ever since my wife died, I've probably been looking at Julie through rose-colored glasses."

"Julie's your only child?"

As in, she's all you've got left of your family. His voice failed him for a moment. She seemed to sense she'd intruded. "Look," she said briskly, "I still just want to see what develops, if anything. I told her not to mention that I was in the picture unless someone really started to hassle her. That you would drop that shoe when you thought it necessary."

"Good. I told her the same thing."

"For what it's worth, it just sounds to me like a standard investigation," she said.

"Thanks, Liz. I'll be by in about a half hour to do those papers. Oh, and should I bring a check?"

"'Fraid so," she said, and named her retainer figure. He gulped mentally, thanked her, and hung up. He had time to go into town during his lunch break, but first had to call his bank.

· · · ·

Jim Hall watched sympathetically as the Public Affairs staff scrambled to prepare the admiral's morning briefing. The executive staff was gathered in the superintendent's conference room on the second floor of the administration building, waiting for the supe, Admiral McDonald. Captain Robbins was meeting privately with the supe, but most of the department heads were present: Operations, Administrative, Public Works, Supply, Management, and the staff JAG. Technically, Jim worked for Operations, but because of the NCIS involvement, he had been asked to sit in. The mood in the conference room was grim; this was not going to be a routine meeting. The Public Affairs officer, a harried-looking aviator commander named, interestingly enough, Berry Springer, was continuously running his hand through his nonexistent hair as he turned sideways in his seat, listening intently to two assistants as they briefed him in stereo.

"Gentlemen, the superintendent," announced Admiral McDonald's rather imperious executive assistant. The admiral came through the door, followed by Captain Robbins. McDonald was a distinguished-looking officer, tall, with bushy eyebrows, keen blue eyes, and a ruddy face that belied the submariner's gold dolphins he wore on his uniform. He went to his chair at the head of the table and nodded at the Public Affairs officer, who went to the podium. Someone dimmed the lights and then the PAO went through a review of press articles and other media interest in the plebe's death. It was not a pretty picture. Normally, when there was an untoward incident at the Academy, the supe would let the press briefing go on just long enough to get the flavor. This time, he let the PAO go through all the articles. No one spoke when he was finished.

"Tell me again how we are characterizing this?" the admiral asked.

"Under investigation; initial speculation from 'informed sources'—that's me—is that it was an accident."

"At that hour of the morning."

"Well, yes, sir, Admiral, but the alternatives are suicide, or worse."

The admiral nodded. "Okay, so how about suicide? Any indicators?"

"None, sir," the commandant said. "He wasn't a star, but the company officer says he wasn't a total goat, either. His roommate discounted suicide immediately. He said Dell was making it. Barely, but making it."

"And this, um, other aspect?"

Robbins shrugged. "We've got NCIS into it, Admiral. The rumor's out. Some questions on it, but Public Affairs says nothing until NCIS completes their investigation."

"They buy that, Berry?"

"So far, anyway, Admiral."

The supe looked over at Jim, who was never sure whether or not Admiral McDonald knew who he was. "Mr. Hall? You were at the scene?"

"Unfortunately, yes, sir, I was."

"No knives sticking out of his back, or other indications of foul play?"

"The body was no longer thick enough for anything to be stuck in it, Admiral."

This comment provoked an embarrassed silence.

"Okay, troops," the admiral said wearily. "We have a dead plebe. We have an NCIS investigation. We have lots and lots of wonderful press coverage. We have the Board of Visitors coming between now and graduation, and we have the vice president of the United States here on commissioning day to make the graduation speech. What we need now is damage control until we have some answers. Berry?"

"Sir?"

"Refresh the executive staff, in writing, about how this works when we're under siege. One point of contact. One source of information. No sidebars with anybody. No speculation as to what happened. Rumor control within Bancroft Hall. You know the drill."

"Yes, sir, I'll have it out today."

"Dee," he said, turning to the commandant, "Let's see if we can get inside the NCIS investigation somehow. I don't want them spooling up any bigger deal than is necessary, and I'd really like to keep it local."

"Aye, aye, sir," the commandant replied, then made some notes. Jim thought Robbins hated being called Dee.

"Senior chaplain, I want to call the parents and reassure them that we're going to find out what happened here just as quickly as we can. Set that up for me, please. And make sure they have a warm body down in Norfolk to hold their hands."

The senior chaplain, a Navy captain, nodded and made his own notes.

"Everybody else: We're very close to the end of the year. I'm saddened and deeply disappointed that we've lost a mid this close to the end. I want everyone to strike a balance, however, between handling this incident and ending the year properly so that the class of 2002 goes out with an appropriate bang. The commandant's office will be the focal point of all incoming information on this matter. The PAO's office will be the focal point of all *outgoing* information. Having the vice president here is almost as big a deal as having the president, from the standpoint of security, protocol, and logistical planning, especially after last year in New York. We want to show proper deference to the Dells' family tragedy, while still keeping the commissioning week train on the tracks. Any questions?"

There were none, or at least none anyone wanted to put to the admiral.

"Okay, let's get to it," the admiral said as he got up.

Ev pushed away the remains of a microwave dinner and vowed once again never to eat another one. He pitched the plastic tray into the trash and went to answer the phone. It was Julie. Finally.

"Dad," she said without preamble. "I think they searched my room."

"*What?* Who? And how do you know?"

"The second class in the room next door. They said they saw those two NCIS people coming out of my room with the OOD just as they were getting back from their last class. Those people who interviewed me."

"Did they take anything?"

"Not that I can tell. Melanie's still checking her side." Melanie Bright was Julie's roommate. He thought for a moment. "This may be serious, Julie. Your cell phone up? You got minutes left?"

She said she did.

"Call Liz DeWinter. Tell her what's happened. If she's willing to come after hours, we can meet here. I'll drive over and get you."

Julie called back forty-five minutes later, confirming that Liz was willing to meet right away. Ev drove over to get Julie, meeting her near the chapel. As he drove up, he saw that she was talking to another midshipman. They had their heads close together, but the mid walked away when he saw the approaching headlights.

"Who was that?" Ev asked as Julie got in.

"Tommy Hays. You remember Tommy. Classmate. Swim team. No sweat—he's cool."

Ev wanted to ask if they'd been talking about what was going on, but he decided not to pursue it. Ever since Joanne had died, Julie had become somewhat secretive about her social life. She gradually stopped bringing other mids home on the weekends, and sometimes took a weekend without telling him where she was going—or with whom. He was pretty sure Tommy Hays was or had been a regular. But everyone on the faculty knew that spring of first class year was a stressful time for Bancroft Hall romances. With graduation, commissioning, and first duty orders rapidly approaching, they either signed up for one of the assembly-line marriages in the chapel at the end of commissioning week or they never saw each other again as they scattered to fleet training schools all over the country. Ev drove Julie back to the house in worried silence.

Liz arrived fifteen minutes after Ev returned home with Julie. She showed up wearing designer jeans, an oversized Columbia University sweatshirt, and carrying what looked like a fat day planner. Ev heard the car in the drive and went to the porch to meet her. He could tell from her expression as she looked around that she was probably surprised by the size of the lot and the house. People who didn't know him wondered how a Naval Academy professor could afford a place like this. She locked the Mercedes and headed for the front porch, where she saw Ev waiting for her in the lighted doorway and waved. He greeted her and led her to the spacious study, where Julie, still in her working blues, was waiting with a worried look on her face. Ev asked Liz if she'd like a drink, but she declined and turned directly to Julie. "Okay, Julie, tell me again what happened."

Ev fixed himself a scotch while Julie talked to Liz. "And no one's contacted you?" Liz was asking. "No official summonses to front offices?"

"Not a word. Since we talked last night, I've been going to classes, working out with the swim team, formation—the usual stuff. Our company officer didn't know anything about this visit, either."

"Or so he said."

Julie thought about that for a moment and then shrugged. "I guess that's possible. But when I signed out in the batt office this evening, no one seemed to care."

Liz turned to Ev, who was sitting on the brick apron of the fireplace.

"I'll take you up on that offer of a drink now," she said.

"I have some single malt," he said. "Straight up?"

"Perfect," she said, apparently surprised that he remembered from the boat party. As he fixed her drink, she looked over at Julie. "Now that you're a suspect, you want a drink, too?"

"What!" Julie exclaimed, her eyes widening. Ev brought Liz her drink and then sat down in one of the upholstered chairs.

"If federal police did in fact come in and search your room," Liz said, "it means they may have a federal search warrant with your name on it. Did they go into your computer?"

"Gosh, I don't think so, but then—"

"Right, you'd have no way of knowing."

"Warrant?" Ev asked. "Based on what?"

"That's the million-dollar question," Liz said. "Until they charge her, they don't have to tell her anything. But they must have something that implicates Julie in that plebe's death, something more than the underwear thing." Then she stopped. "Unless—"

"Unless what?" Ev said. Julie was sitting on the edge of her seat now, just like he was, chewing on a fingernail.

"Does the Academy have the right to search a midshipman's room at any time? Or do they have to go through due process?"

Julie looked at Ev. "I'd have to look in the reg book," she said. "But my guess is, they can if they want to. It's not like a civilian school. They can *inspect* anytime they want to."

"And your company officer knew nothing about this?" Ev asked.

"He failed open when I asked him," Julie said, surprising Ev with the naval engineering expression. "He said he'd find out, but I hadn't heard anything by evening meal hour."

The phone rang. Ev checked the caller ID. "It's a two-nine-three number; that's the Academy," he said. He picked it up and identified himself. "Yes, she is," he said, and then listened for another minute, his eyes on Julie, who was getting a deer-in-the-headlights look back on her face.

"Very well, I'll pass that on, Mr. Tarrens." He glanced at his watch. "Will twenty-one hundred be satisfactory? She's meeting with her attorney right now." Another pause. "That's right. So twenty-one hundred works? . . . Good. And could you please pass something up your chain of command for me? Midshipman Markham will want her attorney present for any further encounters with NCIS regarding the Dell incident."

He saw Liz frown when he said that, but he didn't waver. She probably would have wanted him to wait a little longer before revealing that Julie had counsel, but what the hell. There had to be something going on over there. Something bad. He identified Elizabeth DeWinter as Julie's attorney, then said good night and hung up.

"How'd he react?" Liz asked.

"Audible gulp. Said he'd pass it right along. And twenty-one hundred is when they want you back in Mother Bancroft," he told Julie.

"He mention searching my room?" she asked.

"Nope. Just that he wanted you back at Bancroft, in his office, as soon as possible. He was trying for a little bluster, as in, Right now would be nice, until I mentioned Liz here. He didn't seem to know what to do then."

"Okay," Liz interjected. "I don't propose to spend the evening in Bancroft Hall. If they want to ask more questions when you get back, you reiterate that you're not talking to anyone until your lawyer is present, and your lawyer's not available until normal working hours tomorrow morning. On the other hand, see if you can find out why NCIS agents were in your room. I'll be interested to see what they say, if anything. Especially if they use the inspection pretense."

Julie was shaking her head slowly. "I don't know what's going down here," she said in a small voice. "I haven't done anything. Not to that plebe, nor to anyone else."

"Good," Liz said brightly. "Ev, is this how the Navy usually does business?"

"The Naval Academy isn't the Navy," he said immediately. "But, once you swear the oath, you do surrender a lot of civil liberties when you go into military service."

"So they could go in and search her room just because they wanted to?"

"They can do a room inspection anytime they want to."

"Using NCIS agents?" Julie asked.

"Well, that's a point," he admitted. "But if the OOD was present, they could simply say they were along for the ride while *he* did the inspection." He turned back to Liz. "But look: If military law's been invoked—you know, the UCMJ—and they're getting ready to accuse Julie of something, maybe she needs to ask for a military co-counsel." He paused, realizing Liz might take that wrong. "I mean, um, I don't mean—"

She let him off the hook. "I understand what you're saying. Military law is different. But I don't think we're there yet. Besides, if it comes to that, we don't let *them* appoint a JAG defense counsel. We'll go get our own, preferably from somewhere outside the Academy."

"Defense counsel?" Julie squeaked. Ev could see real fear in her eyes now.

"Normally, I'd tell you to relax, Julie," Liz said, "But what you need to be now is vigilant. They're going to be afraid of me, or at least more afraid of me than they would be of some JAG lawyer *they* appoint as your defense counsel. A midshipman is dead, and that's serious enough. Somehow, it involves you. Beyond that, we don't know squat. Which means our next step is to make them tell us."

Julie just stared into space.

"Why don't I give you a ride back to Bancroft Hall?" Liz said, giving Ev a look that meant, Go with me on this. She put down her scotch, untouched, and got up to emphasize the point. Ev understood and nodded. While Julie went back out to the kitchen to get her hat, Liz said she'd come back after dropping Julie off.

When she returned twenty minutes later, they went back to the study, where she now sampled the single malt.

"So, how'd that go?" he asked.

"Basically, I needed to calibrate the client," Liz said. She told him that Julie was more pissed off than anything else and, unfortunately, more than willing to talk to the authorities if that's what it would take to clear this mess up, especially since she hadn't done anything. "I told her she needed to play by my rules for a while. That you don't talk to the enemy, especially when they're keeping you in the mushroom mode."

"Right."

"I think she got the picture. I told her to be perfectly respectful: no displays of attitude. On the other hand, she shouldn't talk to anyone, not her friendly company officer, not the commandant, not the NCIS, the FBI, or the CIA, whoever and whatever, unless I was present."

"They won't like that," he said.

"Probably not. I reminded her that if she hasn't done anything, they can't make any kind of case against her, unless, of course, she inadvertently hands them something. And that that's rule two, by the way."

"Rule one being never lie to your lawyer?"

"Precisely. I told her that she must tell me the absolute truth with regard to any question I ask. I promised, in turn, not to make value judgments, and confirmed that what she tells me is always protected by lawyer-client confidentiality. I made her promise."

Ev nodded thoughtfully. "And did she? Promise?"

Liz sipped some scotch. "You know, I'd swear she hesitated. Just a fraction, but it was there."

"I'm not entirely surprised," he said. "What you're telling her makes perfect lawyer sense, but it violates just about every principle of ethics and professionalism they've been pounding into her for four years. I can understand that hesitation."

"About telling the truth?"

"No, no, about not talking to them. About clamming up and hiding behind a lawyer's skirts, so to speak. The mids are taught to address issues head-on. To be forthright.

Truthful to the degree of pain. Never to equivocate."

"I suppose. But look: Our legal system is trial by lawyer, not trial by jury. Usually, the best lawyer wins, not necessarily the most innocent client. I can't be the best lawyer here unless I know the truth. And frankly, that's what I think the hesitation was about. Not about hiding behind my so-called skirts."

Ev blinked. "You think she's hiding something?"

Liz waved her hand dismissively. "Hell, Ev, I don't know. But I'm a defense lawyer. My clients tend to be deceptive. I always make them promise to tell me the truth. She did, but she tingled my trip wires in the process."

What has my daughter been thinking? he wondered, frowning. *And was she, God help us all, involved in what happened to that poor plebe?* "Well, I'll certainly reinforce that notion," he said. "That's fundamental."

"Thank you," she said. "Back to rule two: not to offer them anything, even out of some sense of duty. She's dealing with cops now. Nine times out of ten, when cops have nothing, it's the suspect who hands something to them by opening his yap. Remind her of that. Coming from you, it might carry more weight."

Upset by the word *suspect,* he got up and started to pace around the room. "We're so close to commissioning week," he said. "More than just graduation. It's a victory in every sense, victory after four very hard years operating within a system designed to remove a quarter to a third of them by attrition. And here she is, being worked over by federal cops for something some damned plebe did?"

"We're assuming it was something the plebe did; they're acting like somebody may have helped him do it."

"What?" he shouted, whirling around. "Now you're talking *homicide*?"

She leaned back in the chair, a picture of lawyerly composure now. "If NCIS is interviewing people and conducting searches without warrants, then this is more than just a routine incident investigation."

Ev swore and went to refill his drink. This day was truly turning to shit.

"Look," Liz said, obviously concerned that she might have gone too far. "I've upset you, and perhaps prematurely. Bottom line? They're on notice over there. Now we have to wait."

He plopped back down in his chair and tried to get his mind around what was happening. She smiled at him, and it transformed her face, putting a sweetness there. He'd forgotten how attractive she was, with those coloratura features and silken white skin. He unconsciously glanced over her shoulder toward his wife's picture up on the bookshelf. She caught his glance, turned, and looked at the picture for a moment. "That was your wife? Worth told me what happened. That's a lovely picture."

"That was . . . Joanne, yes," he said softly.

"Julie favors her," she said, turning back around. "How are you coping with all that?"

"Poorly," he said immediately, then almost regretted his candor. He didn't know her that well. "I mean, I get by, one day at a time, I suppose. There are places I don't go. Like chapel—I stopped going to Sunday chapel because I'd get too emotional. The senior chaplain—he's an ex-Marine— asked me one day whom I was weeping for, her or me. As in, Stop feeling sorry for yourself."

"That's such bullshit," she said. "Grief suppressed poisons the soul."

"Well," he said with a small shrug. "He did make me think. Didn't take me long to figure out the real answer, either. But I still stopped going."

"Showed him," she said, and he smiled despite himself.

"How about you?" he asked, surprising himself. "Worth said you'd been married before. You have someone in your life?"

"No one of substance," she said. "I was married twice, actually. You know what they say about the triumph of hope over experience? Well, my first ex was a Marine aviator.

That one was all experience. Second ex was another lawyer, and that was hopeless."

He laughed. "I know all about those Marine aviators," he said. "We had a couple in my first fighter squadron. Certifiably crazy bastards, but definitely fun."

"Precisely," she said. "But, trust me, you wouldn't want to marry one." She shook her head and got up to leave. He got up, as well.

"We need to take this Dell matter one day at a time," she said. "It's in their interest to put it to bed quickly, so unless there's some glaring evidence of foul play, that's what they'll do. I'll keep Julie as safe as I can."

"Good," he said. "And I'll keep in touch with you, too. Julie will probably want to talk to me."

"Yes, please do," she said, pausing at the front door. "And if you need to talk—about anything—please feel free to call me."

He looked down into her eyes and saw a smile of friendly sympathy. "Thanks," he said. "I will."

It's me. I'm in computer lab. Finished their stupid little finals project. So, let me tell you how it went. My after-hours town libs, that is. I mean, it was a blast. Met up with the Goths in their lair on West Franklin Street. That's what they call it—"their lair." Okay, so these Johnnie chicks are seriously whacked, but they're hot as hell underneath all those black rags and the weird makeup. What a surprise when you check out the underscene! And they will do anything as long as I play along with their Goth shit. And I mean anything. I'll bet you know what I mean.

It's a rush, especially when I can experience such a total Jekyll and Hyde existence. By day, I'm supermid. Sir! Yes, sir! At the top of my considerable lungs. A-J squared away to the max. Creases on my creases. A military-bearing ramrod stuck so far up my ass that my ears are aligned. Hoo-ah! And then, once the superstraight world of Mother B is asleep, out comes the vampire Dyle. That's right, vampire. Okay, okay, so the whole Goth-vampire–death worship scene is—what's the word, infantile? Fucking laughable? Especially when you realize that they're serious about that shit? Thing is, though, I'm like a dead ringer for the bad guy, especially in costume. One of the girls is in their drama club, so she got her claws on a vampire costume. And that's our town gig—the Goths as bait, and Dyle as the hammer.

You ought to come along. Works like this: past midnight—the girls in their Goth drag: calf-length black dresses, some very white makeup, lots of eye shadow, red, red lipstick, hair everywhere, maybe a dog-collar, laced-strap witch-bitch boots. Those swirling black dresses are slit up the sides, so if they work it right, they can flash black mesh thigh-highs. And that's what they do: They stroll down the street after midnight, ease into and out of the townie bars. Inevitably, a couple of locals will rise to the occasion. Come out onto the street and make their drunken noises. Jeering at the Goths. Calling them "lezzies" "freaks," the usual. The girls pretend to ignore them. Put their noses in the air, supremely intellectual Johnnies, much too high-and-mighty to respond to the provocation of mere village louts. Tossing back quietly muttered words about losers, white trash, the makings of a permanent underclass. But swirl the skirts just a little, enough to flash. Look back. Smile.

The boys follow, of course—they almost always do. Usually, one of them is the alpha dog, the others, onesies, twosies, almost never more than two, the perpetual followers. Not quite sure of what they're going to do next, but enjoying the scene. Everyone shining attitude, which goes pretty quick to sexual taunts: The girls are pros, sluts, whooers, ready to peddle their asses, and hey, the boys are game, right? They've each got two-bits. That'll do it, right, babe? Then the girls begin to ape the walk of working girls on the stroll, laughing at the following rubes, putting an element of challenge into it, but keeping thirty feet or so be-

*tween the boys and themselves, leading them, always lead-
ing them, toward the alley. Toward me. The girls flash some
more leg, attend to a stocking, maybe rub each other on the
ass a little, making sure the rubes are watching. That usually does it.*

*When they get to the alley, they turn on the boys and make
vampire faces at them, hissing, showing teeth, looking
ridiculous, of course, but setting up the play. By now, they've
undone their tops a little, giving the village idiots an eyeful,
then pretending to discover that they're exposing themselves, hissing some more, making witch signs, but grabbing
at their clothes, maybe a little scared now as the big bad
boys approach while the poor defenseless vamps retreat farther into the alley. Toward where I'm waiting.*

*"Who-ee! It's Draculady! Hey, Draculady, bite this.
How 'bout it? Want to suck something? Here it is, witchy
woman!" Grabbing at their crotches and laughing their
asses off as they turn into the alley, their jeers and taunts
becoming more explicit. They're aroused now, sensing the
possibility that they can maybe get some. Hell, there's no
one around. The girls have been flashing T and A for the
past block, begging for it, really. There're three of them and
just two weird-ass St. John's College bitches playing at being vampires or some other equally strange college-girl
shit. The girls stop halfway down the alley, blank brick
walls rising into the dark on either side. They back up to
one of the walls, spread their arms out behind them, flat on
the wall, breasts heaving in obvious excitement, moving
their bodies. The boys are locked on now, alpha dog intent,
responding to a raging short circuit between his brain and
his crank, the followers eager but not sure who's going to
do what.*

*Then the girls start chanting weird shit in unison: "Be-
gone! Begone! Fie on the lot of you." The boys, jeering
again at the vampire act, approach in a loose semicircle.
The girls let their slit skirts part just a little, showing off
some more, but keep chanting. "Oooh, I'm so scared!" the
alpha dog goes, rubbing his crotch again, letting them see*

his action. "Don't bite me. Please, don't bite me!" Trying to laugh, but mostly focused on what they're showing them.

And then: I'm there. Behind them. In full fucking costume: black cavalryman boots that add about two inches to my height. Black midshipman uniform pants stuffed into the boots. White Ballanchino formal shirt with no collar. And the cape: this huge fucking cape, black outside, all red satin inside, sweeping down to the tops of my boots. My face painted dead white. Eyes circled in yellow-looking makeup. Teeth glistening with a little Vaseline. My very big teeth. My shaven head covered in a black rubber wet suit hood. I'm stretching up to damn near seven feet tall, arms wide under the cape, black rubber gloves on my hands. Sometimes I stick two extra-long white plastic fangs on my canine teeth.

The girls know the drill: They look behind the followers, put trembling hands to their mouths, open their clothes up just a little more. Alpha dog, he's on autotrack, can't tear his eyes away. But the followers? They see the girls looking over their shoulders, and they turn around to see whassup. Which is when I let out a sound like a king cobra, the hiss from Hell, causing their blurry, drunken eyes to get as big as saucers and their stupid mouths to drop open like turtles. At which point, I slam their slack-jawed heads together like the pair of cantaloupes they really are. As they go down, alpha dog, who hears the cobra bit, is turning around to check it out, tearing his eyes away from the girls at last, not seeing them lunge for him, grabbing his arms, pulling them behind and up, not even aware they're doing it because all he can see is my face, my painted, hooded death's-head face looming down at him, my eyes coming unhinged as I cross them ever so slightly and bare my glistening teeth, and then—here's the topper— I fucking roar.

He faints. They always do. Get the guy sober, he'd laugh at the thought of a vampire. But drunk? And after the girls

have set him up? It's pure fear, helped along by the girls doing their weird vampire shit. He turns around, suddenly he
can't move, his buddies are flat on the ground, and he's
looking up at the biggest human-shaped thing he's ever
seen, which looks, sounds, and acts like every vampire
nightmare he's had since he was a little kid, and it's right
fucking there, fangs and all, right in his face!

They faint. And sometimes they leak a little. Yes, they do.
The girls run, of course, bursting with laughter. I follow,
but not before I do some things to the big man on campus.
I usually don't really injure him, but he might just hurt a
little—when he wakes up, of course. This last time, we took
his buddies' pants down, arranged the two of them in the
69 position, and called the cops just for grins. But usually,
we just fly out of there, running down the block behind the
bar, back to the lair. A cop car saw us once, the guy driving
so surprised when he got a look at me that he rear-ended a
parked car, which gave us time to disappear through the St.
John's campus and back to their shitty little apartment—
excuse me, Goth lair. Must stay in character, we must. And
when we get back there, guess who's really excited now?
Heh-heh.

We've done it a couple times this year, all to different
town slobs. You'd think the word would get around. On the
other hand, I'd bet it's not like they want to talk about it,
right? Like: Hey, man, listen to what happened to us last
night. Like: You remember when we went after those Johnnie bitches in their vampire costume? And then . . . I don't
think so.

I know, I know: One of these nights, the guy won't faint.
Or it'll be some dude we've done before. But I'm ready for
that, too. In fact, I'm getting more ready for that possibility
every day, especially now that June week is approaching.
Just between you and me, I'm planning a little solo op.
Maybe go lurking in town on my own this time. Let a previ-
ous victim get a quick look. See if I can get him to chase me.
See if I can get him to catch me down in my tunnels. See

what happens then. More good training for my next incarnation in the glorious Corps.

It's like I want to experience some maximum violence before I leave here. Maximum. Like what happened to that plebe. That was certainly extreme, don't you think?

4

As of Wednesday morning, Ev still hadn't heard back from Julie. All through his eight o'clock class, he'd been anxious to call Liz DeWinter to see if she'd heard anything. At the break, he tried her office, but she was already in court. Frustrated, he went down to talk to the HSS division director, Captain Donovan. Ev technically worked for Professor Welles, the chairman of his department, but Captain Donovan was the senior military officer. Growing increasingly anxious, Ev had felt he needed a military opinion, not a civilian one. But the captain had not been helpful. He'd heard about the incident, of course, and also about Julie's involvement. He'd been polite but firm: Let the Academy do its investigation. That way, we get the facts. Then we focus on any required actions. Ev expressed his concerns about the administration possibly using Julie as a scapegoat, but the captain had dismissed that notion. Let them do their investigation. It was the Navy way.

He'd gone back to his office to get ready for the next class, more uneasy than ever, and really wishing Julie would call. He was sitting at his desk, correcting some papers and chewing absently on some folded-up mystery meat, when Liz called.

"Talked to Julie," she said. "Kind of anticlimactic. Her big meeting with the company officer turned out to be a non-event. He just wanted her to know that the visit from NCIS was a room inspection, quote, unquote."

"Sounds to me like your presence has been a shot across their bows, then."

"That was the point, Ev."

"I talked to my boss this morning," he said. "Checking to see what was filtering through the military network."

"And?"

"And he said he'd heard there was an investigation, that Julie was involved, and that she had a lawyer."

Liz thought about that for a moment. "That was quick. So, he's in a neutral corner?"

"He's a division director," Ev said. "That makes him part of the Academy administration."

"As opposed to being an ally of yours."

"Well, he was friendly, and sympathetic. I think."

"Okay. That brings me to something I need to say to you, and it goes along with what I told Julie last night when I dropped her off. *You* need to stop talking to people about this. I know I can't order you to do this, of course, but as Julie's attorney, I should be the primary interface with anyone in the Academy administration from here on out."

He thought about it and then sighed. "Yeah, you're right. So anything I hear or find out about should come to you, then?"

"Yes. And don't go playing detective. The next step is up to them."

"But she hasn't done anything!"

She ignored his protest. "We wait until they want to see her again."

"I just hate not knowing," Ev said. "Since Joanne died, Julie's well . . . well, more important."

Then she surprised him. "Would you like to have dinner with me?" she asked.

"What? Why, sure. Uh, do you have a favorite place?"

"How about Maria's? Tonight. Say seven? Subject, of course, to any breaking developments over in the Yard."

"Roger that. Seven it is. If you have to cancel, call my

home number. In the meantime, I'll keep away from Bancroft so they won't catch me looking in the windows of the interrogation cell."

She laughed. "See you at seven, Ev."

He checked his schedule. He had two more classes that afternoon, a fuller day than usual, which was probably for the best, considering his state of mind. He was surprised when Liz called him again just after three o'clock.

"Hey, counselor," he said. "Change your mind about dinner already?"

"No. But have you heard anything more from Julie?"

"No," he said, sitting up as he sensed the urgency in her voice. "Has something happened?"

She hesitated. "I need her to call me as soon as possible, Ev. I've left her a message to that effect, but she may contact you first."

"What's going on, Liz?"

"There's a rumor circulating through law-enforcement circles that the midshipman suicide case isn't as clear-cut as everyone wants us to believe."

He didn't understand. "What's that got to do with Julie?"

"Hopefully, nothing. And I've got to tell you, cops are the worst rumor mongers there are. Let's make a deal: no Dell case this evening, okay? I'll see you later."

After dinner, they walked up the hill from the Colonial seaport area toward State Circle. Liz's eighteenth-century house was framed inside an iron-fenced compound just off State Circle. They entered a tree-lined, cobblestoned drive through two leaning stone columns that were engraved with the name Weems. Her house was three stories of ivy-covered Flemish lock brickwork outside, with glowing, if somewhat uneven, heart pine floors, plaster and lathe walls, leaded windows, ornate crown moldings and wainscoting, and sixteen-foot ceilings inside.

Liz left Ev in a living room furnished with what looked like period reproduction furniture and went out to the kitchen to get the makings for the Rusty Nails they had talked about over coffee. He first sat down in a lovely Sheraton-period wing chair, which was downright uncomfortable, then moved over to the sofa. He felt apprehensive about being here, in this woman's house. They had enjoyed themselves once he'd overcome his own awkwardness. This was the first time he'd been out with anyone since Joanne had died, and he hadn't been sure what to think of it. Liz had put him at his ease with a steady flow of bright conversation, quick-witted jokes, and stories about clients. Once he'd relaxed a bit, he joined in with equally funny stories about midshipmen and their antics. He'd ended up talking about his own life toward the end of dinner—growing up in Annapolis, the pervasive influence of the Academy on life in the state capital, and the satisfaction of finally returning home after his time in the Navy.

He'd done twelve years in naval aviation before getting out, and then he'd gone to grad school out on the West Coast to get a Ph.D. A week after he'd successfully defended his dissertation, and while he was still shopping around for a faculty appointment, his father had had a heart attack and died. He and Joanne had come back to the East Coast with their eleven-year-old daughter to stay with his mother for a while, and then the appointment in the Academy's Political Science Department had opened up and they'd never left. Once he'd taken the Academy position, his mother, to his surprise, went into what seemed like a deliberate decline, becoming a semi-invalid. One night five years later, she turned her face to the wall and died.

He had explained to Liz that leaving the Navy after almost thirteen years had been Joanne's idea, although he knew the truth to be somewhat more complex. His father had been a strong and domineering man, and Ev's passage into the academy and naval service had been something of a foreordained matter, not really open for discussion. Not that Ev had objected, at least not until he had become a plebe and had all those romantic notions about midshipman life yelled out of him in the first twenty-four hours of plebe summer.

He'd met and married Joanne, a Merrill Lynch stockbroker, while doing an instructor tour in Pensacola, and then watched with chagrin as she underwent a similar experience once he had to return to the real Navy world of sea duty, with a lot of the romance being flattened by the stark fact that naval aviators mostly flew in the away direction. The truth was, he'd been as lonely as she had been when he was cooped up in the hot, crowded, constantly noisy steel catacombs underneath the flight deck. Life as a carrier aviator alternated between two extremes. There was the huge adrenaline rush of being flung off the end of the flight deck while strapped inside a cramped Plexiglas cocoon mounted over a pair of unruly rockets built by the lowest bidder. And then there was the seemingly endless, six-month blear of briefs, debriefs, alerts, training sessions, transits, crowded port visits, duty days, safety stand-downs, no-fly Sundays, punctuated occasionally by the jolt of seeing a squadron mate misjudge a landing and go over the angle in a rending screech of flaming metal into the always-waiting sea. Doing this while missing his new wife, their daughter's early years, and the luxury of life in America made it hard to ignore the fact that the next promotion would mean more deployments and more separation. Even when he had been on shore duty, he had detected a gradual hollowing out of their marriage, as each next deployment loomed ever closer and Joanne began to erect those walls that would support her once he left. Give her credit: She'd never issued any ultimatums, but he had been able to see the choice he would ultimately have to make.

It hadn't hurt that Joanne had some money. She'd stayed with Merrill Lynch during his active-duty career, and her money had paid off his parents' remaining mortgage when his father died and they'd moved into the house. They'd had eight years of a wonderfully normal life in Annapolis as he moved from probationary to tenured status on the faculty. Eight years of coming home every night, waking up in the same place every morning without the crash and bang of jets landing on the roof, or the rattling, scraping sounds of the arresting wires reeling into their greasy lairs to await the next trap, sharing the travails of bringing up just one teenager, actual family vacations over on the Atlantic beaches, the short, sharp spats they both recognized as episodes of cabin fever, the sad subsidence of his mother as she pined away for his father, the care of a home and yard and gardens, secure in the knowledge that he'd probably be around to see the results of his labors. In short, normal American life. He explained to Liz that if he'd never been in the Navy, he would never have appreciated the relative tranquility and productive purpose of his civilian existence.

On the other hand, he'd done nothing to stop his daughter, Julie, from falling under the same romantic delusions about the Academy. Absent his father's political connections, Julie had made it through the grueling admissions process pretty much on her own merits, although it didn't hurt her admissions package that Ev was an alumnus and faculty member. He remembered vividly her comment during parents' weekend, four years ago now, when she had described the downer from the huge victory of getting an appointment to spending the entire first night in Bancroft Hall learning how to stencil her plebe summer whites. He had experienced the very same feelings, and could still smell the stencil ink and hear the upperclassman screaming at him to wash his ink-stained hands, something he'd been trying to do for an hour.

And then Joanne died, he thought, pressing a hand on the smooth fabric of the sofa. Just like that, he realized, his eyes blinking. His whole life here, his normal, post-Navy, happy, real life, had begun with his father's sudden death. And then his mother's. And then Joanne's. Viewed one way, his ultimate homecoming to Annapolis had been a veritable chronology of death. This thought had been at the back of his mind during their entire dinner, and at times, Liz's bright conversation and upbeat attitude had cast a surreal haze around his own thoughts. Liz had skillfully urged him to open up, he realized now, offering small tidbits about her own past, her two ex-husbands, and the challenges of being single at her age. He could not help but notice how other men in the crowded restaurant watched her smile and play with her hair and envied him sitting there, getting her full attention. Despite his emotional fragility, Liz had grown on him, filling his senses and attention. Even so, he'd felt like he was walking through a waking dream, not knowing quite what was coming next but increasingly willing to go forward and see.

Liz came back into the living room. She'd brought a tray with scotch, Drambuie, two snifters, a small sharp knife, a heavy spoon, an ice bucket, and a lemon. She put the tray on the coffee table, tapped a remote to ignite the gas fire in the fireplace, turned on one more table lamp, and sat down at the other end of the sofa. She was wearing a silk pantsuit, and she'd done something to her hair while out in the kitchen. Adjectives tumbled through his thoughts: *lovely, warm, smart, sexy, sweet.* He felt his cheeks warming just a little when he realized he was staring.

"We're in luck," she announced, arranging the things on the tray. "I even had the lemon."

He smiled but didn't say anything, suddenly not willing to trust his voice. A familiar feeling was gathering in his chest.

"So, a Rusty Nail," she said. "One half scotch, one half Drambuie, which I think is scotch-based, and a twist of lemon peel, all over cracked ice. That how you remember it?"

"Yes," he mumbled. "It's been awhile, though." For everything, he thought. And then: I shouldn't have come here.

"I've found a lot of bartenders don't even know how to make one of these," she said, cracking ice cubes against her palm with the back of the heavy spoon. "But they're supposed to be a lot more hangover-proof than most after-dinner drinks." She cracked ice into each snifter, then sliced off a scrape of lemon peel and squeezed the rind side over the ice, filling the air with the pungent smell of citron. Then she poured equal measures of the liquors and passed one snifter over to him. "Here you go," she said. "Long life."

He tipped snifters with her and then they both sat there, holding their drinks, facing each other on the sofa, with the fireplace flickering nearby. He sampled the drink and pronounced it perfect.

"Thank you," she said. "It's been a lovely evening. Thanks for dinner, even though it was supposed to be my treat."

"Your company was treat enough, and it has been very nice," he said. He tried to ignore the tightness in his chest, then found himself nodding absently as if to confirm what he'd just said. He looked into the fire.

Hey, look at her, he thought, not at the damned fire. He caught a glimpse of her out of the corner of his eye as she crossed her legs slowly, letting the expensive silk rustle suggestively. He felt the skin on his face tighten just as his chest had, and he knew, just *knew,* he was going to lose it. It made him so damned mad, but he couldn't help it. He shouldn't have come back to her house; it was too soon, much too soon. And then the tears came, and he felt like a perfect goddamned fool as he put the drink down on the table, trying not to drop it or spill it, and lowered his chin while tears streamed down his face. In a moment, she was there, her perfume filling the air around his face. Her arm was around him and she was saying in her soft voice, "It's all right, all right, let it come. Don't be afraid, just let it come." And then he folded into her and cried his heart out.

After awhile, he took a deep breath, sat up, and muttered an apology. He was afraid even to look at her. He wanted to wipe the tears off his face, and his hands fumbled, looking for a Kleenex.

"For what, Ev?" she said, handing him some cocktail napkins. "For feeling awkward about being here? Unfaithful to her memory? For getting ambushed by memories?"

"For spoiling the evening," he said. "And for watering down this great Rusty Nail."

She laughed quietly and handed him some more napkins. He wiped his face and blew his nose, then tried to figure out what to do with the napkins. Finally, he stuffed them in his pants pocket. He looked over at her. She was sitting back now, both hands wrapped around her snifter. Her eyes were enormous.

"I can't get it right," he said, "this getting-over-it business. It's been almost two years, and you're the first woman I've spent any time with since . . . since—"

"Since she died," Liz prompted.

"Yes. Since she died. I can't even say it unless someone else says it first. Kind of pathetic, isn't it? And you are so very attractive. You're smart, fun, beautiful, and yet I kept asking myself all evening, what are you doing here? I mean me, not you. What am I doing here with someone like you? I should be home in my hole, feeling sorry for myself."

"Instead of out here in the world, feeling like an interloper?"

"Yeah, exactly. I think Julie would be really upset if she knew I was here, for instance."

"Why? Does she think life is off-limits for you now that your wife is gone?"

"Something like that. She wouldn't say it, but she'd let me know it."

"You know, I doubt that. She seems more mature than that. Besides, life alone is a dreary proposition."

"So I've discovered. And it's not like—well, I mean, it wasn't as if marriage to Joanne had been heaven on earth all the time, either. We had a good, solid marriage. With all that entails in real life."

"You apparently did better than I did. And I got two shots at it."

He sipped some of the drink, resisting the impulse to gulp it down. "We used to keep score on that," he said. "Joanne and I. Like we were somehow superior to people who got divorced. Joanne would tell me some couple was splitting up, and we'd shake our heads. Like it was such a pity that other people couldn't manage what we'd managed. And then that little devil voice would say, What would it be like, I wonder, to split up, to start over with someone new?"

"Ever say that out loud?"

"Oh, hell no."

"I did, you see. Worked like a charm, actually."

He smiled. "Julie changed after it happened. Grew up a little. Seemed more like an adult young woman than a college kid. And I saw less of her. She'd go out of town on weekends instead of coming home. After the first six months, I felt sort of cut out of her life. I'm guessing she got close to a guy and preferred to lean on him rather than on me."

"You probably reminded her of what she'd lost," Liz said.

"Probably," he said. "And I wasn't the best of company, as I just demonstrated. And now she's about to graduate and leave. I think that's what's been getting me spooked these past few weeks. And poor Julie, trying so hard not to show how much she's ready to go, as if that's somehow disloyal to me."

"I haven't met all that many midshipmen," she said. "But the seniors, the firsties? They all seem to have this look of desperation about making it all the way through and getting out of there. Is it that unpleasant?"

"It's not so much unpleasant as it is long," he said. "As we used to say, it's a four-hundred-thousand-dollar education, shoved up your ass a penny at a time."

She raised her eyebrows at that. "They all compete so hard to get in, I'm surprised they'd think that way."

"It's hard on purpose, and it gets harder throughout the four years. I'd say half the guys would be willing to drop it and go somewhere else, except that it becomes such a point of honor to beat the system and make it through. They make it a four-year challenge and they never let up. You end up feeling superior to your civilian college brethren, because you have the rigors of the academic program as well as all the military stuff."

"That explains Julie's attitude about this Dell case," she said. "She's angry more than anything else."

"Exactly. Some plebe's mistake might screw up her chances to finish, graduate, and get her commission."

"A plebe who's dead," she reminded him.

"And she's sorry about that, but it had nothing to do with her, and that's why she wants to march into the front office and have it out with anyone who thinks it did."

Liz was silent, and he wondered if he'd said something wrong. They'd agreed, after all, not to talk about the Dell case, and this was why. The good news was that he was over his waterworks. He sensed that it was time for him to leave.

"Thanks for inviting me out," he said. "I needed it, even if I didn't know it. You've been very patient."

She gave him an amused look. "Nobody's ever called me patient before," she said. "But I'll happily accept all those other nice things you said. On one condition."

"Name it," he said, hoping suddenly that he knew what she was going to say.

"That we do it again. Go out. Do something together. Soon."

"Yes, please," he said, suddenly happy that he'd anticipated her. They got up and walked to the front door.

"I meant that," she said. "I like you. I like the fact that your wife's memory can still unhinge you. It shows you're human. I spend most of my time with lawyers. The occasional human is refreshing." She stepped in close, stood up on tiptoes, and kissed him gently on the cheek. He didn't know what to do, so he was grateful when she opened the door and said good night.

He walked back under the streetlights along College Avenue, past the Naval Academy's Alumni House, and then turned left onto King George Street to get home. The blocky brick buildings of St. John's College, almost as old as the town, were on his left. Across the street were the high brick walls of the Academy, and the backs of the captains' and commanders' quarters, which lined the Worden Field parade ground. He kept his mind in neutral, not wanting to dwell on his evening with Liz or the prospects of seeing her again. But he knew he would. He'd embarrassed himself tonight, but in a good way, he supposed, if that were possible. He recognized that tonight had been something of a turning point, because it was becoming perfectly clear that his breaking down like that was not about Joanne, but, just as the chaplain had suggested, all about him. And if this lovely woman wanted to help him climb out of the valley of self-pity, he'd be a fool to turn her down.

5

At the Thursday-morning staff conference, the commandant was in the admiral's chair to take the morning briefing. Jim Hall was sitting in again, this time in place of his boss. The commandant had been complaining that the Dell incident could not have come at a worse time. The papers were reciting the usual litany of recent scandals, the football player rape case, the expulsion of four mids in 1999 and five others in 1998 for sexual misconduct, and the quarterback plebe case in 1997. All the familiar Academy haters were popping back out of their holes, and the alumni were once again viewing the situation with alarm. None of the staffers knew what to say about all that, so they prudently said nothing.

"Okay," Robbins said. "Last item. Mr. Hall, you have an incident to report?"

"Yes, sir. Apparently, the tunnel runners are active again."

The commandant shook his head in frustration. "I don't understand that bullshit," he said. "Why the hell would anyone want to go down there?"

"Because they're not supposed to be down there, sir," Jim replied. "It's mostly a game. We chase 'em; they run. I think it's the same guy or guys doing it, and of course they can get out into town through the tunnels. Running the tunnels has replaced going over the wall."

"When I was here, no one wanted to get out into town that bad," Robbins said.

Jim didn't say what he and probably some others at the table were thinking: Speak for yourself, there, Dant. Jim had had two girlfriends during his last year at the academy, on two different sides of town, and he had always been interested in getting out into town.

Robbins reminded everyone that he was still focused on the emergency at hand—the death of Midshipman Fourth Class Dell. He emphasized the importance of information control through the Public Affairs office. Then he stood up, which was the signal that the morning conference was over. Everyone stood at their seats as the commandant left the room.

Jim hadn't mentioned at the staff meeting that he was more than just a little familiar with the tunnels and the small band of "runners," as they called themselves. After Jim had taken over as security officer, one of the little dears had shut the two main valves for the steam-heating line leading to Bancroft Hall. Jim had decided to take a personal interest. He'd obtained the underground as-built drawings from the Public Works Center, then made several daytime recons of the tunnel complex, compiling a detailed map of the entire underground system. After more than 150 years of operation, the tunnel system was much more extensive and elaborate than he had imagined, with some of the branches dating back to the Civil War.

He had discovered that there were no fewer than five routes out into the city of Annapolis, although three of these were somewhat dangerous as escape routes because of high-voltage cables and transformers. The other two, however, led to places where it would be easy for someone to get into town, especially late at night, without being seen, coming or going. He'd also discovered that there was at least one tagger loose down there, and he had taken some notes on the graffiti designs and signatures. Two months ago, he'd even sprayed over one of the more elaborate territorial markings with black paint, then laid down his own tag, a macabre cryptogram he'd bought from one of the local tattoo parlors, with the name Hall-Man-Chu embedded in it. Two weeks after that, he found that his tag had been defaced, the jaws of a silhouetted shark surrounding it. He'd taken it as a challenge.

After that, he had made some nocturnal excursions to see if he could catch the mysterious runner with the shark tag. Each time, he had notified his own police force and the Public Works duty officer that he was going to be going down into the system. Then the Academy's police chief, Carlo Bustamente, mentioned in passing that the PWC people were listing his nocturnal inspections on their daily maintenance schedules. He changed his MO, telling only the chief when he was going to make a tunnel run of his own.

He hadn't yet escalated his surveillance activities to go hunting, because this was, after all, just a game played by some mids who were defying Executive Department regulations. As security officer, he didn't care if the mids wanted to live dangerously and risk a Class-A conduct offense known in Bancroft Hall as "going over the wall," even if it was technically *under* the walls. He also wasn't sure what he'd do if he actually caught up with one of the runners. He had the authority to put the miscreant on report, assuming it was a mid and not a townie, but he was more inclined simply to count coup and then make the guy knock it off. It was bound to be a firstie, because if a firstie caught a second classman down there, he'd be obliged to put him on report. Whoever it was, he wasn't really damaging anything, and if it was just a game, well, hell, it was just a game. As CO of the Marine detachment, he could never have taken such an attitude, which was one of the reasons, he supposed, that he'd become a civilian. Besides Bosnia.

When he got to his desk, there was a message from Chief Bustamente. Subject: the Dell case. The tunnels forgotten, Jim called Carlo.

Bustamente was a retired Navy chief warrant officer who oversaw the Academy's seventeen-man civilian police force. He'd done twenty-six years in the fleet, starting out as a master at arms, making chief, and then warrant.

Now he was nearly sixty and an old hand in the federal law-enforcement business, having worked in naval base security offices all across the country. Carlo prided himself on knowing what was going on under the floorboards of any installation he'd been assigned to, and he had a large network of contacts in both federal and local civilian law enforcement.

"Hey, Cap," he said when Jim called, in deference to both Jim's now defunct status as a Marine Corps captain and the fact that Jim was his titular boss.

"Chief," Jim replied, observing the protocol, "What's up?"

"You heard any of the details on this flier we had?"

"Only that the powers that be haven't decided whether he was a jumper or it was a DBM—death by misadventure."

"Not misadventure, but maybe AD-venture, Cap," Busta-mente said, lowering his voice. "Did you know our young Captain Marvel was dressed out in lace panties?"

Whoa, Jim thought. That's a detail that ought not to be loose. "Yes, but I'm surprised that's out there," he said.

"An FAK fact," Carlo said. "And I hear through the grapevine that the ME's got some physical indications that he may have had some help in his final moments."

Jim twisted his chair around so that his voice wouldn't carry out into the admin office. "Physical indications? As in?"

"Bruising on lower arms, indicating he may have been gripped, with his arms pinned. Like maybe he was thrown or pushed, instead of jumping. Probably some other stuff, but that's all I have."

Jim was stunned. None of this had come out at the morning conferences—just bland generalities about continuing investigations and heightened sensitivity to indications of suicide or serious depression. This sounded like homicide. If it was true. He said as much to Carlo.

"Yeah, well, my source in town says the ME's report's been snatched up by NCIS and everyone's been told to clamp their yaps and move along smartly, which tells me the rumor's got some legs. I can just imagine how this is gonna play over in the admin building."

"Man. The incident came up at morning staff, of course, but only in terms of a media-relations problem. No hint that it might be more serious than suicide."

"As if suicide wasn't serious enough."

Got that right, Jim thought. According to the JAG this morning, the boy's parents were already asking some pointed questions. "You got any traplines into NCIS?" he asked.

"Well, you know me, Cap," Carlo said. "Nothing I could admit to."

Which meant no, he didn't. "I hear you, Chief," Jim said. "I'm just curious—I have no role in this mess, for which I'm increasingly grateful."

"Yeah," Carlo said with a chuckle. "Don't you just love that exclusive jurisdiction rule, though? Oh, and did you hear about the vampire?"

Jim saw a joke coming. "Haven't heard that one, Chief."

"No, no, not a joke. One of my buds downtown said they had a complaint of some guy getting the shit kicked out of him by Count Dracula."

"Ri-i-ght."

"Seriously. Somebody called nine-one-one, cops came, found two guys passed out, with their pants down in a—what'd they call it—a compromising position. Third guy, on the other hand, had to be scraped up off the concrete."

"Sounds more like a general-purpose mugging."

"Yeah, well, the injured kid claimed they were following a couple of those Goth girls out of a bar. You know, that all in black, abraca-fucking-dabra, white face, green hair scene? Anyway, kid says the girls were hot to trot, despite the weirdness."

"They always are."

"Yeah, right. So our poor vic and his two asshole buddies get misled, probably not for the first time in their miserable lives, an' follow their dicks right into a—*ta da*—dark alley. Where, naturally, things turn to shit."

"What a surprise. And this is when Count Dracula shows up?"

"Ten feet tall, cape, face to stop a clock. The vic in the hospital apparently becomes one helluva witness, comes to this face: dead-white skin, red lips, red eyes like coals, fangs, the whole salami. Had a serious hiss in him, too, apparently. The two nuclear physics majors with him heard the big hiss, but as they're turning around, some *thing* knocks them flat on their asses. Fearless leader says he tried to defend himself, but the docs said he most likely fainted out of fright and *then* got his ass stomped. No defensive injuries, other than he pissed himself. I don't know if that works on vampires or not."

"A vampire in Crabtown. Hey, I gotta know: Did old Drac do his signature deed?"

"Nope, no bites. Count Dracula apparently has his standards. But he did indulge in a pretty vicious beating. Guy's seriously fucked up. Get this: The cops told this guy, he needs to check the mirror the next time the moon is full. See where he's growin' hair."

"I love it. Poor bastard's gonna wonder for a whole month. Guess a working vampire has to be careful these days, all this HIV going around."

Bustamente laughed. "There you go. Safe-sex vampires. Maybe that's why he beat the shit out of the guy. Frustrated. No blood and gore."

Jim laughed and hung up.

And then he had a thought: as the Naval Academy's security officer, should he not be telling his superiors that the word was leaking on a possible homicide? He hesitated. Was this his military mind-set talking? What would a civilian bureaucrat do in this case? A savvy civilian would probably keep his mouth shut and his head down in anticipation of a galactic shit storm, that's what. On the other hand, the supe and the dant were probably operating under the mistaken impression that they had some maneuvering room and time, which, if the rumors were already flying, they probably did not have. He pushed the paperwork aside and picked up the phone.

Cmdr. T. Prentice Walsh, the elegant executive assistant, answered. "Rear Admiral McDonald's office, this is Commander Walsh speaking, sir?"

"Commander, this is Jim Hall. Have some intel for you."

"Ready to write," Walsh said. The EA was very switched in to getting inside information.

Jim told him what he'd heard. Walsh whistled softly. "Damn," he said. "Very well. Thank you." Then he hung up.

Hey. Have you heard? The word's out on campus. Not our campus, silly, the campus of King William's School, founded a few weeks back, in 1696. Now called St. John's. Not sure why old St. John won out over His Majesty, but, whatever. It seems the Annapolis cops have been on the campus, asking questions about the Goths. The Johnnies, being Johnnies, God love 'em, are telling the Filth absolutely nothing, other than there are hundreds and hundreds of Goths, and is there one in particular you might be looking for, Officers? Pretty good for a school of about four hundred lost intellectuals.

Seems like one of the town boys had to be hospitalized after a run-in with—are you ready? A vampire! Yes! A vampire. Right here in River City. The cops apparently talked to one of my tasty little moths, started questioning her about her vampire associations. She's a devotee of Anne Rice, so she comes back with a laundry list of famous vampires, starts in on a regular lecture. Lestat, et al. Annapolis's finest finally figure out they're being diddled and give it up for Lent. But now, of course, the girls want to lay low for a while. Problem is, I don't have awhile. I'm out of here in a few weeks with the rest of my very upstanding, honorable, ethical, and supremely righteous classmates. And I'm enjoying this shit, you know? It's great practice for my upcoming career in the Mameluke Brigade.

So here's the hot flash: I'm going solo, just like I told you before. Only this time, I'm going to lure one of the locals back into the tunnels. My tunnels. Assuming he'll be brave enough.

One little problem, though: It seems as if somebody on the Dark Side has been poking his cop nose into my tunnels. Messing with my art. At first, I thought it was Public Works, you know, the diggers and fillers who chase down steam leaks and electrical grounds. But now I'm not so sure. I found a new cryptogram. Got the impression that, whoever this Communist is, he's trying to tell me something. Like, Stay the fuck out of here.

As if.

Say, what do you hear about the Dell thing? I hear they're questioning midshipmen. Anyone you know? They still think he jumped, don't they? They might be wrong about that.

At 12:45, just as Jim was getting ready to go over to the Natatorium for a swimming workout, his boss, Commander Michaels, stopped him in the hallway. There had been a hurry-up department head meeting, at which it had been announced that the Dell incident might have been a homicide. He instructed Jim to beef up security on the gates to keep media types from sneaking in and interviewing mids. Town liberty for all midshipmen had been canceled under the pretext of the security alert, and the Public Affairs office had been told to apply the "full armadillo" posture to any questions about this development. The Academy chaplain had been ordered to Norfolk to talk to Dell's parents.

Jim went back to his cube and called the chief to pass on the new marching orders. Then, once again, he tried to get out of the building to get his exercise in. This time, he ran into the commandant, who was walking back over to his offices in Bancroft Hall. Captain Robbins indicated he wanted Jim to walk with him.

"That department head meeting was the result of your warning," Robbins said. "Good headwork. Now, I have an assignment for you." He paused for a moment as a gaggle of midshipmen walked by, saluting by the dozen. "You were CO of the MarDet here? Before you got out and took this security job?"

"Yes, sir."

Robbins nodded slowly as they resumed walking. "Why'd you get out, if I may ask?"

Jim knew he had to be careful with what he said. He didn't know whether or not the commandant knew about what had happened in the Balkans that brought him to the Academy in the first place. "I figured out that I didn't want a career in the Corps," he said. "I decided to take some time out, to work out what I really wanted to do with my life. This job came open at the end of my tour as CO of the marine detachment, so I took it."

"Hmm. Yes. Not exactly a young man's job, is it?" They turned up Stribling Walk toward Bancroft Hall.

"It's a job, sir. I give it good measure. But, no, I don't look at it as a career. On the other hand, I may not be the career type."

He thought he saw Robbins smile, which was unusual. "We tend to forget that, those of us immersed in the career Navy," he said absently. "I seem to remember something about a problem in Bosnia?"

So much for that little secret, Jim thought. "I was involved in a friendly fire situation," he said. "Some Brit artillery went blue on blue. I was the spotter."

"Ah," Robbins said. "Were you actually responsible for the error, or were you the designated goat?"

Jim was surprised. Robbins looked sideways at him. "Oh, I know something about how the Corps operates, Mr. Hall. Whenever there's a screwup that embarrasses the Marine Corps, somebody has to take a fall. 'Disciplinary cut,' I think they call it. They pick somebody who was involved, not too senior, hopefully, and hammer him to the satisfaction of whichever general's been embarrassed. Guilty or not."

"It was the Brits who screwed up," Jim said. "To their

credit, they admitted it. The UN commander called it another way, so then the Corps was on the hook. Plus, I had expressed some reservations about what we were doing."

"How convenient. You were a natural target. I understand. Well, here's what I need: I want you to find out as much as you possibly can about the NCIS investigation, using whatever resources you can muster. Ditto for anything being worked in the county or state law-enforcement channels, such as the Anne Arundel medical examiner's office, from whence I suspect the leak cometh."

"I can tap the chief's web for some of this," Jim said. "Bustamente knows everybody."

They had arrived at the Tecumseh monument. "Don't care and don't really want to know," Robbins said, "if you catch my drift. Just feed me as much intel as you can. Directly to me. As you know, I can't lean on NCIS—that Branner woman would squawk command interference. But we need to be in the loop, one way or another, Mr. Hall. This thing is going to get bloody. I'm sure of it."

"It already has," Jim said. "For Midshipman Dell."

Robbins gave him a pained look but then nodded. "I don't for one moment believe that this young man was killed," he said. "A homicide here is just inconceivable. I think this was some kind of end-of-plebe-year stunt that went terribly wrong. But, be that as it may, please be discreet. No James Bond stuff. I don't want anybody on the staff to know you're doing this."

"I'll get right on it," Jim said. He resisted the impulse to salute as the commandant turned away abruptly and headed into Tecumseh Court. Jim turned left and went down along the sidewalk flanking the first wing.

The commandant had been right on about what had happened to Jim's career over there. His commander at the time, a major with very serious career aspirations, had sat him down and told him the bad news after the incident and the ensuing investigation. He was to be relieved of his duties and sent out of the theater. No further disciplinary measures. An assignment to a ceremonial post somewhere. When Jim had objected that he hadn't done anything wrong, the major had just looked at him. You were involved. That means the Corps was involved. Henderson Hall needs somebody to take the fall. You're young, with lots of time to go. I'm at the twelve-year point, with half a career invested. You're the goat. Suck it up, and the Corps will take note of your sacrifice. That's how it works. He'd ended up at the Academy one month later.

Twenty minutes later, he was banging through laps in a side lane of the training pool, called the Natatorium. The Nat was in MacDonough Hall. There was a second, Olympic-sized pool in Lejeune Hall, with seating for one thousand spectators, but the old Natatorium was used mostly for swimming instructions and tests. A familiar drama was unfolding above the middle of the pool. A lone, miserable-looking midshipman sat on the steel grates of the infamous jump tower, a steel platform suspended twenty-five feet above the water, from which every midshipman who wanted to graduate had to jump. The purpose of the drill was to teach the mids what it might be like to abandon a sinking ship.

The exercise was simple, if sometimes daunting. The mids, fully clothed, had to climb a free-hanging steel ladder, ascending from the surface of the pool up to the platform, more than two stories above. They then had to walk to the end of the platform, assume the approved safety posture for the jump, and, on signal from the class supervisor, step off and drop into the pool, come back to the surface, demonstrate the strokes needed to sweep fuel oil out of the way, and then swim to the side of the pool.

Most mids did it without incident. Some were so afraid of doing it, they didn't graduate. In every case, the reluctant dragons were ordered to climb to the platform—which in itself was scary, because the ladder slanted in at an overhang angle as soon as the mid climbed aboard—and stay there until they made the jump. A jump supervisor would remain on the side of the pool to encourage the mid to get it over with. There were mids who had spent the night on the tower. This one had apparently balked during a ten o'clock PE class, and so he had been on the tower for only a few hours, although he didn't look like he was going anywhere anytime soon. As Jim remembered, the next step would be to send for his roommate, who would climb the tower and try to talk him into making the jump. And if that didn't work, they'd detach the ladder.

After fifty laps, Jim still didn't know exactly how he would approach the dant's mission, but his leg muscles were telling him that it was time, innkeeper. He heaved himself out of the pool and grabbed his towel, just as a lone female swimmer did the same on the other side of the pool. Her distinctive swimsuit identified her as a member of the varsity swim team. He also took a moment to admire her very fine figure. That young lady was definitely built for speed, and she smiled through a hank of wet hair when she saw him looking. Then he recognized her: She was the midshipman the NCIS people had been interviewing in the Dell case. Owner of record of the infamous panties.

He grabbed his towel and walked over to where she was drying off. Behind them, the tower jump supervisor, a Marine captain with a shaved head, had begun yelling at the mid on the tower, exhorting him to stop wasting everybody's m-f-ing time and *do* the goddamn thing. That he, the instructor, had already missed chow and wasn't *about* to miss liberty, too.

"I'm Jim Hall, security officer here at the Academy," Jim said.

"Midshipman First Class Markham, sir," she replied promptly, continuing to towel off. Respectful, but cool. And really good-looking.

"Hey, I'm a civilian," he said. "You don't have to call me sir."

She straightened up, draping the towel across the front of her suit as if realizing just how revealing the competition gear was. "I heard the word *officer*," she said. "Besides, you're not a midshipman, you're bigger than I am, and older. That'll get you a sir every time." Hint of a smile.

Older? Ouch. He was maybe six, seven years older than

she was. "Think he'll do it?" he asked, pointing with his chin at the gray-faced mid up on the tower. She turned to look. Strong profile. Her mother must be something, Jim thought.

"That's Captain Mardle over there," she said. "The instructor doing the yelling? We call him Captain Marble. If he starts to take his gym clothes off, that guy'd better jump. He doesn't want to be there if Marble is forced to swim out there and climb the tower."

Captain Marble, Jim thought, staring at the supervisor's glistening scalp. It did look like a marble. An angry marble, now that he thought about it. Getting angrier, too.

"You were a Marine officer, weren't you, sir?" she asked, looking around for her klacks.

"How could you possibly guess?" he said with a grin.

"Haircut, military bearing, the Academy ring. You obviously work out. The way you were looking at the guy on the tower. Like you'd enjoy going out there and lending a hand. Or a foot, maybe." She was still smiling. She bent over, balancing on one foot with ease, to pull on her shower shoes. She'd been looking him over, too.

He laughed out loud. She was right: If it were him, he'd go out there, climb the tower, disconnect the ladder into the pool, and then jump off. "So," he said. "How's the Dell thing going? They know what happened yet?"

Her expression froze. Not quite alarm, he thought, but suddenly guarded. No longer even a hint of flirtation. He moved to reassure her. "I was there when we were lining up the first interviews," he said. "Right after the incident. You were the first one up, as I remember."

"Oh," she said. "Yes."

"My people and I caught the initial call," he said, suddenly wanting to keep it going. "Tell the truth, I wish it had been somebody else."

"You *saw* him?" she asked, her voice suddenly husky. "I heard it was—it was very bad."

"*Bad* doesn't describe it," he said. "Sorry I brought it up. I mean, if you knew him, that is."

"Not really," she said, turning away as if to mask her expression. Is she embarrassed? Jim wondered. "They just wanted to ask some questions. He was in our batt, but otherwise . . ." Her voice drifted off. She obviously didn't want to talk about it. She began gathering her stuff to leave. He didn't want her just to walk away, but he couldn't think of anything else to say without making it really obvious he was either hitting on her or questioning her. She smiled over her shoulder and walked toward the locker rooms, tugging the bottom of her bathing suit. Jim watched her go. Definitely a female. He remembered to breathe.

Captain Marble dropped his clipboard onto the tile floor with a loud slap and bent down to begin taking his shoes off. The reluctant dragon on the tower saw that, got up, and trotted right off the tower as if nothing had ever happened. About a 1.0 for form, Jim thought, but at least the kid did the deed. Markham had been right. He headed for the guest locker room, trying to get back to the problem at hand but not doing all that well. There was no way in hell he was going to fool the flame-headed Special Agent No First Name Branner. Her sidekick, now, was a possibility.

Ev didn't get back to his office until four o'clock. He groaned when his phone announced nine voice mails, but the one from Liz grabbed his immediate attention. He called her back, and she told him that she was meeting with Julie in an hour in her office.

"I can make that," he said. There was a moment of silence.

"Ev," Liz said, "I want to meet with her one-on-one this time. That rumor about a possible homicide is solidifying."

Surprised, he didn't know what to say. She apparently sensed his confusion. "I need to impress upon her that she needs my protection. Not the two of you. She's about to be a commissioned officer. I need her to think in the first person singular."

"O-kay," he said. "I guess I was operating under the assumption that three minds were better than two."

"Sometimes," she said. "Although the usual expression is *two* minds; three tend to divide into sides. But I think Julie's seeking your protection from this investigation as much as mine. I need to have her focused on what I tell her. You can't protect her like I can."

"True."

"And I'm not talking about shutting you out, Ev. It's more a case of calibrating my client. You're paying the bills. I will absolutely keep you informed."

It makes sense, he thought. "Okay," he said. "You're the lawyer. That's what I'm paying for. But please: Let me help with any inside background. You know, the Academy context of what you hear. I believe it will be the Academy that will be calling the shots here, not the NCIS."

"Not if it's a homicide investigation," she said. "If this were simply some outrage to the Navy's dignity at a football game, then, yes, our focus would be on what the Academy was going to do about it. But if it's murder, law enforcement is going to drive it."

"I can't believe a midshipman has been murdered," he said, meaning it.

"I can't, either. That's not what the Academy's supposed to be all about, is it?"

He found himself shaking his head at his desk. "The world turned upside down," he said, remembering what General Cornwallis had ordered his band to play at Yorktown. Then, not wanting to end their conversation on a negative note, he added, "I enjoyed dinner last night. Sorry for the emotional spaz."

She didn't say anything, and he wondered if he'd misspoken.

"You're entitled," she said finally.

"Yeah, but I've got to get over that. I hear it all the time."

"Not from me."

He thought about that. It was true: She hadn't said anything like that. "Well, yes, and I appreciate that." Then he surprised himself. "I'd like to see you again." More silence. Was he getting this right? "I mean, if—"

"Sure," she replied, interrupting him. "When?"

Relieved, he grinned, although she wasn't cutting him any slack whatsoever. "How about tonight? You come out to my place this time. Call me when you leave and I'll order up a pizza. This time, I promise: no waterworks."

"Sounds fine. I like anything but anchovies. Hate anchovies."

Ev loved anchovies, but he decided he could accommodate her. This one time. "Roger no anchovies."

"And Ev? I'm really glad you asked me. See you in a little bit."

He felt his face flush a little as he hung up. For some reason, he felt apprehensive. Why? Being too forward? No, that wasn't it. Julie was the problem. He hoped Liz wouldn't drop an "Oh, by the way, your father and I are going to have dinner tonight."

On the other hand, Julie would be leaving town in a couple of weeks, and then it wouldn't matter.

Right.

Good.

But he decided he was going to get anchovies on his half, just the same. Might as well establish some boundaries here.

Liz arrived at Ev's house at 7:30. She'd brought along a bottle of Joseph Phelps Alexander Valley cabernet. He smiled when he saw it. "Fancy fixin's, counselor. I usually have beer with pizza."

"Force of habit," she said. "Come to someone's house for dinner, you bring some wine."

He took her through to the kitchen and opened the wine, pouring them both a glass. "I know I'm supposed to let this breathe, but—cheers," he said. The kitchen had a spacious breakfast nook that overlooked the backyard and Sayers Creek. They sat on cushioned stools at a semicircular counter facing the windows. Liz hadn't changed from work clothes, and the way she was sitting made it difficult for him to keep his eyes above counter level.

"So, how'd it go with Julie?" he asked.

She reached for her purse and extracted a small boxy tape recorder. "Why don't I let you listen to this?" she said. "Then you tell me what you think."

"You tape your clients?" he asked, surprised.

"Always," she replied, punching on the tape. "For mutual protection. This is interesting."

Ev listened as Liz welcomed Julie to the office and got her some water. She made a comment about Julie looking in her service dress blues like something right out of a recruiting poster.

"They already did," Julie said, and then there were chair noises. "For the catalog."

"I can believe it," Liz said. "And those stars on your uniform—those indicate academic achievement?"

"Yes, they do," Julie said. "Although it took me two years to qualify for them. The really smart kids do it in one."

"Your modesty is most becoming," Liz said. "Now, do you remember what I told you in the car, that first night we met at your father's house?"

"About always being straight with you?"

"Precisely."

There was a pause. "What do you want to know, Ms. DeWinter?"

"Please, call me Liz. And I want you to refresh my memory on how well you knew Midshipman Dell. Take your time to think."

"I don't have to," Julie said. "He was one of about twelve hundred entering plebes this past summer. He ended up being assigned in my battalion for the academic year, but not in my company."

"That means you were in the same building?"

"In the same wing, yes. There are six battalions, five companies in each. There are eight wings to Bancroft Hall, so the battalions overlap, but, for the most part, company rooms are adjacent."

"So you'd know everyone in your company pretty well, but not necessarily everyone in your battalion?"

"That's correct. As a firstie, I know *my* classmates very well. The second class also—they've been right behind us for three years now. The youngsters are last year's plebes, so they're the new guys. This year's crop of plebes are sort of a probationary class: Those who survive into youngster year achieve a class identity."

"So all plebes look alike, then?"

There was a shuffling sound as Julie moved around in her chair. "Not entirely," she said. "There are some plebes who stand out—at both ends of the spectrum. The ones who get with the program, who rise to the challenges of plebe year, become gung ho—they stand out. And the ones who are barely keeping their heads above water—they also stand out."

"What happens to them?"

"It depends," Julie said. "If they're busting their asses to make it, the plebe year system will cut them some slack. Not a lot, but enough to keep them trying. Sort of a subliminal message to penetrate all the plebe year bullshit: You can do this, and we actually want you to succeed."

"And if they're not busting their asses?"

"If they're lazy, dumb, or dishonest—you know, making it, but doing it by climbing over the backs of their plebe classmates—we'll run them out."

" 'Run them out'?"

"Make life so miserable, they ask to quit. Resign."

"The Academy countenances that?"

"The Academy created the plebe year system. They want as many *quality* plebes as possible to succeed, to make it to their youngster year. But they expect some to fail."

"How does that happen?"

Julie gave a short laugh. "A million ways. Look, what I'm telling you is how I see it, as a firstie. The official Academy line would probably be to deny everything I'm saying."

"Okay, I accept that. Tell me how *you'd* do it."

"It's usually not a conscious decision or anything," Julie said. "It's not like we get together and declare someone a shitbird. It's more like a collective conclusion among the upperclassmen. So-and-so's a weakling and doesn't belong here. And that doesn't happen out of the blue, either. Usually, people will try to help a plebe who's struggling. I'm talking about the ones who don't struggle, or who whine and complain, or who try to skate."

"And what happens to them?"

"Basically, a plebe's day is supposed to be split between plebe year stuff and his academics, with a strong emphasis on allowing time to do the academics work. We reverse that. They get eternal come-arounds. They get sent on daily uniform races. They get ordered to roam the mess hall, where they report to a different table of strangers every meal, who harass the shit out of them. They get asked professional questions at meals and then get come-arounds when they show up without the answers. They get no free time, so pretty soon they're on academic probation, too. They get fried—that means put on report—three, four times a week for small infractions: unshined shoes, failing room inspections, having nonreg gear, failure to get to places on time. Any number of things."

"Sounds like piling on."

"Yep. That's what happens. They get loaded down until it's hopeless, and then they resign. Keep in mind, we're talking about the shitbirds here. Most plebes make it, one way or another."

Ev could hear Liz get up and walk around her office. "What personal attributes would line a guy up for shitbird designation?"

Julie said, "I guess it's like art: We know one when we see one."

"But how do shitbirds get in? I've read that there are ten thousand applicants who qualify each year, but only twelve hundred or so get admitted."

Julie cleared her throat. "Everyone here, except the prior enlisted, is on a political appointment. Congressmen and senators from the fifty states. The president, the vice president. All appointments are supposed to be competitive, but—"

"But what?"

"Well, some people are more special than others. Football players, for instance. I can't prove this, but everybody knows that some of them don't belong here, academically speaking. Still, they get preferential treatment—their own tables in the mess hall, special chow, extra academic attention, curved grading. Some minorities get special breaks, too. These hug-'em-and-and-love-'em programs come along, to get people in here from inner-city situations. And some people just manage to fool the system."

"What category was Midshipman Dell?"

"Category?"

"I guess I'm asking if Dell was thought of as someone busting his ass or a shitbird."

"Oh. I think Dell was on the edge," Julie said slowly. "Maybe someone who'd been busting his ass but was now sinking into the failure mode. You know those National Geographic programs, where they show an old or sick animal being eased out of the herd? Like that. I wasn't close to the Dell situation. The people responsible for Dell were the firsties and youngsters in his own company. You'd have to ask them."

"And you didn't really know him in any other context?"

"Why do you keep asking me that?" Julie said with an audible touch of heat. "I've told you, and I've told everyone else—"

Liz interrupted her. "I'm having a problem with the notion that he chose your room at random to go in and heist a pair of your underwear," she said. "Unless he was a panty fetishist, in which case they should have found a stash somewhere."

Julie was silent for a moment. Ev could just see her expression—he'd heard the anger in her voice. "I can't explain that, and I don't know what else they've found. I did not know him, and certainly not on an underwear basis! And I can't help it if you don't believe that."

"It's not just me, Julie," Liz said. There were noises indicating she was sitting back down. "If this is indeed a homicide, the cops are going to pull that string until something emerges. Cops look for connections, in addition to motive, opportunity, and means."

"Okay, so what's my motive supposed to be? And for that matter, opportunity? I was asleep in my bed when he went out that window. Whose side are you on, anyway?"

Ev groaned out loud, but Liz waved it off, as if she'd been expecting his reaction. "I'm on your side. The point of this meeting was to introduce you to the tone and tenor of a homicide investigation. I don't know what the cops have, but something's gone off the tracks with the suicide or accident theory. There was something else going on here, and I need to make sure that you don't know what it is."

Once again, Ev could almost see his daughter, sitting there in a barely controlled rage. She did not reply.

"Julie, look at me," Liz ordered. "Did part of the problem with Dell have anything to do with sexual orientation? Was Midshipman Dell gay?"

"I don't know," Julie said. Ev had heard that tone of voice, too, but not for several years. Joanne sometimes had to be restrained from slapping the shit out of her when she got that way.

"Let me try the question another way: Were there rumors that Dell was gay?"

"Possibly." Ev perked up at that. This was new.

"Oh, c'mon," Liz was saying. "Possibly? There either were or there weren't."

"I don't really know. Sometimes upperclassmen call a plebe a faggot when they don't mean it. Faggot. Maggot. Worm. Shitbird. Fuckup. You know, DI stuff."

"DI?" Liz asked. Ev heard Julie sigh.

"Drill instructor. Look, you're a civilian. I'm not sure you're going to understand all this stuff."

"Try me."

"Okay," Julie said. "The whole point of plebe year is to break down the individual civilian teenager and remold him into someone with a military mind-set. To drive the plebes together so they begin to think like a unit—roommates, a class within the company, then a class within the Brigade. To expose them to pressure, so they learn to think fast on their feet and to organize their hours to get it all done, their schoolwork, their plebe duties, their rooms, their uniforms, all of it."

Liz said, "My first husband was a Marine pilot. He used to talk about Marine OCS. Same kind of thing, but with one big difference, I think: The Marines had professional drill instructors, whereas what I'm hearing now is that this program is run by the midshipmen themselves."

"Not entirely," Julie said. "The program is supervised by the company and battalion officers. There's a whole executive department in Bancroft Hall."

"But basically, at the sharp end, it's kids running kids."

"Well, that's the system we were handed," Julie said sweetly. "We didn't invent it, and it's been succeeding for a hundred and fifty years. I went through it, and earned the right to continue to a commission. This crop of plebes is going to go through it if they want to earn that same right."

Liz changed tack. "Back to homosexuals, whom, I assume, occasionally slip through the admissions process. I thought the official Navy policy on gays was don't ask, don't tell. They keep their sexuality a secret, their hands to themselves, and no one is allowed to go after them."

"That's the policy."

"And? You sound like it really isn't the policy."

Ev could hear Julie sit back in her chair and take a deep breath, as if forcing herself to relax. "The Academy isn't the Navy, Ms. DeWinter," she said finally. "Or so we're often told by the commissioned officers. As in, Don't confuse Bancroft Hall with the fleet."

"What is it, then?"

"My father says that Bancroft Hall is like a big simulator. It looks like the Navy, but it isn't. Same thing at West Point, too, from what I saw during our exchange weekend. Being a plebe in Bancroft Hall is like being in a pressure cooker. Officer Candidate School is, too, but that only lasts three months. Plebe year lasts one whole year."

"So it's a matter of scale?"

"This place takes four years to develop naval officers who can take the heat, who can stand up to steady pressure and not only perform but perform in a superior fashion. Ultimately, it becomes a matter of pride: Keep dumping stuff on my head—the academic load, the required athletics program, the physical tests, the whole plebe year, the constant inspections, the competition for class standing, responsibility for leading the lower classes—and I can not only hack it but do it well. Because I want to, and because I'm going to show them."

"You've been to hack-it school, as my first ex used to say."

"Precisely. It's competitive across the board, from admission to commission, and we're always being tested. Strong men and women, with strong character, visible moral courage, a clear sense of ethics. We consciously address issues of right and wrong. It's a black-and-white world we live in, or at least that's what the system tries to accomplish."

"And you're saying that gays can't fit into that mold?"

"It's not being gay that's the problem, Ms. DeWinter," Julie said softly. "It's the *system* to cope with gays that doesn't fit here. The policy you just mentioned. The don't ask, don't tell policy. It ducks the question. It's basically an evasion. Evasion violates our principles."

"Ah," Liz said. "And so, if someone is suspected of really being gay, he or she could be in trouble."

"Oh yes."

"How do you personally feel about gay people?"

"Poor them," Julie said.

Liz let out a long breath. "Let me try a hypothetical: Is it possible that Dell was suspected of being gay, and that someone or some group threw him out a window? Like some kind of antihomosexual vigilante group?"

"No," Julie said emphatically. "No. Look, when the subject comes up, what you hear is that individuals mostly don't care if someone is gay. What nobody wants to have is some queer hitting on you, whether you're male or female. Plus, there's the practical problem. We're all headed for commissions. Picture a bunch of gung ho Marines taking orders from their second lieutenant if they think he's a fairy. I don't think so."

"And Dell?"

"Dell was a little guy. Not short, but, like, not much heft to him. A diver, not a swimmer. From the few times I worked with him, he was too passive. Not assertive. Not effeminate, either, but maybe just scared. I could see why people might think he didn't belong here."

"But wouldn't it take some balls to sneak into an upperclassman's room and steal underwear?"

"Guys with balls don't wear panties," Julie snapped. "Besides, we don't know that he did that, Ms. DeWinter. Hell, the laundry might have done it. Sent back something of mine in his laundry bag by mistake. I've gotten other women's things back in my laundry. It happens. I told my father that I thought Brian was weak, not gay."

"Brian?" Liz asked softly.

"His classmates called him Brian," Julie said. "And best I know, that wasn't the rap on Dell. And, no, there aren't any Brigade vigilante groups. Against gays or anyone else."

"How can you be sure of that?"

"Because everyone's too damned busy," Julie said patiently. "It would have to be firsties who'd run something like that, and firsties have only one thing on their minds at this stage of the game."

"Which is?"

"Getting the *fuck* out of here," Julie said with a vehemence that surprised Ev. Liz apparently had had the same reaction, and Julie caught it. "Well, you know what they say, Ms. DeWinter. This is a four-hundred-thousand-dollar education, shoved up your ass a penny at a time."

"Yes," Liz said softly. "Your father mentioned that one to me."

"My father?" Julie asked. "When did he tell you that?"

"At dinner last night," Liz said. Ev held his breath when he heard that. He felt Liz looking at him.

"Oh," Julie said.

"Your father is paying the bills here," Liz said. "I promised to keep him in the loop as to what I was doing. But we did have a nice evening, nonetheless."

Ev sensed what was coming next when all Julie said was "Oh" again.

"How do you feel about your father and I seeing each other, Julie?"

"Seeing each other?"

"Yes. Seeing each other. You know exactly what I mean. He's very worried that you'll be upset if he starts seeing someone."

Holy shit, Ev thought, and finally looked over at Liz, aware that he was blushing. There was the hint of a smile on her face.

"Mom's death hit us both pretty hard," Julie was saying slowly. "But I'm out of here in a few weeks. I don't want him living all alone in that big house, so I've got zero problems with him seeing you or anyone else. You've been married before, Ms. DeWinter?"

"Yes, twice," Liz said. "And it's Liz."

"Then you must know what you're doing," Julie said. Ev heard an element of challenge in Julie's voice.

"Meaning?" Liz replied evenly.

"Meaning he's a bit fragile right now. Don't you dare toy with him."

It was Liz's turn to say nothing. Ev tried to imagine the scene in the conference room, the two women glaring at each other. This was a side of Julie he'd not seen or heard before. Liz finally spoke.

"Not that it's any of your business, Julie, but I do understand that your father's been through a rough time. And I don't trifle with men I like."

"I'm glad to hear that, Ms. DeWinter," Julie said. "Have I answered all your questions? I need to get back."

There was a clicking noise as Liz leaned forward to hit stop and rewind. "I guess I'd never thought much past the smart uniforms, pretty dress parades, drums and bugles, and football game rallies in Tecumseh Court," she said. "I didn't realize that day-to-day life inside that big building is so intense. Or that the midshipmen themselves know what they are doing."

"I think Julie's a cut above in considering all that," Ev said, still somewhat aghast. "But she's right: Civilians have no idea. I've often thought about how life at the Academy begins a separation between the officers who come out of there and the American taxpayers, who pay the bill."

" 'Civilians'? Aren't you a civilian?"

"Nope. Never will be, either. Not in my mind. I'm an Academy grad who was also a Navy fighter pilot. Even after all these years in academia, I'm still not a civilian."

"How interesting."

"The place changes you. Julie's right, in a way. If you didn't go there, you probably can't understand just how much it changes you. Or the intense pride one has in getting through it."

She sipped some wine while gazing out over the creek, where twilight was softening the individual features of trees, docks, and houses. She was obviously going to skip right past that part of the discussion involving him. Ev saw her make a token effort to tug on her skirt, but that only made things more interesting. He found himself suddenly very aware of her, physically, and he hadn't experienced that feeling in some time. He felt a sudden urge to pick her up. She was tiny, but oh, my. The silence lingered.

"You graduated when?" she asked finally.

"Class of '73. Seems like a century ago."

"I loved my time at college, law school less so. Would you describe your time at the Academy as being happy?"

"Happy? No. But the Academy's not college. I majored in aeronautical engineering, so I felt as if I had a creditable degree, but the degree was almost a sidebar. Getting through the four years, getting commissioned, that was the accomplishment."

"If Brian Dell had been gay, do you think that would be a reason for someone or some group to kill him?"

Ev shook his head. "No, I wouldn't think so. If he was gay, and groped somebody, he'd get his clock cleaned and be separated. If they caught him doing homosexual acts, they'd separate him. We had two guys in my class who got caught playing drop the soap in the gym. Both gone the next day. One other guy said he was gay, but the word was he just wanted out without having to serve out his obligation in the fleet as a white-hat. But throwing a kid out the window for being gay? Nah. Is that the current theory?"

"I don't know. I was just speculating. You know, the underwear thing."

"But the homicide angle—you think that's real?"

"My source does. I asked the NCIS people what motives there might be for murder in Bancroft Hall. He said the usual: money or love."

"Not many people in Mother Bancroft have money," Ev mused.

"Right. Which leaves love. An Academy romance gone way off the tracks."

"One assumes boy-girl. I suppose in this modern age, it could have been boy-boy."

They were interrupted by the doorbell. Ev left her in the kitchen to go get the pizza. When he came back, he found her looking at a collection of Markham family pictures on a shelf beneath the cookbooks. She was holding one picture in her hand, a group photo of Ev, Joanne, and Julie at about age thirteen, based on the awkward posture and the hint of the good looks to come. Ev, taller than both, was beaming with pride, his arm around both wife and daughter. Joanne was spectacular in this picture, a glowing brunette, wide-eyed, perfectly proportioned face, luxuriant figure, looking back at the camera with practiced ease, knowing that she was beautiful, and apparently comfortable with it. Liz put the picture back as he walked in, then cleared some mail off the counter to make room for the pizza.

"Arrgh," she said when she saw the anchovies.

"I know," he said, "But it's half-and-half. I was going to abstain, but I happen to love the little stinkers."

"Aptly put," she said, wrinkling her nose. He laughed at her.

"I'm going to switch over to beer," he said. "Your half okay?"

"It's fine. I rarely eat pizza, so when I do, it's always good. Although hell on the girlish figure." He got out some plates and silverware, and she helped herself to a slice well away from the offending anchovies.

"Nothing wrong with the girlish figure from where I'm standing," he said, cracking open a Coors.

"One of these days, I'm going to give up and just let myself . . . expand."

Ev laughed as they moved back to the counter.

"Is there a chance Julie might know more about this Dell business than she's telling either of us?" she asked.

Ev felt a protective impulse rise in his chest. Liz kept coming back to this. She saw his concern.

"You want to know why I keep asking," she said. "I sense there's something wrong over there in Bancroft Hall. This is the Naval Academy. Four thousand straight-arrow men and women, the best and the brightest, duty, honor, country, pick your slogan. And yet someone's killed a plebe?"

He stared at her, then down at his pizza. He pushed it away and concentrated on his beer while trying to marshal his thoughts. "You think Julie's lying to you?" he asked.

"Not exactly. I mean, I don't think she had a hand in the boy's death, of course. But I do think she's not telling me everything. I'm just a civilian, you see. She's one of . . . them."

"Them. Right." He nodded slowly, still not looking at her. He was aware of the lights reflecting in small dazzling patterns across the creek. The house was very still.

"I hired you to protect Julie," he said slowly.

"That's correct." She seemed to be waiting for him to understand something important.

"But you can't do that if she's holding back on you, can you?"

"Bingo."

"And you'd like me to do what, exactly?"

"I'd like you to reinforce the notion that if she does know something about this incident, she needs to tell me, and preferably before those G-persons do. Maybe point out that precisely because she's *not* a civilian, the government's investigators might not play nice."

He steepled his hands in front of his face, then nodded again, making up his mind. He'd been on the verge of getting angry, but he then saw the logic in what she was saying. "You've got my attention, counselor," he said. "I'll try to think of something."

"Liz," she said. "So far, I can't get either one of you to call me by my first name."

He laughed. "Liz it is."

They finished their pizza, and Ev made some coffee. They took it into the study.

She stirred her coffee for a moment. "Julie indicated that sometimes there's a collective decision made that a plebe isn't worth keeping. That he's a 'shitbird.' What happens then?"

"Pretty much what she described. In my day, he'd become a target for the entire company's upperclassmen. After a month or so of that, he'd crash and burn and then resign. Nowadays, though, my impression is that the system steps in. The company officers, the kid's academic adviser, his squad leader, his mentoring youngsters, even his sponsor, maybe. That said, they do lose a couple hundred by attrition during plebe year."

"I guess what I'm trying to understand is how much power do the upperclassmen have? Julie implied it was a lot. Even if the executive staff and the faculty get into it, can the upperclassmen run a guy out?"

Ev shrugged. "I'm twenty-eight years out-of-date. When I went through, the answer would have been yes. But he'd really have to be a shitbird. Someone who bilged his classmates, skirted the honor system, or was suspected of stealing—that kind of stuff. It wouldn't happen just as a matter of unpopularity."

"Sounds like extra work for the upperclassmen."

"Actually, they'd set in motion the ultimate sanction: Get the guy's own classmates to shun him. The upperclassmen can run a guy ragged, but if his classmates see that as unfair persecution, they'll help him, carry him even. But if *they* dump him, he's meat."

"I'm wondering if that's what happened to Dell. Julie called him 'weak.' Right from the first, during that plebe summer. She says he appeared to be struggling. If someone combined that opinion of him with an innuendo that he was also a homosexual, he could end up feeling really cornered."

Ev nodded. "But that would imply suicide, not homicide."

She shook her head. "I just don't know. From an outsider's perspective, all I see are lots of windows, but I can't see anything inside. But the civilian system's saying there might be a murderer in there."

"I can't see that," Ev said, shaking his head. "When I was there, there were some plebes who got through plebe year who shouldn't have. We all knew it. Guys with no moral fiber. Liars. Shirkers. Some ex-enlisted who knew how to get by. Guys who held the system in visible contempt. But we also knew that the system would eventually catch up with them: They'd cheat on an exam, or lie, or do something else that would get them sideways with the honor system. And that's what happened."

"You're implying that most midshipmen believe in the 'system,' as you call it."

"Basically, they do. We do. I think West Point says it better than we do: Duty, honor, country. Midshipmen are proud to be there. They want to serve their country. They hold the profession of arms to be an honorable endeavor. They'll bitch and moan about the red-ass nature of daily life in Bancroft Hall, but down deep, they believe in it."

"And yet we have a homicide investigation in progress. We think, anyway."

He sipped his coffee and tried to think of a way to explain what it was like inside Bancroft Hall. The hivelike relationships among the upperclassmen, the plebes, the commissioned officers of the executive department, the companies themselves. A civilian just wasn't going to understand all that. Liz was looking at her watch.

"Tomorrow's a workday, unfortunately," she said. "I'd better go."

"Thanks for sharing that tape with me," he said. "Or most of it, anyway."

"She meant well, I think. I'll call you as soon as I hear anything."

He saw her out, then went back into the kitchen to clean up. The evening had not gone the way he'd envisioned it. He paused over the trash can, his hands full of pizza wrapping. Liz suspected that Julie was holding something back. Surely his daughter understood the danger of that.

He dropped the stuff into the trash can and put the silverware and coffee mugs into the dishwasher. What he hadn't said to Liz was that there was another explanation possible in the Dell matter: that this wasn't a case of a consensus decision on the part of the upperclassmen to drive out an unworthy plebe, but perhaps the work of a single upperclassman, some secret bastard who'd managed to fool the system long enough to rise to firstie status. As much as he would defend the Naval Academy, the midshipmen, and their sense of pride in being part of that duty, honor, country ethic, he knew as well as anyone who had actually been inside that the kids were very different today from when he'd gone through. He'd met enough of Julie's classmates to know that they had experienced more of life than he ever had at that stage. If an evil kid, evil in the Columbine sense, was smart enough to get through the academic program without having to lie, cheat, or steal, he could play havoc in the military school culture of Mother Bancroft. The system was, after all, based on trust and expectations, and Ev had encountered a couple of midshipmen in the past few years who occasionally dropped the mask of military subservience long enough to reveal quite another attitude. What had happened to Brian Dell might have been the work of one of those gifted, smiling psychopaths who live in plain sight and fool all the people all the time until they do something truly unspeakable.

He shook his head to drive away that unsettling thought. With four thousand talented American kids in there, of course it was possible. It was just not likely.

You hope, he thought.

Jim Hall reached the grating entrance behind Mahan Hall at just after eleven o'clock Thursday night. He'd told only the chief that he'd be going into the tunnels tonight, not wanting to alert Public Works. Bustamente had asked Jim to page him once he came back out, but he had not seemed otherwise concerned.

The grating was at the right-rear edge of Mahan Hall, beneath an embankment of grass. During the winter, it exhaled a column of steamy air into the Yard, with the thickness of the column a function of how many steam leaks there were down there. Tonight, the column was visible but not very dense. The windows of the nearby academic buildings were illuminated, in contrast to those of Alumni Hall, which was pretty much at darkened-ship. The difference being in who was paying the lighting bills, Jim thought. The night was misty, with no wind and a promise of real fog later on. The light at the top of the chapel dome was already framed in a halo of moisture. The midshipmen were, theoretically anyway, bedded down in Bancroft Hall for the night.

He was dressed in a one-piece engineering-maintenance jumpsuit, with a black knit watch cap on his head, tropical-weight Marine combat boots, and black leather gloves. He hadn't bothered bringing his cell phone or pager, because the reception in the tunnels was nonexistent. He did carry a Marine combat knife strapped to his right leg, two Maglite flashlights, one large, one small, on his belt, and a Glock strap-holstered in the small of his back. He wore a small lightweight backpack, in which he had a bottle of water, a battery-powered motion-detector box, a compact first-aid kit, and one can of black spray paint.

He lifted the grating that covered the slanting steel ladder, slipped underneath, and then let it back down. He descended the ladder into a concrete pit that ended in a steel door. He had the series key to this and the other Yard entrance doors, courtesy of the chief. For fire-fighting purposes, one key opened all the grating access doors. It also meant that anyone who could get a copy of this key would have free run of the tunnel system, although Jim knew that some of the main communications centers had additional locks. He suspected that there might be other access points inside Bancroft Hall, but he had not found them yet.

He closed the door behind him and looked around. He was standing in a small vestibule facing the main passageway in a T junction. He looked both ways down the tunnels. There were sixty-watt bulbs encased in steam-tight globes every twenty feet, and their yellow light seemed to accentuate the subterranean atmosphere. The only bare concrete visible was on the floor, as the sides and the overhead were covered by cable bundles, various-sized conduits, water pipes, and thickly lagged steam pipes. There was a hum of electricity in the air, audible against a background of hissing steam and the occasional clank of thermal expansion in the pipes. The air was humid and smelled of ozone and old pipe lagging. The pipes were marked at intervals with their contents and pressures. A ribbon of corrugated steel deck plates ran down the center of the five-foot-wide floor, under which ran the main sewage-pumping system.

He consulted his map and turned right, going fifty feet or so to the first dogleg turn to the left, toward the town of Annapolis. The walls being sufficiently covered by the utility lines, there was no room for any graffiti, but he checked anyway, probing the overhead and electrical panels with his Maglite for any signs of spray paint. The tunnel along this branch was one of the modern ones. It was eight feet high, but all the cables and pipes slung along the ceiling made it feel smaller than it was. Behind him, the main tunnel stretched back toward Bancroft Hall, where it branched out into several different loops and legs to the academic buildings nearer the river.

He stopped at the dogleg and listened. He had been careful to walk on the concrete and not the deck plates, but the only sounds came from the steam lines. He stepped around the corner and came to a major telephone vault, a concrete room that branched off the main tunnel and held a bank of signal-relay cabinets, as well as power amplifiers and hundreds of junction switchboards. Its steel door was framed by two large fire extinguishers. The regular keys to the vault were held by the fire department and the telephone company's contractor, with a firefighters' master override box superimposed on the regular locks. Jim did not have the keys to the vaults with him tonight, although he had been into every one of them in the past. Any midshipmen who came down here probably wouldn't want to get into them. They would have other things on their minds.

His objective tonight was to check out the tunnel leading to a steam and electrical junction chamber beneath the St. John's College campus. It was reached by taking this tunnel to the area underneath the senior captains' quarters surrounding the Worden Field Parade ground, then getting through a security door into a branch tunnel that led out under King George Street, where the main telephone trunk lines and two six-hundred-volt power lines entered the Academy grounds from the city's utility vaults. A runner would have to get through the Academy's security door, then turn right into the municipal tunnel and go down about a block, where a similar city security door opened into a branch leading up to the college campus. From there, it was a quick but dangerous climb to the grating access point behind Pinkney Hall on the St. John's campus. Two dangerous six-hundred-volt power lines were lurking in elderly wire conduit cages in a tunnel that was so narrow that any good-sized runner would have to touch the cages to get through. The high-voltage lines were insulated, of course, but they were also old, prompting the power company to spray-paint DANGER—600 VOLTS on signs every six feet to warn its own workers. The final branch line onto the St. John's campus was also unlighted, just to add to the excitement.

Jim tested the doors of the telephone vault before going on around the dogleg and heading up the sloping tunnel toward the parade ground. He crossed two more tunnels, one running under the Academy's Decatur Road, and a second under the portion of Hanover Street that paralleled the Academy's wall. At the top of the Hanover Street tunnel, just in front of the fire door to the city tunnel, he found the fresh tag. It was the Shark again. An exaggerated drawing showing huge, distorted teeth, one baleful eye, a dorsal fin, and the signature SR incorporated into the tail fin. Lightning bolts depicted the shark's wake, and a wide-eyed stick figure, arms and legs in an odd alignment, was directly in front of the gaping jaws. Jim sniffed the paint to see how fresh it was, but he couldn't tell anything. It had definitely not been here before.

Habitual graffiti artists, considered vandals by the weary municipal authorities who had to clean up after them, painted their designs in search of fame among others of the graffiti subculture. Gang graffiti marked gang territory, but this looked more like hip-hop work, the dramatic design crying out for recognition. Jim had to admit the guy was pretty good: The lines between colors were clearly delineated, with no dripping or smeared paint. The design was in proportion and there was even some perspective between the huge shark and the soon-to-be victim. Hip-hop designs normally displayed a three-letter signature, which was often code for the tag team's theme. This one only had two, SR, which probably stood for something really original, such as Shark Rules. But as he studied the design, he noticed two more letters, artfully embedded into the arrangement of the stick figure's arms and legs: WD. That was unusual, and he had no idea what WD stood for. The tag was painted on the only blank section of wall in the tunnel that was close to the entrance to the city's tunnels.

He'd seen other graffiti, but they looked pretty old. This was fresh. And maybe it was territorial. But was it a midshipman or a townie?

He fished the can of black spray paint out and went to work. He painted a large circle around the entire shark design, then drew a diagonal black line through it. A no-shark zone here. Then he drew in a crude fishhook that impaled the body of the shark at the midpoint, and tied that to a line leading to his own signature, an elaborate HMC. He'd spelled it out the last time, so this guy ought to know who was messing with him. He stood back to admire his handiwork. Two drip lines appeared to spoil his work. Not up to the unknown artist's ability, but the message was pretty clear. He restowed the paint can and then let himself through the metal fire door.

The city tunnel was not modern, as befitted a Colonial town old enough to have been the infant nation's capital city. The walls and arched ceiling were lined with oversized brick, and some of it didn't look all that substantial. With close to four hundred years of history, the Annapolis utility tunnels were a hodgepodge of sewer, water, and gas lines that bent down from the statehouse hill. Jim had not been into them except to locate the two most evident rising points for runners from the Academy. At least the Academy tunnels were reasonably dry; these were not, and he was careful where he put his feet. There was a distinct odor of sewage, and when he stopped to listen, he could actually hear the trickle of falling water somewhere, accompanied by the scrabble of little clawed feet in the darkness. He made his way carefully, trying to avoid contact with the badly rusted high-voltage cable cages on either side. He had to use his big flashlight, as there were overhead lights only at intersections.

When he got to the grating access under the St. John's College campus, he found that the lock on the access door had been rendered useless by a wad of putty in the bolt receiver slot. Technically, he had no right to be here, as this was the city's jurisdiction. But if this was a midshipman's doing, he had every right to interfere. He pushed through the door to examine the grating pit, which was very much like the one back behind Mahan Hall. He tested the grating and found a padlock. He twisted the hasp and discovered that it, too, had been jammed open with what looked like some more putty. He then went back behind the access door and removed the wad of goop, pocketing it, while allowing the door to lock behind him. If whoever had taped it open had a master key and was out in town, he would have no problem getting back into the tunnels. If he did not, and he was a mid, he was now in for an interesting evening. There was every possibility that the lock had been gummed open years ago, depending on how often the mysterious runners were operating and how frequently the city crews came through.

He retraced his steps into the Hanover Street tunnel and then back into the Academy precincts. He closed the fire door between the town and government tunnel, making no attempt to be quiet now, as there was no one down here. Then the overhead lights went out.

He immediately dropped down on one knee to reduce his silhouette against the lights, however dim, that were still on in the city tunnel behind him. He had looked down the tunnel all the way through the junction with the Decatur Road leg, and it had been empty. So whoever had just switched off the lights had done it when he'd heard the city tunnel's door clanging shut. He scuttled forward, staying low, until he came to a small alcove on the right side, which led to an electrical junction panel. The alcove was set back into the tunnel wall about three feet, offering enough room for him to squeeze his tall frame under the panel. He wanted to get his body out of the line of sight of anyone looking around the corner, which was about a hundred feet down the tunnel. He felt the comforting lump of the Glock pressing into the small of his back, but then he snorted softly. If this was a midshipman, he wasn't likely to be packing. Remember, this tunnel shit's a game, he told himself. But what if it isn't? his edgy mind asked.

He waited until his legs began to cramp, but there were no identifiable sounds coming from the tunnel system. Just the occasional clinking of the steam pipes, and the periodic rush of water in the lines beneath the steel deck plates. A large vehicle rumbled overhead out on the city side, reminding him that he was most definitely underground. And not alone. He tried to remember where the lighting switch box was for this branch of the tunnel, but he didn't know the layout that well. It had never occurred to him that he might have to operate the lighting system. He decided to remain where he was. Whoever had heard him close that door would have a decision to make. He could keep coming, on the assumption that the door closer had gone out into town, or he'd go back to Bancroft Hall if he suspected someone was waiting for him. He adjusted his legs to a more comfortable position and waited. After twenty minutes, he had about decided to get up and head down the tunnel with flashlight in hand, when he saw a red laser beam probing the tunnel in front of his face.

He froze and blinked his eyes several times. The beam was intermittent but unmistakable. Then he realized that the beam was only visible because of the light mist in the tunnel atmosphere. Otherwise, he would never have seen it.

Them, not it. There were two beams, flashing red lines like he'd once seen at a rock concert. Then suddenly, the beams disappeared. And then they came back, still probing, hitting the top, bottom, and sides of the tunnel, refracting occasionally off the edges of cable brackets or the bright, shiny surfaces of the cable-identifier tags. His own face was only inches from the edge of the alcove, and he could almost feel the cool lances of light when they flashed along his side of the tunnel. He didn't dare look around the corner without knowing the type and power of the laser. Some of those things could blind you with a direct hit in the eye. And yet, whoever was out there had to be visible now, with at least his head and one hand sticking out into the tunnel from the dogleg turn down the slope. He longed to snatch out the Glock and pop a round down the tunnel.

See how long the laser stayed on. But this was almost certainly a mid, not a serious bad guy. Some upperclassman who'd lifted a couple laser pointers from the lecture hall, or built them as a project in the physics lab. And as long as he did not move, the mid would have to come up the tunnel to find out if he was alone.

The beams disappeared again, and Jim felt his breathing relax. It's just a harmless, pretty light, he told himself, but it had been uncomfortable to have those ruby red beams probing the misty darkness in the tunnel. Especially since one other possible explanation was that they had come from the laser pointer on a handgun. But a mid with a gun? No way. Get a grip, James. Mids run the tunnel in search of after-hours booze and late-night women. Just like you used to do. The lasers are just toys—some guy playing at *Star Wars*.

No, he decided. Stay put, see if he comes up the tunnel, and then scare the living shit out of him. He settled back against the wall and waited, focusing his brain to listen for any sounds of movement down the tunnel, and trying not to dwell on the other possibility, that this wasn't a midshipman.

What he finally heard was the sound of steam. Just a light hiss at first, then a steadier pressure, sounding like a distant jet passing at altitude. Now what the hell? he thought. The noise didn't increase, but it didn't decrease, either. He's cracked open a drain valve on one of the steam lines. He could picture the valve arrangement: The decals on the pipes indicated a hundred psi in the line. There were drain lines under every valve and at major junctions in the pipes to allow for condensed water to be removed from the lines after any service evolution. Two valves on each drain line: one isolation, one for operation. The big cutoff valves had been chained and locked in their open position, but the drain valves were not locked.

Okay, he's cracked open a steam valve. To do what? Mask his own sound? Create a fog bank in the tunnel? Based on the sound, there wasn't enough steam escaping to fill the tunnel, or at least not for a long time. Besides, the tunnel walls were cold concrete; any steam might create a mist, but then it would condense on the walls. So he was masking sound.

His own sound.

Which meant he was coming up the tunnel.

Jim lifted the big Maglite off of his belt and tried to position himself so he could lunge out of the alcove. He turned his body in tiny, silent increments to face down the tunnel, flexed his cramped muscles as he began deep breathing, trying to keep as still as possible.

He'd been wrong about the mist effect: The atmosphere in the tunnel was solidifying before his eyes. He blinked to make sure, because the only light was coming from a single bulb thirty feet back up the tunnel. The mist stank of old iron and wet concrete. It was accumulating on the walls and even on the steel cabinet under which he was hiding. He felt a drip of condensation tap the back of his neck, and then a second one.

He put his finger on the Maglite button. His plan was to blind the guy with the powerful flashlight from his crouched position, then to stand up and confront him. The mist swirled visibly now in the murk of the tunnel. Something coming? Had to be. He got ready to snap on the light. The light from up the tunnel was diminishing rapidly, becoming a yellow glow that seemed to suffuse the mist in every direction.

He felt rather than saw a presence, a gathering mass in the mist. Then it disappeared. He almost moved but then froze as he felt it again. There was something wrong: It wasn't down the tunnel; it was behind his left shoulder. The guy hadn't been coming up the tunnel, the guy had been *behind* him, in the city tunnel! Forcing his head to turn as slowly as possible, he saw a definite darkness in the fog, a solidification, shapeless but clearly there. In an instant, he turned the flashlight, pointed it up, and snapped it on. To his shock, he had illuminated a horror mask: a painted face, dead white, with glaring red-rimmed eyes, carmine lips, and huge teeth exposed in a terrible rictus. The face had no edges, but it seemed to disappear into a black-on-black penumbra. He was absolutely paralyzed for half a second by the sight, but just as his brain came back on line, he was blinded by a blast of something sticky spraying into his face, his eyes. He dropped the Maglite to shield his eyes, but the stuff was all over his face and then his hands. He lurched out from under the cabinet and tried to stand up, but something swept his feet out from under him and he fell heavily onto the deck plates, the impact knocking the breath out of him. He heard a horrible fun-house laugh, and then he felt the black mass stepping over him to disappear down the tunnel toward the Academy.

He wiped at his eyes, then stopped when he realized he was making it worse. Suddenly, he recognized the strong smell: paint fumes. The bastard had hit him with a can of spray paint. Wiping his hands clean on his coveralls, he extracted the plastic bottle of water from his backpack, struggled to rip off the top, and then squeezed water into his eyes until the stinging stopped and he could see. After a fashion, that is, for the tunnel was still full of condensing steam, and the lights were still out. He got up and stumbled down the tunnel.

Half an hour later, he emerged from the grating behind Mahan Hall. He hoped he wouldn't encounter a passing police patrol, because he suspected his face would be really something to see. As he secured the grating, he remembered something the chief had mentioned that morning—that bit about the "vampire" thrashing those town boys. Whoever this guy was who'd attacked him, he'd been decked out like Bela Lugosi on a midnight ride. He had to admit that, for a moment there, this guy had managed to scare the shit out of him. And since it had sounded like he'd taken off into the Academy precincts, he was probably a midshipman.

He paged the chief to let him know he was out of the tunnels. He didn't really expect Bustamente to call him back, but when he got back to his pickup truck, he found a message waiting for him on his government cell phone: CALL THE CHIEF, it read.

"Didn't need you to call back," he said when the chief picked up. "Just wanted to let you know I was out of the tunnels."

"It go okay? No bad guys?"

"Not exactly," Jim said, and told him what had happened. The chief whistled in surprise.

"I wonder if that's the same guy who trashed those people over in town. That one guy's still in the hospital."

"He came up from behind me when I was coming back; I was looking down the tunnel, not behind me. He looked like every vampire I've ever seen in the movies, and I have to tell you, that shit stopped me for a second."

"I haven't seen any of those since I quit drinking," Bustamente said.

"Since when did you quit drinking?"

"I mean *drinking*. Look, I'll talk to Allan Wells, chief of D's in town. Tell him what happened. Maybe we can catch this sick fuck."

"Sick fuck is right. I'm having trouble seeing a mid do this. Dress up, scare people, maybe. But assault and battery on civilians—that's different."

"Why don't you let me handle the reporting side?" Bustamente said. "I'm thinking in particular of Public Works. Those guys who work underground all the time aren't gonna like this vampire shit."

"Oh, hell, Chief, it's some guy playing dress-up."

"Yeah, but you see what I'm sayin' here. Those guys who work underground, they tend to be superstitious. We need to be careful. Yard cops start talking vampire shit, ain't nobody gonna go down there. The Johns're gonna back up in Mother Bancroft till the end of time, we're not careful here."

Jim, grinning in the dark, rolled his eyes. Big mistake: The residual paint came after him in stinging waves. "I need to get this paint out of my face. I'll stop over at your office in the morning. Oh, hey, I need to talk to you about this jumper case, too."

"I've heard from a second source that this may not be a jumper case."

"Yeah, that's what I need to talk to you about."

6

On Friday morning, Jim stopped by the Academy dispensary to get some help removing the paint from his eyes. The nurse used a vile mixture of stinging substances to dab the last flecks out of his eyelashes. Looking in his rearview mirror when he got back to his truck, Jim decided that *he* looked like the vampire now. The gate guards gave him a decidedly funny look.

The chief was waiting in his office with tiny cups of espresso coffee ready; kept a machine right there next to his desk. Jim closed the door and inhaled the strong vapors gratefully.

"Interesting makeup," Bustamente said. "And if that's not makeup, there's lots more coffee. You said you wanted to talk about the Dell incident."

Jim sipped some coffee and felt his heartbeat quicken almost immediately. "Yeah. I have a mission, directly from the dant."

"Should you choose to accept it, Jim," the chief intoned with a perfectly straight face.

Jim tried to give him the fish eye, but his lashes were still sticking. "Not exactly," he said. He explained what the commandant had asked him to do.

"You ever get close to Branner?" the chief asked. "Now, you wanna talk about your vampire . . ."

Jim grinned. "I suspect nobody gets close to Branner, other than perhaps her Calvin Kleins."

The chief grinned back. "You noticed."

"She lets you look, but I suspect you better not even think about touch. But to answer your question, no, I don't know her or her sidekick. Young black guy—what's his name?"

"Special Agent Walter Thompson. Nice kid, plays everything cool and loose, but he's no dummy. You should see him shoot. Stands there on the range all casual like, kinda bored, holding the nine down along his leg, and then— badda-boom—his target silhouette's got a see-through heart. Spooky."

Jim looked over at the chief, but Bustamente waved it off. "I know, you can't use that word. But Thompson's cool. Somebody gets racial with Bagger, he can handle it."

"Bagger?"

The chief shrugged. "That's how he introduced himself to me. I believe he's partial to the demon rum."

"Well, he seems easier to deal with than Branner. I'm thinking of maybe taking this tunnel-runner thing over there. Use that as a back-door way to insinuate myself into the Dell investigation. The dant, of course, is worried about NCIS squawking command influence."

Bustamente nodded. "If it weren't for this homicide firefly, I think they'da ruled it a DBM from day one. You know, dumb-ass plebe, screwing around up there on the roof, some kind of plebe year antics, who knows what, falls off. Like that."

"That's what the dant thinks, too. He said homicide was 'inconceivable.' But even with that, if it wasn't suicide, they'd feel compelled to chase down whichever upperclassman incited him to go up there. There has to be accountability."

"There does?" the chief asked, looking skeptical.

"Yeah, there does," Jim said. "The dant is into damage control, of course, but the supe is ultimately accountable for everyone here. I can't feature Admiral McDonald sweeping anything under the rug."

The chief shrugged. "If you say so."

Hey. It happened. That security guy came downstairs last night. Down to my little world. Playing at setting traps. Only he was the one got himself trapped. And a paint job, too. I left him looking like a black guy trying out for the white guy's part in one of those vaudeville shows. Introduced him to the joys and power of steam in confined spaces. I studied that at length, segundo year. And, did I say I was in costume? Was. The vampire Dyle. It had the same shock effect on him that it does on the drunks. Just enough to give me a split-second advantage. And trust me, that's all I need. They say that's the difference between the fighting abilities of a regular Marine and a recon Marine—about a half second.

But he was waiting for me—of that, I'm certain. So now it's officially a game. I love games, don't you? Well, maybe not like I do. Anyway, he'll be back. And so will I. Only he doesn't know the tunnels like I do. And he doesn't have the facilities that I do, either. And now that plebe year's almost over, I'm going to focus on this guy for my fun. Stay out of town, except for the occasional run for Gothic love. But see if I can seduce this guy to come back down to play again. He has no idea of the things I can do down there. It's a lot more fun than terrorizing plebes. Although there was one plebe . . . but I'll tell you about that later. Or maybe I won't. Depends on what the Dark Side does about the case. I'm betting they'll sweep it. What do you think? You think they'll sweep it? Or maybe they'll tag somebody for it? If they do, they'll be so wrong. So very wrong.

Jim met with Agent Thompson right after lunch Friday at the NCIS office. The formidable Agent Branner had gone up to NCIS headquarters at the Washington Navy Yard. She was supposedly on her way back. Thompson showed Jim into a small conference room and offered coffee.

"Coffee'd out, thanks," Jim said, sliding into a side chair, his ears still ringing from the chief's espresso. Thompson sat down and raised his eyebrows.

Jim described his recon work of the past few months in the tunnels, presenting a comprehensive picture of what he'd been doing, leaving out only the fact that he had been messing with the tunnel runner's graffiti. "I didn't consider this any big deal, beyond the obvious security implications that there were ways into and out of the Yard that just about anybody who knew about them could use."

"You've never caught anyone using the tunnels?" Thompson asked.

"Negative. But there are clear signs that they are being used by someone other than the diggers and fillers. I've been assuming that it was just some mids, probably firsties, indulging in some after-hours party times."

"You go to the Academy?" Thompson asked, eyeing Jim's big gold ring. He had been taking notes, but he looked up when he asked this question. Jim suddenly felt like a suspect.

"Yeah, class of '93. Went Marine option. I was CO of the MarDet here a coupla years back. Got out, and walked into this job."

Thompson let the obvious question hang in the air. Shit, Jim thought. This is turning into an interview. Chief was right. "Sure, I ran the tunnels," he said. "Back then, we didn't have town liberty like the guys do now. But let me tell you what happened last night."

When he'd finished describing the attack with the spray paint, the laser pointers, and the vampire getup, Thompson was writing busily in his notebook.

"Thing is," Jim said, "Chief Bustamente mentioned something about some kids being attacked in town. By a 'vampire,' according to the one who was most seriously injured."

Bagger got a pained look on his face. "A vampire."

"Yeah, well, some guy dressed up like one. Big guy, too,

from what I saw. That's what those townies said, too. Big motherfletcher. Came up behind them, surprised them. Clapped their heads together while they were gawking. Then he beat up the third guy."

"And you saw this guy?"

"I mistook the direction from which those laser beams were coming. You know, lasers: They're instant light. He came from the town side of the tunnel. I was hiding down under a cabinet, and he surprised me. I flashed a Maglite into his face, trying to blind him. Instead, there's fucking Dracula. In the flesh. In the moment it took me to get my brain around it, he'd blasted a can of spray paint into my face. Then he ran down the tunnel."

"Why come to NCIS?" Thompson asked, still writing.

"Guy ran back into the Academy side of the tunnels. This is probably a mid."

"Ah," Thompson said. "But it could also have been a townie, who ran the opposite way to confuse you into thinking he was a mid."

Jim shrugged. "That's possible."

"And were you able to follow, to see where he actually went?"

"Nope. Had an eyeful of paint."

"And he was made up like a vampire?"

"He was indeed. I have to tell you, when I got that one look, it didn't register as makeup. It registered as just what it looked like. Big white face, really red lips, a mile of teeth, red eyes. Too many movies, I guess. But man!"

Thompson nodded. "I'da just plain shit my pants, I saw something like that," he said. "Don't much care for vampires and ghost shit."

"Not that we believe in such things, right, Special Agent Thompson?"

"Call me Bagger," Thompson said. "And I don't know what the hell I believe anymore, comes to shit like that. I didn't believe it was possible to have a homicide here at the Naval Academy, either, Mr. Hall."

Jim seized the opening. "It's Jim. And I heard that rumor, via Chief Bustamente. They really have something solid that indicates this kid was murdered?" He used the word *they* to keep his focus ambiguous.

"Solid?" Bagger said, putting down his pen and closing his notebook. "Forensics have some indications. Indications of restraint. Of course, these marks could have been made under different circumstances. You see what I'm sayin'?"

Jim nodded. "Maybe some kind of sexual fun and games that involved the kid wearing panties."

"There you go," Bagger said. "Branner thinks it could even have been some kind of sex domination. Then maybe the kid got so humiliated, he offed himself afterward. But it's also possible someone threw his ass off the roof."

"He was alive when he went down, though."

"That's the indication. You view the body?"

"Vividly."

"Well then, you can understand the forensics problem. Plus, there's major political and media heat. The dant wants accident, death by misadventure, even suicide, anything but homicide."

Jim shook his head. "Whole thing is pretty sordid," he said. "When I was here, we didn't have time for much of anything except studying, classes, sports, and endless tests."

"And yet you ran the tunnels," Bagger said.

"Weekends, first class year, and not many of them," Jim said. "But it was a game, a way of beating the system. Gave you bragging rights, but you kept that within the company classmates you could trust."

"What would have happened had you been caught?"

"Class-A conduct offense, going over the wall. Unauthorized absence. A bunch of demerits, restriction, shitty grease grade."

" 'Grease'?"

"Mid slang for military aptitude. Guys who worked hard at pleasing the officers in Bancroft Hall were known as being 'greasy.'"

Bagger smiled.

"So what happens next with the Dell thing?" Jim asked, trying to keep it going.

"Who wants to know?" a woman's voice asked from the doorway. Uh-oh, Jim thought. The Branner is back. He saw Bagger tense up a little when she strode into the room. Her face was colorfully made up this time, but she was wearing a severe-looking pantsuit as if to compensate. No leg show today, Jim thought as she slipped into a chair at the head of the table. Her hair was copper-colored in the office light. "Bagger and I were talking about how life at the Academy has changed since I went through," he said, trying to deflect any questions on the Dell case.

"Why are you here, Mr. Hall?" she asked.

"Came to report a vampire attack in the tunnels under the Yard," Bagger said with a perfectly straight face.

Branner leaned back in her chair and cocked her head. "A what? Did you say vampire?"

Jim realized that the window of opportunity to talk about the Dell case had just slammed shut. But maybe he could keep something going with Bagger Thompson.

"Bagger here has all the details," he said, pushing back in his chair. "You guys decide whether or not you want to work it. Although I know you're busy just now with this Dell thing."

"I'll call you," Bagger said before Branner could say anything. "Maybe you can show me where it all went down."

Jim handed him one of his cards. "Right. Be glad to take you down there. If this is a mid, we need to catch his ass."

Branner was looking from Jim to Bagger, obviously in the dark and not happy about that. "If this relates to the Dell case," she said, "then please remember we have exclusive jurisdiction."

Jim nodded. "Absolutely, but this has nothing to do with the Dell matter. Bagger, thanks for your time."

Bagger nodded pleasantly and Jim let himself out the conference room door. He pulled it almost all the way shut and walked down the hall, but slowly. He heard Branner ask her assistant angrily what he'd revealed about the Dell case. Didn't fool her, did we? Jim thought as he left the building. Plus, she knows for whom I work. But maybe if I can get young Bagger there to run the tunnels with me, I can get him talking again.

He got into his official security officer's car out in front of the old postgraduate school building. Next stop, the town cops. See what they had on the vampire incidents. But first, he should call the chief. No point in going through channels if Bustamente could get him straight through to the right guy.

At 3:30 Friday afternoon, Jim got a call from Branner, asking him to meet her at the commandant's office in Bancroft Hall. She and Agent Thompson were going to reinterview Midshipman Markham, and she wanted Jim present as an observer. Jim checked it out with his boss, who shrugged. Jim walked over to Bancroft Hall, where he found Branner and Thompson getting set up in the commandant's conference room. Somewhat to his surprise, Branner had changed clothes. She was still wearing visible makeup, but now she had on a see-through blouse, which revealed layers of frilly underwear, and a tight short skirt. Thompson, on the other hand, was positively drab in a plain dark brown suit. Branner greeted Jim politely and told him that they would do the talking.

"What, if anything, do you want me to do or say?"

"Say nothing. Just be here. Afterward, we may have some questions for you."

"Questions?"

"It's our experience that mids don't trust civilians. Sometimes they speak in code. You're a graduate. I'd like you to watch Markham, then tell me afterward if you think she's lying, holding back, or just giving us the CivLant brush-off."

"I can probably do that," Jim said. "She bringing a lawyer?"

"So we've been told," Branner said, and went to sit down at the head of the table. Jim took a chair over to one side, where he could watch Markham and also enjoy the view. Thompson gave him a hello nod, and then the secretary brought in Markham and a very elegant-looking lady lawyer. He saw Branner bristle when she got a look at Markham's lawyer, and he found himself looking forward to a possible catfight. He wondered if Branner had changed clothes to distract a male lawyer.

The agents got up and shook hands with the lawyer, whose name, Jim learned, was Liz DeWinter. He stood to be introduced, and DeWinter gave him a curious look.

"And why are you here, Mr. Hall?" she asked.

"At the commandant's request," replied Branner, lying smoothly. "Mr. Hall is the Academy's security officer, and we've been directed to liaise through him for any support we need from the Academy while conducting our investigation. Today, he's basically an observer."

"Is that so?" DeWinter murmured, raising an eyebrow. Jim wondered if she was buying it. On the other hand, she'd have no way to disprove what Branner was saying. Branner indicated that they should sit down so that the recorder could pick up their voices. The lady lawyer was dressed in an expensively tailored suit. Markham was in working blues, and she looked mostly angry. Liz sat down in a side chair and indicated that Julie should sit on her right, so that she was between Julie and the agents. She put her own voice-activated recorder out on the table, turned it on, introduced herself, and asked the agents to introduce themselves. Neither of them moved to turn on their recorder, which, Jim realized, meant it had been on since Liz and Julie had walked in. Branner took the lead.

"I'm Special Agent Branner, Naval Criminal Investigative Service," she announced, speaking to the recorder. "I'm the supervisor of the Naval Academy NCIS resident unit. With me is Special Agent Thompson, also from my office. For the record, also present is Mr. Hall, Naval Academy security officer, Midshipman First Class Julie Markham, and her attorney of record, Ms. Elizabeth DeWinter of DeWinter, Paulus and Sloane, LLC, One-oh-seven Beale Street, Annapolis, Maryland." Then she recited the date and time.

"What is the purpose of this meeting?" Liz interjected.

Branner blinked once when Liz interrupted the flow of her spiel. "The purpose of this meeting is to conduct an official interview with Midshipman Markham in connection with the death of Midshipman Fourth Class William Brian Dell."

"Is this a homicide investigation?" Liz asked.

"This is an official NCIS investigation," Branner said evenly. "NCIS does not characterize investigations other than as official investigations."

"Is my client suspected of having committed a crime or other infraction of military law?"

"No," Branner said. Then she held up her hand before Liz could ask any more questions. "This interview is suspended at sixteen twenty-three for five minutes," she announced, speaking into the recorder, then reached forward and turned it off. "Look, Ms. DeWinter, this is not an interrogation. Your client is not a suspect. Why don't you take your pack off and just see where this goes?"

Liz had not turned off her own tape recorder. "I have received unofficial information that your investigation is a homicide matter. I'd like you to Mirandize my client now, please, and then understand, if you will, that she will clear her answers to any and all of your questions through me. If these procedures are unsatisfactory to you, this interview will be terminated."

Branner's face colored. "Ms. DeWinter, I should remind you that Midshipman Markham is subject to the Uniform Code of Military Justice," she said. "That said, she does have rights. If she is or becomes a suspect, that's when she gets an Article Thirty-one warning."

"What is that?"

"Like a Miranda, only better, from the suspect's point of view. But I repeat, she is not a suspect."

"Even if she is not a suspect, she does have the right to remain silent, and the right to have counsel present for this interview, correct?"

Branner made a sound of exasperation. "Does your client *want* to become a suspect?"

Liz shook her head. "No. Do you have evidence linking my client to the death of Midshipman Dell?"

"Well, you know we do, actually," Branner replied, glancing at Julie.

Liz stared at Branner. "So let's do that Article Thirty-one warning, then."

Branner hesitated, then looked at Thompson. He shrugged, reached down into his briefcase, and withdrew a single-page form. "It has a waiver line on the bottom, where the interviewee agrees to answer questions voluntarily. Why don't we have her sign that, and you can control which ones she answers? That okay?"

Liz took the form, read it over, and nodded. Thompson filled out the top part, and Julie signed. Round one to the petite lady lawyer, Jim thought.

"Now that we've agreed on the ground rules," Liz said, "let's go back on the record."

Branner rolled her eyes, clearly thinking this was all lawyer nonsense. She punched the recorder back on and announced resumption of the interview.

"Midshipman Markham, do you know how Midshipman Dell came to be in possession of your underwear?"

Julie looked at Liz, who nodded. "No," she answered.

"Do you have any idea of how he might have obtained the panties?"

Julie again looked at Liz, who leaned in close and murmured. "Laundry."

"The laundry might have done it," Julie said. "All our clothes are marked with a laundry number, but we often get back items belonging to other midshipmen."

"Have you ever gotten back male underwear?" Thompson asked.

Liz nodded, and Julie said, "No."

"Did you have or have you ever had an intimate relationship with Midshipman Dell?"

"No."

"Did you know Midshipman Dell in any capacity?"

"Yes."

"Which was? For the record, please."

Liz nodded again, and Julie described plebe summer and the fact that Dell had been in her battalion.

"Was Dell a homosexual?"

Julie blinked. "I don't know."

"Were there rumors to that effect within the battalion?"

"I don't know," Julie said before Liz could give the signal to answer. Liz wrote a note down on her notebook and showed it to Julie. Jim figured it probably said not to answer until instructed to. Julie flushed and nodded.

"Midshipman Markham, do you know of anyone in your battalion who might have wanted to harm Midshipman Dell?"

Liz nodded. "No," Julie replied.

"Did anyone in your battalion have it in for Dell? Want him out of the Academy?"

Liz nodded, but Julie paused, as if thinking about the question. "There was a sense among the upperclassmen that Dell was a little weak. That he might not make it."

"Was there any one person or persons who said that a lot? That Dell ought not to make it?"

Julie thought for a moment, looked at Liz, then said, "No."

"Where were you when Dell went off the roof?" Thompson asked.

Liz put her hand on Julie's arm. "Why are you asking that question?" she said.

"To establish Midshipman Markham's whereabouts at the time of the incident," Branner said. "For the record." Jim realized then that Branner and Thompson had rehearsed and agreed on the line of questioning. If they'd done that, then they were case building. He began to pay more attention.

"You may answer that," Liz said to Julie.

"I was in my rack. Bed. In my room. Asleep."

"Had you been in your room all night?" Thompson asked.

Julie looked at Liz, who nodded. Julie hesitated for a fraction of a second, then said, "Yes."

Branner consulted her notes. Jim wondered if maybe Markham hadn't wanted to answer that question. But had the NCIS people picked up on her hesitation?

"Midshipman Markham, this is a question we have to ask, for the record. It's actually two questions. One, did you kill Midshipman Dell?"

"No!" Julie protested in a loud voice. She hadn't even looked at Liz, who once again put her hand on Julie's arm. This time, she squeezed.

"And the second question is this: Have you done anything, anything at all, in the entire time you have known Midshipman Dell, that might have contributed to his death?"

"My client will not answer that question," Liz announced before Markham could say anything.

"Why not?" Branner asked.

"Neither she nor I has to explain our decision," Liz said. "Next question?"

Branner leaned forward, looking directly at Julie. "You understand, Midshipman Markham, that by not answering that question, you necessarily draw our attention to you?"

"Let the record show that Midshipman Markham's attorney considers Agent Branner's last statement a threat and has therefore decided to terminate this interview."

"Wait a minute, wait a minute. I withdraw that statement. It's just—"

"Next *substantive* question?" Liz said, keeping her hand on Julie's arm.

Branner sat back in her chair and slowly tapped her pen on the edge of the table. She glanced at her notebook. "You are on the women's varsity swim team?"

"Yes."

"Was Midshipman Dell connected in any way with the swim team?"

Liz cocked her head at Julie, then nodded. "Yes," Julie said. "He was one of the managers."

"Managers?"

"It's not like in pro sports," Julie said. "All midshipmen are required to participate in intramural sports, and they are encouraged to try out for varsity sports. Plebes, too. If you try out but eventually get cut, you can sometimes stay on with the team as a manager, a helper bee. They carry equipment bags, act as timers, unload luggage from the bus, stuff like that."

It looked to Jim like this was all news to the lady lawyer, who was taking notes for the first time.

"Would you have had contact with Dell in his capacity as a manager on the swim team?"

Liz nodded. "Not really," Julie said. "He would be helping out with the plebe swimmers, not the upperclassmen. Besides, he was a diver, not a swimmer."

"Does the team travel as a group to away swim meets?"

"Yes."

"But you had no contact with Dell?" This from Thompson.

"He was a plebe. I'm a firstie, a senior. I might talk to or coach another plebe swimmer who swam my own event, but not plebe managers."

"Would he show up for practice sessions here at the Academy?"

"Yes, of course."

"Does the team practice every day?"

"During the competition season, yes."

"So it would be fair to say that you had daily contact with Midshipman Dell during the competition swimming season?" Branner asked, a tiny gleam of triumph in her eye. But the lawyer was ready.

"Don't answer that," Liz instructed. Julie said nothing.

"Why not?" Branner asked.

"Because I didn't like the way you phrased that, Agent Branner. Plus, she's already told you that she had little or no contact with Dell, that he helped out with the plebe members of the team, not the seniors."

Branner started to say something, tapped her pencil three times, and then Thompson picked up the questions. Definitely rehearsed, Jim thought.

"Is the swim team a close-knit organization?" he asked.

Liz nodded. "Fairly close," Julie said. "I mean, we all cheer one another on during the various events. We practice two, sometimes three hours a day, early in the morning and again after class. Swimming is extremely competitive, both within and among the teams."

"Do the women on the swim team tend to hang out with the men on the swim team?"

Julie looked at Liz, who hesitated but then nodded. "Some do," she said. "But most midshipmen date outside of the Academy."

"How about you?"

Liz told her not to answer that. "That's not germane here," she declared.

Thompson, unlike Branner, appeared to take that in stride. "Okay. Do you know if Dell formed any close associations on the swim team?"

"No," Julie said before Liz could give her permission.

"No, what? No he didn't, or no, you don't know?"

"No, I don't know. He was a plebe. He wouldn't have much time for dating in any event. And never an upperclassman."

Thompson consulted his notes. Liz tapped Julie on the arm and pointed to her previous note about answering questions. Julie nodded and mouthed the word *sorry*.

"Are plebes allowed to date upperclassmen?" he asked.

"No."

"Are plebes allowed to date anybody?"

"Dahlgren dates on Saturdays," Julie said. "There are lots of rules. You really have to want to be with someone."

"Did Dell date anyone that you know of?"

"Don't know," Julie said. "He was a plebe. Unless he was in my company, I wouldn't know and wouldn't care."

Thompson nodded equably. "I'm done," he said, looking to Branner.

"I'm not," she said. "Midshipman Markham, are you involved romantically with anyone here at the Academy now?"

"She's still not going to answer that, Agent Branner."

"I think it might be pertinent to our investigation," Branner snapped.

"Then go find out by yourselves," Liz replied. "But based on the tone and drift of this interview, I'm assuming certain things about your view of my client."

"Such as?" Branner snapped.

"Meaning that I think you're investigating her, not Dell. So from now on out, there won't be any more of these interviews. Is that understood?"

"You don't get it, do you?" Branner said, her voice rising. Jim watched with growing interest. "We have the authority to interview Midshipman Markham anytime we please, as long as we execute the Article Thirty-one form. This is *military* law we're talking about."

"Fine," Liz said. "You can, of course, interview her all you want, but she'll have nothing to say, will she? Nor can you draw any inference from her silence, to which she is entitled under *American* law. As for now, this interview is concluded."

Liz stood up and nudged a surprised Julie to do the same. She retrieved her recorder and indicated to Julie that she was to follow her. Neither agent said anything as the two women left the conference room. Jim saw Julie start to speak, but Liz put a finger to her lips until they had walked out of the commandant's office area. Jim got up to stretch while Branner spoke into the recorder, stating that the interview was concluded. Then she turned it off. Branner swore.

"Wasn't all that bad," Thompson said.

Branner tossed her head impatiently. "Goddamned lawyers," she said. "Mr. Hall, what was your take?"

"My job doesn't involve real police work," he said. "The

only interviews I've seen are on television. That said, I think you hit the old blue-and-gold wall."

"Is that like the cops' big blue wall?" Thompson asked. "Like when Internal Affairs comes around?"

"Yeah, I think so," Jim said. "I mean, I can't feature one mid killing another for any reason. But there's always been a cops and robbers atmosphere here, what with all the regulations, rules, laws, procedures. You ever heard the expression, You rate what you skate?"

"No," Branner said, interested now.

"Well, it means basically that you can do what you can get away with. Usually applies to the chickenshit end of the book, as opposed to honor offenses and the serious stuff. And there's a serious taboo against bilging a classmate. You know, ratting out."

"She was a very uncooperative witness," Branner said.

"For what it's worth, I think the lady lawyer was right," Jim said. "You kinda made it sound like Markham was a suspect, not a witness. There was one point, though—when you asked if she'd been in her room all night. I thought she hesitated."

"Thought you said you hadn't done interviews?" Branner said.

"You said you wanted my impressions. You just got one."

Ev heard the phone ringing as he went up the back walk from his boat dock, but it went to voice mail before he got into the house. He'd gone out rowing on the Severn again to take advantage of an almost-perfect afternoon calm. The Academy's varsity eights had swept by in a glorious echelon formation, but he hadn't even tried to keep up. There was a message from Liz to please call her. He showered, changed clothes, and then made a drink. He called her back from the study. She told him that there had been another short-notice interview that afternoon, which is why she hadn't had time to alert him beforehand.

"Interesting. So, how'd it go?"

"Just fair," she said.

That got his attention. "Only fair?"

"Well, it was definitely adversarial. Part of that was a function of my MO when dealing with police interviews: I try real hard to control the flow, and I can be abrasive about it. Part of the problem was that Agent Branner. She came in with a pretty big chip on her shoulder."

"But what were they looking for?"

"As I anticipated, some connection between Julie and Dell. Something besides the underwear thing. Julie did get it on the record that he could have obtained the underwear in a laundry mix-up. Apparently, that happens."

"That's true. Or it did in my day. Although they usually just lost it, period. Or sent it back full of holes. Is this a homicide?"

"They're acting like it, and yet I'm not sure *they're* sure." She reviewed the questions and answers, and explained why she'd shut some of the questions off. "Based on some of the questions, I think they're case building."

"Against *Julie*?"

"Against whoever emerges out of the fog of evidence. With some cops, it's often a toss-up as to whether they want to find the truth or just close the case. The latter outcome is often preferable."

"Shit."

"Yeah. Look, you said you wanted to help."

Ev put down his drink. A mission. "Shoot," he said.

"I learned some things today that neither you nor I knew. For starters, Dell was a manager on the swim team. Which means that Julie could have had daily contact with him during the competition season."

"Wait a minute. He would have been working the plebe bench, so she—"

"Yes, Julie explained that. But in their words, she could have had daily contact with Dell. It is possible."

"But hardly likely."

"You understand that; I understand that. But a jury might not understand the system, the fact that plebes and firsties don't associate, other than in the Sturm und Drang of plebe year."

"O-kay, I guess I can see that."

"You're thinking like a human, Ev. I'm thinking like a lawyer."

He chuckled. "Got it," he said. "And my assignment?"

"I want to know more about Julie's love life, if she has one."

"Why don't you just ask her?"

"I intend to. But I'd like you to corroborate and elaborate."

"Well, as you observed, I might be the least informed in that area, and I don't exactly pry. She is an adult, about to be a commissioned officer." He moved his appointment book to make room for his drink, knocking the book off the table in the process.

"I know, Ev, but she talks to you. I'm just asking for some backup here."

There was some frustration in Liz's voice. Ev reached down to retrieve the book while he considered it. "Sure, Liz, I'll try," he said. "There's Tommy Hays, of course, but I think he's on the outs right now. I can make up a list of the kids she's brought back here on weekends this past year. But I'm going to guess the swim team is the place to look. They're together for hours a day in practice, and then at the away meets, long bus rides, parties after the meets in away towns."

"Do they practice a lot?"

"Oh, hell yes. Actually, I was on the swim team when I went through. That's where Julie gets it, probably. We used to get up before reveille, zero dark-thirty. Hit the pool until zero six-fifteen, then went back to our rooms for regular reveille and morning formation, then did it all again after class."

"Really," she said, and he heard something in her voice.

"What?"

"Well, I wasn't going to bring this up, but they asked her

where she was when Dell died. She told them, asleep in her 'rack,' as she called it."

"Rack, right. Mids love their racks."

"Then they asked her if she'd been there all night."

Well, of course, he thought. Then he understood. "Ah. And she said?"

"She said yes."

"But you had the sense that she would have preferred not answering that question."

"Right."

Ev thought about that. "Well," he said slowly, "if she'd gotten up for swim practice, then technically she was *not* in her room all night. Oh, I get it: If she wasn't in her room, then she could have been what—throwing him out a window?"

"I know, I know, it's ridiculous, but visualize the interview transcript being read into evidence: 'Were you in your room all night?' 'No, I wasn't. I was—' 'Thank you, Midshipman Markham, you've answered my question.' "

"Holy shit!"

"Cops. Case-building cops. That's how they do it, Ev, which is why potential suspects do not go to interviews without their shysters."

"Damn. Does she fully understand that?"

"I think she got a glimmer today, although she's still resisting it. I told NCIS there wouldn't be any more interviews. They can, of course, tell me to pound sand. If they detected what I detected, they're going to pull the string on the early-morning swim practice routine. I'd like to know in advance."

"Well, that's easy enough. I'll find out if there was early practice, and if she was there. I can do that through the Athletic Department. Although, the season's over. And she's graduating. I would guess they're not doing that anymore."

"I need to know, and then I'll sort it out with Julie. And Ev? Let her call you. Let her tell you about the interview. I'm going to go through all of this with her. What I need from you is—"

"Right, 'corroborate and elaborate.'"

She didn't say anything for a moment. "If you're uncomfortable with this, I can do it on my own," she said.

"Hell yes, I'm uncomfortable, but I want her protected. You're the protector. It's my job to help you."

"Thank you. I do understand how you feel." She paused. "There's this eight-hundred-pound gorilla that's beginning to materialize in the back of the room, isn't there?"

"You do have a way with words, counselor," Ev said wearily. "But yes, there is. You're saying Julie, in some fashion or other, might be involved in this mess after all."

"I'm sorry, Ev."

"Thank you. I appreciate what you're doing."

"Hold that thought," she said, and hung up.

At ten o'clock on Friday evening, the two investigators met in back of Mahan Hall, by the grating entrance. Jim indicated the map. "I propose to take you down the way I went the last time. Show you the main tunnels, the access points. See what you think about catching this turd."

"Let's do it," Bagger said.

Jim took Bagger into the main tunnel that ran under Stribling Walk, heading back toward Bancroft Hall this time. He showed the agent the main utility vaults, the access flap doors to the big storm drain, and the branches leading to the various academic buildings. The closer they got to Bancroft Hall, the more pronounced was the hum of machinery and electricity.

"This system is supporting all eight wings of Bancroft Hall, and the four thousand people inside," he said. "Heat, lights, potable water, sewer, telephone, electricity, computer networks, and, pretty soon, chilled water for air conditioning. Every dorm room has water, steam heat, computer lines. Group heads for men and women. It's big."

"Yeah, it is," Bagger said, speaking softly. Something about being in the tunnels had them lowering their voices.

"Can they get directly from Bancroft into any of these tunnels?"

"I don't think so, not without knocking a hole in a basement wall, which, of course, somebody may have done. When I ran the tunnels, I did it from one of the grates, although that one's been moved. You know, diggers and fillers."

They came to a three-way junction, where only one branch was man-high; the other two were filled with utility lines and narrowed down to what were basically crawlspaces. The smell of steam leaking through lagging was strong. "And they run why, again?" Bagger asked.

"It's a game, mostly. The Academy is all about discipline, uniformity, maximum conformity. Some guys like to show a little outlaw attitude."

"That you?" Bagger asked, looking doubtful.

"Nope. I was chasing late-night skirt."

"Yeah, that would be me. What's that archway down there? That looks old."

They followed the main tunnel as it bent around to the right and then back to the left in a gentle S-turn. They came to a section of the tunnel that wasn't made of concrete, but of huge granite blocks. On the left, or bay, side of the tunnel was a recessed alcove, which contained two arched doors side by side. They appeared to be made of very thick oak, reinforced with three-inch-wide cast-iron straps. Bagger played his light over the surface of the left-hand door.

"This area is the old part, the really old part," Jim said. "The Academy was started in 1845 on the grounds of an army fort, Fort Severn. There were underground ammunition magazines in this area, and these tunnels ran from the nineteenth-century seawall guns back to the ammo. No utilities in there. Of course, what had been the seawall in 1845 is now buried in the landfill that created the ground for the seventh and eighth wings."

"Yeah, but look," Bagger said, hunching down into a squat. "Bright metal scratches around the keyhole."

Jim squatted down. Bagger was right. He pushed on the door. The lock held. He looked at his key collection, but he didn't have a key to this door. They checked the other door, but there were no signs of recent entry.

"Where are we?" Bagger asked. "In relation to what's on the surface?"

Jim stood up and studied the map. The lights in this branch of the tunnel were yellow and weak, so he had to use his small Maglite. The map showed that the two doors led to separate tunnels. The left one branched toward Bancroft Hall. The right one branched more toward the entrance to Annapolis harbor. "I'd say we were just to the right of the second wing. The right-front side of Bancroft Hall if you were standing out in Tecumseh Court and watching the noon meal formation. The supe's quarters are back over our shoulder that way, maybe a hundred yards."

"And where does this tunnel go?" Bagger asked, pointing to where the concrete tunnel picked up again.

"There's a service tunnel to the captains' quarters along Porter Road. Eventually, it doglegs down at the end of the row and goes out into town, to the eastern King George Street utility vaults. Double steel doors. I've got keys."

Using his own flashlight, Bagger studied the map. Somewhere back down the tunnel, there was a soft clang of metal, followed by a sustained hiss of either steam or compressed air, which shut off after ten seconds. They looked at each other.

"Company?" Bagger asked softly.

They stood there and listened. Indistinct sounds bounced down the concrete walls, but there was no way to tell how far away they were. Or what they were. They both switched off their flashlights and listened.

Another soft clang of metal, then a sound they couldn't identify. Because of the S-turn, they couldn't see back down the main tunnel, and every sound was being distorted by the background hum of power lines and water pipes. Jim thought he felt a slight change in the air pressure. Bagger had his eyes closed, listening.

Another noise, unrecognizable. Then a sputtering sound. Jim tried to place it. Sputtering. Like a . . . fuse? Bagger heard it, too, and was looking at Jim, who mouthed the word *fuse,* saw Bagger comprehend it, and then there was an explosive roar from the main tunnel, a roar that was approaching very quickly.

Before they had time to react, a red glow lighted up the tunnel and the roar doubled in volume as a rocket of some kind came around the corner, ricocheting low off the walls and then blasting right at them, spinning wildly, chest-high. They barely had time to dive to the deck plates before the thing went blasting over their heads, screaming down the tunnel, where it slammed into the flat concrete wall of the next turn, some fifty feet beyond them. There was a flash of bright green light and a loud bang when it hit. The tunnel disappeared in a cloud of dense white smoke that stank of sulfur, and they had to stay down on the deck plates just to find breathable air. From somewhere behind them in all the smoke, they heard a nasty laugh echoing through the smoke and then the pronounced clang of a metal door.

"What the *fuck!*" Bagger muttered, trying not to cough as the dense trail of smoke drifted down toward the deck plates.

Jim had pulled his Glock. He crouched just beneath the thick layer of smoke, waving it out of his face. "Fireworks," he said. "Some fucker set off a Fourth of July rocket and sent it down the tunnel."

There was definitely a change in the air pressure now, a sudden feeling of release, and, amazingly, the smoke began to retreat, almost as if it were alive, back down the tunnel from which the rocket had come, like a film being run in reverse. Jim saw a blinking red light pulsing through the smoke from just around the corner.

"Smoke detector," he said. "The smoke-evac system's fired up. We're gonna have firefighters next."

They stood up as the smoke shrank back around the corner like a fleeing ghost. They followed it. Just beyond the three-way junction, an exhaust fan in the ceiling was running noisily at high speed, sucking the air from the tunnel and now beginning to squeeze their ears. Another red light was flashing on a sensor panel high in the tunnel ceiling.

"Let's go get the rocket," Bagger said. "Before the firemen show up."

They turned around and went down to the end of the passageway. The rocket body was crumpled up against the door of a telephone equipment vault. It appeared to be made of thick cardboard, two and a half feet long and two inches in diameter, with badly charred fins at the back. The lower part of the rocket body was blackened, and what was left of the front end was smashed flat and also burned. The stink of sulfur was almost overpowering. Jim picked it up and promptly dropped it.

"Yow! Hot motor scooter," he said, waving his hand in the air. "Gunpowder?"

"Yeah, I've seen these. Commercial fireworks. You saw that green flash."

"Still do," Jim said. "Every time I blink."

"How do midshipmen get their hands on commercial fireworks?"

"Brigade activities committee maybe. You know, for football games. They've got that touchdown cannon. I don't know, though. First spray paint, now this. That thing would go right through someone, going like that."

"No shit," Bagger said, examining the simmering tube. "I think we've flushed our sick puppy."

"I'd prefer the vampire scene to being impaled by that damned thing. I think I hear the fire brigade. Let's go tell 'em what happened."

"You better put that away," Bagger said, pointing with his chin at Jim's Glock. "Unless you think Drac's still back there somewhere."

"He'd better not be," Jim growled.

A single fire truck had shown up on the street above the grate in front of Mahan Hall, and a team of three respirator-clad firemen came down into the main tunnel. Most of the smoke had been evacuated by then. Jim identified himself and explained that someone had set off some fireworks in the tunnel. He produced the still-smoldering rocket tube. The firemen, used to midshipman antics, secured the alarm system and took the tube with them to add to their collection of crazy mid memorabilia.

Jim then took Bagger back down the main tunnel and out to the King George Street utility vaults closest to St. John's College. On the way, they passed the original shark tag Jim had defaced with his own pictogram and the words Hall-Man-Chu. At first, Jim thought it was unchanged, until he saw the addition of two small black letters to his own signature: Hall-Man-Chu-mp.

"Our boy offends easily," he said.

"Not bad work for an ex–Jar-head," Bagger said, examining Jim's tag.

"I cheated; got it from a tattoo parlor downtown. There's a bigger one closer to the King George Street doors."

The second tag remained unchanged. Bagger studied it for a long time.

"The shark motif is consistent," Jim said. "That fish with serious teeth. I don't know who WD is, or why the shark is about to bite him."

"This is a white guy," Bagger said.

"How can you tell that?"

Bagger just looked at him. "Trust me. This is a white guy," he repeated. "This the way out to town?"

Jim took him to the utility interchange with the city's vaults. He showed Bagger where they were in relation to the Academy's steam plant across Dorsey Creek. "I've even been under your building," he said, pointing to the location of the old postgraduate school building on the map. "Those are some old tunnels. Date back to the 1920s. Still in use, though."

They stood in front of the steel doors as a large truck rumbled overhead out on King George Street. The tunnel walls were all smooth concrete, but the lightbulbs trembled in their sockets and the steel pipe hangers rattled with the vibration of the passing truck.

"Hate this shit," Bagger muttered. "Don't like being underground."

"Can you imagine working down here all the time?" Jim said, unlocking the door. They stepped through, and Jim closed the door behind them.

"How far to the ee-gress?" Bagger said in reply, and Jim detected some real anxiety in the man's voice. He took him down the King George Street leg and up the sloping tunnel to the grate on the St. John's campus. Two more doors and they were sticking their heads up into the cool night air. Bagger shrugged out of his backpack and wiped perspiration off his forehead.

"Better," he said. "Much effing better."

Jim grinned. "What's not to like?" he said. "Nice wall art, fireworks, the sweet sound of sewage gurgling beneath your feet."

Bagger shook his head and then looked around as if checking for rockets. "I could use a drink," he said.

"Let's hit that Irish pub on Maryland Avenue," Jim suggested. "It's only two blocks away."

They drew some stares from the college kids when they came in wearing jumpsuits and carrying backpacks, but not for long. The singer, an anorexic-looking blonde whose lank hair mercifully hid most of her face, was wailing something about Celtic dreams as she plunked on a much-abused guitar. They squeezed into a tiny booth at the other end of the narrow barroom.

"So what makes it an Irish pub?" Bagger said.

"Fresh Guinness on draft, for one thing," Jim replied. "Never been here?"

"Not exactly a homie place," Bagger said, looking at the small sea of white faces. "And what's a Guinness?"

The bartender, a loudly cheerful Irishman in his forties, took Jim's shouted order for two stouts from across the room. The singer shot them both a hurt look.

Jim nudged Bagger's knee under the table and pointed with a lift of his face over the agent's shoulder. Bagger casually turned around. In another booth halfway down the long, narrow barroom were three girls dressed all in black clothes. They looked to be of college age, although it was hard to tell because of their bizarre makeup. Bagger turned back around.

"Crabtown Goth posse?" he asked.

"Local cops said there were three of them, probably Johnnies. This place is a Johnnie hangout."

The bartender brought two pints of glistening black Guinness stout. Jim dropped a twenty and the bartender left to make change. Bagger tried some and nodded approvingly. The singer gave up her dirge, to the visible relief of most of the patrons. The bartender immediately turned up some Irish background music, and the noise level in the bar went up pleasantly. He brought Jim his change and told them that the kitchen was closing in thirty minutes, if they wanted any food.

Bagger, who had been examining the table menu, ordered a Reuben. Jim said no, but then he asked the bartender about the back-in-black coven three booths over.

The bartender, who recognized Jim as a sometimes regular, laughed softly. "Call themselves Goths. They're harmless. They come in here on slow nights, usually order coffee, and then sit there for hours, trash-mouthing all the straights. Freak show."

"They ever pick up guys?" Bagger asked casually.

"I-don't-think-so," the bartender intoned, rolling his eyes. "I wish a crowd of real Goths would come in one night. You know, those guys with the long hair and horns on their helmets? Bet they'd know what to do with that lot over there." Then he went back to the bar.

"Heard that," Jim muttered. One of the girls might actually have been attractive, but the other two were decidedly dumpy. But with their white-to-pink painted faces, black-rimmed purple lipstick, double lashings of mascara, top and bottom, they looked like vampire mimes taking a break. One of the plain ones had seen him looking and was now whispering to the other two. Jim concentrated on his Guinness to avoid eye contact.

"So, what do you think of the Guinness?" he asked Bagger.

"Ain't half-bad," Bagger said, taking a substantial hit.

"You guys getting anywhere with that suicide?" Jim asked as casually as he could.

Bagger drained the remainder of his Guinness and wiped his lips. "Branner had to go up to DC for a meeting on it. NCIS brass and reps from the SecNav's office. The ME's report raised some questions. Bruising indicates the kid's arms were pinned, which is weird. Navy staff told Branner to go through the motions of a homicide investigation, but more like to rule out murder. Then they'll decide between DBM and a suicide ruling."

The attractive Goth girl had turned sideways in the booth so that she could fiddle with the laces on her witch boot. She wore a studded dog collar around her neck. "I guess a homicide would be tough to prove," Jim said, watching her out of the corner of his eye. "I mean, there're three thousand upperclassmen who have a duty to make life miserable for the plebes for the entire year. Where the hell would you start?"

The girl raised her knee to get a better grip on the laces and her dress parted, revealing a breathtaking length of thigh dressed up in shiny fishnet stockings. Jim tried not to stare, because it had been a very deliberate move. "We start with the girl whose underwear he had on," Bagger said. "Man, what are you looking at?"

The girl put her leg down, slid a seductive smile on and off through all the heavy makeup, and turned back around. "Goth girl putting on a little leg show. Part of the act, I suspect. 'You straight guys all think we're beyond weird, but we can still make you look.' "

"They can *all* make me look," Bagger said, lifting his empty glass so the bartender could see it.

Jim wondered if he should caution Bagger on the alcohol content of the Guinness. "That girl today, the midshipman, I mean, she was pretty damned good-looking," he said. "Maybe the Dell kid was in lust."

Bagger nodded. "She was okay, nice rack an' all, but I

was diggin' that slick little lady lawyer, sexy legs right up to there, phone-sex voice, definitely old enough to know how. You probably noticed—Branner hated her, naturally, but I was being nice as I could be."

"Bet you pulled the wool right over her eyes, huh?"

"Oh yeah." Bagger laughed. "Must have taken her, oh, two, maybe three seconds to see right through my insincere ass. But still. That interview today with Markham? Lady mouthpiece walked all over Sugar Britches."

Jim grinned. "Sugar Britches—that would be Branner?"

"On account of her famously sweet disposition, yeah. Comes with that red hair, I suppose."

Jim still had warm memories of the sight of Midshipman Markham in her spray-on competition swimsuit. The possibly pretty Goth bore a faint resemblance to her, but then he realized, no, it was just those gorgeous wheels. The bartender brought Bagger's Guinness and the sandwich. As he walked back by the Goth booth, one of the girls stopped him and whispered a question. The bartender looked back over his shoulder for a moment at Jim and Bagger, then shook his head and walked on. Jim continued to watch them out of the corner of his eye, still not wanting to make eye contact with them. They'd be just the type to set up something embarrassing in a public bar. As the Academy security officer, he didn't need that hassle.

He wanted to ask some more questions about the Dell investigation, but he decided to let it go for the moment. He didn't want Bagger to suspect he was being pumped for information.

"Man this is a damned good Reuben; you ought to get you one."

"Still trying to preserve my girlish figure," Jim said, finishing his beer. "I'm thinking of getting some motion detectors. Chief knows this guy here in town, does security equipment? Put a series down there in the tunnels, use a timer to turn them on after hours, see how much traffic we've got down there."

"You mean whether this is one dude or maybe a crew?"

"Exactly. Then up the ante a little. Wire the detectors as hunting cues, so when they get a hit, I can be waiting somewhere, like between him and the appropriate exit hole."

"And then?"

"Whack him upside the head with a baseball bat, strip him, tie him up naked to a tree on the Johnnie campus, and then spray-paint his face for him."

"Tut-tut," Bagger said. "And you a federal officer. That would be serious brutality. The tree part anyway."

"Actually, you're the federal officer. I'm just a Navy civilian employee."

"With a sock Glock."

"Well, that's mostly habit."

"And a carry permit, I hope. Damn. This Guinness stuff grows on you. I'm gonna do one more."

"Then don't drive for a while," Jim warned. "Only thing the Irish are serious about is their alcohol."

The pretty Goth girl was fixing her other shoelace. This time, most of the men in the bar were ready for the show, and she did not disappoint them. She gave Jim a fairly direct look, almost as if she recognized him, and then huddled back down with her two acolytes. The bartender brought Bagger his refill. Jim realized he would either have to leave or join Bagger in some serious drinking. He decided he wasn't in the mood, and from the looks of it, he wasn't in Bagger's league as a booze hound, either. Plus, that Goth girl might now know he was with the Academy and be planning some bullshit scene.

"I'm going to secure," he said. "I think the bartender told those Goth girls that we're with the Academy. Don't want a scene in a public bar. Nice legs, though."

"How nice?"

"Really nice, you get all the fetish rags and greasepaint off."

A slow grin spread over Bagger's face. He looked five years younger with the sudden gleam in his eye. He turned around very deliberately to stare at the three girls. The pretty one stared right back, then flicked her tongue in and out of her red-and-black mouth like a snake. Bagger flashed her a smile and turned back around. Jim saw her look back in their direction once, then get up and slink along the bar toward the bathrooms in the back. Standing, she looked ridiculous in the costume.

"Hey, look," Jim warned. "Don't let those freaks lead you anywhere—that's how that vampire mugging shit's been going down."

"Oh, hell," Bagger said with an elaborate shrug.

Jim repeated his warning and then slid out of the booth. "I'll let you know when I have the motion detectors set up. Maybe you could join me, help me control my bad temper. And watch that Guinness."

"Absolutely," Bagger said. "But make sure it's a metal bat. Lots easier to clean."

Jim laughed and left the bar. He hoped Bagger was mostly posturing about making a run on the Goths. There had been three girls, and usually two marks who followed them out into the dark alleys. Bagger could probably handle it if it was a setup, as long as he quit the Guinness at three. He stopped a block away from the bar. Should he go back? Make sure? Across the street, a woman opened her front door to retrieve a cat and gave him a wary look. He smiled and resumed walking down Maryland Avenue toward the Academy's front gate.

Hell with it, he thought. Bagger's a big agent now. Jim was going to concentrate on catching his rocket man.

Ev was reading Andrew Gordon's amazing history of the naval battle of Jutland when the phone rang. He glanced at his watch—it was almost midnight. He picked up. It was Julie.

"Hey," he said. "You're up late."

"I'm on my cellular. The passageway phones are secured."

He thought he could hear the sound of wind blowing into the microphone of the cell phone. "You in your room?"

"Not exactly," she said.

"Tell me you're not up on the damned roof."

"Well . . ."

He sat straight up in his chair, the book spilling onto the floor. "What the hell, Julie? Are you nuts?"

"Chill, Dad. Dudes come up here all the time. It's kind of a firstie rate. There are even chairs—you know, those lawn chairs without legs? It's safe."

"Is that a fact? Recommended by the Brian Dell family?"

"I'm not going to fall, Dad. And no one can see me. I'm way back from the edge, on the bay side. It's just a cool place to hang out."

"Is there anyone with you?"

"No," she said. "We had an interview today. With those NCIS people. I think Lawyer Liz is pissed at me."

"Why would she be pissed at *you*? You're the client."

"She doesn't believe me about Dell. I don't know why. And she was really hostile to those people. Then they started talking like they were coming after me. Dad, I didn't do anything!"

The wind blew across the cell phone again, making a ruffling noise. Liz wanted him to probe Julie's relationships at the Academy. Here was a way in. "Have you told anyone else what's going on?" he asked.

"No," she said miserably.

"How 'bout Tommy Hays? Or is that permanently off?"

"Tommy's, well . . ."

"He's what?"

"He's mad at me, too. Everything's ending here, and he's resisting reality."

"How so?"

"Basically, he's going surface line, which means he goes to Newport, Rhode Island. I'm going aviation, which means Pensacola, Florida. Long way apart."

"He want to get married or something?"

"He wanted some kind of long-term commitment. I won't have time for that, what with flight school and all that."

"College romance confronting graduation day."

"I guess. Tommy's a great guy. Swim team kept us together. But now . . ."

Ev thought of what Liz had said about the swim team. "So the swim team thing is done? No more eight hours of practice every day?"

The wind blew against the cell phone. When she answered, there was a touch of reserve in her voice. "I still swim every day, but it's for exercise. The coaches are mostly working with next year's team. I do some coaching in the freestyle."

"Well, at least you don't have to get up at zero dark-thirty anymore."

He heard Julie sigh. "She asked you to ask me that, didn't she?" Julie said. *"Didn't she?"*

Ev thought about playing dumb, then decided against it. After all they had been through in the two years since Joanne had died, Julie could read him like a book. "Yes, she did. She does think you're holding back, Julie. That you do know something about this Dell case. She can't protect you if you hold back on her."

"Then to hell with her," Julie snapped. "I don't need her. I haven't done anything wrong. I *want* to clear the air with those people. I'm not going to have some damned plebe's problems screwing up everything I've worked for these past four years. No damned way!"

"Now, Julie, listen—" he began, but then stopped. He thought he heard the sound of a car going by over the phone. She *was* on the damned roof.

"Look, Dad, I had nothing to do with what happened to Dell. I'm sorry he's dead. But I'm a big girl now, and if those NCIS people want to talk to me again, I'll waive my rights and tell them whatever they want to know about me, because I had *nothing* to do with Dell."

Ev tried to think of something. "So you really want me to pull Liz off the case?"

"Yes. I don't need *Liz*," she said. "I think maybe you need *Liz* more than I do."

Ev tried to suppress the spike of anger he felt, but failed. At least now he knew what some of Julie's antagonism was all about, no matter what she'd said to Liz on that tape. "Tell you what," he said as evenly as he could. "I'll tell Liz to stand down. I'll tell her what you're going to do, against her advice, of course. But you didn't hire her. I did. So you can't fire her. And I won't fire her. Which is not to say she won't fire you as a client."

Julie didn't say anything. Ev gave her a full minute. He heard another car go by over the cell phone. "So call me if your grand plan doesn't work out," he said finally. "In the meantime, I think you're out of your depth." Then he hung up before she could reply.

Man, what a great night. Perfect night. Caught those two cops down in my tunnels, snooping around. They just happened to come past while I was on my way to see the girls. That security officer and some black guy. Waited for them to get far enough away, then retrieved one of my toys, a game victory rocket. I keep some shit like that down there, hidden in my stash. Set it on the deck plates, ignited the fuse, and watched her go, down that tunnel at the speed of fucking heat. And smoke? Man, was there smoke. Then I had to boogie because the fire trucks came to see what set off the smoke detectors. Taught those two who owns those tunnels, and it's not the Dark Side, not by a long shot.

Better than that, I scored another vampire strike out in town. Had to use Krill, and you know she's not much in the bait department, except for those amazing breasts. Hope that doesn't offend you. But I needed to do it again. Hell, even vampires have needs, right? Better yet, I got the same black guy who'd been fucking around in my tunnels earlier. He thought he was chasing skirt. He ended up chasing me. Big fucking mistake. You'll hear all about it—soon. Or maybe you won't.

Dark Side's gonna be really pissed about this one, and you know how they get when there's a really big fuckup, right? They get real quiet, don't they? No foursquare ethics for them, are there? As if we won't find out. We always find out. They're so pathetic with all that morality and ethics shit. I guess it's just for the classroom, right? They're running scared about lots of shit just now, so close to hat day. Problem is, I'm really liking this shit, you know? They're so helpless, especially if they think those two clowns they sent down last night are going to catch up with my ass. Never happen, baby, not down there. And, actually, now there's only one, isn't there? But you haven't heard about it yet. Let's see if you even do.

Krill was perfect. Got the dude to trail her out of the bar, just like before. I'm slinking along in the shadows, across the street. Eased into Penfold Lane, where there're no streetlights, only those fake gas lights every fifty feet. Nice and dark. Then she slows down, backs up against a building wall, and then—this was so cool!—She lifts the top half of all that black bag fabric, and suddenly she's bare from the waist up. I mean, this is a great scene. The black dude, he is focused, man. Hell, gotta admit, I was focused. Krill is a regular Humpty-Dumpty, but she is something up top. She lets him look, and then, when he gets close, she squats down, starts undoing his belt, rubbing the side of her face up and down against the front of his pants, and he gets all groany and moany. While the vampire Dyle approaches from behind. Dude's so hot by now, I thought I was gonna have to say something, but then, just as she's tugging his zipper down with her teeth, he detects me. Turns his head, but his body doesn't follow, 'cause Krill's still working him up. I do my thing—the big hiss, the roar, the whole bit. Guy freezes, mouth open wide, dinner-plate eyes, total shock. I can smell the booze on him. Then Krill jerks his knees forward and he goes down backward like a ton of bricks, cracks his head on the concrete before I can do a thing. Starts to bleed, man. It looks bad, but then I remember head cuts bleed a lot. Anyway, we book. Get back to her pad for some afterglow. Krill's so excited, she—well, I guess I don't have to describe it in detail. Let me just say it was worth the trip, all around, even with Krill. Especially if that guy was some kind of cop, which I think he was, going down in the tunnels with that security dude. I've never done a cop, but he was scared shitless, just like all the rest. Something about the brain seeing something it fears and freezing up the part that thinks. Something to remember when I get to do this shit for a living. Minus the cape and the makeup, of course. I really love this Jekyll-Hyde shit. Superstraight by day; Dyle the copbanger by night. It's dangerous, it's exciting, and the girls get so hot, I can't believe the things they want to do afterward. You know. And nobody around me suspects a thing—not my classmates, not my company officer, not the faculty dweebs, nobody. Only you know the truth, and you have no reason to tell anyone, do you? Because then I'd stop telling you these things. Admit it, now, you'd miss that. I know you'd miss that. I know you better than you think.

7

Jim rolled over and pushed the light button on his Timex. It was 5:45. Saturday morning, if he remembered correctly. He groaned and rolled back over. He could hear the wind rising outside and the first patter of rain on the deck above the master's cabin. The boat was beginning to move around a little, and he could hear the rubber fenders compressing and then exhaling against the hull. He mentally reviewed the mooring lines, then decided to go back to sleep. At which point he heard the railing gate open and then slam back into place as someone very definitely stepped on deck from the pier. He remembered he hadn't reset the alarm. He tried to listen harder, but a blast of rain swept across the harbor and drowned out the sounds from above. He had a bedside light on and was reaching for his bathrobe when the door to his cabin swung open and Special Agent Branner was swiping her hand along the bulkhead, looking for the overhead light switch, which she found much too quickly.

"What did you do with Bagger Thompson?" she demanded.

"And a brilliant good morning to you, too, Special Agent. What are you doing aboard my boat and in my bedroom at this ungodly hour?"

He could focus his eyes now, and he saw that she was soaking wet, her normally perfect hair bedraggled and her skirt plastered to her thighs. She saw him looking at her body and swore impatiently. "Get your ass out of that bed, Hall. I want to know what you and Thompson were up to last night."

Jim, who slept naked, sighed audibly and obliged her. He walked over to the head without looking at her and went in and closed the door behind him. When he came out, she wasn't there and the lights were on in the main lounge. He put on his bathrobe, grabbed a dry towel, and went through to the lounge. She was sitting in his favorite chair, looking like an angry wet hen. He tossed her the towel and walked through to the galley to fire up the coffeemaker.

She'd made some superficial repairs when he came back out into the lounge and handed her a mug of coffee. She'd taken her soaked suit jacket off, and he manfully tried not to stare at her very wet blouse. Jupiter started bitching under his cage cover.

"Sorry," she muttered into her coffee mug, not looking at him.

"Start at the beginning," he said. "What's going on?"

"Bagger turned up at Anne Arundel General this morning at around zero two hundred," she said. "Someone cracked his skull. He'd been drinking, apparently, which, I can tell you from personal experience, he should not do. He'd told me earlier that he was going out with you on some kind of 'recon mission,' as he put it. Your turn."

"Shit," Jim said, and then gave her an abbreviated summary of the night before. He left out the part about the Goth girls.

"Guinness? You fed him Guinness?"

"He fed himself Guinness. Hey, he's an adult, okay? He'd had two and was talking about a third as I was leaving. I actually warned him about that stuff. How bad's he hurt?"

"Bad enough that he hasn't surfaced yet. Thanks to you."

"Oh, screw that noise," Jim snapped. "How would you react if I told you how many drinks *you* could have, huh?"

She started to say something, stopped, blew a long breath through pursed lips, and then relaxed. "Sorry," she said again. "My partner gets whacked around and I wasn't there to protect him. That's on me, not you."

He crossed the lounge and took Jupiter's cage cover off. The rain was really pounding now, one of those April line squalls that comes sweeping down the Severn to flush the Annapolis harbor from time to time. The boat had stopped moving as the rain beat the harbor waves flat. Jupiter began to bob and weave, trying to get a look at Branner. Jim sat down in the chair across from her. "There's more," he said, and then he told her about the Goth girls.

She shook her head in wonder. "And you think Bagger was lured out of the bar by those girls?"

"I do now. The proof will be when he can talk."

"This is the vampire crowd?"

"Yup. This sounds a lot like another one. I should have stayed with him."

Branner got up and looked out a porthole. The rain was letting up topside and the first streaks of light were painting the eastern horizon over Eastport. Jim admired her wide, strong shoulders, and the unconscious way she let her body jut this way and that. Definitely a female.

"I need to get back to the hospital," she said, standing. "I want to be there when Bagger comes up."

"I've got to file a report this morning on that rocket business. The fire department's probably put one in already. You want me to say that NCIS is going to get into this one?"

"We normally would," she said, turning back around. As if suddenly aware of her semitransparent blouse, she folded her arms across her chest. He noticed that she had green, faintly lupine eyes. Branner as she-wolf. Worked for him. "But this Dell thing has us running," she was saying. "I've been trying not to ask for additional resources. But with Bagger down . . ."

"Why not?" Jim asked. "Calling in a crowd is the government's biggest advantage, especially in a homicide."

"Who said it was a homicide?" she asked, those green eyes flashing.

Jim didn't answer, and then she realized he'd been talking to Bagger. She came back to the chair and flopped down. "Actually, it could go either way," she said. "Something's not quite right with Markham's answers. On the other hand, the ME's report is ambiguous. I'm still trying to decide."

"So it'll be your call?"

"Pretty much. The dant's hating life right now, just wants it all to go the hell away. Here comes all the commissioning week bullshit, the vice president, the Board of Visitors, and they have mids flying off the damned roof."

"Anybody putting the pressure on you to call it a suicide and move on?" he asked.

"Not in so many words," she said slowly. He could see that she was unsure about trusting him. "They're sensitive to the command influence problem. But I've been here long enough to read between the lines."

"You need a statement from me about our little op last night?"

"I guess I do," she said.

"How much you want me to say about the booze?"

"Could you just say what *you* had to drink?"

"Can do," he said. "How about the Goth girls?"

"Yes, you should mention them. My bosses know Bagger."

"I'll have a draft over to you this morning," he said. "You chop it, and I'll smooth it. I don't want to cause him any trouble."

"Appreciate that," she said, holding the jacket out at arm's length like a wet cat. "You and your people pursue the runner. I think this Dell thing's going to come to a head in a few days. Then we'll look into whether or not your runner is connected with Bagger's getting mugged. Then maybe we'll both kick his ass."

"Is that a date?" he asked, just for the hell of it.

She raised her eyebrows. "You asking me out, Mr. Hall? At this hour of the morning?"

"Well," he said. "I guess we are going about it bassackwards. You having already been to my bedroom and all."

She cocked her head and gave him a speculative look. She was standing now with one hand on her left hip, the other holding the jacket out by one finger, as if she were going to twirl it. He saw a flash of amusement in her eyes. Good morning, America: Maybe there's a real girl in there after all, he thought.

"It was just a thought," he said finally, remembering that he had paraded in the buff earlier. He got up. "Seeing as we might be kicking a little ass together in the future, that is."

"Everyone likes a little ass," she began, glancing at his for an instant. "Or so I'm told. Say, you have an umbrella I can borrow?"

"Is that a yes?" he asked. The rain came down even harder.

"Let me call you," she said patiently. "An umbrella?"

Jim waited in line to refill his coffee cup at 10:30 that morning. Saturday mornings were regular working days, and most of the headquarters staff people were in the building. He had already spent a half hour with the fire marshal working up the report on the rocket incident, and he had just finished bringing Chief Bustamente up to speed on the night in the tunnel and what had happened to Bagger Thompson afterward.

Commander Michaels, his boss, joined him at the coffee mess table. Jim back-briefed him on the tunnel business and asked if he wanted a written report. To Jim's surprise, Michaels shook his head.

"Verbal's good enough right now," he said, looking out into the hallway to make sure no one was listening. "But look: This Dell thing is turning into a real media firestorm. The possible homicide angle has leaked. Dell's parents have their congressman into it, and he, for our sins, is on the House subcommittee that has Academy oversight. The supe's so happy, he could just shit."

"And the dant?"

"Lotsa Dant Dance, last time I saw him. He's ready to Class-A Dell's corpse for causing all this shit."

Jim got the picture. "In other words, nobody wants to hear more bad news about a mid going out into town and beating up on locals just now?"

"Especially if he's dressing up as a frigging vampire. Frame that as a breaking story on CNN. So, you're the security officer. See if you and your cops can catch this guy, preferably on federal ground. Keep the story in government channels until we get this other thing squashed. You know, one fire at a time, if we can manage it."

Jim almost told him about the dant's order to get inside the NCIS investigation, but he stopped himself. The chain of command for that had been very specific. "So, I keep you informed?"

Michaels nodded. "Yeah. We don't *know* this is a mid doing this shit, do we?"

"Just a hunch right now."

"Okay, maybe we'll get lucky on this one. We're overdue." He looked around the hallway again and lowered his voice. "Look, we've got two weeks left in this academic year, and then all the firsties become enswines, and the rest of the little dears go off to the seven seas for their summer cruise. If we can just get through this Dell mess, we can maybe get things back to normal around this damned place."

"Whatever normal is," Jim said. Michaels raised his eyebrows.

"Well, I mean, shit," Jim said. "A mid gets himself killed; another one is out there consorting with witches and mugging drunks in back alleys. Is this what normal means here now?"

Michaels, who'd been a carrier pilot until a catapult accident had damaged his neck, was also an Academy graduate.

He shook his head. "Gee-go," he muttered. He filled his coffee mug and left for his office.

Jim stirred his own coffee. GIGO was one of the not-so-secret code words around the office. Garbage in, garbage out. Given all that the Academy had accomplished over the years, it wasn't fair that the 1 percent that was garbage could absolutely demolish the reputation of the 99 percent who were gold. It reminded Jim of his time in the Corps—he had spent 90 percent of his personnel admin time on 5 percent of his Marines.

He went to his own cube to find out the commandant's schedule for the day. Saturdays were more flexible than regular workdays, and he wanted to back-brief him on what he'd learned about the NCIS investigation. Then he wanted to call the hospital and check on Bagger. He still felt bad about the Guinness. He should have been paying more attention.

He wondered if Branner would really call him to go out. That might be more of a thrill than he could stand at his advancing age.

Ev had spent Saturday morning in the Nimitz Library, doing some research on the Uniform Code of Military Justice and its bible, the *Manual for Courts-Martial.* The academic offices in Sampson were only about half-occupied for Saturday classes, especially as the academic year drew to a close. Ev taught mostly seniors, and they were definitely slacking off at this stage of the game.

The rainsqualls had quit just after sunrise and the morning dawned cool and clear, with eye-dazzling sunlight. Looking out the office windows, Ev could see the first clumps of weekend tourists filtering down from the Maryland Avenue gate. Now back in his office, he put a call into Liz at home, got voice mail. He tried her office number.

"Morning, counselor," he said. "I talked to Julie last night. I think we have a problem."

"Now what?"

"Julie wants to unlawyer. My fault, probably. I got clumsy, made one probe too many." He filled her in.

"And it was the question about her getting up for early swim practice that set her off?" she asked.

"Yes."

"Did she actually answer it?"

He thought back for a moment. "No. So I've put a call in to the varsity swim coach to see if they're still doing the pre-reveille sessions, and if so, whether Julie has been involved. But this business about her talking to the NCIS people without you being present . . ."

"You told her that she'd be going against my advice?"

"Hell, I told her you'd fire her as a client."

"I won't do that, not yet anyway. But now you're definitely going to have to get into this, Ev. She obviously doesn't want to talk to me just now, and she won't until they scare her."

"I understand," he said. "Let me start with the coach. I think we need to establish whether or not Julie could have been out of her room that night—or early morning, I guess."

"Exactly," she said. "Oh, I ran into one of the marshals at the sub shop a little while ago. He's heard a rumor that one of the agents from the Academy NCIS office apparently got into some kind of trouble out in town last night. The nice black guy. The word is, he's in the hospital. It gets kinda fuzzy as to what happened, which means the local cops are probably sitting on something."

"Well, maybe that will distract NCIS, vis-à-vis Julie," he said hopefully.

"One can always hope," she said. "But call me when you hear from that coach. I won't do anything until I hear from you."

"Thanks, Liz. For not jumping ship, I mean. She needs you. She just doesn't know it."

"Not to burst your bubble, Ev, but if she won't do what I tell her to, I can't represent her. But let her swim with the sharks for a while, see how she likes it."

"Now there's a comforting image for a father to hear."

"Ev, Julie's well out of the nest. All those kids over there are. Call me at home when you have something."

Ev put down the phone and stared at the wall in front of his desk. It was now past noon, and the Academy weekend had officially begun. He'd changed into his running clothes, then sat back down at his desk to finish reading his notes on suspects' rights. The leather of his chair was starting to stick to the backs of his thighs. Goddamn, Julie. This is the wrong time to get pigheaded. He decided to jog over to MacDonough Hall to see if he could chase down Coach Downing in his office or at the Nat. It being Saturday, he was probably going to fail, but he needed to do something.

He stepped outside, did his warm-up, and then broke into a gentle jog across Radford Terrace and down onto Ingram Field, where there was only the Saturday complement of midshipmen and officers out for their daily running exercise. Physical fitness was an integral part of Naval Academy life, for everyone—faculty, staff, and midshipmen. Even on a liberty day, people were still exercising. Being fat or even out of shape at the Naval Academy was a cultural offense, from the admiral on down to the lowliest plebe.

He made ten circuits of the track to kill some time through the lunch hour and then cooled down by walking over to MacDonough. He went upstairs to the coaches' office complex, which was, as he suspected, already empty for the weekend. He asked a passing mid if he'd seen Coach Downing in the building. The coach was down at the training pool with some Class IV swimmers. Ev went back down to the Natatorium, where he found Downing in the water, finishing up a lesson on the basics of the survival breaststroke. The Class Fours, as they were called, were midshipmen who couldn't swim either because they just couldn't get it or because they were basically terrified to be in the water. The Nat was not designed with a shallow end, so there were several frightened young faces bobbing along the side of the pool. They had also missed the noon meal.

Downing, a sixty-year-old former national diving champion, launched the last two plebes from the side, one with each hand. They thrashed their way to the other side with all the style of a light-loaded ship's propeller that is half out of the water. Then he blew his whistle and sent everyone to the locker room. The clinging plebes came out of the water like so many salmon trying to get up a dam's spillway. Downing climbed out of the water in one graceful spring to the side, and Ev walked over. Because of Julie, the coach recognized Ev immediately.

"Hey, Professor: Come to do a tower jump for old times' sake?"

"Not exactly, Coach. Had a question for you. It concerns the swim team. And Julie."

To Ev's surprise, he thought he saw a flicker of apprehension in Downing's eyes. "Shoot," Downing said, reaching for a towel.

"Is the swim team still doing the zero-dark-thirty practice sessions?"

"Prereveille? Negative. We've just finished up the regular competition season. We're in the maintenance mode these days. And the firsties like your daughter, they're just swimming for exercise, if they're swimming at all. You know, graduation looms. They're almost through."

Ev thanked him, said, "See you," and started to walk away.

"Ev?" Downing said. "This isn't about that Dell mess, is it?"

Ev stopped and almost unconsciously glanced around to see if anyone was listening in, but the pool area was empty. Downing came over.

"I've heard some disturbing rumors," he said quietly. "One involves Julie."

"The underwear thing?"

"So you've heard about that? Well, of course she would have told you."

"It's true. Although Julie thinks it's probably a laundry mistake."

"That he was *wearing* them?"

"No, no, that he had them in his possession. Surely there was nothing going on between Dell, a plebe, and my daughter, right?"

"Not that I ever saw. We have some swim team romances every year; Julie and Tommy Hays, for instance. But no, Dell was a diver. Nice form, but not quite good enough for varsity stuff. I let him stay on as a manager on the plebe bench. Plebes know to keep their distance from firsties."

"Yeah, that's my experience. What else are you hearing?"

Downing shook his head. "Nothing that concerns Julie." He glanced around the Natatorium. "But there's been some talk that Dell was maybe a little light in his loafers. If not gay, then maybe bisexual. One of our assistant coaches heard rumors about some 'special' massage treatments after some of the away meets, involving an unnamed manager. Admittedly, we're talking nineteenth-hand scuttlebutt here."

"Specifically involving Dell?"

"An unnamed manager, I tried to run it down, but . . ."

"You hit the old blue-and-gold wall."

Downing nodded. They walked together toward the pool doors. The surface of the Nat had settled into a vast mirror. "Has that NCIS team been down to interview anybody about Dell?" Ev asked.

"No. Will they?"

Ev nodded. "Yeah, Coach, I think they will. Did you know they're considering that the Dell incident might be a possible homicide?"

"Judas Priest! You're kidding. At the Academy?"

"That's rumor, too. Or maybe it's a preliminary line—you know, to rule it out."

Downing stopped. "That why you got Julie a lawyer?"

It was Ev's turn to be surprised. It must have shown on his face, because Downing patted him lightly on the shoulder. "No real secrets around this hothouse, Ev," he said. "You know that."

There might be one or two, Ev thought, but he didn't say it. He needed to report back to Liz. The swim team wasn't doing prereveille practices. So now it came down to a simple but specific yes or no: Had Julie been in her room when Dell went down?

Jim Hall had been unable to get on the commandant's calendar, so he called the chief instead and asked what he'd heard about Bagger since the last time they'd talked. The chief said the police rumor mill had the story, and that the locals were waiting to see if the G would react as it usually did when an agent went down—that is, bring in a platoon of angry agents. Jim then called the NCIS office to see what further word they had on Bagger Thompson. The secretary pretended not to know what he was talking about, so Jim didn't press it. He called the hospital, hit the same brick wall, and decided just to go over there. There might be a town cop around who could get him in to see Bagger, or at least to find out how he was doing.

It took fifteen minutes to find a parking place at the hospital, and another fifteen to find the hospital security officer's office. He identified himself to a secretary and then told the security officer's assistant that he knew Agent Thompson was there and that there was an official lid on that fact. He asked if could she find someone who could tell him how Thompson was doing. Another fifteen minutes out in the main waiting room produced Agent Branner. She had changed clothes and was looking tired but efficient as she strode purposefully across the waiting room, heels clicking. She sat down next to him and a wave of subtle perfume wafted over him.

"They're moving him up to Bethesda," she said softly, not looking at him while she scanned the almost-empty waiting room. "Major skull fracture. Something unpronounceable is swelling. If they don't get it under control pretty quick, he's not going to make it."

Jim swore. "I had no idea it was that serious. He talking?"

"Hell, he's barely breathing," she said, and he heard something in her voice that made him turn to look at her face. Not tears exactly, but some of that gunfighter toughness was noticeably absent.

"What are you looking at?" she snapped, sniffing.

"Careful there, Special Agent. Don't let anyone see you being human."

"Up yours, Hall."

He let it pass, thought about taking her hand, and then decided not to. If they were moving Thompson to the National Naval Medical Center in Bethesda, it must be serious indeed. That's where the president received his medical care. The vampire mugger was swiftly losing his appeal.

"You going up there with him?" he asked.

She shook her head. "Can't," she said. "Dell."

He nodded. "Want me to go?"

She rolled her eyes. "You've done enough damage," she replied, and then immediately put her hand on his. "Cancel that. I'm just . . . just wigging out. Oh and I called that Irish Pub. He had six of those Guinness stouts."

He didn't say anything for a few seconds. Six was a lot. Then he said, "I'm going into the tunnels tonight. Around twenty-two hundred. I could use some backup."

She was looking straight ahead, seeing nothing. Then she seemed to realize where her hand was and retrieved it. "What?"

He said it again.

"What about your cops?"

"My cops deal mostly with patrolling the Yard, parking control, and tourist coordination. I mean *backup*."

She nodded slowly. "*Hell* yes," she said. "Although it's not likely that he's gonna be there so soon after what he did last night."

"We're not positive our tunnel runner is also the guy who took Bagger down," he said. "And we may be talking about more than one guy, so our rocket shooter might also not be the guy who beat up Bagger."

"What do you think?" she asked.

He shrugged. "I guess I think it is."

"Yeah, me, too. And if it is, he's gone way beyond sophomoric pranks in the Academy underground."

"It's weird," Jim said. "This guy's acting as if this is some kind of escalating game. And I've seen him face-to-face."

"Could you recognize him again in his street clothes?"

"No way. He was wearing serious makeup. But very good makeup."

"If this is a firstie, then he's taking big chances."

Jim agreed. "The locals tracking down those Goth thingies?" he asked.

"They said they are, but you know, with all that Goth makeup and shit, it's the same deal as with you and your vampire friend. They could look like humans by day."

"And if they're from the St. John's campus, the cops are going to strike out all around," he said.

"The lead detective offered to do it anyway. He knows we have our hands full with the Dell case. They're going to work the campus cops."

"Anything more on the Dell thing?" he asked as casually as he could.

"I'm planning to interview the swim team coach on Monday," she said. She looked at her watch. "Shit. I've gotta go back upstairs. Where do you want to meet?"

He told her. She said okay and walked back toward the elevators. Jim watched her go. He liked the way she moved, solid and strong. Everything about her was straight ahead. Minimal bullshit.

Now he still needed to get to the commandant, one way or another.

Ev didn't make contact with Liz DeWinter until just after five o'clock. Since he'd spent the rest of his Saturday afternoon correcting papers in his office, he proposed that she join him for a drink at the Officers Club. As he walked across the parking lot to the club, he worried about what the swim coach had told him. Julie could have been out of her room before or even during the incident. And she could also have been sound asleep, too. But it would have been wonderful to have had an airtight alibi for the time leading up to Dell's death.

The main bar was a comfortable paneled room with tables and chairs. Academy memorabilia covered the walls. It being Saturday, the clientele was composed more of retirees than faculty members or executive staff. He got a table in view of the door and ordered a glass of wine. Five minutes later, Liz walked in wearing an expensive-looking white linen suit whose trim lines nicely accentuated her figure. Two patrons waiting for a table were blocking her way. She was small enough that she could slip between them with an "Excuse me" smile. She sat down before he had a chance to get up to hold her chair. She was obviously dressed up to go somewhere, and for a moment, he wondered where. And with whom. Not that it was any of his business.

"Macallan, rocks," she said to the waitress, who'd already brought Ev his glass of wine. Ev was suddenly conscious of the covert stares from a faculty couple at a nearby table. They'd known Joanne. "What'd you find out?" she asked.

He recapped his conversation with the coach. Liz frowned. "Okay," she said. "So it would have been nice if Julie'd been in the pool with the entire swim team at the precise time of Dell's death, but this doesn't prove she was anywhere *but* in her room, asleep."

"That's what I hoped," he said.

"Problem is, she's the only tie they have right now. Which means they'll call her in again and again and keep probing to see if they can make a connection. In her present mood, she might screw that up."

"So now what?"

Liz looked around and lowered her voice. "My next step is to find out what's in that ME's report that has everyone's nose up."

"Can you do that?"

"I'm working my web. Cross your fingers. But basically, until they lay charges against somebody, we're in the dark," she said. "Maybe the best thing is to just let the NCIS people do their thing."

"And let Julie take her chances?"

"I didn't mean that, although she seems willing to do that anyway."

Ev nodded and drank some wine. The room was filling up, with even some midshipmen coming in now. Firsties were allowed to patronize the Officers Club on Saturdays, and a few had brought along their dates, who appeared to be nervous. The waitress tried her best to put them at ease as she took orders and discreetly checked ID cards. Liz was glancing at her watch.

"Big date tonight?" he asked.

She finished her scotch and looked at him with an amused expression. He flushed and apologized for intruding. She leaned forward and put her fingers over his. "Are you ever going to relax around me?" she asked.

Acutely aware that the faculty couple across the way was watching, he withdrew his hand and ran it through his hair. "I feel like a teenager," he said. "When you came into the bar all dressed up, I wondered where you were going and with whom, and then I kicked myself mentally. Like it was any of my business."

She smiled openly then. "You're right, it's none of your business. But I'm edified that you care. I like you. I think you're a nice guy who's been kicked in the teeth by what happened to your wife and now you don't know what the hell to do. You know those people over there?"

Surprised, he almost glanced over at them. He said, "Yes, they knew Joanne."

"I thought I detected some vibes of disapproval," she said. "I've got to run. I'll call you when I hear something. And you call me if Julie squawks."

"I will," he said, suddenly reluctant to see her go.

"Or just call me," she said quietly as she stood up to

leave. He smiled up at her. She then walked over to where the faculty couple was sitting, leaned down, and said something to the woman, then left the lounge with an exaggerated stride that had every man in the room watching her go. Ev saw the woman's face turn very red, and he wondered what Liz had said. Don't ask, he thought, and then found himself grinning despite himself.

Just call me. Okay, counselor—excuse me, Liz—I will definitely do that. Liz was the only ray of light in his life right now.

Jim listened to a movie themes CD while he waited for Agent Branner in his truck. He was parked in the small lot in front of Alumni Hall. It was just after 10:30 Saturday night, and there was barely any traffic around the Yard. A partial moon shone through fleeting clouds. There was a dance over in Dahlgren Hall, so most of the traffic was down at the other end of the Yard.

He'd caught up with the commandant late that afternoon and given him a quick debrief on what he'd learned about the Dell case, which, of course, wasn't very much. He did not tell the commandant anything about the tunnel runner incident, nor did Robbins seem to know about the fire alarm of the night before. He'd told Jim to keep plugging and then hurried away. If he was pleased with what Jim had told him, he gave no sign. Probably just expected his orders to be carried out, with hardly a thought to the possibility that they wouldn't be. The confidence of command. Or maybe the arrogance.

Branner knocked on the driver's side window, startling him. He hadn't heard or seen her vehicle approach, but there it was, parked right next to his. He rolled the window down and shut off the CD.

"Ready?" she asked. She was dressed as he'd recommended: dark slacks, a sweatshirt, black gloves, a ball cap with NCIS emblazoned across the front, and a dark-colored

NCIS windbreaker. She had a utility belt with flashlight, her weapon, extra rounds, cuffs, and some odds and ends in Velcro pouches.

Jim nodded, swung out of the truck, and locked it up. He was dressed as he had been for his previous excursions, with a different windbreaker to replace the one trashed by the spray paint. He carried a small tool bag with the motion detectors, and he was also wearing a utility belt.

"The grate's over there, behind Mahan Hall," he said. "You okay with being underground? Not claustrophobic?"

"Not thrilled with confined spaces, but I'm not anything-phobic," she said. "Mood I'm in, I hope your bat bird does show up tonight."

"How's Bagger?" he asked as they walked over toward the grate. A fine mist of steam was wafting up through the steel grating.

"Hanging in there," she said, looking hard at the shadows around the underground entrance, unconsciously touching her sidearm. "They've got the swelling problem controlled. Now they're waiting for him to surface."

"Getting whacked in the head—it's not like the movies, is it?" Jim said as he lifted the grate. Branner didn't answer as she inspected the steel stairs leading down into the concrete pit. Jim asked her to pull the grate closed behind her as he led the way down.

She asked few questions as he gave her the grand tour for the next hour. He took her all the way out to the St. John's grate and then back under the utility tunnels serving Bancroft Hall. He showed her where the rocket had left char marks on the concrete, the territorial graffiti, which remained unchanged from the previous night, and where he'd been surprised by the paint-spraying vampire. He noticed that, despite her statement to the contrary, she did seem to be uncomfortable being down in the tunnels. The tunnels weren't exactly claustrophobic, in his opinion, what with the lights and ample room to walk around without bending over, even for someone of his height. Nor was it particularly spooky. Just a collection of pipes, cables, conduits, equipment cabinets, and steel doors leading to vaults along the sides. The air was close and warm; maybe that was doing it.

He set up the first motion detector in the main tunnel, pointing back toward Bancroft Hall. He set it high so as to not detect any rodents that might be operating down here. Branner made a face when he mentioned rodents, but she helped him string the tiny transmitter wire through the overhead conduit brackets back to the T junction with the Mahan Hall grating access. The second one went into the tunnel aimed at the Annapolis utility tunnel access, a few blocks from the St. John's campus, with its transmitter wire coming back to the same point as the first one. He took the steam-tight globes off the two lights illuminating the junction and unscrewed the bulbs. Then they moved into the short tunnel leading back to the Mahan Hall grating, set up the receiver-indicator box, ran the box through its self-test, and sat down on some equipment cabinets to wait. The only sounds came from the steam pipes, with the additional rumble of a vehicle out on the street in front of Mahan Hall.

"Can he get directly out into town, down at the other end?" she asked, speaking quietly. "Down by those old brick arches under Dahlgren Hall?"

"He could, except I locked out the interchange doors last night after that rocket. Assuming he has the regular series lock key, the new locks will defeat him, so he'll have to come out via St. John's."

"And the other detector will get him coming back in, assuming he's already out there?"

Jim nodded. "It being Saturday night, this may be a waste of time," he said. "If this is a firstie, he could just come back through the gates."

"Not dressed up as a vampire, one assumes," she said.

Jim shrugged. "Yeah, but if he's operating with those Goth freaks, he may have a base of operations in the student ghetto somewhere. My guess is that he'll be in costume in the tunnels only if he's on the run. Like after busting some civilian heads in an alley. And it's a little early for that shit."

"How do these things work?" she asked, indicating the receiver box for the detectors.

"The sensors themselves are out there in the tunnels. They get a hit, they send a signal here over those wires, and we get a channel light. Tells us which one is getting the hit."

"Why wire? Why not a transmitter?"

"A wire signal can't be detected. If the detector used a radio to get back to this receiver, it could be intercepted."

Branner was skeptical. "You're assuming your mid would have some pretty sophisticated gear," she said.

"They get to play with sophisticated gear in the double-E labs all the time. You go to any of the football games?"

She nodded.

"You catch the Navy–Air Force game last year? The bus drivers like to put on a falconry display at halftime. The falcons are their mascots. Last year, some mids built a high-powered radar transmitter dish. Mounted it on the back of a pickup truck, with a parabolic antenna and an optical tracking telescope. Parked it outside the stadium, out with the tailgaters. When the falcon started doing his thing, they turned it on, locked a tracking beam on the bird, and drove it nuts. Damn thing went up into the light towers and wouldn't come down."

"Damn."

"Well, we don't especially like the Air Farce. But all of that gear, that was just bench stuff from a missile fire-control lab. Homework assignment. So, yes, he could have a detector that could pick up the fan beams from my motion detectors, if he's worried about stuff like that. I don't think so, though."

"You think he's getting overconfident?"

"I'm hoping so. Although he did surprise me fairly easily, and he had to have preplanned that rocket business."

"He won't surprise me," she said. "And if he comes up with any bullshit like that rocket, I'll cap his young ass."

Jim grinned. "The objective is to apprehend subject young ass, not blow holes in it. Got enough dead mids this week already."

She grimaced at the reference to Dell.

"My chief said he'd heard some stuff about the post-mortem. Said that was where the homicide vibes were coming from." He kept his voice casual, his eyes on the receiver.

"It's cumulative," she said, suppressing a yawn. "There was the panties bit, plus some, um, anatomical aspects that might indicate the kid was no stranger to wearing panties, if you catch my drift. Main thing was the bruising. Upper arms grabbed from the front, probably right before he died. One interpretation would be that he was lifted and thrown. But there are some S and M situations that could cause those bruises."

"Wow," he said. "What's ambiguous about all that?"

"Well, there you are, Mr. Security Officer," she said. "That's why we're looking into it as if it might be a homicide. Tell me, are you technically a cop?"

"Nope. Government civilian, grade twelve. I supervise the people who have police jurisdiction in the Yard and on other Academy property, but I personally don't have a badge. I pack a Glock on occasions like this, but probably not legally. That help?"

She frowned. "Can you make arrests?"

"Not normally. If I get into that situation, I'd be calling the Yard cops, or maybe even you guys. But, no, I'm not a cop. I'm technically an administrator."

"So what've you been doing down here chasing this shit-bird? Why not your own cops?"

"Because he made it personal."

She stared at him for a moment and then nodded. Personal, she understood. "Okay," she said. "So if we catch this guy tonight, and especially if he did Bagger, he's mine, right?"

"Absolutely. As long as you don't shoot him right off. We won't *know* he's the guy who did Bagger until there's been an arrest and some questions asked, right?"

"Right," she said, touching her weapon again. "But if it is . . ."

"We subdue him, cuff him, you take him into custody, read him his rights, and *then* you can shoot him. But do it over in your holding cell, not one of ours, okay? Ours doesn't have a drain."

She grinned, although it wasn't a pleasant sight just now, Jim thought. Then the receiver beeped, and the channel from the detector pointed at Annapolis lighted up.

"Hello," Jim said softly. He moved up to the edge of the tunnel junction, with Branner right beside him. The nearest overhead light was fifty feet down the main tunnel, in the direction of the St. John's campus. Branner had her weapon out. Jim saw it and leaned over to whisper in her ear. "You fire that thing down here in a concrete tunnel and it's as likely to get you as him," he said.

"Only if I miss," she whispered back. "I'll go down that way. Let him go by; then yell halt. If he rabbits, he'll run right into me." With that, she slipped into the main tunnel, turned left, and hurried silently down to a dogleg turn fifty feet toward Bancroft, where she disappeared around the corner.

Okay, I guess we now officially have a plan, Jim thought. Although it would have been nice to have had a vote. On the other hand, she was a trained police agent, and he was not. He waited.

One minute stretched into two, and then three. Shouldn't have taken the guy this long. He reviewed the layout of the tunnel complex to see if there was another branch he could have taken, and decided there wasn't, not if he was headed back to Bancroft. Four minutes. Then he heard a distant clang of metal, as if one of the interchange doors was being closed.

More silence. Three vehicles in succession bumped over the road above his head. Five minutes. He wanted to look around the corner toward the sound of that door, but he held back. The guy would probably see him as he went by the entrance to the branch tunnel, but by then, Jim would be coming at him. He touched the Glock but decided not to draw it. Once he called the guy out and Branner made her presence known, a mid would give it up for Lent. Six minutes.

Then a soft shuffling sound to his right. Something coming down the tunnel. He crouched into a ready stance and drew out his big Maglite. Nothing like a little white light to disorient his quarry for a crucial second or two. Another sound. Closer. Then silence. Then a very soft giggle.

Giggle? Before he could even blink, a stumpy figure in flowing black robes slipped by the entrance to his tunnel, a smallish figure, with a painted white face. He got only a momentary glimpse, then stood up and roared for her to halt just as she went out of sight to his left. He jumped into the main tunnel, saw the figure's back ten feet away, and snapped on the Maglite just as the girl spun around. It was one of those Goth girls, looking like some kind of alien in the harsh blue-white beam.

"Put your hands out where I can see them," he ordered, staying put while he held the blinding light in her face. To his amazement, she screamed. Really screamed. She took a deep breath, clenched her fists, and let one fly, a continuous, top-of-the-lungs, "My baby is being ripped from my womb before my very own eyes" scream. That brought Branner out from behind the dogleg, her own flashlight blazing up the tunnel and partially blinding Jim. Then a jet airplane fired up its engines in the tunnel behind him and he could hear nothing but a huge roar of sound as the girl ran right at him, her face still contorted in the act of screaming, even though the blast of sound from behind him in the tunnel was overwhelming all his senses. He managed to grab her as she tried to slip by, and then both of them were down on the deck plates as he tried to hold on to her billowing robes and keep his sanity in the midst of the incredible noise. His flashlight went flying and he was left grappling in the dark with this surprisingly strong girl. He managed to pin one of her arms and then a second one. She started kicking out, and he ended up dropping across her back, still gripping both her arms, until she stopped it.

He felt rather than saw Branner jump over both of them

as she ran in the direction of the St. John's doors. The blasting noise was getting even louder, if that was possible, and then he felt a billowing wet heat enveloping them both.

Steam. *Shit!* There'd been two of them, and the other one, probably the guy they were after, had opened a steam-line drain valve as he took off back the way they had come in. The girl began to struggle again, but this time it was different. She wasn't fighting him as much as fighting to breathe, and he realized he'd laid his entire weight on her. Being careful to keep his grip, he rolled off her back and yelled at her to keep still, that she was under arrest, but it was pointless in the shattering noise. As he raised his head, he realized he wasn't able to breathe, not at all. His first inhalation brought a hot, wet gulp of oxygen-free water vapor, and he bent his head down immediately to get some air. This was dangerous. The tunnel was quickly filling with steam. This wasn't a drain valve, but one of the main lines. Steam would soon displace all the oxygen. They couldn't stay here. He wondered where Branner was, then decided he had to get himself and his prisoner the hell out of there, or at least behind a fire door. The nearest one was back in the branch tunnel leading to Mahan Hall, so he began dragging the girl toward the junction.

But which way was the junction? In his struggles with the girl, he had lost his bearings. Now he no longer knew which way led to the branch intersection. What little light there had been was being swallowed up in the billowing steam, and his attempts to breathe were bringing in increasingly less oxygen. If he chose wrong, there were no more doors for at least three hundred feet. He felt the girl start to cough and choke in his grip, and he forced her head down to the deck plates, where there was still some air.

The deck plates. There was a channel under the deck plates. Hot steam would rise. There might be air in the channel. Keeping one hand on the girl, he clawed at the edge of the deck plate nearest his hand until he got under an edge. He heaved against it and it moved, but the girl's body was holding it down. He rolled her off of it and tried again. She had stopped struggling and was now down flat on the concrete floor. With one enormous heave, he got the deck plate up and out of its brackets. He pushed the girl down into the trenchlike channel, which was two feet deep and the same distance across, a notch running beneath the tunnel floor where water could accumulate in the event of a major leak, allowing repair crews time to get it stopped. On the bottom of the channel was the top of the main sewage line. He dropped in after her and landed partially on her and into a few inches of ice-cold water. Above him, the steam noise was louder and the temperature was rising fast. He could see nothing but a glow in the billowing mist above the floor. He pulled the plate over them as best he could, and the noise subsided a little.

"Stay down," he yelled into the white blur that was the girl's face, and she got flatter, no longer resisting. He fumbled in his belt for the small, spare Maglite and snapped it on. Where the hell is Branner? he wondered. She doesn't know these tunnels. The channel ran in a straight line in both directions until it disappeared from sight. It smelled faintly of sewer gas and salt water. He felt water starting to drip down from the edges of the deck plate. Hot water. Steam's condensing up there on the cold walls, he thought. He wondered how long it would be before the water started rising in the channel. But there was nowhere else to go. Above them, all the air and oxygen had been displaced by steam, and even at atmospheric pressure, the ambient temperature would be at least 150 degrees, enough to sear lung tissue. They would just have to wait until the steam plant's operators detected the pressure drop, realized they had a leak, and shut down the main steam-supply line to Bancroft Hall. He took as deep a breath as he could stand, then settled lower into the water at the bottom of the channel to wait it out.

After what seemed like ages, the noise began to subside above their heads. He looked at his watch. It had been more like ten, maybe fifteen minutes since the whole thing started. He waited for the roaring noise to reduce itself to a medium blast, and then he jammed his fingers up between the edge of the plate and the lip of the trench. He raised his hand. The air was still hot and wet. When he thought he could make himself heard, he told the girl that they had shut off the steam but that they'd have to wait until there was air up there. She made a noise, and he shone the light in her face. All that white pancake makeup had begun to run off her face, and he was looking at a young and very scared college kid. Not all the moisture streaming down her cheeks was from the steam.

After another five minutes, all the noise had stopped and he pushed the plate out of its channel and sat up in the trench. The water was another inch or so deeper in the channel and running in a visible current around his hips. The air above them was still full of mist, but it was no longer hot and he could breathe. The girl was still flattened down in the bottom of the channel, her black clothes looking like an ink spill. He hoisted himself to sit on the edge of the channel, set the flashlight down on the floor, and lifted her up to a sitting position. He could hear the sounds of a maintenance crew in the distance. He wondered where the hell Branner was, and if she'd caught the bastard who'd done this.

"Did I tell you that you were under arrest?" he asked the girl. She nodded emphatically and started to cry again.

He saw lights coming down the tunnel from the direction of Bancroft Hall, then heard someone coming from the other direction.

"Hall?" Branner called. "You still down here?"

"Here," he yelled back. "You catch him?"

A flashlight stabbed through the swirling cloud of condensing steam and then Branner stepped out of the mist. She appeared none the worse for wear. "Saw him, but he slammed a steel door shut, and I didn't have a key. Then all that steam came and I had to run for it. Found another tunnel behind a door and hid out."

"Well, I managed to hold on to this one," he said, pointing at the bedraggled Goth.

"She'll do," Branner said, crouching down to stare at the frightened girl. Branner had a wolfish look on her face. "She'll do."

The girl began to cry in earnest as the maintenance crew showed up to ask what the hell was going on.

8

It was 1:00 A.M. on Sunday when Branner and Jim got the girl to the NCIS offices. Once out of the tunnel, her defiance had resurfaced and she had refused to say anything to either of them. She was carrying no identification, only a small wallet containing eleven dollars, a condom, and a used movie ticket. Branner had taken her in the bathroom and made her remove all the Goth makeup from her face. While Jim waited outside, she searched her for weapons or other contraband, discovering a nasty little two-inch knife in a flat sheath in the girl's stocking. She also had had a small leather pouch attached to her belt. It was decorated with odd symbols and contained some minute bits of vegetable material, from which Branner had obtained a positive test for cannabis. She'd then locked the girl in the interview room and told her to wait there.

"So we have her for simple possession," she was telling Jim while she made some fresh coffee before talking to the girl. "I can big-deal that up to possession of narcotics on a federal reservation—you know, for scare factor."

"But actually—"

"Yeah, actually, it's peanuts. The knife was concealed, but not long enough for full weapons status. Anyway, I want to know who that guy was I chased into the city tunnels. I'm assuming that he was probably our vampire mugger."

"Was he in costume?"

"Couldn't see, with all that steam. Just that it appeared to be big, male, description, height, weight unknown. He could flat-ass run, I'll tell you that, and he knew his way around down there. I was bouncing off equipment cabinets. He wasn't."

"I wish we could have alerted the gates," Jim said, drawing off a cup of coffee before the percolator finished hiccuping. The coffee was amber instead of black and filled with tiny coffee grounds. He lifted the lid and poured it back in.

"You think he beat it into town and then circled back?"

"If he's a mid, right," Jim said. "While we were in the sauna. You know, I don't think he just thought that steam move up on the fly, either. He's getting into this shit."

"Our boy's a planner and a plotter."

"Our boy's a badass. That touchdown rocket. Live steam. A can of spray paint in the face. He gets chased, he reacts."

"And it works, too," she said. "I thought I was going to be smothered down there when all that steam let go. And the noise!"

Jim tried the coffee again. "Plus, he's no hero. He knew we had the girl, but he took off anyway."

"Either that or he knows she won't say shit. Or, just possibly, she doesn't really know who he is."

"Right now, I'm interested in *what* he is," Jim said. "You do the talking; I'll just glare at her."

Branner nodded, got some coffee and the tape recorder, and then they went to the interview room.

The girl was sitting at the small metal table, her elbows propped on it and her head in her hands. She now had an expression of total boredom on her face, and she didn't even look up when they came into the room. Branner sat down at the head of the table and set up the tape recorder. Jim remained standing to one side, fixing the girl with a steady stare. Without all the Goth paint on her face, she looked much younger, a sophomore maybe. Moon-faced, pasty complexion, limp black hair, the beginnings of a double chin, outsized front, dull, dark eyes, red, dishwater hands with nicotine stains on her right forefinger, exaggerated, extra-long fake nails. A real beauty.

Branner turned on the machine, identified herself and Jim, and then took her through the required time, date, and Miranda warning for the record. When Branner asked her if she wanted a lawyer present, the girl stared straight ahead, saying nothing. Branner stated that she was taking that as a no, and then she asked the girl to identify herself. The girl gave her a surly look but said nothing. Branner paused the recorder and sat back in her chair.

"Listen, sweet pea, we have you for criminal trespass on a federal reservation, assault on a federal officer, destruction of government property, resisting arrest, carrying a concealed weapon, and possession of a controlled substance on federal property. You're in no position to play hardball with us."

"What destruction?" the girl asked.

"Causing steam to vent into the Academy's utility tunnel complex. Destruction of electrical and telephone equipment from water damage. Hope you or your family carry lots and lots of liability insurance."

The girl blinked when Branner mentioned her family. "I didn't do that," she said.

"You were the only one down there," Branner said, cocking her head to one side. "Right?"

The girl started to say something, looked quickly at Branner, and then clamped her jaw shut. Branner leaned forward. "More to the point," she said, "you are the one we apprehended. So if someone else did open the steam valve, it really doesn't matter to us. Unless, of course, you want to tell us who that was."

The girl set her jaw and said nothing. Branner looked at Jim. "Mr. Hall, there's a fingerprint kit and a Polaroid in the main office. Could you bring them in here, please?"

Jim left the door open and went to look for the camera and the cardboard fingerprint forms. He could hear Branner explaining what she was going to do. He found the camera, ink pad, and forms and took them back into the interview room.

"Are you going to tell us your name?" Branner asked.

The girl stared back at her. "You said I had the right to remain silent. Guess what?"

"O-kay," Branner said. "Mr. Hall, do your police have a holding cell?"

"No. If we need to hold someone, we take them downtown to the Annapolis station. Let's see, at this hour? They'll probably put her in the women's drunk tank. She'll have an interesting intercultural experience."

"Are you willing to cooperate and let me take your fingerprints?" Branner asked. The girl stuffed her hands into the folds of her black dress.

Branner deactivated the recorder and terminated the interview. "It's too late for this bullshit," she said. "We'll take her downtown. The night-shift cops can get her booked in. She gives them shit, they'll get a couple of those sumo matrons to help out. I'll file the charges Monday morning, and she can call her parents. They're going to be so proud."

She reached across the table and snapped on handcuffs, locking the girl's wrist to the ring on the table. They left her in there, closed the door, and went back to the office with the camera and the identification kit.

"What we need here is a good dungeon," Jim said.

"That one would probably enjoy a dungeon," Branner replied. "She could hang upside down and hiss a lot."

"What do you figure?"

"She's too old to be in high school," Branner said, getting out her Rolodex. "So I'm guessing St. John's." Branner found the number for the Annapolis police. "Do you think she could have been in that group Bagger tangled with? In that Irish pub?"

"It's possible," Jim said, rubbing his eyes. He could still feel the steam heat on his skin. "But with all the makeup they were wearing, I couldn't tell one from another. There's more attitude than brains in that one."

"I know some of the state attorneys," Branner said. "I'll get one of them to lean on the parents. Talk about big fines."

Jim didn't think any of that would work. He doubted there had been any real damage done down in those tunnels. Those equipment rooms were built to protect against leaks of water or steam. The steam plant people had come down, closed one valve, and put the system back in operation. The vent fans had exhausted all the steam in about five minutes. Bancroft Hall probably hadn't even noticed the outage.

They had missed their real target. Again. Branner was dialing the number.

"I'll ride with you downtown, if you'd like," he offered, stifling another yawn.

The game continues! And tonight I got a twofer. The security guy brings along a babe this time. Redhead, packing serious heat. From the NCIS no less. How do I know this? Because I have ways of seeing in the tunnels, that's how. Learned long time ago, if you have the time, prepare your ground. Marines do that, whenever possible, and they're the masters of small-unit tactics. So these two come waltzing down into the main complex, and set up some—are you ready for this?—motion detectors! How do I know? Because they talk about them. And I can not only see; I can also hear down there. So I step into a quiet zone just outside and make a quick call to Krill, my most pliable Goth moth. Krill's up for anything, as I told you earlier, because her prospects in life are, shall we say, limited. I mean, how far will boobs get you these days? Krill's not the brightest bulb in the circuit, in other words. How she got into St. John's is beyond me. Suspect some money changed hands in alumni channels somewhere, because those people, as weird and liberal as they are, also have to be fairly smart. Anyway, Krill comes a-running, all decked out in serious Goth cloth. I pitch her into the main complex, send her down Broadway, and wait for the big bad law persons to do their thing. Then as soon as they say the magic word? I cut open a steam-line drain valve directly off the 150-psi heating main, and—presto—the tunnel fills with hot, wet steam. And me? I decided to call it a night and go on back through the Maryland Ave. gate, just like I rated it. Which I did, of course.

This security guy must be taking things seriously. I've tapped into his E-mail terminal, but he doesn't use E-mail for his cop stuff. I've scanned into the Yard cops freq., but that's all seriously routine, total admin crap. You wondering how I do all this? It's easy, really. Well, you know, they teach us how. All those years of electrical and electronic engineering, computer science, mechanical engineering, materials, chemistry, physics, and lots and lots of math? Well, shucks, I actually use it. Most of my classmates are welded to the get-through treadmill. You know, grind through the courses, pass the daily quizzes, pass the weekly tests, scurry for the Gouge, and then sweat through the exams. And then what do they do? They do a core dump and set up for the next required course. They learn nothing.

Not me. I actually learn it. I actually like it. But, of course, I see all the tests and exams beforehand. And if my classmates treated me better, so would they. It isn't hard, you know. The faculty dweebs are basically lazy. And they're bureaucrats. Which means they use test questions from a database (and all God's databases were made for me to break into). AND, they have to get the test approved by the department head. AND, they use E-mail to do the approval process. AND, I can read any E-mail riding the Academy's intranets. Piece of cake. They don't even really encrypt the stuff—of course they have fire walls to protect against outside penetration, but not from someone who can place his own fire-wire port in the faculty server bank. Most importantly, they don't expect us mids to do this shit. They expect us to hunt for Gouge, but not to read their internal mail.

But I'm not just any mid, am I? Not by a damned sight. I came from nothing much, but everywhere they sent me, I learned all about working the system. There's always a system. Now we wait to see what the security wienies do next. So little time, so many opportunities for fun down below. Eventually, they'll figure out they're playing on my ground. And if they bring a crowd, well, hell, I'll go have a beer in the Goth lair. Or maybe in my own lair. I do have one, you know.

Did you know that black cop who met up with the vampire Dyle the other night was NCIS? Just like the redhead who got a steam bath last night. I'd better be careful, right? 'Cause NCIS is also investigating the Dell incident. They get lucky, it might be them getting the twofer. . . . You, too, need to pay attention now. This Dell thing's like an oil spill in water. It can spread out and get all over you.

Ev went into his office at nine o'clock that Sunday morning. He had twenty-three senior term papers left to grade, and nothing in particular holding him at home on a Sunday morning. In fact, Sunday mornings were not a good time for him to be at home. Too many memories, and that intrusive silence in the house.

An hour into the exercise, the words began to run together. Yet another dissertation on the World War I naval battle of Jutland by yet another midshipman who obviously had missed the entire strategic point of the battle. Suddenly tired of things academic, he stepped outside into the sunlight, thought briefly about finding a cigarette, then walked up Stribling Walk toward Bancroft and found a park bench halfway up. Chapel services were in full swing and he could hear the enormous Moeller organ rumbling away in the Academy's cathedral-sized, 2,500-seat "chapel." There were some early-bird tourists walking around the grounds, but, compared to the hustle and bustle of a Saturday morning, the Yard was empty. The few people strolling around the brick walks, passing among the aging bronze cannons and marble monuments, actually looked more like townies than real tourists. Except for the couple coming down the double walk from the chapel precincts. An older-looking man was pushing a woman in a wheelchair. The man was overweight, with a reddish face, steel-colored gray hair cut short, and a weary expression on his face, as if he'd been pushing that wheelchair for a long, long time. The woman in the chair was wrapped up in a voluminous blanket. She was also round, but she had an unhealthy pallor, lank gray hair tied back in a bun, and an oxygen line clipped to her nostrils. The chair had an IV stand attached, on which hung the green oxygen bottle. Ev watched them pull abreast of his bench and then look around at the beautiful vistas of the Yard. The Severn River shone like a big blue mirror between the white academic buildings down the walk. The couple was close enough to Ev's bench that he felt obliged to say good morning.

"Your first visit to the Academy?" he asked.

They both looked at him, but it was the man who answered. "Nope. Been here once before. August. Hotter'n hell. This is much better."

"August?" Ev said. "Parents' weekend?"

"Yup," the man said, turning the wheelchair so that the woman didn't have to crane her neck. "Much good that it did us."

Ev didn't understand that comment, but he let it pass. It must have been a real effort to bring this woman into the crowds of parents' weekend. That was when parents got to see their sons and daughters looking like midshipmen for the first time. The transformations were always something of a small but proud shock. The woman was having trouble breathing, and Ev suddenly realized that she was weeping.

"Is there something wrong?" he asked, leaning forward on the bench. "Can I help you?"

The man wiped a tear out of his eyes. "Don't think you can," he said, patting the woman's shoulder. "See, our boy's dead. Our Brian. That's why we're here. There's gonna be a memorial service. Up there, in that big church. This afternoon. We got here too early."

Ev felt a chill settle over his shoulders. These were Midshipman Dell's parents. He tried to think of something comforting to say, but his voice was stuck in his throat.

"You work here, sir?" the man asked.

"Yes, I do. I'm a professor in the Social Sciences Division. I teach naval history."

"You know our boy, maybe? Brian Dell?"

"No, Mr. Dell. I didn't. I teach mostly first classmen. Seniors. Your son was a plebe. I—I heard about what happened, of course. I'm very sorry for your loss. We all are."

"Doubt that," the woman wheezed, speaking for the first time. "Sumbitch who killed him isn't sorry."

"Killed him?" Ev said, and then felt stupid. Of course they would have learned of the rumors. "I thought he, um, fell."

"He fell all right," Dell's father said. "But there're some folks think he had him some help. That some bastard pushed him, maybe."

"I really can't imagine that," Ev said. He thought he should stand up, but then he'd be towering over both of them.

Dell's mother grunted, and then concentrated on her breathing for a long moment. "Brian was small," she said, exhaling. Her voice was raspy and wet at the same time. "Kids picked on him in school. He shouldn't oughta come here. Everyone's too big. Like you."

"Well, not everyone," Ev said, thinking of the women midshipmen. Then he thought of Julie, who was hardly petite. "And everyone gets picked on for the first year. Even big guys like me. It's part of the program."

"You say so," the woman said, and then began to cough. Her husband did something with the oxygen bottle's valve, and the coughing subsided. She closed her eyes and concentrated on her breathing again.

"You go through here?" Mr. Dell asked.

"I did. Almost thirty years ago. And I have a daughter who's about to graduate."

"How come you're a professor, then? How come you're not in the Navy?"

"I was in the Navy for thirteen years. Flew carrier jets. Got tired of it, being away all the time. Having a wife and daughter I rarely saw."

The man nodded. "I was a lifer," he said. "Twenty-two years. Signalman chief. Brian was my son, by my first wife. Lost her to the cancer." He had tears in his eyes again. He wiped them away with his sleeve.

"I lost my wife to a drunk driver," Ev blurted out without thinking.

Mr. Dell's eyebrows rose, and then he nodded. "Then you know," he said. "You know."

Ev wasn't entirely sure what it was he knew, but he understood the sympathy. A foursome of young civilians came down the walk, passing the Dells on either side, trying not to stare at Mrs. Dell.

"Didn't send him here to die, goddamnit," Mrs. Dell said, loudly enough that one of the girls looked back over her shoulder in surprise. "They took him because he could do that math. And he was a diver. A really good one. Supposed to throw his hat in the air one day. Be a Navy officer. Now he's in a drawer in some morgue somewhere. Goddamn people won't even let us see him."

"Uh, that's probably a good thing, Mrs. Dell," Ev said. "They're doing that for your protection. For what it's worth, they never even found my wife. So I know something of what you're feeling, although losing a child is really tough. But they're not bastards."

She turned her face away from him and stared angrily down the walk. From her tone of voice, he had the feeling that she would have spit on the ground if she could have.

"She's real upset," Mr. Dell said. "We both are. They're being as polite as they can, but nobody can say for sure what happened. We're beginning to wonder."

Ev couldn't bring himself to tell them about his relationship to the incident, or that he knew anything about the investigation. "Well, they're not hiding anything, Chief, if that's what you're worried about. There's an official investigation going on. NCIS. Those things take time. You probably remember—they never say anything while the investigation's still going on."

"We met with the superintendent, that Admiral McDonald. In his office. This morning. We showed up early, so they had to go get him. He said he was very sorry that it happened. I believe he meant it."

"I can assure you he meant it," Ev said. "He feels responsible for every midshipman here. We all do. Faculty and staff." Even as he said it, he could hear the official line creeping into his words. Mrs. Dell, who still wouldn't look at him, was clearly not buying it, although the chief seemed mollified.

"We're gonna walk around some," he said. "It's been nice talking to you, Professor . . . ?"

"Markham. Ev Markham," Ev responded, standing up and offering his hand to the chief. "And I meant it when I said I was sorry for what happened to Midshipman Dell. We all are. Truly, we are."

"Well, we thank you for that," Chief Dell said, and then pushed the chair down toward the Mexican monument. As Ev sat back down on the bench, Mrs. Dell turned around in her chair. "Didn't send Brian here to die," she said in a surprisingly clear voice. "There's something wrong with this place. Bad wrong."

When Ev got to his office, he found Julie waiting for him. She was standing by the windows behind his desk. She was dressed in service dress blues, probably for chapel, he figured. When he had gone through, attendance at chapel on Sundays had been mandatory. Now it was optional. She didn't turn around when he entered the office. He stopped in the doorway.

"Going to church services?" he asked, and then realized that services were already in progress. He kept his tone cool. If she was here to apologize for that crack about Liz, he wasn't going to make it easy.

"I was," she said. "Then I changed my mind."

"What's happened now?"

She turned around and he saw the worry in her eyes. "There was a company-wide room inspection yesterday. The OOD hit four plebe, four youngster, two second class, and two firstie rooms. One of them was ours."

Ev frowned. Saturday room inspections were not unheard of, but it was a bit unusual for the officer of the day to hit first class rooms on a weekend.

"Who was the OOD?" he asked.

"Commander Talbot," she said. "First Batt officer. Hard-ass."

"I guess if I had the OOD duty on Saturday, I'd be a hard-ass, too. So?"

She went over to one of the chairs in his office and sat down. "So, when I got back in last night, I found a form two—a report chit. I was ICOR—in change of room. Talbot fried me for having nonreg gear—namely, men's uniform items—in my locker. An Academy T-shirt, athletic shorts, and a Speedo swimsuit. In *my* closet. Up on the shelf."

Ev didn't understand—what was the big deal? A boyfriend's clothes in her room—okay—a ten-demerit pap. It wasn't as if the OOD had burst in on them making out in her bed. Except Julie looked like that was exactly what had happened.

"And?"

"And the report chit specified the owner of the clothes." She looked up at him. "Dad, the clothes belonged to Dell."

He walked over to his desk and sat down behind it. "Dell? What were they doing in your room? I would think they'd have picked up all of his personal effects by now?"

"I don't have any idea. I know this: They weren't there when I went out Saturday morning. Dad, I think someone's trying to frame me for what happened to Brian."

Ev frowned and tried to think it through. First Julie's underwear on Dell's body. Now some of Dell's clothes appearing in Julie's locker. "Laundry marks again?"

"I guess. The report chit said the clothes were 'hidden' behind a stack of towels."

"Didn't those NCIS people look through your room right after the incident? If these things had been there, they would have found them."

"*If* they had been there then, sure. But they weren't. I put clean towels in that locker day before yesterday. We get laundry back on Fridays. This stuff was not there, and I sure as hell didn't put it there."

"Okay, if that's true, then somebody else put it there."

"What do you mean, 'if that's true'?"

"I was stating a logical case, Julie. If you didn't hide Dell's stuff in your locker, then obviously someone else did. Now, who, and why?"

"Someone's trying to implicate me in what happened to Dell," she said again.

"I say again, who, and why?"

She got up and started pacing around the office. "I have no goddamned idea!"

"You have real enemies?" he asked. Then he remembered what both the swim coach and Julie had said about her ex-boyfriend, Tommy Hays. "You said you broke up with Tommy. Could he be doing this?"

She shook her head vehemently. "Tommy's not like that, not at all. Besides, I think he's still . . . still—"

"You think he still cares for you?"

"Yes. He's angry, but I think he's more hurt than angry. I mean, it's not like I dropped him for another guy. I'm just facing reality. He isn't."

"Any other lovelorn corpses bobbing in your wake?" he asked.

She gave him an exasperated look. It reminded him of looks he used to get when she was a teenager. And sometimes from Joanne. "No-o," she groaned.

The chapel bell began to toll. "Okay then, let's play this out," he said. "There are rumors circulating that Dell's fall was a homicide, not an accident or suicide. Say it's true, that it was a homicide. There's a fair chance that who-ever's planting this stuff is probably the guy who did it. It would just about have to be another midshipman to have this kind of access to your rooms. That or one of the company officers."

Julie sat down again. After a moment, she nodded. "Yes, it would. Anybody else messing around in rooms, someone would notice. Even if it was one of the Executive Department officers."

"Where was your roommate yesterday?"

"She's on an authorized weekend. So the room was empty for most of the day."

"You weren't there?"

"I was . . . away."

Away, he thought. As in, That's my business. "All right," he said. "So let's hit this from another angle: Who might want Dell dead?"

She shook her head. "I don't know. I mean, the whole notion of a midshipman wanting to kill another mid—it's outrageous! We don't have people like that at the Naval Academy!"

"Well, there's a notion that might now be in doubt. I mean, there was that case a few years back, where those two cadets killed another kid. As I remember, one of them was Air Force Academy, the other was Naval Academy?"

"But that was different. That was some warped boyfriend-girlfriend thing."

"Like that never happens here? Two guys getting into it over the same girl? All of them midshipmen?"

"Well, yes, I suppose, but not to the extent where they go get guns or anything."

"If Dell was killed, and of course we still don't know that, it wasn't with a gun, Julie. But he was wearing your underwear when he hit the pavement. So there was something pretty weird going on there that didn't come out of the Academy reg book. Now look: Dell was on the swim team. You were on the swim team. Was there someone on the swim team who might have hated you both?"

Julie sat there, shaking her head from side to side. "I don't know about Dell," she said slowly. "I mean, he was just a manager. But no, I can't think of anyone. We're a team first, individual winners second. No superstars, no goats. That's the whole point."

But there was something in her voice that got his attention. Not evasion exactly, but just a whiff of artful casualness. If he'd been talking to just another midshipman, he would not have detected it. But this was his daughter, Julie, who used to tell some barefaced whoppers in precisely that offhand tone of voice when she was a kid. Back then, he would have braced her up about it. But now, with graduation, commissioning, adulthood visible on the horizon, he just couldn't do it. This was Julie, but she was also Midshipman Markham, almost Ensign Markham, USNR. She was already mad at him for seeing Liz. He realized what he was really afraid of: saying something that would pull down a real iron curtain between them.

"Well, think about it, Julie," he said. "When that report chit gets into the system, those NCIS people are going to be all over it. They're going to sound like a broken record: Why was Dell wearing your underwear? Why does a room inspection come up with some of Dell's clothes in your room? What connects you to Dell? And if not you, who's doing this shit? And why?"

Julie nodded but didn't say anything for a moment. Then she said, "You're mad at me, aren't you?"

He hesitated, terribly aware of all the possible permutations. But then he thought, Hell with it: She wants to be a grown-up. "Yeah, but you started it," he replied.

"What I said about Liz DeWinter?"

"Yes. As if I'm somehow being unfaithful to your mother. Your mother is dead, Julie. Living alone in that house is beginning to wear me down. All of my friends, the close ones anyway, are forever telling me to get back into the world. The first time I do, my own daughter goes off on me?"

She opened her mouth to reply but then shut it. He thought about softening what he'd just said, then decided to hold fast. Finally, she nodded, got up, said, "Okay,

Dad," and walked out of his office, closing the door gently behind her.

He threw a pen across the room. Well done, Professor, he thought. Now who's she going to talk to? Then he had an idea. Turn this to advantage. He'd call Liz, tell her what had happened, get Liz to call Julie. He had a feeling that Julie might need Liz more rather than less come Monday, when that report chit lighted some fuses. He put in a call to Liz's office, then remembered it was Sunday. He called her home number, and she picked up.

"Good morning, Professor," she said brightly.

"Good morning to you, counselor," he answered. "You're sounding chipper this morning."

"Well, so I am. What's up?"

He told her Julie's news about the room inspection.

"This has to be a setup," she said immediately.

"Yeah, that's what I think. Even if Julie had been involved with that plebe, she sure as hell would not have left some of his stuff out in plain sight, and certainly not after coming under the gun this past week. Somebody's fucking around."

"To say the least," she said. "Where are you?"

"Office."

"Ah. Sunday morning."

"You've been down this road."

"I have indeed. Look—I have a boat. Sunday afternoons, I usually go out for a couple of hours. Care to join me? We can talk about this."

"Love to," he said immediately. Anything to get out of the Yard just now. Plus, he wanted to see her. No matter what his daughter thought about it.

"Okay. It's a stinkpot, so you won't have to crew or anything. I'll stop by the Greek place, get some lunch stuff. You bring the beer. I like anything dark. Slip forty-seven, AYC. Bring a bathing suit—it gets hot out there."

"Roger that. See you in forty minutes or so."

He hung up the phone and sat back in his chair. Annapolis Yacht Club. Sometimes he forgot she was a successful lawyer with her own firm. Julie, he reminded himself. This is all about Julie. But he had to admit that talk of bathing suits had perked him right up.

Jim was giving the *Chantal* a freshwater wash-down when he spotted Branner coming down the pier. He had brought Jupiter up on his shoulder for some sunlight R and R. It was fairly safe; the parrot had tried a short flight just once, when he'd first moved aboard. Even with his primaries clipped, he had managed to flap over the side and then down into the harbor. Jim had had to fish him out with a swab. Ever since then, Jupiter had hung on with his version of a Vulcan death grip whenever Jim brought him up on deck.

Branner let herself through the visitors' gate and came down his dock. She was wearing wraparound shades, jeans, flat white tennis shoes, and a sleeveless white blouse. He paused to watch her progress, and she gave him a crooked smile when she saw him watching. The guy on the Hatteras across the pier walked into a deck chair while doing his own surveillance. Special Agent B for Branner, on the strut, Jim thought.

"What's that you're wearing?" she asked as she came up the gangway. "Is that a bird bib?"

"Exactly; Jupiter's medium housebroken when I carry him around down below, but up here, he acts like any damn seagull. What's the word on Bagger?"

She plopped herself down on the edge of the hatch leading down into the main salon and shrugged. "He's holding his own, but barely. In and out of consciousness. His ex-wife is with him."

"Is that good or bad?"

"Not sure. The theory is that seeing her will scare him into full consciousness. Otherwise, the docs are babbling the usual oatmeal."

"Want some coffee?" he asked, indicating the percolator perched on the binnacle.

"Yes, please," she said. "Black and sweet."

He went below, grabbed a relatively clean mug and the box of Domino Dots, came back up topside, and got her coffee. To his amazement, she popped one of the cubes between her front teeth and started sipping the coffee through the cube.

"I can get you a glass," he said. "Which one of your parents was Russian?"

"M'mother," she mumbled around the cube. Jupiter wanted a cube, so Jim gave him one. He promptly began reducing it to powdery bits.

"Okay," he said. "I have to ask: What's your first name? Bagger wouldn't tell me."

"Special Agent?" she said, popping the sugar cube out into the mug. "And Bagger wouldn't tell you because he doesn't know."

A huge motor yacht sounded its horn imperiously as it got under way from the Annapolis Yacht Club across the way. A dozen swirling seagulls screamed back at it. Jupiter joined in, momentarily deafening Jim. He reached up and flicked Jupiter's beak with the tip of his finger. Jupiter dropped a bomb down the back of the bib and made to bite Jim's ear.

"Nice birdie," she said. "What's deep-fried parrot taste like?"

Jupiter, hearing something hostile in her tone of voice, went into range-finder mode, swinging his head back and forth and glaring at her.

"If that *thing* flies over at me, I'll smack it clean across the harbor," she said pleasantly. "Nothing personal, you understand."

Jim laughed, swiped Jupiter off his shoulder with his right hand, and began scratching the back of his neck. The parrot, mollified, closed his eyes, although he peeked occasionally at Branner as if to say, I'm watching you.

"Your Goth slag still in the pokey?" he asked.

"They let her out this morning. Some ponytailed faculty adviser of uncertain gender assumed responsibility for her. Made lots of noise about jackboots and storm troopers. The town cops were way impressed. They'll bring her back in for a hearing when and if I make formal charges. *Her* first name, by the way, is Hermione. Hermione Natter."

Jim leaned back against the life rails, enjoying a sudden bloom of sunlight. " 'Hermione'? I think I'd become a Goth, too. What were her parents thinking?"

Branner shook her head. "Mom must have been getting even for a tough labor. Anyway, she wouldn't give up the other runner, so we're nowhere with that little problem."

"You have enough for charges?"

"Nah. The laundry list of heinous crimes and misdemeanors either works right away or it doesn't. Then lawyers set in. It was worth a try."

"You going to let the downtown cops work on her for the muggings?"

"I've talked to the case detective, but there's no probable cause to connect this girl with those incidents. You know, all Goths look alike: uniformly grotesque. So tomorrow, I'm going to get back on the Dell case. I need to find some leverage on Markham. Get her to talk to me."

The wake from the big motor cruiser rocked the *Chantal* gently. "I still can't feature midshipmen offing other midshipmen," Jim said. "I mean, those bruises could have come from a hand-to-gland class the day before he died. Or a boxing class, or a wrestling class. They put the plebes through the whole gamut in their first year."

"I know; I'm one of the coaches for the Academy judo sports club."

"I didn't know that. You coach just the girls?"

She grunted. "I coach them all, the long, the short, and the tall. When I get a guy whose attitude exceeds his ability, I hum that airline commercial song, 'Come Fly with Me.' . . . You ought to try it sometime."

"Sorry, there, Special Agent. When I clinch with the ladies, it's for purposes other than throwing them across the room."

"Or getting thrown, maybe?"

"Guess I'm a lover, not a fighter," he said.

"Sometimes love's a fight," she shot back. "Think about it. Back to Dell: Who would have his class schedule?"

"Any prof in the academic department could call it up on the faculty intranet," Jim said. "And I suppose the officers in the Exec Department could, too. You get into Dell's computer?"

"Not yet; we have the box, but that was Bagger's specialty. Dude was a total whiz with those damn things. Now we'll have to import a lab rat from Washington. It'll be low priority as long as it's a suicide case."

"And that's where you are with Dell? Suicide?" Jim asked as he went to get himself some more coffee. He refilled her mug.

"That or DBM. Homicide's looking shaky just now. The data well dried up."

"I think I'd talk to Dell's roommate," he said. "Plebe year roommates have no secrets. They're under attack from the upperclassmen as a room, if you will. You know, room inspections, uniform races, one guy's gear adrift bilges the entire room. Like that."

"We questioned him briefly, of course," she said. "But he says he was asleep when the thing went down. He only realized who was dead when Dell didn't show up at morning formation, and then we called him in."

"Yeah, but this time, pull the string on Dell's life as a plebe. Who his friends were. What he did on weekends. Whether he had a girlfriend. If he got mail, and from whom. And aren't there suicide profiles? Questions you ask to establish a predisposition?"

Branner gave him a look. "You want a job?" she asked.

"Got a job."

"Oh, right." She sniffed, looking across the harbor.

He sat down on the deck, his back against the rails. Jupiter squawked at almost getting squished. "Okay, what's that supposed to mean?"

"I don't know. It's just that—well, security officer at a military academy? I would expect some fifty-year-old retired officer to be doing that, not a young Studly-Dudley like yourself. I mean, most guys your age I know are hot and heavy into their careers. This job seems like a side pass. What'd you do before this—weren't you a Marine officer?"

"Yeah. CO of the MarDet here at the academy. Packed it in when my obligated service was over."

She gave him a puzzled look. "How come? Seems to me that CO of the Academy marine detachment would be a pretty high-vis posting. Good for the old career."

"My career was over before it began. Little operational problem in Bosnia." He gave her the same version he'd given the dant.

"And you had to take the rap for that? I thought the Marines were straight shooters."

"Most of the time. Unless it involves embarrassing the Corps. Then they have other rules. It wasn't personal, just the system. I didn't go away mad, just went away."

"I'd say you got screwed."

He wanted to tell her there was more to it, but let it go. "Yup," he said. "Shit happens, going west. But then life goes on. And, hey?" He paused, gesturing at the beautiful harbor, the fine morning, even the good coffee. "Life ain't so bad, is it?"

Across the harbor, two guys in full yachting costume were trying to be seriously traditional by sailing their fancy yawl out of the city harbor without using the engine. With both of them wrestling the sails, no one was watching the navigation, and Jim saw that they were headed straight for a mudflat. The sunlight reflecting off the water was almost bright enough to hurt his eyes.

"So you're parked? Is that good enough for you?"

"I think I'm not career material," he said.

"A career isn't necessarily a life sentence, not if you're doing something you enjoy."

"You enjoy being a government cop?"

The two guys on the yawl achieved a sudden, spectacular mast-bending stop on the mudflat. One pitched over the side and popped up, squawking for help until his buddy told him just to stand up. Older salts along the city dock were grinning at the spectacle.

Branner shrugged. "Yeah, most of the time. I've got my own shop, small as it is, at an early age. The NCIS has plenty of opportunities for women."

"Well, there you are. Sounds like you're all set up."

She laughed, putting up her hands in mock surrender. "Okay, okay, I withdraw the comment. Obviously, you're not hurting for money, so maybe this all makes sense."

Stung, Jim wanted to defend himself, but then he forced himself to relax. He suspected that Branner went through life provoking other people. It must be the red hair, he thought.

"You ever take this thing out on the open water?" she asked.

"Almost never," he replied. "It's a place to live. Like having a condo where I also happen to own the building. And besides, sailing something this size takes crew. I'm not into group efforts anymore."

"But you do know how to sail it?"

"Oh yeah," he said, wondering if another challenge was coming. "I grew up in my father's boatyard down in Pensacola. I could not only sail her; I could build her. But she's just a glorified houseboat now. Dock ornament."

"Sounds like you and the boat are perfectly suited," she said, looking across the harbor.

He was getting a little tired of her critical attitude. "So," he said. "You come out here for a specific reason this morning, or did you just get up and feel like breaking balls?"

"Bit of both, I suppose," she said with a small yawn. She had put her mug down and now put her hands behind her head, leaned back on the boom, closed her eyes, and arched her back so she could turn her face to the sun. He had to admit the effect was spectacular. "I guess I'm partial to strong, purposeful men," she continued. "I don't really mean to break balls; it's just, I don't know, some guys are more fragile than others." She opened her eyes and looked over at him. "But actually, what I need right now is some full-time help with this Dell case. I need someone who's been inside Bancroft Hall, who's been a midshipman, but who's not a part of the Bancroft Hall Executive Department."

Jim tried not to laugh out loud. He could suddenly visualize a tiny commandant devil sitting on his other shoulder, whispering urgently into his ear, Say yes, yes! Immediately!

"Help doing what?" he asked as casually as he could.

"What you just did, there, earlier. Suggesting a line of questions for the roommate."

"So you want, like, a consultant."

"Basically. For the most part, our office works what I'd call 'admin crime.' Fraud, theft, drugs, contractors cheating the Supply Department, mids cheating on exams. But this case is different, and I think you're right—solving it is going to turn on penetrating that blue-and-gold wall, as you called it. I can't ask the officers in the Executive Department because their boss initiated the investigation."

"Go on."

"Thing is, we both know what the administration wants in a case like this."

He thought for a moment. "To solve it, of course," he said. "To right all wrongs, root out evil, so that justice and the American way prevail."

She laughed out loud, the sound echoing over the water between the docks. "Yeah, right," she said. "Think about it? I'll even stop trying to break your balls."

"That would be nice," he said. "You feel obligated to put men down?"

"Only men who go through life at half power," she said, not giving him an inch. "But give me a hand with this Dell thing, who knows? You might like a real investigation."

"Will I get paid extra?" he asked with a straight face.

She laughed again. "How's an NCIS ball cap sound? Or, hell, maybe we'll figure something else out." She gave him a mock leer, but then her face grew serious. "I'm going up to Bethesda today. Hopefully, talk to Bagger. Call me tomorrow morning? I do need some help with this. For the Academy's sake, and maybe for Dell's."

"Sure, what the hell," he said, trying to hide his elation. "The chief runs the day-to-day bits of my nothing job anyway. The only thing I have going is the vampire runner gig. And protecting my gonads from transient redheads."

"Oh, lighten up, Hall," she snorted. She got up, shot an imaginary finger gun at Jupiter, said, "Bye-bye, birdie," and set off. "And thanks for the coffee," she called to Jim as she went down the brow.

He watched her go up the dock, slim legs pumping. Jupiter muttered something unkind. No halfway measures with that one, he thought. Casually busting my hump, and I still don't know her first name. He almost called her back to tell her the rest of it. But she steamed right out of sight. Life was still unfair.

A pleasant young man dressed in the Annapolis Yacht Club work uniform asked if he could be of any assistance as Ev walked down toward the restricted dock area. He gave the young man Liz's slip number and was then politely escorted to the proper dock, where the man waited to see if Ev was indeed a legitimate and expected guest. Occupying slip 47 was Liz's so-called stinkpot, a gleaming white Eastbay 43 power cruiser with the name *Not Guilty* spelled out in bronze letters on her transom. Liz, dressed in white short shorts, a red halter top, wraparound sunglasses, and long-billed white ball cap, waved him on board as the young man dutifully disappeared back toward the parking lot.

"I have a boat," he announced as he handed over two six-packs of beer. "It's about eight feet long and powered by Norwegian steam. This, on the other hand, is a *boat.*"

"Yeah, it is," she said, indicating he should come below. The main salon was fully enclosed, decorated with rubbed teak, stainless steel, and lush carpeting. There was a U-shaped galley, a center island–style master stateroom, a guest stateroom with upper and lower berths, a head with shower, and storage compartments everywhere. Liz stashed the beer in the reefer and gave him the full tour. Ev realized this must be a half-million-dollar yacht at least.

"She can range four hundred miles, has a top speed of twenty-four knots on a good day and with a following sea. Twin Cat diesels. Forty-three-foot overall and a great seakeeper. I mostly cruise the bay, but she can go offshore with the best of them."

"It's magnificent. Do you just buy something like this, or do you take out a mortgage?"

She smiled at his question. "As the broker would say, if you have to ask . . ."

He put up his hands in a gesture of mock surrender. "Okay, okay. And I would have to ask." Although, he thought, you wouldn't, would you? On the other hand, he knew he would never spend a huge amount on a boat, remembering the old adage about the three things in life a man should always try to rent, not own.

"Come topside while I get her lit off," she said, and went up the polished companionway to the bridge area. Ev followed, enjoying the sight of her slender legs and full figure climbing ahead of him. Follow you anywhere, he told himself. The day had bloomed into one of glorious sunshine and a twenty-knot sea breeze that was already rippling the Annapolis harbor with tiny whitecaps. Julie and her problems were suddenly forgotten.

"Stinkpot—that means powerboat?" he asked.

"In sailboat language. As opposed to the much more politically correct and environmentally considerate *sailing vessels*. Annapolis is the premier sailing harbor on the East Coast. Just ask any sailor. We heedless Philistines who dare to sully the sea breeze with diesel fumes, engine noises, and big wakes are held in some long-nosed contempt by our bay-hugging betters."

"Hoo-boy," he said.

"On the other hand, our popularity rises somewhat when there's a dead calm out on the bay and our purist friends have zero chance of getting back in before sundown on a Sunday afternoon, unless of course one of us Philistines offers them a tow."

"You do that often?"

"Often enough to get enormous satisfaction when it happens. Have a seat while I do the checklist."

He watched as she sat up on the captain's chair, her legs not quite long enough to reach the deck, and flipped switches. A few minutes later, she brought the two big Cats to life. Ev was directed to bring in the mooring lines, and then she backed the big boat expertly out of the slip, brought her about, and headed for the channel at the prescribed idle speed. She motioned for him to bring up the fenders, then beckoned him back up to the bridge.

"You don't take your scull out of the river, do you?"

"Did it once," he said, rubbing on some sunblock. "On one of those dead-calm days you talked about. Then came fog."

"Yow," she said. "I'll take some of that."

He obliged by standing behind her while she sat at the wheel and rubbing the sunblock cream on her shoulders, upper arms, and back. "And you under way with oars? What'd you do?"

"One of these enormous 'stinkpots' came by, idling in on radar," he said. She had wide shoulders and surprisingly taut muscles for such a petite woman. Then he remembered that she swam regularly for exercise. He stopped when he got to her waist. "He was going really slow, so I fell in behind him, following his wake. Ended up in a marina, hoisted out, and took a cab home to get my car and trailer. Felt like a proper idiot."

"I'll bet they never knew you were back there."

They were passing the Naval Academy on the port hand as they headed for the entrance of Spa Creek, another river estuary. Bancroft Hall rose in gleaming splendor beyond the landfill hump of Farragut Field. They could see tourists swarming around the visitors' center, and there were several knockabout-class sailboats trying not to collide with one another around the Santee Basin on the Severn side. When they pulled abreast of the Triton Light monument, which memorialized all the lost American submarines now on eternal patrol, she brought the speed up and pointed fair for the bay itself.

Ev wedged himself into a corner of the pilothouse and watched as she concentrated on maneuvering the big cruiser through all the smaller powerboats, dinghies, fishermen, yachts, channel buoys, and even two YPs out into the more open waters of the bay. He could see a large tanker plowing its way up toward Baltimore about five miles out, seemingly motionless until he lined it up visually with a distant buoy and saw the buoy appear to move.

"Get yourself a beer and bring me up a Coke, if you would, kind sir," she said, checking the radarscope. "We'll go down past South River and then anchor for a swim and some lunch, if that's okay."

"This is glorious," he said, looking around at the sparkling water and grateful that his sunglasses were polarized; the glare was very strong. "Whatever you want to do suits me."

She flashed a mischievous smile over her shoulder and then went back to her driving. He went below and got the drinks. The interior air conditioning was on, and the salon was already wonderfully cool.

An hour later, she turned in toward the bluffs below the South River estuary and began paying attention to the depth finder. She asked him to go forward and release the anchor stopper chain. When the depth finder read twenty-five feet, she slowed, stopped, backed the engines gently, using them to point the yacht's bow into the breeze, and then released the anchor. She backed slowly, veering chain until she had it set, veered more chain, and then shut down the engines.

"This is good holding ground," she said. "But we'll just watch for a few minutes to make sure."

Now that the boat was no longer under way, it was suddenly hot and muggy up in the pilothouse, even with the sea breeze. "How will you tell?" he asked.

"And you were in the Navy how long?" she asked, staring down into the cone of the radar display.

"I was a naval aviator. Navigation, piloting, that's blackshoe stuff. Shipboard duty, that is. Our idea of a boat was ninety thousand tons, a thousand feet long, with a crew of six thousand people who did the nautical stuff."

"I see," she said archly. "So your ignorance of seamanship, navigation, boat handling, rules of the road—"

"Is damned near infinite," he said before she could continue. "Hell, all we did was fly our trusty, if aging, warbirds onto the flight deck at a hundred and eighty knots and hope the frigging arresting wire didn't break. The ocean was just something that kept the carrier afloat and provided a soft spot to land in if we had to eject."

Liz laughed at that and shook her head. She checked the radar again to make sure the range rings weren't moving downwind. Satisfied the anchor was holding, she suggested a swim. He got his suit and went below to change while she deployed a sea ladder and a buoyed line off the stern. By the time he came back topside, she was in the water. He looked around to see if there were any other boats in view, but they had the shoreline to themselves. As he headed for the transom, he spied that red halter top on the aftermost cushions. He went over the side and swam toward her, coming up alongside her fifty feet from the transom of the yacht. She was treading water, with only her neck and face bobbing above the slight chop.

"What's this for?" he asked, grabbing the buoy line with one hand. He tried not to look at anything other than her face.

"For just exactly what you're doing. Also, if you get tired, or catch a cramp, you can pull yourself back to the boat with a minimum of effort. You'd be surprised at how often the Coast Guard finds perfectly intact boats out here with no crew aboard."

The waves were just big enough to require some effort to keep his face out of the water, and he found himself having to work his legs to stay in one place. She was doing the same thing, and their legs touched from time to time. The water was cool, almost cold, and a nice relief from the humid air. The upper part of her body was a blue-green blur. He felt a flush rising in his face that wasn't entirely due to the sun.

"I was a swimmer back in my Academy days," he said, determined to keep things totally normal. "But I never once went into the bay."

"Why not?" she asked. There were little beads of water glistening on her forehead, and he wanted to wipe them off her perfect complexion. He realized what he really wanted to do was touch her. She'd left the sunglasses back on the boat, and her eyes were laughing at him.

"Didn't like the thought of all those creatures swimming around down there and looking up at *their* lunch. Plus, we used to go hunting for sharks' teeth along these bluffs. Some of those teeth were serious."

"And all a hundred million years old, too," she pointed out. "Biggest problem out here are the damned jellyfish, but it's too early." She ducked beneath the water for a moment, then came back up, flipping her hair back. Her bare breasts nearly popped out of the water, and this time he found himself staring. She was wiping the water out of her eyes. "Ready to go back?" she asked.

"Yep," he said, a slight catch in his throat. They pushed off together, their legs and hips touching again, just for an instant. He was the more powerful swimmer, arriving at the ladder first, but he moved aside to let her go up. She rose out of the water like a sleek mermaid. Those white shorts were now thoroughly transparent. She was sufficiently well made to carry it off, and he almost forgot to climb the ladder himself once she was on deck. Realizing he was getting an erection, he hesitated at the bottom of the ladder long enough for things to calm down. It had been two years since he'd really even looked at a woman, and he was surprised at the strength of his reaction.

"You coming aboard?" she called from the top of the ladder. He forced himself not to look up.

"Uh, yes, right," he answered, and pulled himself up the ladder, trying to turn sideways as his own wet trunks clung to his thighs and exposed his arousal. When he got on deck, she was rubbing her face and hair with a towel, and her breasts swung gently in time with her efforts. He reached quickly for a towel and unconsciously, and absurdly, began drying off his middle.

"Dry my back, please?" she said, turning around. He used his own towel to dry off her back and shoulders. She stood there, slightly bent at the waist, and it was everything he could do not to reach around to her front. Then before he knew it, she had turned around and was pressing her towel up against his chest and around to his upper back, their faces inches apart. He held his breath as he felt her fingers rubbing across the back of his neck and her warm breath close to his face. In their bare feet, the difference in their height was very obvious, and suddenly, as a wave rocked the boat, she was standing very close, the tips of her breasts touching his stomach and her hands coming around to run the towel slowly across his chest and then his stomach. He closed his eyes, swallowed once, and took a deep breath.

"You can look at me now," she said in a husky voice, and he did, fully aware of the heat rising from her body, her arm wrapped around his neck, pulling him down, and the press of her lips on his. And then he wrapped his arms around her and pulled her in tight, his longing driving the breath right out of her. He pulled her down onto the cushioned bench seat, where they kissed as their bodies melted together. He almost came when she thrust her belly up against his and held herself there, the wanting palpable. Then she stopped, her eyes huge, and stood up. She unbuttoned her shorts and beckoned for him to come to her. He leaned forward in front of her, holding her hips while he consumed her from top to bottom, until she pulled his bathing suit off, rolled on top of him, and rode him like a bronc rider for what he later felt was far too short a time. Then after a few minutes and without a spoken word, they went below into the air conditioning of the master stateroom and tried it all out again, slower this time, concentrating on making sure nobody got left out.

Afterward, he lay on his back beside her, deliciously spent, staring at the polished ceiling in quiet contentment. He realized that she had ambushed him, and he had been so ready that it had taken all his effort not go off in the first minute like some randy teenager. She lay quietly next to him, her face on his chest. He rolled over, to find her watching him.

"I had no idea," he said.

"I know," she replied. "But I did."

"And thank God for that," he said, surprised at how grateful he felt.

She chuckled and rolled over onto her stomach as he sat up on one elbow and began to stroke her back. She was a study in feminine roundness, with smooth skin and yet muscles from top to bottom. He leaned over and kissed the hollow below her collarbone. Her skin tasted of salt.

The boat was rolling steadily now as the sea breeze picked up and the wave action increased. They decided to get up, check the anchor, and have lunch. An hour later, they got under way and headed back toward Annapolis. The wind had backed to the north, and the big Cats were driving the boat into the chop with a thumping authority. She kept it at a speed that covered ground but didn't make the ride too rough. She offered to let him drive, but he demurred, preferring to watch her work, even though the red halter top was back in place. The wind was whistling hard enough to make further conversation difficult, and he saw that there were several other boats apparently intent on getting back in before things got hairy out on the bay, which was notorious for changing the odds in a hurry.

As they drew abreast of the South River, they came under a partial lee from Sandy Point to the north, and the waves diminished a bit. The visibility was unlimited, and the sky was a ferocious blue, darkening somewhat as the day sloped into late afternoon. Ev felt more alive than he had in years. More years, he realized, than Joanne had been gone. He felt a wave of guilt at that disloyal thought, but there was no getting around it. This woman excited him, surprised him, challenged him in a way that Joanne never had. He wondered if that was simply the toll of many years of marriage talking, or if he and Liz were better suited than he and Joanne had been. That's unfair, a voice whispered. He wondered what Julie would have thought of his Sunday afternoon.

Julie.

That problem hadn't gone away. They hadn't even discussed it, either. He wanted to seek reassurance from Liz that it would go away, but he was unwilling to break the spell. Liz signaled to him to look at something with the binoculars while she slowed the big boat and brought her up directly into the wind.

"Over there—starboard bow. Is that a boat capsized? I thought I saw a sail in the water." She had to raise her voice to make herself heard over the whipping wind. The yacht was starting to wallow a bit as the power decreased and her bow began to bump into the seaway. He had to wedge himself to hold the binocs steady.

He searched but saw nothing. After looking at Liz again to see where she was pointing, he refocused and saw a blur of white in the water. Then he noticed a flash of metal as what looked like a mast surfaced briefly and then went back under.

"Yes. There's a boat over. Sailboat. Can't see people." Then he could, or rather, he glimpsed a single white arm waving once before disappearing into the whitecaps. "Whoa, there are people out there. I just saw an arm."

"Okay," she shouted. "I'm going to head over there. You get that life ring, snap it to that coil of line right there, and get up on the bow. Get into a life jacket first—they're in that locker by the companionway. When you get up on the bow, sit down, wedge your legs, and hold on to the lifeline until I get her alongside."

He saw several other boats passing behind them, all oblivious to the capsized boat ahead. As Liz drew closer, she got on the radio and called the Coast Guard station to report a capsized boat and their radar position.

He got into a life jacket, grabbed the ring and the coil of white nylon line, and went forward. He was immediately soaked by a wave that slapped salt spray all over the bow. The boat was pitching more dramatically now as she crept forward. After what seemed like a long time, they got close enough to see the boat, or its bottom anyway. Something, probably internal floatation gear, was keeping it from sinking. He could not see the people, even when they were only fifty feet away. His perch was pitching rhythmically now, dousing him with spray and even the occasional greenie. He was glad for the life jacket, although it seemed positively flimsy compared to the Navy's kapok jackets. He saw an arm again, and then a head. A woman's head, from the looks of it. He turned to see if Liz had seen the woman, and she nodded vigorously, adding power to the engines to get closer while still keeping the bow into the wind and sea.

Ev got on his knees, wedging himself between the pilothouse and a lifeline stanchion. There was a constant thrash of water coming over the deck, and the wind was going to make it very hard to throw a lifeline anywhere. Liz brought the big yacht within ten feet of the capsized boat, then surprised Ev by sounding the horn in one long blast. Then he saw why: The woman in the water hadn't actually seen the *Not Guilty*. Now she looked up and shouted something, but her words were whipped away in the wind. She appeared to be holding on to the overturned hull with one hand while supporting something else with the other. Another person?

Was that a child? She was as white-faced as the waves and visibly exhausted.

Liz eased the yacht to a position ten feet beyond and upwind of the overturned boat, then held her there with powerful thrusts of the engines as the wind buffeted the *Not Guilty*. Ev rose up on his knees, skinning them on the nonskid surface of the deck, and heaved the life ring upwind of the capsized boat. The ring hurtled past it and then fell into the water, dragging the line right over the woman's head.

Shit, he thought, she never even saw it. She must be about done. As he reeled the line in, he turned to the pilothouse and signaled that he was going to go into the water to get her. Liz shook her head violently, motioned for him to wait, then disappeared. She popped back into view a moment later, just in time to gun the port engine to reposition the yacht. Then she opened a window and slid two life jackets down to him.

He grabbed the jackets before the next wave could snatch them off the bow. He understood now that he had to get the life jackets on the two people, then try to bring them back to the yacht. He'd been about to make a big mistake, just swimming over there. He snapped the two extra jackets onto his left arm, slid the life ring around his right shoulder, made sure his line was clear and secured to a cleat on the bow, and then slipped over the side. The bow immediately rose up on a big wave and very nearly knocked him senseless when it came back down, barely pushing him away in a rush of water. He could no longer see the capsized boat, but he remembered where it had been relative to the yacht. He struck out in that direction, doing the sidestroke so he could keep an eye on the yacht to maintain direction. The water seemed colder out here, but he hardly noticed as his adrenaline kicked in.

When he thought he was where the overturned boat should be, he looked back at Liz, who was pointing to his right while she wrestled the yacht. He spun around in the water and nearly impaled himself on the tip of the semisubmerged mast. He grunted with the pain, and then a wave took him under. He would have been in trouble if not for the fact that he was in great shape, had once been a competitive swimmer, and had the life jackets. Being underwater was no big deal; he only wished he had goggles.

He grabbed for that mast tip to keep himself off of it, but that proved to be a mistake, as it was being whipsawed by the punishing waves. He pushed away from it, surfaced again, bobbing high with the life ring and the extra jackets, and swam around the overturned hull until he spotted the woman. She was hanging on to a small length of line. She was not wearing a life jacket; her eyes were shut, but her fingers were grasping that line in a white-knuckled death grip. With her other arm, she held on to a small child, who was almost invisible, bundled in an adult life jacket. The child was looking right at him, as if he were some kind of sea monster.

He tried yelling at her, but she couldn't hear him in the sea noise. He swam right up to her and grabbed the same line she was holding. She opened her eyes, and he yelled at her to hold on, to stay still, while he worked to fit a life jacket onto her. He was barely conscious that the *Not Guilty* was close by, but it took all his concentration to fasten a jacket onto her upper body and then pass her the life ring. She put her arm through it but then gripped the boat line again. Her eyes were partially unfocused, and Ev realized he was going to have to do everything for her. The child was obviously terrified, but in no danger of sinking. The line back to the boat was alternating between being slack and then taut as the yacht's bow bounced around in the waves, but Liz was maintaining perfect position.

"You hang on," he yelled. "I'll take the child back to the boat, then come back for you."

The woman just stared at him, and then there was a glimmer of understanding. A big wave washed over all three of them, and he said it again twice more, until he was sure she understood. He tied the bitter end of the small boat line to the life ring and made her put her head and one shoulder through it. That'll make it easier for her to hold on, he thought. As long as their boat doesn't sink. He let go of the remaining life jacket, reached his arm through one of the straps on the child's jacket, and then pulled them both through the water back toward the *Not Guilty*. Liz, of course, couldn't help, because she had to keep the yacht in position, as that light nylon line would never hold the two boats together. When he got alongside the boat, he realized there was no way to get up the high sides of the bow. He let go of the line and drifted back with the waves down the starboard side, the child held close alongside, until he banged up against the bottom of the folded-up sea ladder. He grabbed the ladder, extended it, and hoisted himself and the child up on deck. He took the child down below to the main salon and put her—a little girl, he realized—down on the deck and forcefully told her to stay there. Her lower lip popped out and she began to cry, but she obeyed.

Ev raced back on deck and got himself back up to the bow. The light line was still attached to the overturned boat, although he could no longer see the woman. Liz nodded and pointed, and he dived over the side this time and swam directly to the downwind side of the capsized boat. The woman was still there, her head thrown back in the life ring, both arms holding on to it, with only the small boat line holding her to the gunwale of the wrecked boat. Ev came alongside of her, touched her back, and got her to open one eye. Then they rode through a set of three big waves, which submerged them each time, and Ev felt something happen underwater. The boat was finally going down, and he didn't have a knife. The woman was oblivious, but Ev felt the suction beginning under his legs and realized she was tied to the sinking boat. There was no way he was going to be able to get that line untied, or the ring untied in time. Without warning her, he went underwater and simply pulled her out of the life ring and away from the dark shape that was settling into the depths below. Holding on to her life jacket, he pulled her away and up to the surface in a gasping thrust.

The *Not Guilty* was no longer close, and the light nylon

line from her bow cleat to the submerging life ring was now taut as a wire; then it parted with a vicious crack, its end lashing the *Not Guilty*'s pilothouse window hard enough to crack it from top to bottom. The woman was limp in his arms, which was probably a good thing, he realized. He did the sidestroke again, aiming for the starboard quarter of the *Not Guilty* and that ladder, very grateful for the life jackets, which took a lot of the work out of it. Liz saw what he was doing and kicked the stern around to provide a momentary lee. A few seconds later, he was at the ladder and so was Liz, helping to pull the nearly unconscious woman up on deck, where they deposited her like a wet sack of potatoes.

"Is she breathing?" Liz asked.

As if in reply, the woman turned sideways, vomited a huge amount of water all over the deck, and then went into a paroxysm of coughing and heaving while they both held her. She was a small woman, fully dressed in slacks, a blouse, and flat tennis shoes. She was very pretty, Ev realized, even though she was barely on the plus side of a drowning equation. The *Not Guilty*, with no one at the helm, began to wallow as her head fell off into the seaway.

"I put the little girl down below," he told Liz, who immediately went down into the main salon. She appeared back on deck a moment later with the little girl still swaddled in that huge life jacket. The girl tottered over to her mother, shouting, "Mommy, Mommy," and Ev helped the woman to sit up and embrace her daughter. The boat began to roll heavily as she came fully sideways to the running seaway, and Liz hurried back up to the pilothouse to straighten her out and ease the ride. The woman was getting some color back in her face and had begun to breathe more normally as she realized she was finally safe.

"My husband," she began, but then stopped, staring at her daughter's wet head, and bit her lip as if she'd said something wrong.

"Let's get you below where you can dry off," he said. "We'll stay in the area and look for him." But even as he said it, he knew whose life jacket the child had been wearing. The woman gave him a long, bleak look that told him she knew, too, but she didn't say anything. He took them below and into the master cabin. He made them both lie down, wet clothes and all, right on the rumpled bedclothes where he and Liz had made love only a few hours ago.

"Just rest for a few minutes," he said. "We need to contact the Coast Guard, let them know we have you, and set up a search. What was the name of your boat?"

"Windsong," she said, her voice low. She said it again, louder. "Just the three of us on board."

She had anticipated his next question. He pulled a blanket over them both, told them to sit tight, and went back topside to the pilothouse. Liz had the boat pointed in toward Annapolis harbor.

"There was a man on board," he announced. "I think the kid had his life jacket. We need to tell the Coast Guard."

"I marked the position," she said, pointing to an *X* in grease pencil on the chart. "But I didn't see him."

"I told her we'd do a search," he said, feeling suddenly a little weak as his adrenaline began to crash. Liz glanced at his face.

"Okay, now you sit down. We'll hang around the area until they show up. Although it's pretty hopeless."

"Are we okay in this shit?" he asked, looking at the solid green waves coming at them like white-capped infantry, angry at losing their prey.

"Hell yes," she said. "This is nothing. This is a trawler hull, basically. Tarted up inside, but she's a pretty tough seakeeper. You did quite a job out there today. You okay?"

"A little winded, but, yeah, I'm fine. It was the sex that wore my ass out, I think."

She grinned and gave him a thumbs-up, then brought the yacht around to head back to the area where the boat had sunk. Ev saw the flashing lights of a Coast Guard boat behind them. It was banging through the waves, sending up dramatic V's of spray. Liz switched over to the emergency band and checked in with the approaching boat. Ev was content just to sit there in a corner of the pilothouse. And Sundays used to be such quiet, peaceful days, he thought. Then he remembered that there were a woman and child down below, a child who had probably just lost her daddy. He heaved himself upright and went below decks.

Down in the master cabin, the survivors were huddled together under all the blankets and sheets on the bed. Ev wondered if he should find the air-conditioning thermostat and turn it off, but they were probably experiencing the cold of exhaustion. The little girl appeared to be asleep, but her mother was staring fixedly at nothing when he came in. He sat down gently on one corner of the bed.

"Can I get you anything? Some water? Coffee? A drink?"

She shook her head. The boat was corkscrewing now as Liz took her across the seas toward the sinking datum. Being inside wasn't pleasant.

"The Coast Guard boat is almost here," he said. "We're staying in the area for a search. They'll probably send a helo out, too."

The woman reached down and put her hand over her daughter's upturned ear. "He's gone," she whispered. "I saw him go down. He put his jacket on Lily. Then the mast hit him, right on the head. Hard. His eyes rolled up and he was gone. I couldn't reach him and still hang on to her."

He sighed and nodded. "How long were you in the water?" he asked.

"Forever," she said, still speaking softly, not wanting to wake the child. "I didn't thank you, did I?"

"No need. It was Liz who saw the sail. Liz DeWinter. This is her boat. We almost went right on by."

"Several boats did. They couldn't see us, I suppose."

"I couldn't see you until we were damn near on top of you." The boat began to roll again as Liz slowed and turned parallel to the seas. Ev could hear the deep-throated engines of another boat close by. "Get some rest," he said. "There's no point in transferring you to the Coast Guard boat. We'll take you in. I'm sorry about your husband."

"Thank you," she said almost mechanically. "I don't think it's really penetrated yet."

"I lost my wife two years ago," he said. "To a drunk driver."

"And this Liz DeWinter? Who is she?"

Ev looked down at her, startled by the question and the vaguely disapproving expression on the woman's face. The yacht hit a large wave and shuddered.

"Right now, she's saving my life," he said. "Now get some rest."

He got up and turned out the lights. As he was shutting the cabin door, he thought he heard her say she was sorry. You don't know the half of it, he thought. But you will.

9

Jim Hall wrote a quick note at his desk, sealed it into an official envelope, marked it "Eyes only, personal-for RADM-Select Robbins," and asked a secretary to give it to the commandant's admin assistant. Then he went to meet Oberst-sturmbannführer Branner over in Mother B.

Branner was waiting for him in the rotunda. She was wearing another tight short skirt outfit, and she was tapping one high-heeled foot impatiently. There was a fat briefcase sitting on the marble floor beside her. Two firsties walking by gave her an unabashed once-over until she looked back at them, at which point they found an urgent reason to pick up the pace.

"We have a development," she said without preamble when he joined her. "It seems that Midshipman Markham turned up having some of Dell's clothes in her room."

"And how did we find that out?" he asked. He was conscious of the fact that their voices were echoing around the cavernous room.

"Room inspection," she said. "Apparently one of those random things. Markham was in charge of the room for last week. She was placed on report for having nonregulation gear in the room. They called me this morning just before I left to come over here."

"Was it truly random, or did you put a word in to the Exec Department?"

"Moi?" she asked sweetly. "Actually, no. Fortuitous, but random. We're meeting with Dell's roommate in five minutes."

She picked up the briefcase and they headed for the commandant's conference room. "What do you want me to do in there this time?" he asked.

"I'll ask the questions. If you think of something, chime in. This kid's not a suspect. I'm going to concentrate on what he knew about Dell, not the incident. I will tape it, so you'll need to ID yourself at the appropriate time. Otherwise, follow my lead."

"Anywhere," he quipped as they stepped behind the partition. She ignored the remark. They went into the commandant's outer office and the secretary led them into the conference room, where Midshipman Antonelli was waiting nervously. He stood up to attention and sounded off when they entered the room. He was a tall, rangy kid with heavy shoulders, a bony face, crooked nose, acne, and the regulation buzz-cut hair of a plebe. Jim guessed he played sprint ball.

"Midshipman Fourth Class Antonelli, sir!" the plebe shouted. Then he realized that one of them was a woman. "Uh, ma'am. Sir!" He blushed furiously, staring straight ahead, hands pressed flat to his sides, tucking his chin in even harder.

"Please sit down, Midshipman Antonelli," Branner said.

"Yes, ma'am!" Antonelli all but shouted.

"And carry on, plebe," Jim said in a calm voice.

"Sir, aye aye, sir!" the boy replied. He sat down in one of the side chairs and folded his hands in his lap. He still sat semirigidly. Branner took the chair at the head of the table, and Jim sat down next to her. They brushed knees for an instant, and Jim moved his chair, trying to ignore those shiny stockings. Branner fished the tape recorder out of the big briefcase and set it up.

"Midshipman Antonelli, I need you to relax, please," she said. "We're here to talk about Midshipman Dell, but not about what happened to him, understand? You are not a suspect or even a formal witness. We're just trying to find out more about Dell as a person. What kind of a roommate he was. What kind of guy. How you two got along. Like that, okay?"

"Yes, ma'am," the plebe said, lowering the volume just slightly and giving Jim a sideways look.

"And this is Mr. Hall, the Academy security officer; he's helping me with my inquiries. Now, I'm going to tape this, so we'll do the introductions all over again for the tape." She saw him frown and moved to reassure him. "The tape's no big deal—it just keeps me from having to take a bunch of notes, okay?"

The plebe nodded and then Branner took him through the audio ID process. "So, Mr. Antonelli, tell us about Brian Dell. What kind of guy was he?"

"We got along," Antonelli said after first licking his lips. He was obviously very nervous. Jim wondered how much of it was due to having to do an interview in the commandant's office with NCIS, and how much of it was due to what had happened to his roommate. Branner looked over at Jim as if to say, You take it.

"Tell us about your plebe year," Jim said.

"We were getting through it," the plebe said. "I mean, like, there were three of us in the room at the beginning of plebe year. Frankie Browning dropped out at Christmas, so then it was just the two of us. That made it a little tougher."

"I understand," Jim said. "I graduated in '93. Went Marine option and then got out. So I understand what plebe year's all about and what you've been going through. What was Dell's plebe year like?"

Antonelli shrugged. "Tough, I guess. He wasn't very big. Kinda quiet. Kept his head down and his mouth shut, like most of us."

"You go out for sprint ball, by any chance?"

"Yes, sir," Antonelli said with obvious pride.

"But Dell—he wasn't a big jock, was he?"

"No, sir. Kinda small. He had some trouble with that. I mean, with all the phys ed classes. Boxing. Wrestling. Hand to gland." He reddened when he realized what he'd just called the self-defense course, but Branner just gave him a neutral smile. "But swimming, that he could do. Actually, he was a competition diver. He even went out for the varsity swim team. Got cut but stayed on as a manager."

"How about academics?"

"Brian was a math geek," Antonelli replied. "Otherwise, he kept a two-nine, three-oh QPR. He saved my ass in math."

Jim nodded. "Did you ever get the impression that the upperclassmen were actively singling Dell out when they ran the plebes in your company? You know what I mean? Like when they really come down on a guy? Hound his ass until he puts his chit in?"

Antonelli hesitated but then nodded. "I know what you mean, sir," he said. "Brian had to go roaming for a coupla weeks, during dark ages."

"What's that mean, 'roaming,' 'dark ages'?" Branner asked Jim.

"Plebes are assigned to company tables in the mess hall," he explained. "They rotate once a week to a new table, but always within the company. That way, the upperclassmen get a shot at all the plebes. When you go roaming, you report to a new table for every meal, and these are tables outside your company area."

"So?"

"Well, every meal means hitting the wall with hostile strangers, who all know that you had to be something of a screwup to get sent around the world in the first place. That's what it was called when I went through. Trust me, it's very unpleasant."

"I see. And 'dark ages' refers to the time right after Christmas leave?"

"Right," Jim said. "January and February in Annapolis. Dark and dreary. When it seems like plebe year will never, ever end, right, Antonelli?"

"Seems that way still," the plebe said, relaxing a bit when he heard Jim speaking in familiar terms.

"How many days till you climb Herndon, then?"

"Ten and a wake-up, sir!" Antonelli replied, the volume back up.

"And was there anyone in the company who was especially hard on Dell?" Branner asked.

The plebe thought about it for a moment. He shook his head.

"That mean all the upperclassmen ran him the same as everyone else?"

"Yes, ma'am."

"Who was his squad leader for this striper set?" Jim asked.

"Mr. Edwards," Antonelli said.

"He and Dell get along?"

"Um. Not that good, sir."

"You're saying that Dell's own squad leader disliked him?" Branner asked.

The plebe was obviously uncomfortable with the question. "Well, ma'am, Mr. Edwards, he's kinda hard-core."

"What did Dell do on hundredth night?" Jim asked.

"I was kinda busy on that night, sir. But I doubt Brian would have done much at all. Especially to Mr. Edwards. Like I said, Edwards is hard-core. He's going Marines." The expression on his face said that that explained everything.

"You going Marines, Antonelli?" Jim asked.

"Hope to, yes, sir," the plebe said, squaring his shoulders. Jim repressed a grin.

"Did Dell ever talk about the swim team? Personalities on the team? Anyone he might be buddies with?"

"He'd tell me about the meets, especially the away meets. How they did. Who the power guys were. The best divers. I went to some of the meets here. You know, yell for Navy. Support my roomie."

Jim looked over at Branner, who asked the next question: "Did he ever mention a Midshipman Markham?"

Antonelli nodded. "Yes, ma'am. He said they called her 'Hot Wheels.' " He stopped, looking from Branner to Jim in sudden embarrassment. "I mean, they all did. She almost always won her event, and she—she . . ."

Branner sat back in her chair, crossed her legs dramatically, and then smiled at the struggling plebe's red-faced reaction. "And she has a magnificent rack and all the guys who see her in a competition swimsuit fantasize about her? Is that about right?"

"Y-y-yes, ma'am," Antonelli stuttered, looking even more miserable. Jim could empathize. He had done a little fantasizing himself. Markham was gorgeous.

"What we need to know," Jim said gently, "was whether or not Dell had a thing for Midshipman Markham, or she for him, something that went beyond what any normal red-blooded American male would think about when he sees a beautiful woman?"

Antonelli looked horrified. "But she's a firstie," he said. "That would be serious dark-siding. No way, no day. Sir."

They had their answer. "Did Dell get a sugar report from anyone on a steady basis?" he asked. "He have a girlfriend back home somewhere?"

Antonelli shook his head. "No, sir," he said. "He got mail once a month from his 'rents. They'd usually spot him a twenty, you know, gedunk money. But if he had a girl, I didn't know anything about it. He kept to himself pretty much in that department. It's not like we had a lot of free time. It's only now slowing down a little."

"Who was his youngster?" Jim asked.

"He didn't have one, not since Christmas leave. Guy didn't come back. Put his chit in and went back to CivLant."

"Interesting. So would it be fair to say that Dell was a loner? I mean, where did he go during his free time? Who'd he hang out with?"

"Free time, sir?" Antonelli said, as if Jim had asked about Dell's Rolls-Royce.

Jim smiled. "Point taken," he said. Plebes didn't get any free time, except during study hours. And even then, stuff could happen.

"Would you say that he had been depressed over the past few weeks?" Branner asked.

Antonelli hesitated again. "You're asking if he was suicidal?"

"No, not that extreme," she said. "But was he unusually down?"

The plebe thought about it but didn't answer.

"Did he say anything that might lead you to believe he was in trouble?" Jim asked. "Like he was wondering if he was going to make it through the year?"

Antonelli shook his head slowly. "He was getting by," he said. "Head down, mouth shut, counting days to Herndon. Just like the rest of us."

"So who sent him roaming, then?" Jim asked suddenly.

"Uh, actually, I think it was Mr. Edwards, sir," Antonelli said. He looked embarrassed again.

"Anybody outside your company running him, then?"

Antonelli frowned again. "Brian'd sneak out at night sometimes. I always thought it was to study. Guys do that, get together in somebody's room after taps, hold a Gouge session. I'd see him go, but not come back. Sometimes, next morning, he'd be kinda down."

Jim gave Branner a look. She raised her eyebrows, but he shook his head. Then she thanked the plebe for his help, told him they might want to talk to him again, and asked that he not discuss any part of the interview with anyone until the investigation was completed. She switched off the tape once he'd gone.

"What?" she said.

"A plebe's own squad leader sends him roaming? There had to be a major problem there somewhere. Usually, it would be someone else, and his squad leader would be in that guy's face, raising hell about it. You look after your plebes. That's the whole point."

"So we need to talk to this Edwards guy, then?"

"Absolutely."

She checked her case notes and discovered that they had already interviewed Edwards. "He didn't come up with any-thing unusual," she said. "Typical dumb-ass plebe, lower than whale shit, et cetera, et cetera. But we didn't detect any personal animus."

"I'd have asked about that roaming thing. And whether or

not he knew about the late-night Gouge sessions. Antonelli assumed that's what they were."

"Okay, maybe we'll pull that string again. What was that 'hundredth night' stuff?"

"A hundred nights before graduation, the plebes and the firsties reverse roles for a few hours. The plebes get to run the firsties. Like payback time. It gets real noisy."

"Is plebe year over after that?"

"Nope."

"So one would have to be careful how far he went with that?"

"Very."

"I think I'm glad I asked you to get involved in this. I'd have never caught that bit about the roaming."

"Some of it's the blue-and-gold wall," he said. "But you saw his reaction when we suggested there was something between Markham and Dell?"

"As in, Never happen," she said. "Hot Wheels. I love it."

"It's a good thing you never went through here," he said with a grin, glancing at her legs.

She gave him an arch look. "Eyes in the boat, sailor," she said. "And right now, I want to get Markham back in here. I want an explanation for those clothes."

He shook his head. "Interesting timing with those clothes, don't you think?" he said. "Look, I've got paperwork piling up. Call me when you round her up, and I'll come sit in again. By the way, how's Bagger?"

"The same. The docs are of two minds. Most still say he'll come out of it."

"How the hell do they know?"

"Because he hasn't died yet?"

Jim tackled his in-box for an hour, attended a department meeting with Commander Michaels, and made a call to Public Works in search of the senior tunnel supervisor. Just before noon, he called the commandant's admin assistant and asked if he could get three minutes. The assistant said no way. There was a Saudi delegation visiting the Yard, and the commandant was joined at the hip to the duty prince for the entire day. As Jim was about to go find lunch, the assistant called back.

"I lied," he said. "Come over right now. You got three minutes."

Jim hurried out of the admin building and raced over to Bancroft Hall, where noon meal formation was just concluding to the boom and blare of the much-maligned Midshipman Drum and Bugle Corps. Jim saw the commandant standing on the front steps with several uniformed Saudi officers and one impressive-looking sheik in flowing white robes. He went in through the doors of the first wing, then trotted up one deck and through the corridors to the commandant's office. By the time he got there, Captain Robbins was standing behind his desk, doing a rapid scan of his messages. Jim stood there in his doorway for a minute, and then the commandant looked up. "Report," he ordered.

Jim gave him a quick summary of what he'd been doing. The commandant's eyes lighted up when he heard Jim was actively participating in Branner's investigation.

"And you're a civilian, too," Robbins said. "That gives us plausible deniability, somebody starts squawking command influence. Perfect. Well done. Now, suicide or accident?"

"No data, yet, sir," Jim said. "But Midshipman Markham, the one whose—"

"Yes, yes, I know. What about her?"

"There was a room inspection this past weekend. Random OOD hit. Some of Dell's clothes turned up in Markham's room. OOD fried her for nonreg gear."

The commandant sat down. "Son of bitch," he murmured. "Then somebody's lying."

"Possibly, sir. Or somebody's setting her up. If she were involved, she'd hardly keep anything belonging to Dell in her room, not with NCIS on the prowl."

"What does she say now?"

"We're going to interview her again, probably this afternoon. I'm waiting for Agent Branner to call and tell me when."

Robbins looked at his watch. "My deputy, Captain Rogers, is occupying the prince for lunch in King Hall," he said. "I have to get back. Dell's parents were here Sunday. Tough scene. They're asking questions. They're not buying the accident theory, and they can't believe suicide. Of course, the parents never do believe suicide."

"Unfortunately, I'd say the case was open, sir," Jim ventured, even though he knew his three minutes were up. "Branner is tough. With me helping to steer her questions, I think we'll find out."

"At this juncture, Mr. Hall, I'm not sure I can stand all the possible answers," Robbins said. "And what was this incident with a goal rocket in the utility tunnels the other night?"

"I've been investigating a runner. It seems like he's aware of it, and wants to play games."

"Not a midshipman, I hope?"

"I actually think it is, but I can't prove that. We arrested his companion, a Johnnie, but couldn't hold her. It may be also related to a couple of beating cases in town." He didn't elaborate on his use of the "we," not wanting to make a connection with what had happened to Bagger Thompson. He didn't want the commandant calling for reinforcements. The runner was his. Just like Branner wanted an exclusive on the Dell case.

The commandant shook his head and looked at his watch. "All right. Thank you, Mr. Hall. Keep me advised. I've instructed my people to get you in whenever you call. Use that privilege sparingly, please."

"Aye, aye, sir," Jim said, more out of habit than anything else, as the diminutive commandant hurried by.

When he got back to the admin building, there was a message from Branner. Markham was to be on deck in the conference room at 1430. He looked at his watch. That gave him time to work out, get a sandwich, and still make the meeting. He went to the locker room, got into his running gear, and headed outside.

After a half hour out on the track, he fell in with another runner, someone he'd seen before. They paced each other through the noon-hour running crowd and then walked together along the Severn River seawall to cool down. An Academy YP boat sounded its horn as it got under way, bright signal flags fluttering on both yardarms. The glare off the river was intense.

"Jim Hall, security officer," Jim offered.

"Ev Markham, Political Science Department," the other man said.

"You're a prof?" Jim said. "You don't look old enough."

"Thank you, I think. Actually, lots of folks tell me that. But I've been here for almost ten years."

Jim stopped to redo a shoelace, and Markham stopped with him, wiping his face with a small towel. "I graduated in '93," Jim said. "Must have missed your class."

"I teach firstie history," Markham said, stretching an incipient cramp out of his calf muscles.

"Can't say I did very well in history," Jim said, wishing he'd worn his shades. "Still wouldn't. Can't remember all those dates. One of the reasons I went Marine infantry."

"And now you're security officer? Isn't that a civilian position here?"

"Yep. Got out and moved sideways. I was OinC of the Marine detachment here for two years."

"Lemme guess: After two years of dress parades, honor guards, and funeral details, you felt your classmates had passed you by?"

Jim was surprised. "Close," he said. "You ex-Navy?"

"Yeah, flew carrier aviation. I was class of '73."

Jim looked him up and down. "Never know you were almost fifty. Good work. Didn't I see your name in the crab wrapper this morning? Something about a rescue out in the bay?"

"So I've heard," Markham said, wiping his face again. It

was the warmest day of the spring so far. "Happened to pass by an overturned boat. A quick swim to get two people off the hull. Fortunately, I've been keeping in shape, so it was no big deal. Woman lost her husband, though. Big deal for her."

"I saw that water yesterday. I work out regularly, but I'm not sure I'd have been ready for that."

"It was salt water and I had a life jacket on," Markham said. "You run every day?"

"Sometimes I swim, but usually I run, out in town. The women are better-looking."

Markham glanced sideways as two fairly attractive female midshipmen jogged by, as if to say he wasn't so sure about that.

"Those are girls," Jim observed, turning back toward the admin building. "I'm talking about women."

"My daughter's a firstie," Markham said. "She'd probably argue with you."

Holy shit, Jim thought. That Markham. Whom he was going to interrogate—no, interview—in about forty minutes. And he hadn't thought of Julie Markham as a girl that day at the pool. "No offense," he said quickly. "But I'm on staff and still enjoying the bachelor life. I observe the sandbox rule."

"Good thinking," Markham said, staying with him as they jogged up the steps toward Michelson Hall. "I don't know how the administration here deals with all those raging hormones. You know, four thousand healthy boys and girls jammed together in Mother Bancroft. All that pressure."

Jim was beginning to wonder if their meeting had been entirely accidental. Next thing he knew, Markham might start talking about the Dell case. He wasn't sure what the ground rules were now that he was working with NCIS, but when they reached the top of the steps, Markham waved and headed toward the Mahan Hall complex. Jim breathed a sigh of relief. Markham's daughter had to be talking to her father about what was going on in her life. The next time he ran into the professor, the exchange might not be so cordial. He made a mental note to do his noontime runs in town for the next week.

Ev Markham didn't give his interchange with Jim Hall a second thought by the time he got back to his office, especially when he read the message slip from Julie. "Meeting with NCIS again at 1430. Called Liz, but she was out. Please inform her. Julie."

And here we go, he thought. He looked at his watch: The meeting would start in twenty minutes. Should he go over there? He assumed it would be in the commandant's conference room. He dialed up Liz's office phone number, but she was in court for the rest of the day. The secretary asked if he wanted to leave a message. He told her to have Liz call him, gave her his home and office numbers just to be sure, and hung up. Liz had instructed Julie not to attend any meetings with NCIS unless she, Liz, could be present. But that was before Julie had had her little tantrum. Even as her father, he had no standing to attend such a meeting. Julie would be on her own. Based on their last meeting together, she might actually prefer it that way. He hoped she would remember some of the things Liz had told her.

He called Lieutenant Tarrens, Julie's company officer, to see if he knew about the meeting. The lieutenant did not. Ev asked him what might be going on. The lieutenant had no idea. The summons had probably come through the watch organization in the battalion office. He assumed it was about the Dell case again, but the commandant's office wasn't in the habit of clearing a summons like that through the company officer.

"They're doing an investigation, Dr. Markham," Tarrens said. "Word is that they're calling people in, asking everybody a shitload of questions. Dell's roommate, his squad leader, his company officer. They'll probably question all his profs next. Hell, maybe even the mokes. I don't think you should worry. This is routine."

Ev thanked him and hung up. It might be routine for NCIS, but it was not routine for him. The bells rang for class break. It took all his self-control not to cancel his next class and go over there right now. But what would he say to her? She'd as much as said she wanted to cooperate with them and dispel this cloud of suspicion. Hell, maybe that was the way to play it. If she'd had no part in this incident, what did she have to worry about? He sat there tapping a red pencil on the desk. He really wanted to talk to Liz. And not just about Julie.

Jim went directly to the conference room, where Branner was already set up. Midshipman Markham was due in five minutes. He had bummed a cup of coffee from the receptionist.

"Once again, how do you want me to play it?" he asked Branner. She had everything in place and was sitting at the head of the table.

"If we have a homicide here, then she qualifies as a potential suspect, as far as I'm concerned. So I'll do another Article Thirty-one warning. If she's willing to talk without her lawyer, I'll try to take her from the clothes to a connection with Dell."

"You want me to chime in when I sense the wall?"

"How about making notes and passing them? If she turns out to be involved in this kid's death, I don't want any ambiguities about your being here tainting testimony. That way, the tape will have only me and her in the interview. You'll be identified as being present, but that's all. You okay with that?"

"Absolutely. I want to help, not screw the thing up."

"Marvelous," she said brightly.

"What?" he asked.

"A man who can take direction from a woman without a bunch of bullshit."

"Heck, I often take direction from women," he said with a grin. "But it's not called an interview."

"Believe it or not, I can relate to that, too," she said, brightly. "Okay. Let's get our grillee."

Julie was dressed in her working blues, which consisted of not particularly flattering dark blue, almost black trousers, a long-sleeved black shirt and tie with the collar insignia denoting first class rank, and black shoes. Next to Branner, she looked almost asexual. She glanced quickly at Jim. He was pretty sure she recognized him. Branner asked her to sit down and then led her through the Article 31 warning procedure again.

"Are you willing to make a statement without Ms. DeWinter being with you, Midshipman Markham?" she asked.

"I am," Julie said. "I've got nothing to hide, and I want this over with. I suppose this is about that report chit?"

"Yes, it is. The deputy commandant's office alerted me to what the report chit contained. My first question is, What were those clothes doing in your room?"

"No idea," Julie said. "They weren't there before. When you and that other agent searched my room."

"We did not *search* your room," Branner asserted. "We accompanied the officer of the day on an authorized room inspection. That does not mean those uniform items weren't there at the time. It just means the OOD didn't find them."

"Well, this one did," Julie said impatiently. "Bottom line? I don't know. And I still don't know what Dell was doing wearing some of my underwear. The only connection I had with Dell was that we were both on the swim team. I think we've been through all this."

"We have," Branner said. "Was there anyone on the swim team who had it in for Dell?"

"Not to my knowledge," Julie replied. "We're a team."

"No resentments? No stars who got all the glory while the rest of the team just swam heats?"

"A Navy varsity team doesn't work that way, Agent Branner," Julie said. "Everyone's busting his ass. If you're just there for personal glory, you usually don't stay."

Jim could agree with that. None of the midshipmen were eyeing million-dollar contracts in professional or Olympic sports after graduation. They were going to get commissioned and spend the next five years serving their country. He also noticed that Markham had become a little more assertive in her demeanor. No more automatic "sir" or "ma'am" to civilians like Branner. He wondered why the lady lawyer wasn't here.

"If you weren't stashing those clothes, then perhaps someone put them there, most likely to implicate you in the Dell matter. Why would someone do that?"

"To implicate me in the Dell matter, I suppose," Julie said patiently.

Branner bristled. "Someone have it in for you, Markham?"

"Not that I know of. I broke up with another firstie a few weeks ago, but it wasn't a jealousy scene or anything. He wanted to keep going after graduation, and I'm going to be too busy for that."

Branner asked for his name and company, which Julie gave him. "So he wouldn't be plotting against you?"

"He's had his feelings hurt, but he'll live. It's not like I dumped him for someone else."

"Okay, then, who else? You strike me as a go-ahead young lady. Some men can't handle that. You beat out someone for promotion, or status here in the Academy? Class standing, or grades in a particular class?"

"All those things happen constantly," Julie said. "That's the system. Class standing. Academic standing. President of the Glee Club or any other ECA. Everyone competes here, and if they don't, the Dark Side will notice."

"The what?"

Julie colored slightly. "The senior officers. The people who run the Academy. The supe. The dant. They *are* the system."

Jim found himself nodding in agreement. No one would get killed because he had advanced over someone else in class rank or standing. Branner was appearing to read her next question from her notebook, but that pen was tapping again.

"So you had nothing to do with Midshipman Dell, and you have no idea of who might have done something, anything, to Dell that would have resulted in his going off the roof?"

"For the last time, I hope: Yes, that's correct."

"Will you be willing to take a polygraph test to that effect?"

"No," Julie said promptly. Branner stopped tapping her pen.

"Why not?"

"Because a guilty person has nothing to lose by taking a lie-detector test, while an innocent person has everything to lose if he or she happens to fail it."

"Who told you that?"

"Read it in a novel."

Branner sat back in her chair. "And you believe that?"

"Yes, I do. Simple probabilities. A lie detector is a machine being interpreted by a human. That's a two points of failure scenario, and one point of possible influence."

Branner obviously didn't know what to say to that.

"Look," Julie said, leaning forward in her chair. "I *know* I didn't do anything to Dell. If somebody put some of his uniform clothes in my room, then that's the dude you want to find. In the meantime, I'd like you to leave me the hell out of this mess, unless you have some *evidence* to the contrary."

"You're an evidentiary expert now?"

"I know that the clothes thing, both sides of it, aren't evidence of homicide. That's what you're looking for, isn't it? Evidence of homicide?"

Branner controlled her expression and just looked at her, waiting.

"Okay, tell me this: You people picked up all of Brian's personal effects after he died, correct?"

Branner nodded.

"Did you do an inventory? Because we all have a speci-fied uniform allowance, especially plebes, who are required to maintain a full seabag at all times."

"Assuming we did?"

"If the clothes found in my room are included in that in-ventory, then someone's hit your evidence locker. And if they're not, then someone else had them on the day he died. Find that someone else."

"Who says we haven't?"

Julie groaned in frustration. "Meaning me? I say so. You people went through my room that day. These clothes were found behind the towels in the closet. Any room inspector looks there. They reach behind the stacked clothes and swipe for dust. *You* would have looked there."

"So maybe you had them somewhere else, then."

"And then what? Brought them back to my room and put them out practically in plain sight? This *after* you've called me a suspect?"

Branner didn't answer that, and Jim made his first note. He passed it over to Branner, who read it, nodded, and an-nounced that the interview was over. She excused Julie, who looked from Branner to Jim for a moment, then got up and left without another word.

"Okay," Branner said. "I shut it off. What'd you hear?"

"Deflection. Let's play the tape back."

She rewound it, fast-forwarded past the Article 31 prel-ude, and then set it on play. When it got to the point where Julie said that she *knew* she didn't do anything to Brian Dell, Jim stopped it.

"She asserts that she knows *she* didn't do anything to Dell. She does *not* assert that she doesn't know who else might have done something to Dell. You asked her a two-part question, remember? She's ducking the second part of your question. And I'll bet that's why she refuses to take a lie-detector test. I think she does know something."

Branner rewound the tape and listened to it again. She seemed unconvinced. "She might just not have thought to say both things," she said.

"She's projecting a different attitude. Today, she was on offense. When she was with her lawyer, she was on defense, deferential, and it was the lady lawyer who was confrontational. Her demeanor just now is not typical of a midshipman in the presence of authority."

Branner stopped the tape and began tapping her ballpoint pen. After thirty seconds of that, Jim was ready to swat it.

"Okay, suppose you're right," she said. "How do we get into her backfield and find out?"

"We pulled in Dell's roommate; now let's pull in Markham's."

"I don't know her schedule."

"The deputy dant does, and he's right next door. But I think you should do the asking." He checked his watch. "It's just after fifteen hundred. She might be free."

In the event, Julie's roommate was available, and she arrived at the conference room twenty minutes later. Her name was Melanie Bright, and she looked like her name. Tall, athletic, sparkling blue eyes in a Nordic face, and a friendly, engaging smile. Even Branner smiled back at her when she introduced herself and sat down.

"Midshipman Bright," Branner said, "NCIS is investigating the Brian Dell incident. You are neither a suspect nor a designated witness. We'd simply like to talk to you in order to fill in some background relating to this regrettable incident. Will you help us?"

"Yes, ma'am, if I can." Midshipman Bright had a fairly broad California accent, and Jim was pretty sure she had a wad of chewing gum stashed back in her mouth somewhere.

"Good. You are Julie Markham's roommate. Have you and she talked about the case, and her interactions with us so far? Including today?"

"Yes, ma'am," Bright said. "Although I haven't seen Julie since today's noon meal formation. She said she had to come in and, like, see you guys this afternoon."

"Right, we've just spoken to her. You're aware of the special circumstances that connect Midshipman Markham to Midshipman Dell? The clothes?"

Bright's smile dimmed somewhat. "Yes, ma'am. Our room went down for that this past weekend. I wasn't there, and Julie was ICOR—So, like, she's the one who got fried. I can't explain the clothes bit, either."

Either? Jim thought. Maybe she *had* seen Julie since her 1430 interview. And yet, this young woman looked completely guileless.

"To your knowledge, was there anything going on between Julie and Dell? Other than that they were on the same varsity team?"

"No way," Bright said. "I mean, yes, they were on the same team. But he was a plebe."

"I understand that," Branner said. "How about between Julie and any other members of the swim team?"

"Well, there was Tommy. Tommy Hays? He's a classmate. But they broke up a while ago. They'd been dating since second class year, I think."

"And no one else? Maybe outside of the Academy?"

Bright shook her head. "I don't think so. Not after her mother died and all. I mean, there were a couple of times when she and Tommy had some ups and downs—you know, the usual stuff. Didn't see each other. Like that. She saw some other guys then, but nothing serious."

"Does she get mail?" Branner asked, looking down at her notepad.

"Mail? Well, yeah, bills, stuff like that." Bright patted her hair self-consciously.

"No, I mean personal mail. From friends outside the Academy?"

Bright thought about it for a moment. Jim suddenly had the impression that Miss Bright Eyes here might be putting on just a little bit of an act. "You're talking about snail mail, right?" she said. "Because personal stuff? That's going to be on the Net. I mean, I don't know anybody who actually writes letters."

Jim made a note to find a way to get into Markham's E-mail account. He looked up when Branner asked her next question.

"Where were you on the morning Dell went off the roof?" she asked.

"Me? I was in my rack, I guess. I mean, I don't know exactly when it happened. I didn't find out about it until morning meal formation. Gross." She made a face.

"Was Julie in her rack? When you guys got up at reveille that day?"

"Yes, ma'am, she was." Jim wrote another note and passed this one to Branner. She glanced at it before proceeding.

"Midshipman Bright, if Julie had gotten up earlier, would you have noticed?"

"You mean like for early swim practice? She did that all the time, although I think they're all done now. But no, I'da slept right through that. I mean, if you're gonna get up early, or come in late, you don't wake your roommate."

"Early swim practice?"

"Ya. The whole swim team does it. They go down to the pool at zero dark-thirty and swim until reveille. Then they go to their classes, and practice again after that."

"Are you on the swim team?"

"No, ma'am. I run track and field."

"Do you know people on the swim team?"

"I guess I know my classmates on the team, or most of them anyway."

Branner glanced momentarily at Jim, as if considering whether or not she should ask the next question. But then she went ahead. "Midshipman Bright, we're really trying to figure out the business with the clothes. Julie's and Brian Dell's, if you follow me. Julie states that she has no idea of how they got where they got. Assuming that's true, who else might have done that?"

"You mean put Dell's uniform stuff in her locker?"

"Yes."

Bright shook her head slowly. "No idea," she said, looking back at both of them and turning that smile back on. Jim once again felt that Bright might be just blowing them off.

Know nothing, saw nothing, and, like, heard nothing. He knew that if his roommate had ever gotten across the breakers with the NCIS, they would have talked out every tiny detail. He passed another note to Branner.

"Are there any weirdos in your class, Midshipman Bright? You know, heavy dudes, guys who are known or thought to be . . . well a little different?"

"I'm not sure what you mean, Agent Branner," Bright replied, that smile still pasted on her face. "I mean, this is the Naval Academy. People like that? My high school had some, you know, out-there guys, the kind that some people thought might show up at school with guns one day? Like, to do a Columbine? But here? The system wouldn't put up with that sh—um, with that attitude."

"So this place is strictly for Boy Scouts, then?" Branner asked with a faint note of challenge in her voice.

"And Girl Scouts," Bright said, coming right back at her. The smile never wavered.

Branner shot him that "What next?" look. He shook his head, and Branner ended the interview. Once Bright had left, Branner turned off the tape recorder. Jim realized he had not seen her turn it on, and then he remembered that she had been fooling with it just before Bright had walked in. Branner being sneaky.

"Well?" he asked.

"Well, I think she's shining us on," Branner said. "I'm so pretty. I'm so full of personality. I'm so . . . so very Bright. Yes, that's it," she said in a singsong voice that sounded remarkably like Bright's voice. Jim was laughing by the time she'd finished.

"They've not only talked about it; they've probably agreed on what Bright would say or not say."

"Gosh, you think?" Branner said drolly.

"Yeah, I think. Roommates are damn near married—it's usually that close, especially by first class year. Way back in the real old days, midshipmen used to call their roommates 'wives.' We need to check to see how long they've been roomies. If it's been a couple of years—and that's not unusual—then this was smoke and mirrors."

Branner made a quick note. "At least a little contrived," she said. The commandant's secretary stuck her head in and asked if they were finished, as the room was scheduled. Jim helped Branner pull her stuff together. "The important thing I'm finding out here is that the midshipmen are perfectly willing and able to close ranks," she said. "Buncha guys with a code of silence. Remind you of anyone?"

"That's a little extreme. Part of it is the system here. The conduct system, where people get put on report for about a million different infractions, large and small. Getting 'fried,' as it's called, becomes a bit of a cops and robbers game. But two rules do apply: One, it's a cultural crime to bilge someone else."

" 'Bilge'?"

"Get someone else in trouble, especially a classmate. Think rat squad. And it's even worse if you do it to save your own ass, or to gain advantage. I'm talking of infractions outside of the honor code, of course. That's different."

Branner paused in the doorway, ignoring the hovering secretary. "How is that different?"

"That's rule two: Rule one doesn't apply in honor cases, because an honor offense is an offense against everyone. I'm talking cheating on exams, lying, stealing, like that."

"How about covering up for someone?"

"If you lie to do the cover-up, it's an honor offense. If you're asked a direct question by a competent authority, you're supposed tell to the truth. What you don't do is slip into the deputy dant's office after hours and bilge someone for offenses, other than honor offenses."

They moved out of the anteroom and into the hallway. "So if the roommate was covering for Julie—that is, if she knows Julie did go out of the room early that morning, she'd be obliged to tell us that?"

"That's what the system expects."

"Now who's equivocating? Is that what the system always gets?"

Jim shook his head. "I'd have to call that a gray area. See, the midshipmen are always watching. The administration tends to forget that the honor system is a two-way street. The mids watch to see how the Academy administration comports itself, too. Every time something bad happens, like this Dell case, they watch to see how the administration's response squares with what they think to be the facts."

"In other words, if they think the administration is trying to cover something up, then it's okay for them to play cover-up, too?"

"It may not be okay technically, but now they'll play the game. Or at least that's my take on it."

Branner thought about that for a moment. "This is going to be hard, isn't it?" she said. "Finding out what really happened here?"

Jim looked around to see who was listening. Nobody appeared to be. "Yes, it is," he replied. "Fact is, we might never find out what really happened, especially if the administration persists with this 'accident' spin."

"The mids recognize spin when they hear it?"

"Oh yes. Plus, there's the basic fact of leadership: Whenever the leader goes into the 'Do as I say, not as I do' mode, he forfeits his moral right to be the leader. That's the problem with teaching a bunch of smart kids about leadership: They learn."

Branner shook her head again and started walking down the corridor. They didn't speak until they were out on the steps leading up to the rotunda.

"I've got to do some thinking," she said. "Hate that."

"What do you mean?"

"I may not be able to keep this case to myself after all."

"I'm still willing to help," he said.

"But you're not really on the inside, in Bancroft Hall," she said. "I mean, I appreciate it all to hell, but we've got to break through this wall."

"Let me think about it, too," he said. "If we can inject the honor system into the problem, we might be able to crack that wall. You really think someone killed that plebe?"

"I'm not hearing any substantiated reasons for him to commit suicide," she replied. "Other than that he was a little guy who kept mostly to himself. As I told you, my orders were to rule homicide *out* first. If I can do that, then it becomes a question of accident or suicide. That's a whole lot less pressing than homicide."

They stood there on the wide marble steps while midshipmen came and went around them. "I've never understood suicide," Jim said. "But if you were a guy and you were depressed, despondent, suicidal even, would you kill yourself wearing women's underwear?"

"One might," she said. "In theory, suicide is very often a statement. A final 'Screw you, world. See what you made me do? Now it's all your fault. And by the way, I was a flaming faggot, and now you know. So there, world. I showed you.'"

"But there was no suicide note. The roomie says Dell was making it through. Nobody was on Dell's ass so hard that the roomie was willing to point a finger. You said that the parents reported no indication of a suicidal frame of mind."

"All true. On the other hand, he's wearing Markham's panties, and forensics indicates he may have had some help going off the roof."

"So what the hell was this?"

"I don't know," she said.

Jim thought about those clothes. He had a bad thought. "What if Dell wasn't the real target here?" he said. "What if the real target was Markham?"

Branner blinked. "Whoa," she said. "Kill Dell to frame Markham? That's pretty damned cold. You're talking psychopath now."

"Dell jumps wearing Markham's underwear. *X* days after Dell goes over, some of *his* uniform items turn up in Markham's locker. She even picked up on it: If she had been involved in Dell's death, she never would have allowed those clothes to show up anywhere near her."

"But that brings us back to a connection between Dell

and Markham, something more than their being on the same sports team."

Jim kicked at a small stone. Circles. "Yeah," he said. "I know."

"But it does, as a theory, bring us right back to Markham," she said. "Again. Funny how that keeps happening."

A plebe walked by, eyed Jim, and finally, just to be safe, saluted. Jim nodded back at him distractedly. "But if I'm right, and I hope I'm not, Dell's getting killed may actually have been incidental."

"As in target of opportunity?" Branner said softly. "Like I said, you're implying a psychopath got through the Academy's admissions process." She looked around. The late-afternoon sunlight was filtering through the green haze of new leaves on all the big trees guarding the Yard. There were lights on in some of the rooms facing inner courtyard rooms, and they could see the figures of midshipmen passing by windows. The hum of ventilation systems mixed with the sounds of the Brigade settling into Mother Bancroft for the evening, as one more day in a 150-year tradition subsided. The gilt in the dome of the chapel gleamed its approval.

"The service academies are all about honor, duty, country," Jim said. "Like you said, Boy Scouts. Young men and women of integrity who want to do something patriotic." He paused as a final gaggle of mids hurried by, anxious to get into Bancroft Hall before some magic bell went off. "Both sides here are supremely idealistic, when you think about it, both the candidates for admission and the administration. With all those sincere expectations, would they ever see a real psychopath coming?"

"I think I need a drink," she said, looking at her watch.

"I need to get back to my office, see what's shaking," Jim said. He was halfway tempted to ask her over to the boat, but it was clear she'd been very disturbed by his theory. She was definitely going to be working this evening. Besides, he hadn't forgotten that remark about his current career, or lack of one.

"Let me call you when I've had time to think," she said. "I want to get a second opinion on the forensics report, and I need to talk to my boss. I do appreciate the support, Mr. Hall."

He smiled. "I'll tell you my first name if you'll tell me yours," he said.

She gave him a bright smile. "What's yours?"

"Jim."

"That's great, Jim. You can still call me Special Agent, I'm afraid."

"I knew that."

Ev was gathering up some papers and his briefcase when Liz called. "I've heard from Julie," Liz announced.

"How'd it go with the gestapo?" He tried not to sound too anxious, although Julie had not called him.

"Pretty straightforward, actually. They were following up on the clothes in the locker. Wanted to know how they got there. She told them she had no idea. She also reiterated that she had nothing to do with what happened to Brian Dell."

"How'd they react this time?"

"They wanted her to take a polygraph test. She told them no."

"Good girl. Did they ask where you were?"

"Apparently not. She just kept repeating that she didn't do anything to Brian Dell, not then, not ever. She says she basically told them to chase somebody else."

"How did they leave it?"

"The interview? That woman just terminated it, after the security officer passed her a note."

"What? The Academy security officer?"

Liz told him what Julie had said about Jim Hall being at the interview, and that he'd been there when she had accompanied Julie for the last one.

"You mean the black guy wasn't there?" Ev asked. "This is the Naval Academy security officer we're talking about?"

"I guess so."

"Interesting. I ran into him today while I was out for a run. We just sort of fell in together. You know how that goes when you're running around a track. Now I wonder if that was as accidental as it seemed."

"I'm not sure what his role in this case is," Liz said. "The first time, he was just an observer, as Branner put it. But he was definitely there today, and the black guy, Agent Thompson, was not there. As I said, Hall apparently passed her a note and then Agent Branner shut it off."

"How'd Julie like going solo with the cops?"

"She was brave, but I think she's getting the picture. I told her that she was living dangerously; then I shut her off."

"Prolong the feeling of exposure." This is Julie you're talking about, he reminded himself.

"Exactly. But the security officer being there bothers me a little bit. That sounds like the Academy might not be keeping itself at arm's length from this investigation. I'm going to make some calls, see what I can find out."

"Anything I can do?"

"No, I think we should let it play out for now. They might just move on to some other track."

"Okay, you're the boss on that, no matter what my darling daughter says."

"See the article in the paper today?"

"I did, finally. They never found that guy, I suppose."

"Not yet," she said. "The bay doesn't always give her victims back."

"Well I know," he said without even thinking. The comment caught Liz off guard.

"I'm so sorry, Ev," she said quickly. "That was heedless of me."

He sighed. "Yesterday was . . . perfect. Until life intruded again."

"Think of it this way," she said. "We—but mostly you—saved two people's lives yesterday. I saw their faces from the pilothouse. They were finished. That makes it a pretty damn good week, in my book."

"I was talking about us. You."

"I know, silly. We can deal with life and us, if we play our cards right."

"Okay, then, how about coming out to my house tonight?" he asked. "You're as positive as it gets for me right now."

"Listen to you! Give me an hour. No—make it two. I think I'm going to take a chance on something."

Jim went back to the boat after checking in with his office and the chief. Nothing out of the ordinary happening, other than the usual semifrantic preparations for commissioning week, the logistical and security issues caused by the presence of the vice president, the hand-holding sessions being set up for the Board of Visitors, and the media siege over the Dell incident. As he drove through the eternally crowded streets of the harbor area, he wondered if he should lay out his own theory on the Dell case for the dant. Probably not. He wasn't a trained investigator. Even Branner wanted to consult with her own people. And he could be so wrong. Hell, the kid might have gotten depressed, gone up on the roof to stew about it, and tripped. Plebes were, by definition, screwups.

As he passed by the small marina office, Charlie Mack, the dock manager, stuck his head out the door. There was a woman standing behind him in the office.

"Yo, Big Jim, you got a visitor."

Jim stopped as Charlie stepped aside and a tiny but fully equipped brunette came out of the office. "Mr. Hall?" she said. "I'm Liz DeWinter. Remember? Julie Markham's attorney? Can we talk?"

"I'm going to have a beer," Jim said as he turned on more lights in the main lounge. "Can I get you something?"

Jupiter was perch-walking, trying to get a better look at the lady lawyer.

"Thanks, no," Liz said. "I'm a scotch drinker, but I still have to drive home."

"I've got some twelve-year-old Laphroaig back here," he said, pausing at the door to the galley area.

"Well, in that case," she said. "Make it a truly wee dram, though."

"One wee dram coming up," he said. "So, how'd you find me?"

"Some serious investigative work. The phone book? You were the only Jim Hall. The other three were all listed as James."

"That'll do it," he said, returning with her scotch in a snifter and his glass of bright black Guinness. "Cheers and confusion to the redcoats."

"Remember Culloden," she replied. She tasted the single malt. "Lovely, as always."

"DeWinter," he said. "That was your boat yesterday? Picked those people up? You and Professor Markham?"

"Small world, isn't it?" she said. "And now you're wondering why I'm here."

Jim sat down across from her in one of the big leather chairs. She was probably ten years older than he was, but definitely a Slinky Toy, even if she was only about five-one in her stockings. Nice stockings, too. He smiled instead of answering, then waited.

"I talked to Julie Markham today, or this evening, actually. She told me that you were present for an NCIS interview on the Dell case. Again. I'm curious."

"You're wondering why the Naval Academy security officer's involved in an NCIS matter."

"More specifically, still involved in their investigation of what happened to Brian Dell."

He told her about what had happened to Bagger and his offer to help, leaving out any reference to the tunnel incidents or the dant's instructions. "NCIS has a two-man office here. Without Agent Thompson, she was on her own. I offered to help, and she took me up on it. I have no official status in her investigation, though."

"So how can you help Agent Branner?"

"I'm an Academy grad. She needs an interpreter. Someone who can translate what the mids are saying when she does her interviews. A consultant."

"And what they're *not* saying?"

Whoops, he thought. Careful: This one's switched in. "Yes, and what they're not saying. I'm going to help her look through the blue-and-gold wall. If I can."

Liz nodded. "I'm having similar difficulties with that wall," she said. "What do you think of my client?"

"She was there without her lawyer," Jim said with a smile. "Not as smart as she looks."

Liz inclined her glass at him in a small salud.

"Actually, I've met her three times," he continued, in case this was a test. "The first interview, the one today, and a chance encounter at the Natatorium, where I sometimes work out. But you should understand that I didn't participate in the interview. I was just there, observing and listening."

"And passing notes. Julie said you passed Branner a note and that then she terminated the interview. If you're willing to share, I'd like to know what was in that note."

He frowned. This lady was a defense lawyer. He worked for the government, and, while not really a police officer, he wasn't sure what he should be telling a possible homicide suspect's lawyer.

She put down the snifter and shifted in her chair, revealing a flash of great legs. "Look, Mr. Hall, I'm not asking you to divulge details of a government investigation or anything like that. But if I understand the process correctly, the NCIS investigation was turned on by the superintendent. You work for the superintendent. You being in that room gives the administration a direct line into the NCIS investigation, which is supposed to be conducted entirely independently of the command convening it. As I understand it, of course."

Jim heard more mental warning bells. She was talking directly about command interference. "I could quibble, I guess," he said. "The investigation was turned on by the commandant, not the supe. Either way, there's command influence only if I'm reporting back to the administration."

"Tell me something: Do you think Midshipman Dell was murdered?"

Jim tried not to blink. "Don't know," he replied. "I believe that's what Special Agent Branner's trying to rule out."

"You're a graduate. Do you think it's possible? Murder at the Naval Academy?"

He sipped some beer to give himself time to think. "Possible? Anything's possible, I guess. It's a high-pressure place. But likely? No. I'd hope that the admissions process was better than that. Let me ask you one. Do you think your client caused Dell's death?"

"I guess I'd have to say that that's between my client and me, Mr. Hall."

"Well, there's a one-way street," he said with a smile. "But that wasn't a definite no."

"You shouldn't infer anything from what I said or didn't say, Mr. Hall, especially when I'm crouching down behind lawyer-client privilege. Is that where your investigation is going right now?"

"It's not my investigation, Ms. DeWinter," he reminded her. "I'm just helping the NCIS with its inquiries."

She gave a short laugh, finished her scotch, and stood up. "Thanks for your time and the wonderful scotch," she said. "It seems we're too much on opposite sides of this thing to share information."

He got up to show her out. "You could always ask Agent Branner," he suggested with a straight face.

"Oh, right, sure I could," she said, and they both laughed. Over in his cage, Jupiter chuckled agreeably.

Jim followed her up the companionway. She was tiny, but extremely well made. Up on deck, she glanced around. "Nice boat, Mr. Hall. Consulting pays well, I take it?"

"Consulting pays nothing, unfortunately," he said. "Guess I'm not doing it right."

"You must be doing something right," she said. "I don't think Agent Branner suffers fools gladly."

"Agent Branner *hunts* fools on her days off, for fun and pleasure. You shouldn't attach any significance to my being in this picture, Ms. DeWinter. I'm helping her read the mids when she interviews them. Sometimes they speak in code. Mids don't think much of civilians."

"So I've discovered, talking to Julie." A large yacht glided by under power, headed out of Annapolis for the bay. They watched it for a minute. "The more I get around the Academy, the more I think it's an anachronism in today's America."

He nodded. "It probably is, although I think there's still a place for duty, honor, country in today's America. Maybe especially in today's America."

They both glanced over at the gray mass of Bancroft Hall. The stoical buildings, with their regimented squares of light in rows and columns, dominated the shoreline of Colonial Annapolis. Jim watched the lawyer out of the corner of his eye. Her head came up to about the level of his upper arm. She seemed to be making up her mind about something. He could just detect her perfume.

"Look, Mr. Hall—"

"Call me Jim, if you'd like."

"Okay. Jim. I'm a civilian. I was married to a military guy once, but he didn't go here, so I've got the same problem that Branner has. Basically, I've been hired to keep the system, as everyone seems to call it, from railroading Julie Markham."

"I suppose that's possible," he said slowly, thinking of the commandant. "But Branner sure isn't approaching it that way. I believe she's looking for answers."

"Do you?" she asked. "Or maybe you've been invited into this investigation for another reason."

"Which is?"

"Most of my clients are politicians in trouble. I know how that system works. Whether you know it or not, you might be running top cover for Branner."

"I don't get it."

"Suppose they've already decided to lay this off on Julie. Outsiders perceive a midshipman's death as an Academy failure. This way, they'll have you to stand up and say that, no, Branner didn't just go through the motions. You can say you were there and that she conducted a fair and square investigation. Defend her, like you did just now."

"I still don't get it," Jim protested. "I think she is conducting a fair and square investigation."

"Or she's going through the motions for your benefit, the decision having been made by the commandant that Julie Markham's going to take the fall."

"Branner's not that devious, counselor. What you see is what you get with her, like it or not."

"Well, tell me this, then: Whom does Branner work for, as the resident agent for NCIS at the U.S. Naval Academy?"

He thought about it. Her government paycheck came from the NCIS, of course, but her performance ratings would be cosigned, at the very least, by . . . by—the dant. The dant was the customer. She watched him work it out.

"Who've you been talking to?" he asked.

"Ev Markham, for one. Julie's father. He's a grad, too, and he's worried."

Jim nodded. Professor Markham. "He the one who hired you?"

"Yes."

"Well, look. I appreciate your insights. But I'm going to continue helping Branner, if she wants me to. I can give you this much: If I see any signs that her investigation is some kind of Kabuki, I'll call you. Fair enough, Ms. DeWinter?"

"More than fair. And now you can call me Liz."

"Good deal. Why only now?"

"You just showed a flash of fair play, Jim. Were you by

any chance a Marine before you took this security officer job?"

"Aw shucks, does it show?"

"My first ex was a Marine fighter pilot," she said. "You can take the guy out of the Marines, but you can never take the Marines out of the guy." She stepped through the gate, being careful of her footing. "Thanks for seeing me this evening, Jim. And if you sense . . . well, what we talked about, I'd really appreciate that heads-up. Julie Markham doesn't deserve this."

"I hope you're right about that," he said.

"Meaning?"

"Meaning it might not be a railroad deal here. It might not be the system. It might in fact be Julie."

She frowned. "Julie what?"

"Has Julie Markham been absolutely straight with you? Completely forthright? No signs of deception? At all times?"

Liz pursed her lips but didn't say anything.

"Uh-huh," he said, nodding. "Stay tuned, counselor. We might all be wrong about what we're seeing here."

Liz thought about it, then shook her head. "I don't think so. My bet stays on the Academy trying to whitewash this, find somebody they can pin it on, and then make sincere pronouncements about closure."

"Well, I guess we wait and see," he said. "You have a good evening, Liz."

She smiled up at him and left. He went back down the companionway, closing the hatch behind him.

Goddamned career women, he thought. Lawyer Liz insisting he call her by her first name, Lock and Load Branner insisting she didn't *have* a first name. But both world-class manipulators, if not ball-breakers. He recalled the image of Liz steaming up the pier, tiny but definitely sexy, and yet she'd driven right over him. No wonder she was an *ex*-wife. Maybe it was something in the Annapolis drinking water.

Jupiter let out an unhappy screech when Jim came back into the lounge.

"Don't you start, feather merchant," he growled. "I've got places to go tonight."

At 10:50 P.M., Jim stood in the main tunnel. Ten more minutes, he thought, and then the PWC will do its thing. In the past forty-five minutes, he'd walked the entire length of the main tunnel, from the Bancroft Hall sector, where the rocket had been fired, all the way to the King George Street access doors. He'd tested all the electrical access panels, the two doors to that big air-conditioning compressor chamber, and the doors on every one of the telephone equipment cabinets. He'd checked out each of the cross tunnels for signs of intrusion. The only thing he hadn't done was to pull up the steel deck plates lining the center of the main tunnel, and only because that would have taken all night.

He didn't expect his runner to be on the move on a Monday night. The town bars would be pretty much dead as the party-hearty crowd sobered up after the weekend. Midshipmen would be grappling with the start of the working week, recovering from Monday-morning pop quizzes and getting some much-needed sleep after the exertions of weekend liberty. The motion detectors were still in place, but he had disconnected the receiver box and had it in his backpack.

He stood at the junction between the main tunnel and cross tunnel that led down to Michelson Hall. He could almost feel the weight of the concrete ceiling and the ground above pressing down on his head from inches away. The by-now-familiar odors of steam, hot lagging, and ozone permeated the air. From off to his right came the occasional clanking of traffic passing over a steam grate out on King George Street. He looked at his watch again: 10:59.

At precisely eleven o'clock, all the tunnel lights winked out. The main tunnel and all its branches went completely dark. He didn't move, but he did close his eyes. The only sound now was the hum of a nearby electrical panel. After a few minutes, he opened his eyes and stared into the darkness. The first thing he noticed was that the darkness was not complete; he could still see. Up and down the tunnel, there were small lights, most of them green but some amber, mounted on the front of the electrical panels. The green lights indicated conditions normal, while the amber lights indicated that power was present in the panel. There was a red glow in the far distance to his left, which probably came from the transformer bank recessed into the tunnel wall next to the telephone amplifier vault.

Okay, he thought. Only partial success. He had wanted to see if it was possible to put the tunnels into complete darkness on command. He had talked to the PWC people and they had figured out a signal that could be detected on their utility control panels in the Academy's power plant. All Jim had to do was to go up to any electrical panel, open the main breaker, and then close it again. An alarm indicating a power interruption would flash on the PWC's control console, and that would be the prearranged signal to kill all the lighting circuits in the tunnel for fifteen minutes, as long as the alarm popped up during a designated time period. Jim had designated the time window before going down into the tunnels.

His objective had been to lie in wait for the runner, using his motion detectors. Once he detected movement, he'd plunge the tunnel system into darkness. Then with night-vision goggles and whatever faint ambient light came from the indicator lights on the electrical panels, he would have the advantage over his quarry. The problem was that there were too many indicators producing too much ambient light. He might have the advantage for the first minute or so while the runner's eyes adjusted to the sudden darkness, but then the runner would be able to see, at least well enough to react. Jim couldn't get away from the feeling that the runner knew this labyrinth better than he did.

Okay, he thought, I'll have to get some electrical insulating tape. Go down the tunnels and tape over all but a very few of these lights. But that's going to take a lot of time.

Shit. This isn't going to work. Unless he got some backup. He could always call in the Yard cops, but the tunnels didn't lend themselves to having lots of people operating down there. The runner had always managed to sniff out Jim's presence very quickly, so more cops meant fewer chances of surprise. Assuming the vampire had some place in town to ditch the costume, he could always go back through the main gate if he had to. That would mean risking being hit with a conduct offense, but there would be no way to tie him to what had been going on out in town.

Think, Jim told himself. You're after one guy. You've locked him out of one of his main avenues of escape, at least until he figures out how to get through those locks. You know the way he's been coming back—through that grate on the St. John's campus. So put a surveillance team on the grate? But that would mean Yard cops operating out in town, on the St. John's campus, where they had zero jurisdiction. He didn't want to bring Annapolis cops into this, either, in case it was a midshipman. The Ops boss had made it very clear they didn't need another scandal popping up just now. Which meant he needed to take this guy on federal property.

The lights all came back on in a hum of fluorescent starters. He blinked at the sudden brightness and realized he'd been thinking in circles. He had an idea, but first he wanted to check something. He walked down the tunnel toward the King George Street access doors until he came to the shark tag drawn on the concrete wall. There had been no change since the last alteration, after he'd put his own tag down. He fished for the can of spray paint, which was still in his backpack. Standing close, he sprayed ONE-ON-ONE, followed by the numerals 2400. Below the shark figure, he sprayed on IF YOU'RE MAN ENOUGH. Then signed it HMC.

He stood back and examined his handiwork. He'd have to alert PWC to make sure they didn't clean off the tag now that it was getting bigger. Then he'd come back tomorrow night, around nine or so, to see if there'd been some indication his runner had seen it. Some kind of a reply. Then maybe aim at Wednesday night to set up for his first real try. Get some backup, but put it in the Yard, out of general sight but close enough to the major grates within the Yard for quick response time.

He started back toward the Mahan Hall interchange. Just for the hell of it, he began counting indicator lights. He'd seen thirty-seven by the time he reached the interchange. Far too many. Plus, the night-vision headset would make for a cumbersome hand-to-hand situation. But he still might use the lights-out maneuver. Mask out his own eyes for five minutes, then send the signal, see how well he could function. The question he still hadn't answered was where his runner was getting *into* the tunnels. Had to be down at the Bancroft Hall end, although those tunnels were jam-packed with pipes and cables. The only other tunnels down at that end were the old Fort Severn magazine tunnels. Wait a minute, he thought. The night of the rocket, Bagger had pointed out some bright metal scratches on the lock of one of the doors to the Severn magazine tunnel. In the excitement, Jim had forgotten that. He decided to go down there and look again.

The splotches had been cleaned off the concrete where the rocket had gone ricocheting down the S-turn. When he got to the alcove leading down to the magazine doors, he found the overhead light was out. There were no lights in the alcove, which ran for about ten feet before reaching the two doors. He turned into the alcove, went down three stone steps, crossed the ten feet, and knelt down in front of the oak door on the left-hand side. He shone his Maglite on the antique lock. Hard to tell. It was humid enough down here to encourage corrosion, so shiny metal scratches could have dulled down by now. He couldn't see any scratches, and yet they had been visible before. He put his finger to the keyhole and rubbed it around. Something came off on his finger, some gooey-gray substance. And there were the shiny scratches.

Well, hello, he thought. Someone has been covering his tracks here. Then the hair went up on the back of his head. He sensed the presence of someone or *something* behind him. Not right behind him, but very close. His heart began to pound slightly. The ambient light seemed to be different, but the bright beam of the Maglite made it difficult to tell. He worked to control his breathing and the urge to whip around to take a look. He kept the Maglite on the keyhole but focused all his senses on what was behind him. A vision of that terrible vampire face floated up in his mind. Trying not to make any sudden moves, he dropped his right hand casually to his ankle, as if to scratch an itch, and began to lift the hem of his coveralls to get at the Glock. When he had his hands on the butt, he yanked it out and spun around in place, pointing it up at the arched entrance to the alcove. But there was nothing there. Just a rectangle of dim light framed by the old stone walls.

He swore and stuffed the Glock back into the ankle rig. Goddamned place was spooking him. He stood up and exhaled. He'd have to get keys to these oak doors. He didn't care about the right-hand tunnel—it didn't go in the correct direction. But the left-hand tunnel might get close enough to the Bancroft Hall basements that this could be his runner's access point. No, on second thought, he'd do this the right way, the safe way. He'd get the PWC guys to open the doors, make sure the atmosphere was safe down there, and then he'd get proper gear to make an exploration. With the PWC people knowing he was down there, time in, time out, and preparations in place to retrieve his young ass if something went wrong. Those old brick tunnels were dangerous as hell, and the magazine complex appeared to be surprisingly large. Go into that by yourself and probably nobody would ever know what became of you.

He started back up the alcove, climbed the three steps, and emerged into the modern tunnel. He stopped to listen, but there were only the familiar sounds of the utility lines. Nothing from above ground penetrated this sector. There wouldn't be any vehicle traffic on the Yard streets above, and the mids would all be in their respective trees for the nights, excepting the poor bastards who were failing courses. They'd be in their closets with flashlights, or in their racks with a blanket over the flashlight, desperately memorizing the Gouge as they tried to get ready for the next morning's pop quiz.

As he came to the S-turn under the front of Bancroft Hall, he thought he heard something. He froze and reached down for the Glock again. The lights in this sector were all working, but the S-turn would make an excellent place to start some shit. Then he definitely heard something. He recognized it as the unmistakable sound of a tennis ball being smacked right in the sweet spot of a racket, and then bouncing along the concrete floor from side wall to side wall, through the S-turn, until it rolled out practically at his feet. It made a surreal sound down among all the pipes, cables, and concrete. He heard a clang and felt a pressure change in his ears as he scooped it up and discovered that there was something written on it. Two words.

YOU'RE ON.

Liz helped Ev clean up after a supper of cold steamed crabs she had brought from the harbor market. They took their wineglasses out to the back porch and settled into chairs. It was fully dark, with the only lights coming from inside the house and across the shimmering black waters of the creek.

She had told him about visiting Jim Hall at the marina, and that she was still bothered by his involvement in the NCIS investigation. He wasn't so sure that it was all such a bad thing, understanding as he did the difficulty civilians would have getting through to the inner workings and hidden mechanisms of life in the Brigade of Midshipmen.

"It's a strange world in there," he said, pouring them both some more wine. "Stranger than even I remember it, because now there are women on board. It was probably a whole lot easier when it was all guys."

"You don't think women belong in the military?" she asked.

"Now there's a loaded question." He laughed. "But the truth is, no, I don't. I mean, I understand the equal-opportunity issue—that women shouldn't be denied the right to serve their country as officers or anything else. And I'm very proud of what Julie's managed to do, getting through and doing it well."

"So?"

"Well, I just don't think that military service is suitable for women. I think their role in life has more to do with nurturing a family, bearing and having children, and acting as the sanity counterbalance to the aggressive and often dumb-headed things we men do to screw up their lives and other people's. Like charging off to war, drawing lines in the sand, getting even, showing off. Women are too valuable to waste in military service."

"Not all women want to do the things you just mentioned."

"Agreed. And I know my views are not politically correct these days."

"But shared perhaps by more people than you know," she said. "I often wonder if it's fitting for the nation's women-folk to be on the front lines. But maybe now that the front lines have come to downtown America, we'll have to reevaluate. Personally, though, I'd rather see women in the professions. How does Julie feel about it?"

"She's going Navy air, so it should be obvious. But I'm not sure I know how she really feels."

"Trying to be the son you didn't have, perhaps?"

"It's possible, although I've never laid that rap on her. Besides, look at her. A tomboy she's not. But she's been somewhat remote since, you know."

"I grew up the elder of two children. My brother always gravitated toward our mother when it came time to let hair down, and I gravitated toward my dad. How was it with Julie?"

"Her mother," he replied, sipping some wine. "I wasn't really aware of that until . . ."

"Until Joanne died?"

"Yes."

"You shouldn't be afraid to say the word, Ev."

"I know."

"Anyway—Julie? Maybe being remote is her way of grieving."

He was silent for a moment. "She was pretty torn up by the whole thing. And then suddenly, she seemed to take an emotional deep breath and ploughed back into her life. Kids are strange."

"Someone over there in Bancroft Hall may have asked the same thing your minister asked you, 'Whom are you weeping for?' "

"Yeah, probably."

"Do you miss Joanne?" she asked.

He thought about what to say. They'd started something yesterday, and he didn't want to derail that, not now. "I think I miss the life we had. The stability. What seemed like predictability. My career was on track. She'd been taking courses to get back to speed in the financial-planning world. Julie was making it through the Academy. Our house was paid for. It looked like all we had to do was keep on trucking and life was going to be all right. Then it wasn't."

"But now it can be," Liz said. "You can choose to come out of the cave. Like you did yesterday. And I'm awfully glad you did."

He smiled across at her. "It was a pretty irresistible package," he said. The phone began to ring in the house. Ev got up and went into the kitchen to get it. It was Julie.

"Dad," she said.

"Himself," he replied. "What's up?"

"I went to that interview today. Did Liz tell you?"

"Yes," he said, glancing at the silhouette of Liz's head through the kitchen window. "She said we watch and wait."

"I guess," said Julie. "And I read in the *Capital* about what you did yesterday—saving those two people? That was shit-hot."

"It was worse for them than for me," he said. "All I had to do was swim fifty feet through a medium chop, twice. They'd been hanging on for an eternity. And they lost a husband and father, it looks like."

"Were they from here?"

"Don't think so. Once the medics got to them, I never saw them again."

"Lucky for them you were right there. That was Liz's yacht?"

"Yes. We'd gone out for the afternoon. She apparently goes out on the bay every Sunday. Invited me along this time."

"Just the two of you?"

He took a deep breath before answering. "Yes, Julie. Just the two of us." He saw Liz's head turn when he said that. He waited.

"She's pretty impressive," Julie said finally. "She's tougher than you might think, too."

"From your perspective, that should be good," he said.

"I suppose, but I don't want you hurt. I guess I'm getting tired of all these surprises, and I haven't even made it out into the world yet."

"From what Liz told me, you did well today. Especially by refusing that lie-detector test. You knew the old rule about those, did you?"

"Yep. I watch TV, too, Dad."

He laughed. "Have to admit, that's where I heard it. Okay. Let me know if anything else pops up."

"Is she there now, Dad? Liz?"

None of your damn business, he thought. "Good night, Julie," he said, and hung up. He went back out to the porch.

"Why'd she call?" Liz asked.

"To find out what I was doing on your boat yesterday, unchaperoned."

"Ah," she said. "You know what?"

"What?"

"Seems to me," she said softly, setting her glass down, "that we're unchaperoned right now."

Monday night and all's well. Sort of. That security dink's been poking around in my tunnels again, and, guess what? This time he issued a challenge. Like, I think he wants a duel. Mano a mano. *As if. Hasn't he been keeping score? So far, he's had his face painted, a singular chance to become a rocket man, and a steam bath. All courtesy of yours truly. And, as you know, he's even been scoping out the Goth scene in town at our favorite public watering hole. As opposed to our favorite private watering hole, where we tend to get everything wet, don't we.*

I think it's time this nosy bastard has himself a near-death experience. Those are my tunnels. I see all and hear all. This dimwit puts up listening devices and motion detectors and I don't know what, and thinks I can't see those, either. I can. I can even make them do things I want them to do, if I put my mind to it. Except time is short, for both of us, really. If we had a year, I could make his little toys light up his life, so to speak. Connect one of his little transmitter cases to a six-hundred-volt line. Make it malfunction. Get him to check it out. To handle it. Just for one night— wouldn't want to hurt any of the permanent tunnel rats from Public Works. You should see what a couple of those guys do down there after hours. My, my. Big strong men like that— you'd think they'd like girls.

So maybe I'll up the ante, even if time is short. He's been creeping around, going into places that aren't safe. I'm sure Public Works has told him those places aren't safe. And they really aren't, because I've already been there, and I've made some arrangements. I could make him just flat disappear, you know that? I can make anyone here disappear. Except you, of course. I can't make you disappear. And don't want to, not yet anyway. But I can make your life increasingly—what's the word? Interest-

ing. You spin your little tales; I'll spin mine. In the meantime, HMC needs to watch his back. Or front. Haven't made up my mind yet, but either one will do, when the time comes.

10

On Tuesday morning, Jim met Mike Carrick, the PWC utilities manager, at the Stribling Walk down ramp into the main tunnels. He'd asked the manager to bring along the keys to the Fort Severn tunnels. Above them, the sky was darkening fast with the approach of a spring thunderstorm. They hurried down the concrete steps and into the main tunnel just as the rain began. When they got down to the descending alcove leading to the big oak doors, Jim found a small crew already there. They had the left-hand door open. A battery of portable air handlers was doing a fresh-air exchange into the normally sealed tunnels.

"Gas-free engineering," Carrick shouted above the roar of the Red Devil blowers. "No telling how much oxygen's down there. Or how little."

"How much longer?" Jim said.

As if they'd heard him, the crews switched off the blowers and began retrieving several feet of bulky air hose from the tunnels.

"They've given it thirty minutes of air exchange," Carrick said. "Let them do their tests, and then you can go in."

"Not coming with me?"

"Not on your life," Carrick said. He stepped forward and tapped the top of the brick arch nearest to the doorway. A fine snowfall of masonry dust wafted down. "You want to go down there, be our guest. But I'll require that you pull an air line with you for when it caves in."

"*When?* Is it really that bad?" Jim asked, eyeing the moldering brickwork.

"It might be, although we haven't had a cave-in since the eastern gun gallery tunnel collapsed. But that was some years ago. Arches are Roman engineering. Pretty strong. But those are basically mud bricks, well over a hundred years old."

The test engineer went into the left-hand tunnel for a distance of about thirty feet and tested the air for free oxygen and any explosive gases with his instruments. Then he backed out. "You want us to do the right-hand tunnel?"

Jim shook his head. "The map shows it's a mirror image of the left-hand side. Is that correct?"

Carrick nodded, looking at his diagrams. "It ends up in a magazine that's right under the front walls of Lejeune Hall," he said. "The map doesn't show it, but I think there's a connector tunnel between the two branches. Probably caved in by now."

"I'm only interested in this left-hand side," Jim said.

"How come?" Carrick asked.

"I think some mids have been into it," he said. "Can I have your site map?"

"Right here. Layout's pretty simple. Two tunnels, parallel for two hundred feet. Then they branch left and right, respectively, into the magazine vaults. That's where I think that cross tunnel is, but, like I said, it isn't on the map."

"Okay," Jim said.

"From the magazines, there were two tunnels that kept going out to where the gun pits were. That would be under the landfill now, and they've collapsed. Sealed them with cement-block walls. The main tunnels are one level below where we're standing right now. The magazines are one level below the main tunnels. Steel doors, no locks. Oh, and the left magazine is flooded, by the way. Okay so far?"

"Yep."

"There's no lights, no power down there. The air exchange may not have reached the magazine alcoves. You start getting dizzy, have trouble breathing, you back out."

"Okay."

"There's a liquid manometer outside the main magazine chamber. If there's water visible in the manometer, then that's the level of the water in the magazine. Don't open the doors."

"Big magazines?"

"Big enough: fifty by fifty, arched dome, twenty-foot ceilings."

"No ammo or guns, I take it?"

Carrick laughed. "Long gone. If there was powder down there, it would be marvelously unstable. No matches or flames down there, by the way—there could be methane. That Maglite is okay."

"I'm having serious second thoughts," Jim said.

"You want to quit now, no hard feelings."

Jim took a deep breath, wondering if it was going to be his last. But he had to go. Those scratches on the lock had been deliberately obscured. Had to be a reason for that. Even if the magazine itself was flooded. He shook his head. "No, I have to take a look."

"Suit yourself. I'll have two guys stand by while you're down there. They hear a rumble, they'll start air into the hose and get the recovery crew in. Here's your air hose, and here are those spare keys you requested."

He handed Jim the antique iron keys, the tunnel diagrams, and the end of a reinforced air hose, which had a tiny sound-powered telephone wire wrapped around the outside. "The hose is graduated," Carrick said. "If you get a cave-in, it'll tell us how far into the tunnel you are. That there is a microphone where we can talk back and forth, assuming you survive it."

Nobody was smirking, Jim realized. These guys were obviously taking the possibility of a cave-in seriously. "Don't bother to bring the air hose out when you come back; we'll use the cable reel to retrieve it. How long you going to be in there?"

"Half hour, max," Jim said. "I want to make a quick tour, see what I see. I'll back out as soon as possible."

"You back out if you think the structure is giving way. Don't stop. Don't think. Run like a striped-assed ape."

"I think you're scaring me."

"That's the idea. And good luck."

Jim took the end of the air hose in hand and went down the stone steps into the left-hand tunnel. Behind him, the PWC crew unreeled the hose for him. By the diagram, the right-hand tunnel led directly out toward what had been the original banks of Spa Creek, which in turn fed into the Colonial harbor of Annapolis. Subsequent landfills to expand the Academy grounds had long since buried the original shoreline, but Fort Severn's foundations were supposedly still there, along with these underground facilities.

The left-hand tunnel, on the other hand, branched back toward Bancroft Hall. If their runner was using it, this would be the one. The diagrams might not be that accurate, so there could be a tie into the basements.

The Maglite threw bobbing shadows along the brick walls as he walked forward. The arched tunnel ceiling was barely an inch above his head, increasing the feeling that he was taking a walk in a burial vault. The air was musty, smelling of old lime. Tiny little avalanches of mortar dust trickled down from between the odd-shaped bricks in the side walls as his footfalls disturbed the silence. He shuddered when he realized the entire massive weight of Dahlgren Hall was pressing down on all this crumbling ancient brickwork right above his head.

The floor appeared to be hard-packed dirt until he scuffed it with his toe and uncovered more brickwork under an inch-thick layer of white dust. Mortar dust, he realized. Good deal. The joints between all the bricks were recessed at least a quarter inch. He thought about testing one to see if it was loose, then thought better of doing that. Hate to find out I'm right, he thought. He kept tugging on the air line until he reached the first intersection, about two hundred feet from the alcove entrance. One tunnel went left and sloped down. The other, presumably the gun pit tunnel, went straight ahead and then branched left. He stopped fifteen feet back from the intersection, squatted down on his heels, and examined the dust.

There were regular depressions in the fine dust. Not exactly footprints, but spaced at about the right intervals. He realized he should have come down here sooner. The mortar dust was the consistency of confectioners' sugar, so it didn't hold the definition of a footprint or the ridges of a sole or heel pattern. But the depressions in the dust were regular, about two feet apart. He put the Maglite down on the tunnel floor, but that didn't help. Still no definition.

Just then he heard a low, ominous rumble echoing down the tunnel, and his heart jumped. But then he recognized it: thunder. The storm must be overhead. As he worked to control his breathing, there came another clap of thunder, louder and more pronounced. He shone the light back down the tunnel. The tiny metal bands that bundled the air hose and the phone cable winked back at him through a fine mist of falling masonry dust. A third thump of thunder, and the mist thickened momentarily. He swallowed and wondered if he ought not to give this shit up right now. But there had been thunderstorms before, and the tunnels were still standing. He decided to go on.

Then he realized that the intersection was actually a three-way junction. The left turn went down to the magazines. Straight ahead were the blocked-off gun pit tunnels. To the right was another oak door, smaller than the main entrance. He pushed on it, but it was locked. He tried the keys, and one worked the lock. This had to be the cross tunnel. He relocked it, turned around, and took the left turn down toward the magazines. The tunnel floor sloped down noticeably, and he wondered how far underground he was. He should be beyond the massive granite bulk of Dahlgren now, and approaching the right-hand edges of either the sixth or the eighth wing of Bancroft Hall. Or maybe even the tennis courts. He voted for the tennis courts. The air hose was getting much harder to pull, and he was tempted to leave it. The magazine doors were visible twenty feet away, framed by an arched alcove. It looked as if they were made of cast iron, not steel, with rivet heads visible in the harsh white light of the Maglite. There were wheels under the doors, and, based on iron semicircles embedded in the floor, they apparently swung outward against the alcove walls. He checked for more depressions in the dust, but they weren't as obvious on the sloping floor of this tunnel.

When he reached the doors themselves, he found the manometer to one side. It was a thin vertical glass tube about four feet long and an inch in diameter. It was supported by a bracket at each end, and there were tiny brass valves above and below the brackets. Small pipes led through the masonry at top and bottom so that the water level in the tube would always match the water level inside the magazine. And there was definitely water, right up near the top of the manometer.

Okay, so much for that. Based on where the manometer was mounted, the magazine was flooded at least eight feet up from the bottom sill of the doors. So nobody could be in there. He'd have to ask the PWC manager if the water level varied, but it probably didn't. The magazines were simply sealed underground chambers that had been abandoned for over a hundred years. Okay, then what were those depressions? Then it hit him: They said they inspected the tunnels every five years or so. Those were the footprints of the last inspection team. There had been nothing to disturb them once the men had backed out. Another rumble of thunder echoed down the tunnels. More mortar dust. He imagined he felt the earth itself shifting under his feet. Then the steel doors in front of him moved.

Again he froze. Had he imagined it? He hadn't actually seen them move, but he had heard them stir on their ancient iron rollers. A trick of the acoustics down here. He waited, and then remembered to breathe. He stared at the doors. Another boom of thunder, the sensation of movement, a slight pressure in his ears, and, yes, by God, the door moved. Less than a fraction of an inch. Air pressure. Somehow, the storm was modulating the air pressure down here, and the doors, being at the end of a tunnel, were being affected. While his logical brain worked that out, his lizard brain was beginning to sound a repeating refrain: Let's go, let's go, let's go. Great damned idea, he thought, and, dropping the air hose, he started back up the tunnel.

Another thump and boom from the storm up above, and the answering veil of mortar dust streamed out of the arched ceiling.

I will not run. I will walk. If I run, my footfalls could disturb the brickwork even more.

I will not run.

But I can trot. Or do a fast shuffle, maybe?

And he did, keeping his footfalls minimized, trying not to make any big vibrations, wiping the perspiration off his face and realizing it was gritty, fixing his eyes on the beam of white light ahead of him as he followed it back up to the intersection. He was terribly aware of the tunnel roof right above his head, and he stepped out and picked up the pace. Eighty feet from the entrance, he heard a crack from the brickwork, somewhere behind him. I will not run. I will not run.

A moment later, he bounded up the steps past the two crewmen who were watching with knowing grins. A boom of thunder let go that sounded as if it had gone off down here in the main tunnel, but the sound was obviously just coming down from the various gratings in all its beautiful fury.

"All done today?" the older of the PWC guys asked him as the other one began to crank on the reel of the air hose. "Look a little white around the gills."

Jim wiped his face and saw that his entire hand was white. "That thunder was starting to move shit around down there. Scared my ass."

"Yeah, it does that. Compresses the air. You were at the end of the pipe. It's interesting shit."

"That's one word for it," Jim said, and all three laughed.

"At least you didn't rabbit. We had the PWC officer himself back there, Captain Johnson? Same thing happened. He damn near went over the crew's backs to get out of there."

"Wasn't like I didn't want to," Jim said. "I was afraid of making vibrations."

"You ought to try it when there's a storm out on the bay and we get big waves. The waves hit the seawall out on Farragut Field. That's all packed landfill, you know, rammed earth. Transmits the vibrations back into the Fort Severn foundations. That's really interesting. Sure you don't wanna go down this other tunnel?"

Another boom of thunder bellowed down the concrete walls. "All the same to you," said Jim, and the guy nodded. Jim asked if he could help with the cable reel, but they thanked him and said no. Then he asked why PWC didn't just fill these death traps in.

"Money," the man said. "They shoulda done it a hundred years ago, but there you are. Army then, you know. Army does everything half-ass."

Jim thanked them again and headed for the surface, forcing himself to walk through the tunnel at a normal pace. When he reached the Stribling Walk access doors, he could hear rain streaming down the steps. There was a more pronounced gurgle under the steel deck plates out in the middle of the tunnel floor. He decided to wait it out.

So what had he learned? That he was scared of underground chambers. Okay. But why had there been scratches on the lock, and why had they been covered up? His runner take a tour one night and have the same reaction? He should have gone down that other tunnel while it was open. He knew they wouldn't open it again anytime soon. But there was just no way. When that huge damned door moved, it had taken all his self-control not to drop that air hose and just bolt.

A small tingle at the back of his brain told him he was missing something here. He tried to think. Shit. He realized he should go back down there right now and explore that second tunnel. He wouldn't get another chance unless some really hard evidence precipitated opening up and gas-freeing the complex again.

Another clap of thunder blasted seemingly right above his head, rattling the steel door and the gratings above. He felt the pressure in his ears and thought he saw the overhead lights sway.

Go back down there? Screw that noise.

Branner called Jim after lunch and asked if he could come up to the NCIS office to meet someone. There had been a staff meeting called for 1400, which Jim was more than pleased to skip, so he said he'd be right over. There was still intense media pressure relating to the Dell case, and the commandant was all over the Public Affairs office to control the spin. The Yard police had caught a television crew from CBS national news hawking the Nimitz Library steps, trying for interviews with midshipmen. The mids had turned them in immediately.

"Mr. Hall, this is Mr. Harry Chang," Branner said, making introductions in the conference room. "Mr. Chang, this is Mr. Jim Hall, Naval Academy security officer."

Jim almost did a double take. Harry Chang appeared to be a clone of Mao Tse-tung. The same broad, round face, thickset body, thinning grayish black hair, and black eyes gleaming with wily intelligence. He grinned when he saw the look on Jim's face. "Scary, isn't it?" he said, shaking hands.

"Mr. Chairman" was all Jim could manage, and Chang laughed out loud. "See?" he said to Branner. Then to Jim: "I understand you were a Marine?"

"Yes, that's right," he said, wondering if he was going to get another query about what he was doing here in the security officer job.

"I was, too," Chang said, gesturing for everyone to sit down. "Enlisted. Intel specialist. Four years. Saw some interesting times in Nam. But that was thirty years ago or thereabouts. I joined up with NCIS when it was still called NIS."

"Mr. Chang is from headquarters," Branner said. "He's a homicide specialist. Actually, I should say he is *the* homicide specialist."

"Actually, I happened to be *the* homicide specialist who zigged instead of zagged when Agent Branner called in yesterday," Chang said with an easy smile. "Our senior directing staff told me to butt in."

"I briefed him on what we've done up to now," Branner said. Jim noted her choice of "we" and wondered how that sat with the senior NCIS people.

"She said you proposed an interesting theory of the case, Mr. Hall," Chang said. "Could I hear it in your own words?"

Apparently, his participation in the NCIS investigation didn't bother their headquarters people. Jim nodded and went through it again, saying that maybe what had happened to Dell was incidental to something aimed at Midshipman Markham. Chang stared at him the whole time he was talking. His expression revealed absolutely nothing.

"As Agent Branner here observed," Jim concluded, "that would mean we might be dealing with a sociopath, if not a psychopath. A midshipman, in all probability."

"A psychopath at the Naval Academy," Chang said. "That raises all sorts of interesting problems, does it not?"

"Got that right," Jim said. "The Dell case. The system here. The admissions process. If I'm right, it's not going to be a very popular theory."

Chang nodded emphatically. "Our brief," he said, "is to pull the string on the possibility that what happened to Midshipman Brian Dell was a homicide. The emphasis coming from our overseers is to *dis*prove homicide. Then maybe the current media circus can be damped down somewhat."

"That's coming from the supe?"

"That's coming from the SecNav. Or so I've been told."

Jim considered this news. If the SecNav's office was involved in this case, then the stakes were considerably higher than he had thought. "Hell, it's just a theory," he said.

"And now you're feeling like the messenger who's set himself up for a shooting," Chang replied.

"My Marine experience showing," Jim said. "But now that you're here, maybe the two of you can develop an alternate theory. I'll be more than happy to butt out, if that's what you want."

Chang was smiling again. "You said he was smart, Agent Branner. But actually," he said, turning to Jim, "I'd like you to stay connected, if you can. I should say *we'd* like you to stay connected. My boss's bottom line is that a midshipman's dead; go find out what happened."

"That's pretty straightforward," Jim said.

"And having you involved on an informal basis has one other advantage, Mr. Hall. Can I assume you are back-briefing the commandant on what NCIS is doing?"

Jim colored. They'd known all along? Branner was studying the edge of the table, not looking at him. "Yes, of course," he admitted. "We have to protect the NCIS investigation from any charges of command influence, which is probably why he chose me."

"Exactly," Chang said. "Thanks for not bullshitting me. And that suits us, too. We have to strike a balance here. We'll focus on finding out what happened to Brian Dell. The Academy will focus on mitigating any damage to the institution, the system, as everyone seems to call it, from what comes out of our investigation. Tell me, you find this investigation interesting, Mr. Hall?"

Jim was somewhat thrown off balance by Chang's quick shifts in directions. "I do," he replied.

"Okay. Here's our deal: You stay involved. According to Agent Branner here, you've been very helpful, in terms of insight into the midshipman culture. You can tell your bosses whatever you want to about what we're doing. We ask for only one thing: If you sense that *they* are going to get in the way of finding out the truth of what happened here, you give us warning."

Jim sat back in his chair. Mr. Harry Chang was being extraordinarily straight with him. And this was what Liz had been talking about, too. But where did his own loyalties lie? Branner's request for his help had made it possible for him to do what the dant had asked him to do, and he'd pocketed the advantage. He could still do that. As to their one condition—he would not want to be part of anything that smacked of cover-up or a railroading. He'd had enough of that crap in the Corps. It had cost him any chance at a career. But then he remembered what else Liz DeWinter had said.

"Okay," he said. "With the proviso that if *I* think I'm being used by NCIS, I back out and we part as friends."

" 'Used by NCIS'?" Chang asked. "How?"

"Let's say, NCIS headquarters and the superintendent strike some kind of deal to produce the required right answer, with me being inside the investigation so that later I could corroborate that it all looked like the real deal to me."

"Wow," Chang said. "You overestimate NCIS headquarters. Nobody up there is that clever."

"There are some folks down here who are," Jim said, thinking of the dant, although he actually didn't think Admiral McDonald would play a game like that.

"Fine," Chang said. "That's okay by us. We could always flood the problem with a special team brought in from a larger NCIS office, but that would hurt Agent Branner's feelings. And none of us wants to be on her shit list." He was smiling as he said it, but the expression on Branner's face was not one of amusement.

"Back to your theory of the case," Branner said. "Have you thought of a way to explore that?"

"Possibly," Jim said. "During the interview with Markham, I got the impression she's hiding something. Not something she did, but something she knows. I've also spoken with her lawyer, who came to see me last night, by the way."

"She *did*?" Branner looked truly surprised.

"Yeah, I meant to tell you. She'd learned that I was there again for the Markham interview. She just dropped by at the marina to ask why. I tried to do a little soft-shoe routine, but she brought up the business of command influence."

Chang frowned and glanced over at Branner. "How'd you answer that?" she asked.

"I told her I was there to interpret midshipmanspeak for Agent Branner here. She seemed to buy that. Anyway, I asked her if she thought her client was telling her the whole truth and nothing but. She gave me the impression that the answer was no."

"Is Markham being deceptive, or just a mid dealing with a civilian?" Branner asked.

"Well, there you go," Jim said. "I guess that's what I'm here for—to make that interpretation. As someone who's lived through the Bancroft Hall experience, *I* think she was acting out of character for a midshipman the other afternoon."

"And what's that got to do with your theory?" Chang asked.

"Let's say Dell's death was not an accident. I have to ask myself, What could Markham have done that would make another mid kill Brian Dell and then try to pin it on her?"

"She's a good-looking young woman," Branner said. "She turned somebody down?"

"The boy-girl thing down here that intense?" Chang asked. "I mean, would a normal guy go to these lengths to get back at someone for that?"

"I'm thinking this isn't a normal guy," Jim said. He could see from Chang's expression that he seemed to be having trouble with this logic. And Jim suddenly had the feeling he was missing something crucial, as well. "I know," he said. "This is a reach. It's entirely out of character for the Naval Academy and the kind of people who want to come here. But I've met Markham a couple times now, and I simply can't feature her throwing Brian Dell off the roof, if that indeed is what happened."

"Well, that's something you could help us with, Harry," Branner said. "Get the forensics people to sharpen up the focus of their report. One way or another. I think we're both struggling with the concept of murder at the Naval Academy."

"And even more so with the idea that somebody did this to Dell simply to destroy Markham," Jim said. "I could just be all wrong, you know."

"I sure as hell hope so, Mr. Hall," Chang said. "But from what Agent Branner here tells me of the clothes evidence, it does seem a little too pat for my tastes. Could a psychopath get into the Academy? And if he got in, wouldn't they catch him?"

"We've talked about this," Jim said. "If he got through the admissions process, he'd have to lead a totally double life. Look like one thing but think and do shit totally out of character for a midshipman." Then it hit him: a double life—like running the tunnels at night, dressing up like a vampire, hanging out with the Goth crowd, and beating the shit out of drunks out in town. And almost beating an NCIS agent to death. The thought struck him like a bucket of water in the face. Branner saw it.

"What?" she asked.

Jim hesitated. If he told Chang what he'd just thought of, NCIS would absolutely bring an army down, if only because of Bagger. And he, Jim Hall, would then be the proximate cause of doubling the scandal already whirling around the Dell matter. No way, José. He decided to run it by Branner, but only after Chang left.

"No," he said, shaking his head, "I had a thought, but it's too outlandish. But I did have an idea of how we might test my theory. I think we need to invoke the Academy's honor system. The part about knowledge, as opposed to conduct."

"Meaning what, specifically?"

"If someone is caught lying, cheating, or stealing, he or she is down for an honor offense. Punishment can range from dismissal to lots and lots of demerits. But let's suppose a mid goes back to his room and finds his roommate looking at a copy of tomorrow's final math exam, which someone else has filched and put on the intranet. He goes, 'What the hell?' The roomie says, 'Hey, dude, you don't want a look at this? Go get a Coke somewhere. I'm failing math and I need this Gouge.' By the code, that mid is expected to go down to the batt office and drop a dime to the math department. They immediately ask, 'How do you know the exam's loose?' The mid says, 'I saw my roommate going through it on his PC.' The roommate goes down in flames, and an investigation is launched to see who else got a look."

"And what happens to the first guy?" Chang asked.

"Well, there you are. He played by the rules. The guilty roomie, however, is probably gonna tell everyone else who goes down that it was *his* roommate who dropped the dime. He's managed to bilge a hundred of his classmates, and chances are he will experience what the Brits used to call 'Coventry.'"

"He'll be ostracized."

"Yeah, I think so. Or maybe worse. But the thing is, that's an example of *knowledge* of a potential honor offense. You swear not to lie, cheat, or steal. That mid's got a tough decision to make."

"So what would really happen?" Branner asked.

"That really happens," Jim said. "Or at least it did once. But the other way is for the mid to make an anonymous phone call or send an E-mail to the math department, letting them know the exam has been blown. That way, the opportunity to cheat is excised, and supposedly no one will get directly burned."

"'Supposedly'?" Chang asked.

Jim smiled. "Yeah, well, that's where the system would come into play, depending on the commandant. If the math department can corroborate that, yes, the exam was compromised, and, yes, it looks like a copy got out on the Brigade intranet, the administration would then turn around and announce at noon meal formation that anyone who saw the exam is to take one step forward. Now you have a real honor system dilemma. It's clear that somebody must have seen the exam, because of the anonymous phone call. But they've now put the mids who did see the exam in danger of two honor offenses: one for looking at the exam, one for not reporting that it had been compromised."

"What happens if nobody steps forward?"

"I think they'd ask each one individually: 'Did you see a copy of the math exam on the intranet last night?' If he says no, and they can later prove that, yes, he or someone using his PC did access that file, he's expelled for three honor offenses: looking at a compromised exam, not reporting the situation, lying when they asked the question. If he answers, yes, he did, he may or may not get expelled—probably not, since he didn't add a third honor offense to the first two."

"Consequences," Branner murmured.

"You play with the honor system, you play with fire," Jim said. "And that's true right up to graduation eve."

Chang raised a finger. "Are you saying that if they don't ask in the first place, he doesn't have to tell?"

"I'm saying that if they don't ask, he's not *likely* to tell. He was always *required* to tell."

"Damn. That's a lot for a twenty-year-old to handle, what with his entire Academy career riding on the answer."

"Sure as shit is, which brings me back to Markham: She's a senior, homing in on graduation and her new career. If no one asks, I think it's likely she is not going to tell. I'm new at this investigation business, but I think we need to find something to ask about, something that presents her with a clear honor situation. If she's the straight-arrow type everyone says she is, that might break this thing open."

"And if you're wrong?" Chang asked.

"Then I'm wrong," Jim said. "Been there a couple of times, too."

"Haven't we all," murmured Harry Chang.

The phone rang in Branner's office. She got up to go take the call, striding out of the room at her customary thirty knots. Chang got up to get them some coffee. They could hear Branner raising hell with someone.

"She's a pistol," Jim said.

"On full auto, most of the time," Chang said. "But she's pretty good at what she does. That's why she's in charge down here."

"I have to ask," Jim said, but Chang waved him off.

"I don't know," he said. "We all call her Special Agent. Safer that way, from what I gather."

Jim laughed. Branner had the entire NCIS wondering what the hell her first name was? "How's Bagger Thompson doing?" he asked. Branner was shouting now.

"Fair, just fair. They say he'll pull out of it, but you never know with head injuries. The head doc says it's unknowable. Let me ask you one."

"Shoot."

"Back there when you looked like you saw a ghost. What was that all about?"

Jim gazed into Chang's black eyes, which suddenly seemed implacable. "Let me kick it around with Branner," he said. "If she thinks you ought to hear it, I'll leave it up to her."

The older agent continued to look at Jim, who got the sudden impression that Mr. Harry Chang would be one tough bastard on the other side of an interview table. Then Chang smiled.

"Mr. Hall, haven't you wondered why there hasn't been a horde of agents down here after the Bagger thing?"

"Yes, I have."

"And Branner has told you, 'This is my turf, and I don't want any damn horde. I want this prick all to myself.' Right?"

"Right."

"Well, there are two possible answers to your question, especially when we're talking about a prickly pear like Branner. One is that Branner's a really clever lady, and we're all asleep at the switch up in the Navy Yard."

"Possible, but now that you put it that way, not likely."

"Not likely, Mr. Hall. No. So what's the other possibility?"

Jim hesitated, although he thought he knew the answer. "Rope," he said.

"Yes, Mr. Hall. Rope. Let Branner run with this hairball. Give her lots and lots of rope. That way—"

"Okay, I understand," Jim said. "Palace games. But you didn't see what I saw—the day Brian Dell fell out of the sky. In my book, that trivializes any palace games."

Chang just stared at him. Then Branner came back. She dropped into her chair with a small bang. "Piece of shit maintenance pool," she growled. Chang flashed a warning glance at Jim and stood up. "I'm going back to the Navy Yard," he said. "For now, I'm your point of contact on this matter, Agent Branner. I don't have to tell you that time is of the essence."

"I think we already know that," she said briskly. "And you're going to put a boot up the forensic lab's ass for me, right?"

"Not in so many words, but yes," said Harry Chang with a wry grin. He looked over at Jim, and the smile lost some of its warmth.

Branner plopped down at the conference table after escorting Harry Chang out to the front door. "I heard Harry say you saw a ghost. I caught it, too. Give."

"We were talking about the possibility of a psychopath getting through the admissions filter. How he'd have to live a double life."

"Yeah, and?"

"By day, he'd be Mr. Clean. Maybe super–gung ho. Hard-core, full bore. But by night, maybe he'd run the tunnels, do graffiti, go out in town, consort with the most anti–establishment crowd out there, those Goth freaks, and maybe, in his spare time—"

"Beat the shit out of drunks. And Bagger. *Motherfuck!* You think?"

"If our runner is a mid, then yes, it just might be."

"Which would mean your theory of the Dell case goes from being off-the-wall to on the mark."

"Not like I have any evidence, though," he said, getting up to dump his coffee cup. His nerves were starting to jangle. He raised his eyebrows at Branner, but she shook her head. "I mean, all I know about this guy is that he's game." Then he told her about the tennis ball.

"You figure he knows who you are?"

"I figure he knows I'm someone in authority here at Canoe U. Specifically, no, not unless he figured out my cryptogram, Hall-Man-Chu."

The phone rang back in Branner's office again. She got up to get it, and Jim went to the whiteboard to lay out a list of what they did know about the runner. He was halfway through it when Branner came back in and punched a button on the speakerphone.

"Detective, I've got you on a speaker," she said. "With me is Mr. Jim Hall, security officer here at the Academy. Mr. Hall, this is Detective Sorensen, who's got some news. Go ahead, Detective."

"Right," Sorensen said. "As I was telling Agent Branner, we've got a missing persons report in from the college. One Hermione Natter. Remember her?"

"Yes," Jim said. "The Goth girl we picked up in the tunnels."

"That's the one. You guys didn't file any immediate charges, so we ROR'ed her. Well, now her faculty adviser is back to us, asking if we picked her up again, because she missed all her classes yesterday and her morning ones today."

"Kids skip all the time," Branner said.

"Yeah, but this adviser—name's Evelyn Wallace—had our Hermione on a short tether since we picked her up. Supposed to report in at the end of each day kinda thing, plus no more all-night flights with the rest of the coven. Well, she didn't show. Adviser asked around, found out she'd gone AWOL."

"She go home?" Jim asked.

"Pulled that string. Parents didn't have a clue. In fact, didn't know she'd been in trouble with the cops. Did know she was doing the Goth scene."

"But they hadn't heard from her."

"That's a negative. Now they're all spun up. I told them to call Professor Wallace. She called back here, saying Hermione's roommate hasn't seen her for *three* days. The college cops are involved now, so we're gonna have us a situation here, I think."

"Is the roommate into the Goth scene, too?" Jim asked.

"Don't know. Professor Wallace simply gave me the facts. Said the parents are coming down to Annapolis from D.C. this afternoon. They're both civil servants, apparently."

"Well, we don't have her and haven't seen her," Branner said. "Are you gonna work it?"

"Unless I can find someone else to, yeah, I'll work it. They'll want to talk to you guys."

"We're available. And she's just flat gone, huh?"

"Well, with that Goth crap, who knows? You know how they get, all into doom, death, despair, vampires and shit. Maybe she flew off to Transylvania for some OJT."

Jim and Branner smiled. Then Jim remembered he hadn't told the dant about catching the girl in the tunnel. "When you come to the Academy, come through me if you can," Jim said. "I need to go up my tape so nobody gets surprised."

"Better go now, then," Sorensen said. "The only reason we saw her was because of you guys."

"Will do," Jim said, and gave the detective his office phone number. Sorensen thanked him and hung up.

"I've gotta get over to the admin building," Jim said. "I told the Ops boss about the runner, but he didn't want to go up the line with it because of the Dell incident. I don't need the dant getting blindsided."

"Okay, you do that. Then let's meet and get going on Markham. I'm assuming this Natter bullshit won't knock Dell off the top of the dant's priority list."

"How about this other problem, the runner? I'd planned

to go back down tonight to see if he got my message, but he made it clear he already had. So now I'm gonna set up some backup with my guys and go after him tomorrow night."

She thought about that. "If he's tied into this Dell business, maybe sooner would be better. Get him, we might not need Markham."

Jim shook his head. "My theory's interesting, but hardly solid. We need Markham. I still think she's the key to what happened to Brian Dell. I'll call you from my office."

Jim found the operations officer having an early lunch at his desk, the *Washington Post* spread out under his sandwich.

"Only time I ever get to read the damn paper," he said. "What's up?"

Jim told him about the developments with the missing girl, and that someone would be coming to see the Academy authorities soon.

"Oh, great," Michaels groaned. "Just what we need—more bereft parents."

"I need to back-brief the dant on where we are with the Dell case. I can bring him up to speed on this stuff, too."

"He's gonna ask why he didn't hear about it before—the runner bit, I mean. And that's my fault."

"Actually, he did, at one of the first Dell meetings. Picking up the girl will be news. I did that. He won't have time for getting pissed off."

"He probably won't have time to see you, either," Michaels said, pulling out the executive calendar sheet. "He's got a dry run for the Board of Visitors briefing. He'll be with the academics all day today. That'll put him in a great mood."

"I'll check with his admin guy; the dant said to come see him when I had news and that he'd work me in."

"Take your flak vest, matey," Michaels said. "And if there's any shit over my not bringing the runner problem up the line, I'll go fall on my sword later this afternoon."

Jim grinned. Commander Michaels was in his swan-song

tour, with retirement coming in less than a year. He definitely did not sweat the career load. Jim called the dant's assistant but struck out. Everyone was with the dant over in the Mahan Hall auditorium. Jim asked the secretary where the commandant would be for lunch.

"With the supe in quarters," she told him. "He'll swing back through here for five minutes at around thirteen-fifteen. And no, you can't see him then."

"Tell you what," he said. "Tell him I need two minutes on the Dell matter. I'll be waiting in the rotunda."

"I'll tell him, Mr. Hall," she said. "But with his sked today, you've got those famous two chances."

She was wrong. Jim was summoned a few minutes later. The dant was standing behind his desk skimming through a stack of staffing folders. His assistant stood at his side, making notes. Three lines were blinking on hold on the console phone. Jim stood in front of the commandant's desk for three minutes before the dant finally looked up.

"Report," he said.

Jim had done some thinking about what to say in the allotted 120 seconds. The dant would not be interested in theories. He wanted to know where NCIS was with the case.

"Sir, they're pursuing a homicide investigation," he began. The dant put down the folder he had been reading and stared at him over the top of his reading glasses.

"Ruling out or ruling in?"

"In my opinion, ruling in." He told the dant about meeting Harry Chang and that they were going to pull a board together to review the forensics package. "And there's a possible link to another problem I've been working, sir. The tunnel runner."

The commandant decided to sit down in his chair. "Tell Mary to tell the dean I'll be delayed ten minutes," he said to the assistant, who left the room. Jim then reviewed what had been going on with the runner, including the news that more parents were inbound.

"There's a possibility that this guy was responsible for

beating up that NCIS agent, Thompson, last week, plus some other incidents in town. Assuming he's a mid, we've got a really bad apple loose in the Brigade. If that's all true, and I know there's a lot of assuming going on, I believe he might be connected to the Dell case."

"You have evidence of any of this?"

"No, sir. Nothing direct. But Special Agent Branner thinks it might be possible. I'm setting up a full court press to catch this guy, and then we'll see if there's a link to the Dell case."

"I'm not sure I understand," Robbins said, frowning. "What link?"

"Sir, given the time press right now, it would take too long to explain that. I'm inside the NCIS investigation, and they're comfortable with that, including that Harry Chang guy."

"Hang on a minute," Robbins said, and hit the intercom button. When his admin assistant responded, he said, "Pren, the subject is NCIS. Find out who Harry Chang is. He's at their HQ."

"Aye, aye, sir," the assistant answered. The commandant turned back to Jim.

"These are our problems, Mr. Hall," he said. "A dead midshipman. The Board of Visitors. The press. Dell's parents. Commissioning week. The vice president. We need the Dell matter *resolved,* not expanded. Understood?"

"Yes, sir."

"And if there's any doubt or ambiguity about this being a homicide, we need a determination that it *wasn't* a homicide, and we need that in public, and now would be really nice. I'm not pleased at all to hear about ruling in rather than ruling out. You sure this isn't some kind of ego trip with that Branner woman?"

Jim hesitated. Branner's ego was obviously formidable. And she'd wanted no outside help with the Dell case. And the same thing with the runner—if this runner was the one who got Bagger, his ass was hers. But then, Chang had hinted that maybe Branner was being set up for a fall, for being too independent. "I guess that's possible, sir," he began. "But—"

"No *buts,* Mr. Hall," Robbins said. "I'm ready to weigh in at the highest levels in NCIS or above if that's what it takes. It is preposterous, in my opinion, to think that Dell was murdered. No one has turned up any mortal enemies, and my sources tell me he was surviving, if not exactly prospering, as a plebe. His parents avow that he was not overly depressed, and definitely not suicidal. I think he fell off the damn roof by accident, and unless there is direct and palpable evidence to the contrary, that's the ruling I'm looking for. And, like I said, today would be nice. Right now would be nice."

"Sir?" came the assistant's voice on the intercom.

"Go."

"Mr. Harry Chang is the number-three guy at NCIS. He's an SES, directs all their criminal investigations. Big kahuna."

"Thank you," Robbins said, and turned back to Jim. "Was this how he was introduced to you, Jim?"

"Not exactly, sir," Jim said, flushing a little. "Branner said he was in charge of homicide investigations." Mentally, he swore. Had Branner and Chang been screwing around with him at that little meeting?

"Isn't that interesting," Robbins said. "Okay, I'm out of time. Keep going, but brief me daily, starting tomorrow. Go tell the deputy dant everything you know about your tunnel runner and the arrest of that civilian girl, but, for the moment at least, leave out any tie-in with the Dell case. Go do that now. He'll handle any further inquiries on that problem. That's all."

Jim nodded. As he left the room, he overheard Robbins telling the assistant to get the deputy commandant on the line ASAP. He assumed there was going to be some political precalibration. He'd wait ten minutes before going next door to see him. In the meantime, he needed to talk to Branner.

•   •   •

It was three o'clock by the time Jim had finished briefing the deputy commandant on the tunnel runner situation. He had called the chief in so that he could bring him up to speed at the same time. About the time Jim was finishing up, the deputy's secretary had announced that a Detective Sorensen of the Annapolis Police Department was on the line and wanted to speak to him about a missing college girl. Rogers had waved Jim and the chief out of the office with a grim smile. Both were glad to escape with at least part of their afternoon still intact.

The chief gave Jim a ride back over to the admin building as the Yard filled with midshipmen returning from afternoon classes. He parked on the Maryland Avenue side of the building, pulling into the superintendent's official slot, but kept the engine running. "You keep this up, you're gonna have to go get a job as a detective," he said. "I haven't seen you so involved with your job since you got here."

Jim gave him a sideways look, and the chief put up his hands. "No offense, boss," he said. "It's just that us old-timer Yard cops have always kinda wondered what, um—"

"Don't start, Chief," Jim said testily. "Talk to me about backup and a plan of action for catching this little fuck."

Bustamente nodded earnestly. "Right, boss. So, I think tonight would be too soon. I need to get a gander at those maps of yours and talk to my sergeants. We have to coordinate some overtime, figure out where we need to put people, and how to do it without attracting attention. From what you say, this guy's got pretty good antennae."

Jim agreed. Tonight would be too soon to set up a coordinated operation. And it was only Tuesday. Wednesday night would be a much more probable window for the runner to make an excursion, because there was no town liberty on Wednesday night. "Come inside and I'll get you those maps. I also want a PWC boss to know about it, but not everybody in PWC. This guy's managed to get keys; he may have penetrated their internal control system, too."

Jim met with Branner at 4:30 back in the NCIS office. Her phone rang just as they were getting coffee, so she had to go take care of that first. As he sat at the conference table, he tried to work out what, if anything, to say about the commandant's earlier comments. Probably nothing at all. Harry Chang might have been all about putting Jim at ease, while at the same time sending notice to the Academy that there was adult supervision being brought to bear on the local NCIS office. And yet, Branner hadn't seemed to have been overly deferential or even worried about Chang's senior rank. But then, we're talking about Branner, aren't we? he thought. A woman who would never win the Miss Deferential contest.

The second issue was the Dell case and Midshipman Julie Markham. He thought he had that worked out. He was about to go get some coffee, when a pale Agent Branner came back into the conference room. The expression on her face made him forget what he'd been thinking about.

"What?" he said.

She sank slowly into the chair at the head of the table. "Bagger Thompson. He died an hour ago. Stroked out. Blood clot got him."

"Oh shit," Jim said. "I'm truly sorry."

Branner nodded numbly, staring down at the table. She seemed to shrink into herself, and for a moment, Jim wanted to get up and go to her. But he kept his seat, knowing fury would follow her shock at losing Thompson. And of course it had been Jim who'd taken Thompson out into town and introduced him to the black Irish beer.

"Don't blame yourself," she said, as if reading his mind. "Bagger always drank too much. And when he did, all his inhibitions and most of his training went right out the window. He liked to fight, too. You'd never know it, behind that mild-mannered office face. But he came up from a tough neighborhood. Positively loved to rumble."

"What happens now?"

"That was my divisional supervisor at the Navy Yard. They're convening a board to decide what to do next. They have my report from when it happened. My guess is that they'll get with the Annapolis cops and start a circus."

"I met with my chief this afternoon. He's setting up for tomorrow night, when we're gonna try to nail this guy."

"I *will* be there," she said, still not looking at him.

"Goes without saying," he replied immediately, although he hadn't planned that she would be along. But now . . .

"This business with the missing Goth girl. I got Harry Chang on his cell phone, gave him the background on that. He's wondering if she might have been 'disappeared' by this guy, whoever the hell he is. Because *she* knows who he is."

"Whew," Jim said. "But how would he know that we arrested her? Or what she might have said to us?"

"She told him? And then said she hadn't given him up to the cops?"

"And he—what? Assumed she had? And then did something to her? I don't know, Branner—that's stretching it a little bit."

"Not if he's the guy behind what happened to Brian Dell."

Hoo boy, Jim thought. That theory was my contribution, wasn't it? "Maybe we're getting a little ahead of ourselves here," he said. "If we've got some guy, mid or civilian, who's responsible for people dying, maybe it's Bureau time. This shit's getting out of hand."

"Not necessarily," she said. "I'd get laughed out of court with all these theories based on the evidence we *don't* have. Look, we, or you, know those tunnels better than anyone right now. Let's take a shot. If he gets by us again, then I'll declare defeat and get the bosses to initiate a monster mash."

"The dant will need to know about Bagger."

"Certainly. And I'm going to have to go up to D.C. this evening. Probably stay the night. I'll brief my boss on what we're gonna try tomorrow night. You'll have manpower?"

"I'll have to get the overtime authorized, but, yeah, I'll have every cop we own on it. Especially when the word gets out that this guy may have taken Bagger down."

"Okay, then. Back to Dell."

"Right. Dell. And Markham."

"You said you had a plan," she said. Her face was tightening with the anger he'd been expecting.

"I said I had an idea. Right now, we think Markham is holding back. She's been able to answer no to every question, which, if she's playing the honor game, means we haven't asked the right question."

"How do we beat that?"

"We get them to convene the Brigade Honor Committee. Bring Markham before the committee. Tell her that we are pursuing the Dell investigation as something other than an accident or suicide. And then ask her, in front of them, if there's anyone who might want *her* harmed, who might also have harmed Dell. Remind her that failure to tell the truth now would be an expulsion-level honor offense."

"Suppose the answer really is no? Or she just lies? Says that no, there isn't."

"Then I'd ask her if she's ever been involved in the Goth scene, either in Annapolis or elsewhere."

"Again, no, or she lies. What have we accomplished?"

"If she's telling the truth, we've done no harm. If she's lying, then we've put her in the honor box. Either way, what we do then is request that the committee investigate the possibility that there's something behind the first question. They have to do it if requested."

"What's that get *us*?"

"It gets us behind the blue-and-gold wall. Midshipmen investigating midshipmen, with all the clout of the Honor Committee. Honor offenses are the third rail of conduct offenses. A mid might lie or quibble or evade when *we* come around asking questions, but no mid would lie to the committee."

"A liar's a liar. Why wouldn't a mid lie to the committee?"

"Because an honor offense is an offense against the entire

Brigade. They'll bend the rules behind the blue-and-gold wall to protect one of their own from what they see as unfair treatment: The little shit. Ten demerits and two hours marching offenses. But they'll expose an honor offender and push him, or her, right through the wall and into the system's claws."

"I'm not sure I understand this."

"It's because the system stands for something. Something that's good and clean and honest and fair. That's what the honor system is all about. It's what these kids signed up for when they came here, because it totally distinguishes them from the 'outside,' with all its equivocal don't ask/don't tell bullshit. The only way they justify the wall is by guaranteeing they'll draw the line at honor offenses. They'll play cops and robbers with the officer of the day, or the midshipman officer of the watch, about room inspections, unshined shoes, being two minutes late, after taps high jinks, illegal stereos, nonreg uniform gear, cars in the Yard, even booze in Bancroft Hall—all the game offenses. But not when it comes to honor offenses. And the system accepts that. The Executive Department plays the game with them, for four years. Both sides get pretty good at it. With that one proviso."

"If they draw the line at honor offenses, how about that example you cited—the guy coming in and seeing his roomie looking at a compromised exam?"

"The last time that happened, a hundred-odd mids went down the tubes. Exposed by their own roommates or classmates."

Branner thought about it. "There was something else you said, something about the mids always watching. That if they thought the system was playing fuck-fuck, then they would, too, right?"

And now I know why you are the head of this office, Jim thought. "You're exactly right. The one thing the administration could do to make them all go deep and rig for silent running is to compromise your investigation, say by declaring a desired right answer: This was an accident, or, worse, suicide."

"But isn't that what they want to do?"

"Don't know," Jim said, wincing inwardly at his own evasion. He knew that was certainly what the dant wanted to do. "But that's certainly a possibility. If this was indeed a homicide, some hoary cultural tectonic plates are going to tilt around here."

"So we need to move quickly, then, with this Honor Committee thing."

"Yeah. I'd suggest you contact the deputy commandant, Captain Rogers, and request that the committee be convened. Tell him what you think about the Dell thing, although I wouldn't emphasize the possible connection between our runner and the Dell case. Ask him to move on it immediately. Within twenty-four hours. Time is of the essence."

"Shit," she said. "Maybe you had the right idea—bring in the Feebs. They love hairballs like this."

"They'll push you right out of the room," he said. "And they'll never get behind the wall. *You* have a chance. To solve both incidents."

"And what about you?" she asked. "What do you get out of this?"

"I owe it to Bagger," he said. "And if some psychopath made it into this place, I want his ass found and burned, preferably before he gets to the fleet or the Corps."

She looked at him. "You believe in all this, don't you? This duty, honor, country stuff?"

"Yes. More of us do than don't."

"I wonder," she said. "Especially when I hear the dant wanting a 'right' answer. When the big dogs get their paws around a 'right answer,' it's often best for the little dogs just to go along."

"That what you expect me to do?" he said, a little anger in his voice.

"Don't get pissed off. It's just that if this thing recoils in our faces, you might get burned. I work for NCIS. You work for them. You could find yourself out of a job."

"Well, Special Agent," he said as evenly as he could, "you keep telling me it's a nothing job, right?"

She smiled and said, "Touché." Then she went to look up Rogers's phone number. Jim tried to figure out why he was mad. Was he just possibly looking for some payback of his own?

Jim checked in with the PWC before going down into the tunnel at 10:00 P.M. Tuesday evening. He'd previously briefed the chief that he was going to make another recon, and that he was still looking for a direct access between Bancroft Hall and the tunnel complex. The PWC people had been requested to call the chief if Jim didn't surface within two hours. He'd also asked the chief to alert the Yard police patrols that he was down there, and for them to be alert to any suspicious activities around the principal access gratings in the Yard until midnight.

He first checked the shark graffiti: No changes. The atmosphere in the main tunnels was normal, permeated with the scent of steam and ozone. Some of the burned-out lightbulbs had been replaced, so the light was more homogeneous than before. The door to the King George Street city utility vaults was locked. On the way back, he checked his motion detectors, but they did not appear to have been disturbed.

As he walked through the main tunnel, he realized that the guy might not ever come down here again, the little note on the tennis ball notwithstanding. Assuming it was a firstie who'd been doing this shit, he would have to know they were going to keep trying to catch him. Graduation and commissioning were only days away. Why put all that in jeopardy just to satisfy some macho pride? How about because the guy was a nutcase?

He came to the intersection of the Stribling Walk tunnel and the hinged flaps of the big storm drain leading down to the Severn River seawall. No sign of intrusion there, and besides, half the time the drain's mouth was underwater. No, this wasn't the way in. He had to find something that was physically under Bancroft Hall, something bigger than those electrical cableway lines. This guy had been tracking him when he threw the tennis ball. He had to have a direct way back into Bancroft in order to just disappear like that.

After verifying that he was in the vicinity of the Bancroft Hall foundations, he spent the next hour checking out every equipment cabinet, utility vault, steam pipe, and chilled water transfer plenum. Every one of them led into Bancroft somehow, but it was all via cableways, piping bundles, and wire conduits—nothing big enough to accommodate a human. Twice he passed the big oak doors leading down into the buried remains of Fort Severn. He touched the keys in his pocket, knowing he did not really want to revisit that crumbling brickwork anytime soon. He explored the branch tunnels that ran out to Lejeune Hall, the field house, and the city harbor utilities, but the farther he got from Bancroft, the less useful they would have been. He retraced his steps, ready to call it a night. As he passed the oak doors for the third time, he noticed that the gas-free engineering equipment was still there, piled in an alcove across the passageway from the big doors. He stopped.

He had never resolved the problem of the painted-over scratches. The PWC people had not done that. Only someone trying to conceal the fact that the door had been unlocked would do that. Ergo, someone had been using that old tunnel for something. Had to be.

He stood in front of the door and considered his options. For getting into Bancroft Hall, the right branch wasn't possible. It had to be the left-hand tunnel. He felt for the keys, tried one, then the other, and the big door on the left side swung inward slightly with a creaking noise. Half-expecting a vampire to leap out at him, he pushed the huge door all the way open. Light from the main tunnel spilled down the steps, but no farther. Beyond was the familiar darkened arched ceiling. He pulled his Maglite and shone it down the dusty passageway. No snowfall of mortar dust—yet. He checked his watch. He had about twenty-five minutes before he was supposed to call in. Time enough to walk down the magazine tunnel to the powder room and take another look.

He wondered if he should pull some of that air hose with him, but the Red Devils weren't set up. Besides, it would take too much time.

He stepped down into the alcove below the floor level of the main tunnel. Then he went back to the door to see if it could be unlocked from the inside. It could. He tried it, then adjusted the bolt, leaving it protruding to prevent the door from closing if some back draft occurred out in the tunnels. Then he set out for the magazine room. He walked quickly this time, although as softly as he could, not wanting to set up any significant vibrations. The skin on the back of his neck crawled with the anticipation of falling dust, but actually the mortar seemed to be undisturbed this time. He looked behind him as the arched frame of dim light back at the entrance diminished into a smaller and smaller block. Then the tunnel bent slightly to the left and the light bled away. The only light now came from his flashlight, and it seemed to magnify all the cracks in the mortar joints between the old bricks. Once again, he thought he could feel the massive granite weight of the buildings above bearing down on him.

When he reached the magazine anteroom, he saw the glint of railroad rails embedded in the stone floor. He hadn't noticed them before. He rubbed the dust off the rails with his foot and saw that they led under the heavy metal doors. Probably for ammunition wagons. The rails went on up the sloping passageway to the intersection with the gun pit tunnel. He shone the light around the entire anteroom but noticed nothing else of significance. He still couldn't see any clearly defined footprints in all the mortar dust, not even his own from earlier that day. He stood there, thinking. This area was certainly near the foundations of Bancroft Hall, if not under the eighth wing. But he had to be at least twenty, thirty feet down underground, so how the hell . . .

He went back to the doors and felt the cold steel with his bare hand. Cold steel. He glanced at the manometer again, then ran his hand up the door to about where the air-water interface should be inside. No discernible temperature difference. Wouldn't the water be colder than the air? Or, after all these years, would they simply be in equilibrium? He looked at the hinges, which were huge round pin-type fixtures, four per door. The doors must weigh a thousand pounds each, he thought. He thought he felt the air shift around him, and he listened carefully. He heard nothing, not even the subtle vibrations from street level that could be heard out in the main tunnels. He studied the hinges again in the harsh white light of the Maglite. The rivets holding them to the door were rusted. They probably had used dissimilar metals, not understanding the corrosive effects of galvanic cells.

He stared at the doors. He was missing something. He was sure of it, but for the life of him, he—Wait, he thought. There was a crack visible between the door frame and the door itself, especially next to the four hinges. Not much of one, but definitely a crack. He put the Maglite right up to the crack and tried to look through it. He couldn't see anything. He fished for his pocketknife, unfolded a flat blade, and poked it into the crack. It slid right in.

So where was the water?

He walked back over to the manometer and then figured it out. There were two isolation valves, one at the top and one at the bottom. He tried to turn first the top and then the bottom valve to the right. Righty-tighty, lefty-loosey, he said to himself. The valves didn't budge. That's because they're not open, he told himself. They're shut tight, Einstein.

The clever bastard. He'd closed the bottom isolation valve, filled the manometer with water, and then closed the top valve. Any passing inspector would see the full manometer, assume the space behind the door was flooded, and never open the doors. But of course it *wasn't* flooded. On the other hand, he'd better check.

He opened the bottom valve on the manometer, then the tube's drain valve. Then he cracked the top valve. The water quickly poured out into the dust, forming tiny glittering beads in the white lime carpet before disappearing. Then he fully opened the top isolation valve. If the space behind the doors had been flooded, there should have been an arterial stream shooting out of the bottom of the manometer. But there was nothing. Not a drop. The clever bastard.

He went to the center of the two doors. There were iron ring plates bolted to the doors, and he pulled on one. It didn't move. He pulled on the other. He thought he felt it move a fraction of an inch. He stooped down to check the bottom and found a vertical latch disappearing into the thick dust. He grabbed it with both hands, expecting it to be rusted shut. To his surprise, it lifted easily, almost too smoothly, and the huge door actually edged out toward him. He backed away from it, not wanting to catch a foot or hand underneath, but even the big rollers operated smoothly. The door was perfectly balanced, and it came open with hardly any effort at all. On greased hinges, no doubt, he thought. He pulled it all the way open and shone the light inside.

The powder room itself was about fifty feet square, with a smooth, twenty-foot-high domed ceiling that appeared to be made of concrete. No, he thought, it only looks like concrete. White cement had been parged over the brickwork of the roof, although imperfectly, as patches of brickwork shone through when he put the light on it. Heavy wooden racks lined the four walls, but they were all empty. In the two back corners of the ceiling, there were dark holes, about three feet square, which he figured had either been ventilation holes or pressure-release pipes in the event of a fire in the powder magazine. The hole on the left had a steel grating. The one on the right was open, and the steel grating was down in the dust on the floor, leaning up against one of the racks. What looked like the bottom of a wooden ladder protruded down out of the right-hand hole and rested on the top shelf of the closest rack.

Bingo, he thought. That hole leads up the surface. Or probably into the basement of Bancroft Hall. He couldn't be sure of where he was in relation to the surface. He felt another subtle change in the air pressure and stopped to listen again. He heard nothing, only the sound of his own pulse thumping in his ears. He walked over to the hole and shone the light up the ladder, but he could see only blackness above the top of the ladder.

He looked at his watch. Only ten minutes left. No time to climb the ladder, and he didn't particularly want to climb into yet another, smaller hole. He'd taken the maps of the Fort Severn tunnels home but then forgotten to bring them with him tonight—he'd had no intention of ever coming back down here. But the maps should tell him where this pressure-release pipe came out up on the surface. Now he had a decision to make: He could climb up there and pull the ladder down. Then somehow lock those steel doors from the outside. Or touch nothing and close the place up. Leave everything as it was. That way, if they secured the other possible routes into the tunnels from the Yard and then watched the oak doors, they'd have a better chance of catching their quarry. As long as he didn't see Jim's footprints in the dust, or notice that the manometer was now empty.

He decided to leave it as he'd found it. Turn the old Fort Severn tunnel into a trap. He backed out of the magazine and got the door shut and latched. Wait—the latch. It was outside the door. So how did the runner unlatch the door from the inside? He opened the door back up and checked behind it. Sure enough, there was a block magnet, probably lifted from a large stereo speaker, stuck to the door halfway up. Okay, that's how. He closed the magazine back up, then went over to the manometer. He closed all the valves and then used his penknife to tap the glass in the lower half of the tube until a small crack appeared. If the runner checked, this would explain the loss of the water. Then he took off his shirt and swept it over the floor of the anteroom, trying to obliterate his footprints in the mortar dust. A low cloud of dust coiled up from the floor like a fat white snake. He made a final check of the latches and then headed back up the tunnel to the intersection with the entrance to the collapsed gun pit tunnel.

Once at the intersection, he turned off his flashlight to see how far the anteroom light penetrated. It didn't. The darkness was absolute. The curve—you're forgetting that the tunnel curves, he told himself. He snapped the light on again; then, holding the tight white beam down at his feet, he walked toward the oak doors. His feet made no sound in the flourlike dust. When he figured he had rounded most of the curve, he turned the flashlight off again. To his surprise, the dim arch of light he'd been expecting to see as he neared the doors wasn't there anymore. Jim stopped dead. No light meant one of two things: Either the door he'd bolted open was now closed. Or the main tunnel lights had all gone out.

He flattened himself against the left-hand side of the tunnel and tried to think. He felt a tickle of mortar dust against the back of his neck. The bricks pressing against his right hip seemed to move a tiny bit. They felt like ceramic snake scales. He forced the image out of his mind.

He hadn't shone the flashlight down the tunnel. It had been pointed at his feet. It was still almost a hundred feet, maybe even more, to the anteroom below the oak doors. His footfalls were not audible. So if someone was waiting for him up there in the darkened anteroom, he shouldn't know that Jim was approaching. He tapped the Indiglo light on his watch. Three minutes until his call-in time. Hell, he could just wait right here and let the PWC crew come looking. Except they wouldn't know he'd come into the Fort Severn tunnels, would they? Shit.

He realized he'd had his eyes shut in the darkness. He opened them. No change. The total darkness of a cave. Or tomb. He listened but could hear nothing, either from the tunnel or the surface above. After a minute, he imagined that he could hear the fine sound of mortar dust falling on the floor. Like the sand in an hourglass. He bent down and lifted the Glock from his ankle holster. It wasn't chambered, and if he did chamber it, that noise would definitely carry down here. As he stood back up, his belt caught on the exposed corner of a brick and it moved. Definitely moved. And then it slid out of the wall with a small sound and thudded down into the deep dust by his ankle. Then another one came out, and suddenly he felt the whole wall press out against his back. He froze in place, straining his back muscles to hold the tottering masonry in place. He felt his heart beating wildly as he thought about the arch over his head. If the wall gave way, would the arch come down? Hell yes.

He flattened his shoulders and pressed against the wall as another brick slid between his legs and landed with a click against one of the first bricks. Then a third popped out of the wall and landed on his right shoulder, perching there for an instant before dropping into the dust. Then things stopped moving. He felt a sneeze coming on as the air filled with dust.

Gotta move, he thought frantically. Which way? Left, of course, up the tunnel, toward the oak door.

Sure about that? Or was the door to my right? I didn't turn around, did I? Another brick slid down the back of his pants leg and clicked against one already on the floor.

Hell with this shit, he thought. First, he racked the slide and chambered a round. The sound seemed enormous in the darkness. Unmistakable, too. Then he pumped himself off the wall, going to his left, and switched on the Maglite. Behind him, a whole section of the wall slumped to the floor in a muffled rattle of bricks. Amazingly, the ceiling didn't come raining down behind it. He switched the gun to his left hand and walked fast up toward the anteroom, holding the flashlight out in his right hand while keeping his body pressed to the left side of the tunnel, just in case someone started shooting. But when he reached the anteroom, it was empty. He made sure, even sweeping the light up over the ceiling to look for suspended vampires.

He shone the light back down the tunnel from which he had just come. It remained empty except for an ominous cloud of white dust that seemed to be approaching like some kind of billowing ghost. His heart in his throat, he pulled on the huge door. It swung gently back, spilling white light from the main tunnel back into the anteroom. He poked his head and the Glock out into the main tunnel, but everything was as he'd left it. A little more noise from all the utility lines, but the place was definitely empty. He looked behind him as the white cloud expanded silently into the anteroom. Glancing at his watch, he realized his time was up. He stepped up into the main tunnel, pulled the big oak door closed and locked it, then hurried up the tunnel to the first available grate where he could get topside and use a cell phone to call the PWC people. Assuming he could get his voice to work—his throat was dry as all that mortar dust. He shivered as he thought of that tunnel collapsing all along its length. And nobody would have known he'd been down in there.

He drove back to the marina after checking in with PWC. As he was getting out of his truck at the marina parking lot, a thought hit him like a small hammer. He had left the bolt protruding on that damned door to keep it open. But it had been completely shut when he got to it. So who the hell had moved the bolt? It would have taken a key to do that. If it had been their runner, then there would be no trapping him in the Fort Severn tunnel. Not now that Jim had been detected down there. He swore out loud, startling a couple getting into the car next to his. He gave them a weak smile and headed for the boat and a badly needed drink. He wondered if Branner was back from D.C. yet.

Branner called Jim on his cell phone an hour after he got back to the boat. She was back from Washington and just entering Annapolis. He invited her to come over to the boat for a nightcap, and she arrived fifteen minutes later. He poured two snifters of single malt and told her about what he'd found down in the abandoned tunnels. He showed her the probable exit point on one of the maps.

"I took a look, although it was dark. I'm guessing it's a light standard," he said. "One of these towers along here that light the tennis courts behind Bancroft Hall. Or a manhole. They probably hit the magazine vent pipe by accident when they put the lights in and just left it. Those standards are hollow."

"So he doesn't have to use one of the Yard grates?"

"Right. Nobody, not even PWC, goes into the old Fort Severn tunnels. They're lethal. They weren't very happy about my going down there."

"Where the hell did he get keys?"

"Those locks are old, very old. The doors are solid oak. I think those locks could be picked with a thin screwdriver. The point is, no one's been looking. The guys who maintain the utility tunnels couldn't imagine anyone being dumb enough to go into those death traps."

"You included?" she said, eyebrows rising.

"Trust me, having been down twice, I don't want to go back. But there's more." He told her about the bolt being moved after he had left it protruding.

"Shit. So you think he was down there? And knew you were down there?"

"Not the first time, either," Jim said. "The tennis ball came down the tunnel right when I was there to see it. He knows when someone else is in the tunnels after hours."

She sighed, sat back in her chair, and sipped some scotch. She looked really tired. "So, how'd your trip go?" he asked.

"Frustrating. There are two camps at headquarters. One wants to flood the mugger case with agents—ours, Feebs, marshals, whatever. NCIS doesn't lose agents."

"Except that he was on his own time, wasn't he? I'll bet there are people saying this wasn't an operational loss."

She nodded. "Yeah, that's right. And of course he has family, and, officially, the agency doesn't want to say that Bagger hit a bar, got drunk, followed some girls, and got whacked."

"So what *was* he doing—a follow-up to an ongoing investigation? Conducting a joint investigation with the Academy security officer, who was looking into unauthorized intruders into the Academy's underground utility areas?"

"Something like that," she said. "They were wondering if you'd go along with that."

"Absolutely," he said. "The bosses know the real score. No sense in dissing Bagger's good name. Anything on the Dell case?"

"Harry Chang's running some kind of game with that one, I think. Strong sense that SecNav's office wants the Dell case put to bed. As in, Lose the homicide angle."

"That would sell well here. But what about my theory— that the two cases are related?"

She finished her scotch and put the snifter down on a table. "I'm not sure. Harry's intrigued, but there's no real evidence. He told me after the main meeting that the only way he could hold off the 'send a mob' crowd is by saying that it might spook the runner."

"Who could, if he wanted to, just decide to stay in Bancroft Hall, run no more, and then graduate right on time and take his sick-ass, criminal mind out into the world of commissioned officers."

"The thing is," she said, "if this is the guy who did Bagger, we want him clean and prosecutable. Not mired in some complex web with the Dell case."

"Well hell," Jim said. "Then we need to move out. Stop talking about it."

She rubbed her face with her hand.

"You look beat to shit," he said, getting up. "Why don't you go home, get some rest, and then I'll come over to your office in the late morning? Then let's go see the deputy dant and stir up the Honor Committee bees. Or did you already do that?"

"I called Rogers. I declined to tell him what it was about, only that we needed to move out smartly. He said to bring it on."

"Okay, I'll snoop around the admin building first thing in the morning. Word of your call will have come through by then. I'll see what the walls are saying."

She agreed with that and they walked up on deck. The harbor was silently beautiful in the moonlight. The gray granite bulk of Bancroft Hall shone across the glimmering black water, although most of the room lights were out by now. "I don't know," she said, looking across at the Academy precincts. "I think I'm perfectly willing to let the Dell case fall out however the elephants want it to. This shit with Bagger, though . . . I want the sumbitch who did that."

Jim nodded. "I want him, too, especially if he's a mid. He's a fucking alien."

Better and better. I hear someone's going before the Honor Committee. Right before graduation, even. Anyone you know? My little web is beginning to close. Wonder who the BIO will be? Wouldn't it be rich if they use Tommy Hays? Man, but I love to screw around with the system, and it looks like the system is going to do exactly what I want it to do. There are consequences when people cross me. Especially when they were once my friends. Well, for a little while anyway. Can't say as I have any friends at this place, but then, I never expected to. All these shiny white faces, all with parents who have the same name as they do. I've often wondered what it must have been like, growing up in one of those perfect, made-for-television families. With each kid getting his or her own room. New clothes every year. A car. Being able to cruise the malls with people just like them.

The Shark, you see, never had any of that. In a sense, that's how he became the Shark. We are solitary beings. And let me tell you, the juvie system will damn well teach you what solitary means. Whether in Juvie Hall or in a foster home, you'd better be solitary. Otherwise, it's the gangs, with all their hip-hop secret sign bullshit, scabby women, and tribal boundaries, or maybe it's foster daddy creeping the back stairs at night, looking for what foster mama doesn't want to give him anymore. It's going to school, year after year, even the parochial school, knowing you don't belong there, because you're not like them, not like any of them. It's a solitary feeling, but I'm cool with it now, be-

cause it's the source of my strength. When you operate alone, when you hunt alone, when you crush your enemies all by yourself, no one can rob you of the victories. No one can betray you. Hell, most of the time, no one can even see you. Just like my classmates here at Canoe U don't see me. They don't want to. They know I'm different, and if it weren't for a few overachieving cells in the math and science part of my brain, they'd have had my ass out of here a long time ago. My own classmates!

Which is why I undertook to screw the system. To lie, cheat, and steal with vigor. To role-play by day and then consort with the other end of the human spectrum by night. Not just to run plebes but to terrorize plebes. To taste, whenever possible, the bounties of some of these lovely mids, and then to degrade them. I know what they really think of me, and I feed their preconceptions. Big, shaved-head, bruising Dyle, who shouldn't be here. Strong in body, no getting around that, but hardly the kind we'd want to see at the Officers Club cotillion. Book-smart in the techie world, but gets mysteriously good grades in the bull world, too. Looks like he couldn't even read. Going Marine option, we understand. Snigger. Snigger. That fits: What the hell does a Marine need with being able to read and write? Look at him: six-feet-plus tall, six feet across the shoulders, six feet through the chest, Man Mountain Dean in the flesh. Makes all that noise. Can march like a robot. Face like the Terminator. Shoes to blind the uniform inspector. Creases on his creases. A perfect rack in his room, but no roommate, we understand?

They can laugh, but what they don't know is going to hurt them. The whole class will be tarred with what I do in the next week. I expect to get away with it, but if I don't, well, hell, screw 'em all if they can't take a joke. My being here has been a joke, a bad one, I'll grant you, but that's what you get when you allow the Navy's premier penitentiary to indulge in a little social engineering. And I'm all set for those two featherweight cops who've been sneaking around my tunnels. They think they're going to trap me down there.

Well, there're traps, and then there're traps. Oh, am I waiting. I have the most interesting surprises set up for them. And maybe one or two for you, too. You just think it's over, don't you? Not hardly.

11

At 10:30 A.M. Wednesday, Ev was in his office editing a
PowerPoint presentation for an upcoming group lecture-hall
class. The secretary called in and said Captain Donovan
wanted to see him in his office.

"He say why?"

"Surely you jest."

Ev smiled and went downstairs to Donovan's office.
When he got there, he was surprised to find a small gathering of the faculty waiting for him. A Coast Guard commander was there, along with the commandant. Captain
Donovan deferred to Robbins.

"Professor Markham," the commandant said, "this is
Commander Bell, representing Admiral Johnson, commander of the local Coast Guard district. He has something
to present to you for your lifesaving efforts in the bay this
past weekend."

The commander stepped forward to read a citation for a
Coast Guard Silver Lifesaving Medal awarded to Professor
Everett Markham of the United States Naval Academy. Ev
was a little embarrassed when he listened to the citation; he
thought the woman he'd saved must have embellished the
circumstances somewhat. There was a round of enthusiastic
applause, and then Captain Donovan, ever the master of
short and sweet, invited everyone to get back to work. Ev

asked Commander Bell about the missing husband; the commander shook his head. "No real chance, based on what she told us. She said the mast was whipping around in the waves, whacked him pretty good."

"I remember that mast," Ev said. "Vividly. Still have a bruise."

"Well, it was still a very nice piece of work all around," the commandant said. "And apparently some smart seamanship on Ms. DeWinter's part."

Ev was surprised. And, he wondered, does the dant know that Liz is Julie's lawyer? As if in answer, the commandant, after a few more pleasantries with the Coast Guard commander, took Ev's elbow and steered him out of Donovan's office and into the marble-floored hallway.

"Amazing, isn't it?" he said. "The Navy would have taken six months to work up that medal. The Coasties do it in a day. Congratulations."

"Thank you, sir," Ev said, waiting for the other shoe.

"About the Dell matter," Robbins said. "We've still not made a determination as to what happened."

"My daughter continues to interest the NCIS," Ev said. "She's getting pretty upset about all this, so close to graduation."

"From what I know about their investigation, she is not the focal point," Robbins said.

"Let me ask you something. Why is the Academy security officer involved in an NCIS investigation?"

Robbins's eyebrows rose. "Mr. Hall? I wasn't aware that he was. Involved how?"

Ev told him about Hall being present at the interviews. The commandant frowned, and then he appeared to remember something. "Oh, yes," he said. "Jim did mention that. Agent Branner wanted him there to act as sort of an interpreter. Sometimes the midshipmen are a bit opaque in their dealings with civilians."

"Doesn't that sort of compromise the independence of their investigation?"

"Oh, I don't think so. Agent Branner doesn't take orders from me. Or anyone else, based on what I know of her. How's Ms. DeWinter?"

It was a clear challenge, and Ev met it head-on. "Lawyering as before," he said. He paused as two firsties walked by them in the hall. "And also wondering about Mr. Hall's involvement in the Dell investigation."

Robbins dropped all pretense of amicability. "If your daughter wants to graduate and be commissioned on the appointed day, I'd suggest she be a lot more cooperative. Lawyer or no lawyer."

Ev unconsciously crumpled the Coast Guard citation letter. He looked down into Robbins's face. "I'm tempted to give that comment the *Washington Post* test, Captain Robbins. You okay with that?"

"Don't fuck with us, Professor Markham," Robbins growled. "There's a lot of high-level interest out there in this Dell case. Your daughter is being less than helpful. That may have consequences."

"Such as?"

"Such as this: The rest of us are all still going to be here the day after graduation. She can be on her way as an ensign, or still be a midshipman. Her choice. Why don't you pass that on? To her, and to your good friend, her lawyer."

"If I thought she'd get a fair shake, I would. But I think you're looking for a scapegoat. I won't permit that."

Robbins began to bounce on the balls of his feet. "You are not in a position to permit or not permit. This is an Executive Department matter. We can't terminate you on academic grounds without a big stink. But we can terminate you for interference in a government investigation. Don't let that tenure label confuse you. *Professor.*"

Robbins stalked away toward the main doors. Ev was furious, but he held his tongue. He wasn't worried about himself, but he was definitely worried about what they could do to Julie. The Academy's supposedly benign objectivity was beginning to show its teeth. He headed for his office to call Liz.

• • •

At 10:30, Jim met with the chief in his office over at the naval station. Bustamente had his three section sergeants, plus a rep from the Marine gate guards detachment present. He laid out his plan to cover all of the access grates with covert surveillance teams, beginning after the evening meal in Bancroft Hall. The Marines were requested to check out all vehicles leaving the Yard to ensure there were no midshipmen on board. The chief had obtained a radio retransmitter set from the county cops that would get signals up out of the tunnels, giving the entire Yard team a way to establish a radio net with the personnel underground. He had also obtained permission from the city police and campus security to set up a surveillance team in the building on the St. John's campus overlooking the grating nearest to King George Street. A campus cop would be with them.

"The deal is, the campus cops will arrest anyone coming out of or trying to get into that grating. If it's a mid, they hand him over to us. If it's a civilian, we all go downtown to sort it out."

"This guy has already abandoned one civilian accomplice in the tunnels," Jim said. "He's probably capable of sending out another stalking horse to see if anything's up."

"Okay," the chief said. "Let's do this: If someone comes out of the grating, we follow and apprehend out of sight of the grating. If someone goes down into the system, we report it to the underground team, and you guys nail him when he comes through."

Jim agreed with that. "That way, he'll be on federal property. I like that better."

"Who's going to be underground, Cap?" the Marine sergeant asked. He'd been there when Jim had been the detachment CO.

"I will, with Special Agent Branner. Actually, she'll be in charge." He told them about what had happened to Bagger Thompson, and that they thought this guy might be the one who'd done that. The professional casualness bled out of the meeting. They went over communications and stationing procedures, talked a little bit about deadly force authorization, and then the meeting broke up.

Commander Michaels was rushed, as usual, so Jim briefed him as they walked down the hallway to a department head staff meeting. He told him that he and Branner were setting up a small task force to see if they could capture this runner who was tearing things up down in the utility tunnels. Michaels waved him off, not seeming to care much about that. The Dell case was reaching crisis proportions now that a congressman was asking very pointed questions and the local papers were editorializing about a cover-up. He told Jim that a senior civilian from NCIS, a Mr. Harry Chang, was meeting with the dant and the supe as they spoke.

"I've met him," Jim said. "At the NCIS office. What's he doing here?"

"The answer to that is way above my pay grade, but apparently there's a lot of stick and rudder coming down from Washington. As usual. Whatever you're doing tonight, keep it under the media radar if you can, okay?"

Jim said he'd try, and Michaels hurried into the conference room. Jim went back to his own cubicle and put a call in to the commandant's assistant, asking for five minutes on the dant's calendar, preferably before the dant went off to the luncheon being held for the winners of this year's Naval Institute Prize Essay contest. The assistant said he'd call him. Jim got some coffee, moved some paperwork from his in box to his out box for a few minutes, and thought about what he had put in motion for Julie Markham by getting Branner to call the Honor Committee. Only days before graduation. The summons would scare her to death. The phone rang. It was the dant's assistant.

"Five minutes. Now, please."

Jim trotted over to Bancroft, and then had to wait while

the commandant took a phone call. Finally, the assistant waved him into the inner office.

"What's this about an honor hearing on Midshipman Markham?" Captain Robbins asked without preamble.

And a hearty good morning to you, too, Jim thought. "We think—"

"Qualify that," the dant said. "Who's 'we'?"

"Special Agent Branner and I," Jim said, and then paused to see if Robbins had anything to say about that. But the dant just made a gesture for Jim to continue. The phone rang outside, and a light began to blink on the dant's telephone console.

"We both think Midshipman Markham knows more than she's telling about the Dell case."

"So I've heard. She lying to you?"

"No, sir, I just don't think we've asked the right question."

The commandant thought about that. "Blue-and-gold wall?" he asked.

"Possibly. My idea was to use the Honor Committee to get behind the wall. She might play games with us, but not with them if she thinks she's being set up to take an honor fall this close to graduation."

Robbins grunted. "Now you're starting to think like an executive officer, Mr. Hall," he said approvingly. "But do you think she's guilty of some involvement in what happened to Dell?"

"No, sir. I don't. Nor do we have any direct evidence that she's concealing something. It's just a hunch. Mostly on my part. In reality, if she stands pat, we're nowhere."

"You and NCIS might be nowhere, but I won't be," the dant said, and then waited to see if Jim understood.

"You mean," Jim said, "that if we don't get anywhere with this, then the Academy will make a ruling?"

"NCIS was told to develop *evidence* of a homicide—if they could. Doesn't seem like they can. Our position, therefore, is that it wasn't a homicide. We need to end this matter, Mr. Hall. We really do. I talked to the assistant director of NCIS today, that Mr. Chang. He seems to agree with our conclusions. By the way, he also told me that their junior agent here in the Annapolis office has died as a result of injuries sustained in that mugging? I didn't realize he'd been that seriously injured. Did you know about that?"

Shit, Jim thought. He'd forgotten to pass this news up the chain. "Yes, sir, I did. The incident was reported, I believe. You and I discussed it briefly."

"I don't recall that," Robbins said distractedly. "But then, there are a lot of issues flowing over my desk. Anyway, Mr. Chang says that you and agent Branner are working that case, as well. He said they think that you and Branner have a better chance of finding this guy than they would if they brought a horde of agents into it. True?"

"We're getting closer," Jim said. "The bad news is that I'm more than ever convinced that he's a midshipman. Probably a firstie. If we catch him—"

"If you catch him, we get to deal with more shit in the fan."

"Yes, sir. Especially if we can tie him to what happened to agent Thompson. Lots more shit in the fan."

"That's just great, Mr. Hall. Sometimes I wonder if we're accomplishing anything here at the Academy. But I hope you're wrong."

"Yes, sir. I hope I am." But I don't think so, he thought.

The commandant was standing, so Jim got up as well.

"Remember one thing about the honor system, Mr. Hall," the dant said. "We can put that machinery in motion, but it's the mids who will bring it to conclusion, and we almost always have to accept that conclusion. Your gambit here could end up destroying Markham."

"Even if she's totally innocent?"

"She's not cooperating. And no midshipman is ever totally innocent. You rate what you skate, right? You went through here, just like I did. You know that."

"Yes, sir, but—"

"Think of it like a tax audit, Mr. Hall. We can always find something."

"With respect, sir, we're not the IRS."

Robbins gave him a cold smile. "Do you know what you get when you put the words *the* and *IRS* together? *Theirs,* Mr. Hall. In that respect, we are very much alike. Keep me informed. That's all."

At 1:30 that afternoon, Jim and Branner went into the commandant's conference room in Bancroft Hall. They'd been waiting for half an hour in Captain Rogers's office while he signed the necessary paperwork to convene the Brigade Honor Committee.

While they waited, Jim had explained how the system was set up. Each company had four honor reps—two first class, two second class. Midshipmen interested in serving on the Brigade Honor Committee put themselves forward as candidates for selection. If the company officer approved, a vote was held. The top fifteen candidates from the thirty companies went through a further selection process to select ten for interviews in front of a board made up of officers, faculty, and midshipmen. Those ten were further whittled down, ultimately by the commandant and the superintendent, to a final seven. The seven positions on the Brigade board were chairman, vice chairman, education director, deputy in charge of investigations, secretary, academic liaison, and honor program coordinator. They would be meeting today with the chairman, investigations deputy, and secretary. Captain Rogers would sit in.

Branner was dressed more conservatively today. Severe pantsuit, black shoes, almost no makeup. Jim, used to her flashy style, thought she looked positively drab. She also still seemed to be preoccupied with something. She had a brown envelope in her lap, but she had not told him what was in it.

"You sure you want me to pitch this thing, and not you?" he asked.

"You know the lingo," she said. "We're agreed on the objective. I'll get into it at the appropriate time."

"The dant warned me this morning when I went in to

brief him. Said we stood the chance of really damaging Markham once we turn the Honor Committee loose."

"It was your idea—you want to back out?" she asked.

"I want to know what she knows," he said. "But she's so close to graduation—I hate to smear her reputation."

"If she knows something that bears on a possible homicide, she should have told us," Branner said, tapping her foot impatiently. She looked at her watch. "What's the damned holdup?"

"But if I'm wrong? And she really doesn't know anything?"

"Can't do this 'what if' shit, partner. Our job is to find out what happened to Brian Dell. Nobody else is speaking for him just now, because the little dude's dead. If this Honor Committee can't find anything, then we try something else or give it up for lack of evidence. The fact that the committee asks her some questions should not constitute a smear on her personal reputation. If it does, their system here is really screwed up."

Captain Rogers came out and motioned for them to come into the room. "Apologize for the delay—we needed to get Midshipman Markham's Academy service records."

The waiting midshipmen stood up. "The chairman is Midshipman First Class Magnuson. He has the authority to make decisions. The DCI—that's deputy chairman for investigations—is Midshipman First Class Hays. He will take investigative action, if action's warranted. The recording secretary is Midshipman Second Class Vannuys."

He pointed to chairs, and then everyone sat down. Jim started it off by saying that he was assisting Special Agent Branner of the NCIS in an investigation into the death of Midshipman Brian Dell.

"As I'm sure you all know, Midshipman Dell was killed in a fall from the rooftop of the eighth wing. In the course of the investigation, agent Branner determined that Midshipman Julie Markham might be tangentially involved in this matter."

"In what manner, sir?" one of the midshipmen asked.

"Is this conversation privileged?" Branner asked, directing her question at Rogers.

"Yes, it is," he replied. "What's said here stays here. The board secretary will write up summary minutes for the record, which the chairman will approve. But given the possible consequences to anyone who's being examined by this group, the board keeps it all close-hold."

"Okay, then," Jim continued. "Midshipman Dell was wearing women's underwear when he died. Specifically, underwear that belonged to Midshipman First Class Julie Markham."

The three midshipmen looked at one another but said nothing. Jim noticed that the DCI, Hays, didn't seem surprised. For some reason, the name Hays was sticking in Jim's mind.

"Naturally, the investigation focused on Markham in the context of whether or not she knew Dell, or had possibly even been intimate with him. She denied the latter, but she did state that she knew who Dell was, and that she had had dealings with him."

" 'Dealings'?" the chairman asked.

"In the course of his plebe summer," Jim said.

Magnuson nodded and made a note on his legal pad.

"There were two other connections, the varsity swim team, and the discovery of Dell's clothing in her room." He went on to describe that.

All three midshipmen took notes. He went on. "We are exploring the possibility that someone may have either influenced Dell to commit suicide or done something that resulted in Dell coming off that roof."

"You mean you think someone *killed* him?" asked Captain Rogers in a surprised voice.

Apparently, he had not heard the rumors, Jim thought, although the three midshipmen did not seem surprised by this information, either. "Yes, sir, that's a possibility. Because one of the things that's come out of the investigation is that no one who knew Midshipman Dell thought he was suicidal."

"Could it have been grab-ass up there on the roof?" the chairman asked.

"With a guy wearing panties?" said Vannuys, the recording secretary. This produced a faint smile on the chairman's face. Branner slapped the brown envelope down on the conference table, startling everybody. She slid it across to the chairman.

"Those are some pictures of Brian Dell," she said. "After he hit the concrete. Take a good look, Mr. Magnuson. See if you still think this is funny."

The chastened midshipman stared at the envelope and then at Captain Rogers, who nodded. Magnuson fished the pictures out, took one look, blanched, and passed them to his left. Hays looked at each one before passing them to Vannuys, who was visibly aghast at what he saw. The recording secretary got up and gave the pictures to Captain Rogers, who avoided looking at them, tidied them into a neat pile, and slid them back across the table to Branner.

"That's what we're here to talk about, gentlemen," she said. "In barracks terms, this is serious shit, in case you didn't notice. And that puddle of human flesh was not what Chief Petty Officer and Mrs. Dell expected from their son's Academy experience, okay?"

All three nodded, almost in unison.

"Here's our problem," she continued. "Based on interviews, it is our opinion that Midshipman Markham does know something about what happened to Dell. Either something that would explain why he'd jump or something that would point a finger at someone else who might have been involved. The cross-dressing means something. Grab-ass, homosexual activity, or even sadomasochistic behavior. We don't know. But we think Markham does."

"And you want us to do what, exactly, ma'am?" the chairman asked. Branner glanced sideways at Jim.

"Make the fact that she knows something but isn't telling an honor issue," Jim said. "Do what you guys do in such a manner as to find out what she knows."

"But it's not," the chairman said.

"Not what?"

"An honor issue. What she knows is not an honor issue. You're confusing us with West Point. Their code doesn't tolerate anyone who lies, cheats, or steals, or who has knowledge of those who do. Our code stops at the word *steals.*"

"Knowledge might constitute a *conduct* offense," Rogers said. "Knowing of an honor offense and not saying anything constitutes an offense against the Academy's regulations."

"But that's not an honor offense?" Jim asked.

"No, sir," said the chairman.

Jim, surprised, didn't know what to say. Branner leaned forward. "What if she said she knew nothing pertinent but she actually did?"

"That would be a lie. That could be an honor offense."

"Then once again, how about you finding out what she knows?"

"Did she tell you that she knows nothing about what happened to Dell?" asked Hays.

"Yes," Branner said. "So if you could find an indication that she knows something about this, other than what we've told you and shown you, then—"

"Agent Branner, ma'am," Midshipman Magnuson said, "with all due respect, I have no idea of how to do that, or if we even *should* do that."

He looked over at Captain Rogers as if for moral support, and the captain indicated he should go on. "Ma'am, the Honor Committee investigates *actions.* Someone tells a lie and gets caught out. Someone steals something. Someone is seen cheating on an exam—crib notes written on his forearm—again, actions. But we don't investigate anything until there's been an accusation made, and the matter's already been discussed between the accuser and accused. That's step one: Approach and discuss. I don't know how we would prove that she knows something about the Dell incident. DCI, you want to comment?"

"I do," said Hays. Of the three midshipmen, he was the largest. Jim figured him for a varsity athlete. Wide shoulders, big, rangy physique. That look of watchful aggression.

"Go ahead," Rogers said.

"Normally, I'd assign a BIO," Hays said. "That's one of our Brigade investigative officers. But given that," the DCI said, pointing at the pictures, "I think that I should talk to Midshipman Markham."

"How would you proceed?" Branner asked. "I mean, why should she talk to you?"

"Because of who I am on this board," Hays said. "And because of what I can do. I'm the DCI. I can call in everyone who knows her. Her roommates, past and present. The other members of the swim team. All the firsties in her company. The people in her academic classes. Her instructors. Her extracurricular activities officers. I'd tell 'em we're doing an honor investigation, and that I want to know what they know about Midshipman Markham."

"That's a lot of people," Jim said.

"That's the point, sir," the DCI said. "If there's anything weird about her four years here, one of those people will reveal that. And she'll know that. Everyone here has some bones in his locker."

Jim remembered the commandant saying basically the same thing. "And you think she'd tell you what you want to know?"

"I happen to know Julie Markham," the young man said. "Actually, we've dated. So ordinarily, I'd recuse myself. Someone else would have to do it. But seeing as we're this close to graduation, I'd feel comfortable getting the ball rolling. And because we have, um, history, I think I could find out something faster than anyone else."

Jim finally recognized the name. Tommy Hays, the ex-boyfriend. Branner leaned forward. "If she knows something about the Dell case, then you'll declare an honor offense?" she asked.

"No, ma'am. If she tells me something, I'll take that to the chairman here." The DCI looked over at the chairman, sending a silent message, Jim thought. "The first thing he'll do is to take it to you and Mr. Hall. Then it would be up to you to come before the Honor Committee and make an accusation that she lied to you. An action constituting an honor offense. *Then* we'd formally appoint a BIO, and handle it as an ordinary honor offense." He stopped for a moment. "Assuming that's what you really want," he added.

Jim sat back in his chair to consider what Hays was saying. If he understood the subtext, Hays was letting him know that if they let him do it his way, they might get what they needed without tagging Julie Markham with an honor offense.

"Deal," he said, looking sideways at Branner to confirm that she was going to go along. Branner nodded but said nothing. "But time is of the essence. You need to have that discussion today. This afternoon."

"No problem, sir," Hays said. He nodded at the recording secretary, who got up and left the room.

"Then we're done here?" Branner said.

"Yes, ma'am, I think so, unless you've got something else for us," Magnuson said. Jim sensed tension in the air, but he couldn't be sure. The perplexed look on Rogers's face made Jim think that Hays's offer might even have been rehearsed.

The meeting broke up, and they followed Captain Rogers out of the room. The midshipmen remained behind. Rogers said that the chairman would be in touch as soon as they had something, and that he would have to brief the commandant on what had transpired. Branner had no problems with that.

Once Rogers left, Branner looked at Jim. "What happened in there?" she asked.

Jim explained what he thought was going on.

"Okay, I'll buy that, unless, of course, she's an accessory."

"If she's an accessory to a homicide, she's got bigger problems than an honor offense. Those guys are pretty smooth, aren't they? Let's step outside."

They went through the waiting room to the executive corridor, and from there to the rotunda. To Jim's surprise, the

big midshipman, Hays, was already there, obviously waiting
for them.

"Yes?" Jim said as he approached them.

"Sir, I need to speak frankly?"

"Shoot."

"Like I said, I know Julie Markham, so I'm not exactly,
um, unbiased. I like her a hell of a lot is what I'm saying.
Most of her classmates do, too. But here's the thing: If what
she knows is because somebody else has something he's
holding over her, would you go after Julie or the somebody
else?"

Jim was tall, but he still had to look up to measure the
young giant's expression. Hays seemed sincere. Before he
could answer, Branner chimed in.

"We're not after Julie Markham, unless she threw Dell
off the roof, or stood by and watched, okay?"

"No fucking way," Hays said quietly. "Ma'am."

"You sure?"

"She's tougher than you might think," Hays said. He
frowned as he thought for a moment. "And she's deeper than
I thought. But she's no killer."

"Okay," Branner said evenly. "Then we're looking for
who did throw Dell off the roof. Assuming someone did.
Our target is not Markham, unless we see evidence—hard
evidence—that she did something to Dell."

The midshipman nodded, then exhaled. "Got it," he said.
"I've got to talk to some people. And exams start this week.
Makes it harder."

"Call this number," Branner said, handing him a card.
"And remember those pictures."

"Yes, ma'am. Serious shit. And ma'am?"

"What?"

"The officers are always saying not to confuse the Academy with the fleet, the real world? You shouldn't confuse
the mids with the officers, either, okay?"

Branner looked at Jim, who nodded. "Got it," he said.

"Yes indeed," Branner added.

Hays nodded, squared his shoulders, and walked away.

"And thank you," Branner called after him, her voice echoing in the rotunda. She turned to Jim. "That was interesting," she said. "So they do know something?"

"I think *he* does."

"Then why the hell hasn't he come forward before this?"

"Because they're so close to getting out of here. So close to achieving what they've all worked their asses off for these past one thousand four hundred and sixty days, and they do count them, every day. And up to now, they probably thought the investigation would find the answer."

"So what's changed?"

"Maybe now they're sensing a cover-up in the making?"

"Why would the firsties care?"

"Because Dell, even if he was only a plebe, was a mid. One of them. Remember what I told you about the rules of the game here. This is going to get very interesting."

By 3:30, Jim and the chief, accompanied by an elderly PWC engineer, were walking the ground behind the tennis courts, trying to match the tunnel maps with a possible location for the top end of the shaft that led down into the old ammunition storage room. Branner had gone back to her office to update her case file with her notes from their meeting with Captain Rogers and the midshipmen. Jim had scheduled a briefing for the entire tunnel surveillance team, including Branner, for 4:30 at the Academy police building over at the naval station.

"There's nothing that we're using that would go down that far," the PWC engineer said. "This whole area was recovered from the river forty years ago and filled in. That ammo bunker's gotta be thirty feet down."

"Well, there was a ladder going up, but I couldn't see how high, and I wasn't going to climb up in there by myself."

"Shit," the engineer said, looking at the diagrams. "I won't go down there at all. That old brickwork's like marzipan. One good vibration, the whole damn thing would come down."

"Well, there's nothing around here that looks like a ventilator shaft or storm drain or any other thing," the chief said. "I wonder if it connects underground to something that goes into Bancroft Hall."

They studied the diagrams. There were no utility tunnels or even lines anywhere near where they were standing. There were only the eighty-foot-high light towers, which illuminated the courts at night.

"Okay, I give up," Jim said. "That whole ammunition bunker complex should be beyond the eighth wing's foundations. If that shaft comes up, it has to be around here somewhere."

"Hold on a minute," the engineer said. "The eighth wing is built entirely on landfill. The original Bancroft had six wings, and a street between the end of the fifth and sixth wings and the seawall. I was here in 1956. The seventh and eighth wings weren't here, nor was the land they're built on."

"Which means this diagram's wrong," Jim said. "Fort Severn couldn't have been where this diagram shows it. It would have had to be back alongside the—what, sixth wing, right?"

The PWC engineer nodded. The chief was confused by the wing numbering. Jim explained that the wings were numbered second, fourth, sixth, and eighth on one side of Bancroft, and first, third, fifth, and seventh on the other side. "Like channel buoys used to be—right side were even numbers, left side were odd numbers. Naval tradition stuff."

"Okay, then, if Fort Severn was back here," he said, pointing on the map to the building right behind the eighth wing, "then that vent shaft would be coming up . . . very near the eighth wing. Not out here in the tennis courts. So we need to get into the basement of the eighth wing."

They folded up the maps and walked back toward the eighth wing. "I wonder how many other errors there are in these diagrams," Jim said.

"The diagrams of the active utility tunnels are correct," the engineer said. "The Fort Severn stuff goes back over a century and a half. I'm not surprised it's been displaced.

Someone was probably supposed to survey it, and got scared."

"And then faked it," Jim said.

"Yeah, probably. Can't blame him."

They entered the eighth wing through the doors beneath the sixth wing–eighth wing overpass bridge. There were dozens of doors in the eighth wing's basement. They led to storage rooms, utility bays, extracurricular club rooms, and laundry and trash collection areas. "Hell," Jim said, "This'll take a week to search."

"We don't have to search this," the chief said. "All we gotta do is catch the sumbitch coming out of that oak door into the modern tunnels. Do we really care how he gets into the Fort Severn tunnels? Now that we know it's probably feasible?"

"You're right," Jim said. "We don't. Let's go."

Using the access grate near Dahlgren Hall, they went down into the main utility tunnel and examined the oak doors again. They were still locked, and there were no further signs of anyone using a key or a jimmy to work the locks.

"I've got my surveillance team setting up motion detectors throughout the tunnel complex," the chief said. "We'll set one here, pointed at this door. They're low-level lasers. Break the beam, it sends an alert and its location number to a central station. Size of a pack of cigarettes. We can track him through the tunnels, take him where we want to."

"How will these things communicate with the outside?"

"They don't; so we'll need a comms node underground. I'll cover all that at the briefing."

"All right, I guess we're done here," Jim said. He turned to the engineer. "We need this whole op to stay hush-hush, so please ensure that there's nothing about it on your internal LAN, okay?"

"Gotcha covered," the engineer said. "The Public Works officer knows about it, but that's it."

"Good. Chief, I'm going back to my office. I'll bring Agent Branner over with me at sixteen-thirty. See you at the briefing."

. . .

Ev didn't get through to Liz until just before five o'clock. He told her about his run-in with the commandant.

"Did he directly threaten to do something to Julie?"

"Yes," Ev said. "He threatened to delay her commissioning. That would put her date of rank permanently behind her entire class. I'd call that a threat."

"Because he thinks she's withholding information?"

"I think someone's telling him that, yes."

Liz didn't say anything for a moment.

"I mean, I don't know what the hell to do about this. Julie's not listening to either one of us."

"That's the problem," Liz said. "Maybe I'll have another go at that security officer, Jim Hall."

"You think he'll talk to you?"

"Maybe. He's a graduate. He might be sympathetic to Julie's situation."

"This is really frustrating," Ev said. "You should have seen Robbins. One minute all sweetness and light in front of my colleagues, presenting me this stupid award certificate, the next acting like some sort of gestapo director."

"They're under a ton of pressure," Liz said. "Media, congressional, the Secretary of the Navy, probably. Let me see if I can talk to Hall. Want to get together later tonight?"

"I'd probably be lousy company," he said. "I want to smack somebody."

"Go for a long run. Or take your boat out. Push it hard. I have to go out to a chamber of commerce dinner. I'll be back by ten. If you're still all stressed out by then, we'll figure something out."

Smiling in spite of the tension he felt, Ev promised her he'd be there. He hung up and thought about how direct she was. He couldn't imagine Joanne being so forward. And bedtime with Liz was also very different, although, to be fair, he and Joanne had been married for a long time. But Liz was exciting, direct, challenging without being threatening. He couldn't imagine being in the mood for sex right now, given everything that was going on with Julie. But Liz was right: Go beat up your body, bleed all this stress into the river, and then go see her. As long as Julie was being obstinate, there wasn't anything he could do to help her. So he'd go do something about his situation. With Liz. There, he thought. That wasn't even hard, was it?

By 10:00 P.M., the entire team was in place. The topside surveillance people were set up at all the Yard grates and were up on a tactical radio net. Jim and Branner were down under Stribling Walk in the main tunnel complex, set up in a telephone switchboard vault. The motion-detector string was in place, ready to transmit alerts via a separate radio frequency, which would be detectable underground. The chief and one radio operator were set up in a mobile CP in the radio van they'd borrowed from the Annapolis cops. The van was hardwired to the retransmitter underground.

The switchboard vault was ten feet by ten feet and filled with equipment cabinets, which kept the room at a humming ninety degrees despite the air-conditioning. Branner was in her NCIS tactical field gear, and Jim was similarly outfitted. Both wore shoulder transceiver mikes provided by the chief. There were no chairs in the switchboard vault and very little room to move around, so Jim and Branner sat shoulder-to-shoulder against one of the equipment racks. The door to the main tunnel was almost closed, but open enough to show a slit of light from the main tunnel.

"This is cozy," Jim said. "But kind of a boring date."

"If you and I ever go on a date, that's a word you'll never use," she replied, looking at her watch for the umpteenth time. Jim wondered if she'd get the ballpoint out pretty soon and start tapping again.

"It's after twenty-two hundred. Did Midshipman Hays ever get back to you?" he asked.

"Nope," she said. "You think our vampire's going to make his move tonight?"

"It's a Wednesday. They're not allowed off the reservation on Wednesdays—sort of a reminder of who grants them liberty. The rest of the time, he could just walk out the gate after evening meal."

"The Annapolis cops said there hadn't been another vampire mugging since Bagger," she said. "So maybe he got scared."

Jim remembered the brief look he'd had into the guy's face. "I don't think *scared*'s in his lexicon," he said. "This is one big game to him; the more danger, the bigger the thrill. Plus, the fact that Bagger died isn't common knowledge here at the Academy."

"Maybe we ought to announce it," she said. "Let the fucker know what he did."

"If anything would force him into deep cover, that would certainly do it. We need him to keep doing this."

She didn't say anything, just looked at her watch again. Then she leaned back and closed her eyes. "You pretty confident Hays will give us something?" she asked.

"It might take a little longer than he thought. At some point, he has to talk to Markham. She may go ballistic, or just clam up. But, yeah, he'll come back with something. He wasn't exactly ambivalent about the whole thing."

They waited some more. Then the radio squawked quietly in their shoulder mikes. It was the chief, making a comms check. There were seven teams in place, including themselves and the team out on the St. John's campus. The chief's call sign was team zero. Each team responded with its number. Branner answered for both of them. "Team three, in position, no contact."

"Team four, no contact."

"Team five, no contact."

"Team six, no contact, no nothing."

"Team seven, no contact, no vampires."

"Okay, people," the chief came up. "Remember, this is surveillance. No contact just means the game hasn't started yet."

There was an instant of silence, and then a new voice

came up on the circuit. "This is station eight. I've got lots of contacts."

Another moment of silence, and then the chief was back on. "Who's fucking around?" he called.

No one answered. Jim looked at Branner. *Station* eight? Not team eight? Neither had recognized that voice as being one they'd heard on previous comms checks. Then the motion detector board lighted up.

"We have motion in the cross tunnel under Buchanan Road," Jim announced to the net. A second light came up. "Going past the supe's house. Moving toward Dahlgren."

Branner leaned down to study the light panel. Using a grease pencil, Jim had drawn a rough diagram of the tunnel complex onto a piece of plywood. He'd put numbers next to *X*'s on the diagram, indicating where the chief's team had placed motion detectors. Then he'd coded a map of the streets and major buildings above ground to indicate where each numbered detector was. Each team had a copy of the coded street map.

"Team four, watch your grate," the chief ordered.

"Team four," came the laconic acknowledgment. As in, What do you think we're doing?

"He's past four's grate," Jim announced on the net, still puzzling over the "station eight" call. "Four, you're now in position to get behind him."

"Roger that; say when," four answered.

A third light came on, indicating that something had turned the corner at the dogleg turn and was now headed up the main tunnel.

"He's going pretty slow for a runner," Branner said, watching the lights. "And what was that 'station eight' bullshit about 'lots of contacts'?"

"Don't know," Jim said, concentrating on the lights. "But when he passes team six, that'll give us two teams behind him and us in front. That's when we go."

At that moment, there was a loud clicking noise as all the lights out in the main corridor went off, followed a moment later by the lights in the switchboard room. The PWC watch officer, who had been monitoring the tactical net, came up and announced that the tunnel lighting breakers had been thrown in the vicinity of the dogleg turn.

Branner had her flashlight out, pointed into a tight white cone at her feet so as not to reveal their position to anyone out in the passageway.

"Where exactly is that breaker box?" Jim asked.

The PWC watch officer described the location, and Jim pointed down to the diagram. "The lights indicate he's here, but that breaker is behind that position. Two of them?"

Before Branner could answer, they both felt a movement in the air, and the door to their vault swung open on silent hinges. The air moved again, as if a pressure differential had been created somewhere down the tunnel.

"Team four," Jim ordered. "Enter your grating, head toward the river and turn left up under Stribling now. Possible contact a hundred feet in from your entry position. Team six, stand by."

"Four, roger, coming in now."

"Six, standing by."

"Let's go," Jim said to Branner. "Whatever's coming up the tunnel's only a hundred and fifty feet away."

"Suits me," she said, getting to her feet and checking her stun gun. They'd elected to equip each team with the stun guns, rather than take chances with ricocheting bullets down in the maze of concrete tunnels. Given some of the things the runner had already done, however, everyone still had a sidearm.

Jim pulled the shoulder mike into his left hand and kept his Maglite in his right hand. Branner could cover both of them if there were shooting to be done. That station eight business was still nibbling at the edge of his mind. 'Lots of contacts'? Then he had a thought: Was it *him*? Had their runner broken into the tactical net?

They stepped out the opened door and felt a definite movement of air in their faces. Almost a draft, not too strong, but coming toward them. Why? Where was the air coming from? Jim tried to review the tunnel layout in his mind, but the darkness had his attention. They stood just outside the telephone switchboard vault, and the light board down on the floor was still visible. He glanced back and saw yet another light blink on. Whatever was coming up the tunnel was closer by fifty feet.

"This is zero, what's happening, three?"

"This is three; stand by," Jim said, and then nudged Branner. "Lights," he said, and they both shot bright white beams down the main tunnel in the direction of what was coming. What they saw startled them both. It looked like a huge metal sphere. It filled the tunnel and was rolling right toward them. Their flashlights reflected off the smooth surface as if it were glass, but it was definitely moving.

"We have a metal sphere coming down the tunnel right at us," Jim announced to the net, wondering why the sphere wasn't making any noise.

"What the fuck is that thing?" Branner whispered, pointing her stun gun even as she realized it would be useless. The huge sphere kept coming, not too fast, but not slowing down, either, rolling right at them. Jim felt the weight of the concrete ceiling bearing down on him as he just stood there watching this thing.

"Three, this is team four; where are you?"

"Standing just outside our hidey-hole. There's this *thing* going up the tunnel. Where are you?"

"Right behind it, three," the other voice said. "It's a big metal ball of some kind. Rolling all by itself."

"I'm gonna shoot it," Branner growled, reaching for her Glock.

"Negative," Jim shouted, batting her hand down. "Four's right behind it. I know what that is—it's a balloon! It's a Mylar weather balloon. That's why we can't hear it." He called out on the net that the thing was a weather balloon. When it reached them, Jim put his hand out. His finger pressed into it, and then the huge sphere bounced off his hand and stopped rolling.

"If I can't shoot it, I'm gonna pop it," Branner said, angry now that someone had been screwing around with them. She pulled a knife and jabbed at the balloon, which popped with a dull bang and then deflated. They were left facing the flashlights of team four, two Yard cops who were staring down at the puddle of metallic plastic between them.

"Okay," one of them said. "What's up with this shit?"

At that moment, the radio went off. "Hey there, boys and girls," the station eight voice said. "Are we having fun yet?" This was followed by laughter, and then silence. Then the lights flashed back on in the main tunnel. Jim looked down at the mike in his hand and swore.

The teams convened back at the naval station police building thirty minutes later for a debrief. Branner kicked things off.

"It's obvious those tunnels belong to this guy as much as they belong to PWC," she said. "He was into the retransmitter freq from the git-go."

"It almost sounds like he has a closed-circuit TV system down there," the chief offered. "I mean, it's like he could see what was happening, where people were."

"How the hell did he control the lights?" one of the cops asked.

"The lights are on lighting transformers," the PWC engineer said. "They're set out in blocks along the tunnels, so you don't lose all the lights if one fixture has a ground or other problem. It's marked LIGHTING TRANSFORMER right on the box."

"Did you guys have lights when you came down?" Jim asked the men on team four.

"Yeah. It only got dark when we came around the corner. We were confused when our lights reflected off that balloon thing."

Jim looked at Branner. "I think I want to go back down there," he said. "I want to see where the lighting transformers are that control the passageway lights near where we were holed up."

The chief, conscious of his overtime budget, asked if the

rest of the cops were done for the night. Jim said yes, and the meeting broke up.

Jim and Branner went back over to the Yard, and down into the main tunnel from the Stribling Walk grating entrance. They retraced their steps to the telephone vault, then looked around to see if they could find the control box for the passageway's overhead lights. Just past a point where the main tunnel did a small zigzag, they found the nearest electrical panel marked LIGHTING TRANSFORMER and opened the front cover. They found a surprise inside—a message written in black grease pencil on the inside of the box cover. HMC: YOU SAID ONE-ON-ONE—READY 4 THAT ANYTIME. The message was signed with a smaller version of the shark logo from the big tag down the passageway.

"And this means something to you, right?" asked Branner.

"Yup. And he had to have been right here, outside the vault door. These switches look like local control to me."

"He knew where we were, and he was able to get down here, kill the lights, set that big balloon in motion, and be gone by the time we came out and those other cops came down here looking for us," Branner said.

Jim looked around the empty tunnel. "If he was gone," he said. "Hell, he may have been hiding in one of these utility rooms the whole time. None of us searched the place after that balloon thing."

"So how come the motion-detector string didn't tag him if he was moving around out here?"

"Good question," he said. "I asked the chief to leave all those things in place and just take the control box back with him. Let's see, the nearest detector set should be down there, where the flap doors for that big storm drain are."

They walked down the tunnel in the direction of Bancroft Hall. The tunnel expanded into a vestibule area next to the storm drain access, the flaps of which sloped down from the floor at a forty-five-degree angle. The flaps, hinged and spring-loaded, would open with water pressure on the tunnel side, but otherwise they'd remain closed to any access from the drain itself. They searched the cableways, lighting fixtures, and electrical junction boxes until they found the diminutive detector-transceiver. It was taped to the underside of a telephone system amplifier and pointed out into the main passageway. The mirror was in place directly across from it. There did not appear to be anything amiss with the installation—the wires were in place and the box was intact, its tiny laser aperture pointing correctly across the passageway at the receiver.

"This thing should have worked if he came up the tunnel this way from Bancroft," Jim said.

"But if he knew where it was, couldn't he have simply crawled under it?" Branner asked.

"Yeah, but these lasers are not in the visible light range. It's not like he could see little beams of light shining across the tunnel. Unless he had a detector of his own. And there's no way he could have that."

Branner shook her head. "*I've* got one," she said. "On the dash of my car."

Jim thought about it. "You mean like a police radar detector? But he'd still have to be in the beam to get a detection."

"Not necessarily," she said. "That thing shoots a laser beam across the tunnel. The mirror here reflects it back. Something intrudes, the detector sends an alarm. But there has to be some scattering of the refracted light. Down here in a concrete tunnel, that would go everywhere. All he'd have to do is carry a laser detector in his hand to know that these things were down here. Then he could go looking for them."

"And getting on our tactical freq—all that would take is a police-band scanner. It wasn't as if we were encrypted."

"Right. Not much magic to it, once you think about it."

"But at least some familiarity with electronics. So we're looking for some whiz kid in the double-E lab."

"Got any of those here at the Naval Academy?" she asked.

"Only a couple hundred," he said. "And the thing is, he's had time, lots of time, to rig his own shit down here if he wanted to. For all we know, he's got a motion-detector net of his own. These mids have access to real radars, advanced computer networks, acoustic transducers, video-based fire-control systems—you name it, they're taught it."

"Let's get out of here," she said. "This place is giving me the creeps."

Jim had been thinking the same thing. The silence, the strange-smelling atmosphere, the feeling of being pressed in by all the bare concrete, and a mental image of that vampire face had been working on him ever since they had come back down. That and a feeling of helplessness when confronted by the fact that their quarry could just as easily be their hunter.

Once back outside, they both took a moment to breathe in some fresh air. The night was clear and almost warm, with a small breeze carrying a hint of salt air in from the bay. Bancroft Hall was lighted up as usual as the midweek press of the regular academic load and the impending approach of exams kept the midnight oil burning.

"So how'd he do the balloon?"

"Inflated it in the tunnel—they use a cylinder of helium. Not very big. And then he wedged a grating door open to create a pressure gradient toward us. It wasn't rocket science."

"This guy's defeating us," Branner said.

"There's still one window open," Jim replied, heading for his truck. "That one-on-one challenge. I started that with a mark on his tag. He replied that night when he sent that tennis ball down the passageway. Now he's come back with it."

"What's the HMC bit?"

"I put that over his tag—Hall-Man-Chu. HMC. Tagger bullshit."

"You're not seriously thinking of going down there alone, are you?"

"I'm seriously thinking of making it look like I'm down there alone." He grinned at her. "You up for an adventure?"

"I'm up for getting him down there and then filling the tunnels full of carbon monoxide," she growled.

"He's probably got a detector for that, too. Wal-Mart sells them, as I remember. Where's your Bronco?"

"Out by the Maryland Avenue gate. Assuming the locals haven't boosted it."

"My ride's right over here, in front of the supe's quarters. Want to come back to the boat for a nightcap?"

She stopped and looked around at the Yard. Globed streetlights shone through the spidery branches of black trees. Down along the river, the big academic buildings were still fully illuminated. Behind them the looming silhouette of the chapel blacked out an entire chunk of the night horizon. "I feel really shitty about what happened to Bagger," she said finally. "I should go back to the office. Check voice mail, messages. The thing is, I don't much want to go back to the office. Or to my apartment tonight."

"There are two guest cabins on the boat," he said. "C'mon back with me. You can take your pick. We'll get some wine, sit up on deck until the dew gets too heavy."

She gave him a brief, weary smile. "Why not?" she said. "Can't dance."

"Follow me," he said, suddenly happy for her company. "I'll give you a lift to the main gate."

An hour later, they sat watching the lights across the harbor from the cockpit of his boat. It turned out she kept an overnight kit in her Bronco, and she'd changed into a loose-fitting workout suit. He'd given her a sweater and a ball cap, and he'd changed into jeans and a sweater. Jupiter was in his cage, partially covered against the night breeze coming in from the bay. Jim had some single malt; Branner had opted for wine.

"Where are you from originally?" he asked.

"Omaha," she said. "My parents were both cops. He was a detective before he retired, and she worked for Internal Affairs."

"If she's was as good-looking as you are, she must have been downright lethal."

"Thank you, sir. And she was. Lethal, I mean. She could drink any man under the table and they'd tell her anything. Not that we had a big police corruption problem in dear old Omaha."

"You do college?"

"Creighton, right there in town. Jesuit school. Took a prelaw curriculum."

"Wow. So what happened?"

"Met too many lawyers," she said. "Even married one, just for grins. Big mistake. All fixed now, though."

He decided not to ask what "all fixed" meant. He told her about growing up in Pensacola at his father's boatyard. He admitted to her that he didn't really enjoy going very far out into the Gulf.

"Truth be told, I'm prone to seasickness," he said. "Which is why I don't take this beauty out on the bay, either."

"I'm with you," she said. "Being from Omaha, the ocean was just about the biggest damned thing I'd ever seen. And then a marine biologist told me one day at the beach that they called the first two hundred yards out into the water 'the feeding zone.' So now I just look at it."

"I'm sure there's plenty of sharks out there in the bay," he said. "But the big threat around here are the damned jellyfish."

"There you go," she said, settling into the sweater, which she had thrown loosely over her shoulders. "Another reason to stay on nice dry land. I don't like the water, and I don't like confined spaces, either."

"Like tunnels."

"Exactly."

He was a little surprised. After all that redhead bluster, Branner was actually scared of a couple things. Although, he had to admit, she'd gone right down there with him.

"You date much around here?" he asked.

"Nope. Mostly work. I was seeing this guy up in D.C. for a while, but he faded. A couple of Sunday nights getting home on Route Fifty during beach season took the fun right out of it. How about you?"

"Nobody special. The female mids are too young, and most of the tourists are too old. I party with the marina people once in awhile, but that's a pretty wet-drunk scene after about eleven at night. Occasionally, things work out."

"Never married?"

"Nope. Not against it, mind you, but . . ."

"It's overrated," she said, but did not elaborate. She looked smaller now, all tucked into his big cable-knit sweater, her legs curled under her in the soft deck chair. If he closed his eyes, he could still visualize those legs when she was decked out for business. Copper hair, green eyes, small, almost pug nose, pale white skin with a few freckles. In-your-face sexy.

"Where'd you go, cowboy?" she asked, and he opened his eyes and saw that she was smiling at him. It dramatically softened her face.

"I was thinking," he said.

"Uh-oh," she said. The challenge was back in her voice.

"Yeah. Of how pretty you are, sitting over there. And how tough and hard-boiled you are in your day job. I was going to say, how tough and hard you try to be, but the fact is, I think it's *not* an act. I was wondering why?"

"Simple," she said with a small sigh. "I'm a redhead."

"Uh, yeah?"

"What do think of when you see a redhead?"

He thought about being diplomatic. Nah. "Trouble?" he said.

"There you go. Men expect nothing but trouble from a redhead. So I oblige 'em. That way, they think they have me figured out, and when the occasion calls for it, I can surprise them."

"Is all that necessary?" he asked. "In the NCIS business, I mean?"

"Absolutely," she said. "Most male agents meet a reasonably attractive female agent, or any government professional, they get hung up on the reasonably attractive parts."

"Go on."

"You meet another guy, you put a pleasant expression on your face and you shake hands, and that's that, right? Guys meet me, they check out my face, legs, my front and back, legs again, and then ask, after I've already told them, what I do. It takes everything I've got not to tell them I'm a nine-hundred-dollar hooker, just to see what they'd do."

"I think I might hit the ATM machine myself."

She laughed out loud. "Studly guy like you?" she said. "Tell me you've never paid for it."

"Only as a Marine in WestPac, and of course, over there, as we all know, it doesn't count."

She laughed again and sipped some wine.

"So why the provocative clothes?" he asked. "More dazzle?"

"Yep," she said. "It works, too. That's why I'm the boss of my own little resident agency, such as it is, at age thirty. What you see is what you get. That's my approach."

"But they don't get it, do they?" he said with a grin.

"Nice one, Mr. Hall," she said. "Does that shower work down there, or is there some special maritime incantation to make it produce hot water?"

"It's complicated, but you can do it. Turn the left-hand knob, the one marked with the *H*, to the left and you'll be good to go. In fact, you'd better turn the right-hand knob, too, or you're going to be red all over. So to speak."

She cocked her head at him, finished her wine, and gathered herself to go below. "Thanks for the company," she said. "And thanks for not making some clumsy pass. You're a very attractive man." She stopped, as if wondering if she'd said too much. "I'm really bummed about Bagger, and I have this feeling that the Dell case is falling out of my hands." She smiled up at him. "Takes the romance right out of it, you know?"

"I understand," he said. "If you get bored later . . ."

"Yeah? What should I do if I get bored later, Mr. Hall?"

"Jupiter here plays a mean hand of gin rummy," he said with a straight face.

She straightened and slowly smoothed the front of the exercise suit over the contours of her body, letting him watch as she did it. "I'll keep that in mind," she said. Then she went below.

Jim relaxed in his chair and poured some more scotch. He

tried to think about the case of the tunnel runner, but his mind kept coming back to Branner. He wondered what it would take to get through all that armor. And then he realized that nothing would get through all that armor until and unless she decided to take it off.

"She's a tough one, bird," he said. But Jupiter already had his head under his wing. Bird, he decided, had the right idea. He gathered up the sleeping parrot and went below himself. He put Jupiter into his big cage, doused all the lights, set the alarm system, and then went into his own cabin. He read for fifteen minutes before the rack monster sounded its siren song and he turned off the light. He couldn't quite figure Branner out. It was as if she were appraising him, as if she hadn't made up her mind whether or not she liked him. Actually, *like* was the wrong word. Respect. Branner was all about respect. He drifted off.

He woke up to the sounds of somebody moving around out in the lounge. He looked at his watch and saw that he'd been down for no more than half an hour. He lay still, wondering if Branner was looking for something. There was some light coming through the portholes on either side of his cabin, enough to let him see the door clearly. The boat was moving gently in tune with the harbor's tidal currents.

The alarm panel light was steady, so it wasn't an intruder. Had to be Branner. A moment later, he saw the door handle turn down, but the door did not move. Then the handle moved again, and the door slowly opened wide. It was Branner. She appeared to be wearing nothing but an oversized T-shirt, which didn't reach much below her hips. She stood there for a long moment, barely visible in the dim light, her hair down around her shoulders, the curves of her hips and thighs lovely. She had an expression he hadn't seen before. He didn't move, curious to see what she'd do.

"You awake, Hall?" she asked softly.

"I am now. You want a light on?"

"No," she said, coming over to the bed. She sat down sideways on the bottom edge, tentatively, as if she didn't trust the bed to hold her. "I need to know something."

"Shoot."

"You said you got in trouble, over in Bosnia, when you were in the Marines. I'd like to know what really happened. If you want to tell me, that is."

He lay back on the pillows and put his hands behind his head. "It was a blue on blue—friendlies firing on friendlies. I was the spotter—the guy who can see the bad guys when the friendly artillery can't. My job was to call artillery fire down on this fifty-seven-millimeter cannon some Serbs were using to pick off schoolchildren trying to get across a street. Serbs' idea of sport."

"Who were the friendlies?"

"An Italian peacekeeper squad. They were emplaced on a hillside below the Serbian position. Serbs didn't know they were there, but the Italians couldn't do anything about the cannon."

"Couldn't or wouldn't?"

"Couldn't. It was going to take artillery of some kind—mortars, bigger guns. The Italians had rifles. Anyway, I called the mission 'danger close,' meaning there were friendlies close to the intended target. The Brit radio operator told his arty people that it was danger, but not danger close."

"And that made a difference?"

The boat rocked gently as something went by in the darkened channel. The curtains swayed, changing the light in the cabin. "Yeah, that made a difference. 'Close' means the artillery folks hedge their bets with the fall of their rounds. Remember, they can't see the target, so they shoot the first one near the target. My job was to watch to see where it fell and then adjust their fire-control solution. Danger close, that first round is always fired long, or beyond the target, just to make sure."

"And?"

"They dropped a one-oh-five round on top of the Italian position. Got 'em all. I wasn't sure they'd been hit—I was three thousand meters away—but it looked bad. Not knowing, I went ahead and adjusted the fire onto the Serb position. They got on in three rounds, and then fired ten for effect. Hamburgered 'em pretty good. But the Italian local commander couldn't raise his people, so they sent some folks to go look."

"And they blamed you?"

"Well, there was an inquiry, of course. I had been up there solo. My radio operator was in the rear with the gear, down with Tito's revenge. The Brit radio operator said I called danger, not danger close. The Italians were furious, in their inimitable style. They went up the UN chain of command, looking for blood. My bosses were terribly embarrassed—Marines are supposed to be experts at this spotting business. It got public."

"Could you prove your story?"

"Not initially. He said/they said, deal. But then, after I'd been relieved of all duties and sent out of theater, a British signals intelligence outfit came out of the weeds and said they'd had a multitrack tape recorder monitoring the local tactical circuits. They had me on tape. They took it to the Brit artillery people, who fessed up. Like I said, the Brits did the right thing, but by then, my bosses had publicly hung me out to dry, and they weren't willing to admit they'd screwed up twice. The Marine Corps had been getting ready to court-martial me. Instead, they gave me the choice between the court or taking the ceremonial detail posting to the Academy. Naturally, I took it."

"How many people died?"

"All nine of them. Direct hit. The Marine Corps kindly made me go face the families. Not fun."

"God. And afterward? After it came out that it wasn't you?"

"Came out? Nothing came out. And no one was going to convince the signoras. That damage was well and truly done. Bosnia, Kosovo, that whole peacekeeping scene was a major cluster fuck. I still feel guilty, even though I didn't cause it to happen. I was part of it."

"So your career in the Marines went permanently south."

"Yup. The Corps never forgets."

"Did the people here at the Academy know the story?"

"The Marines did. I assume somebody briefed the supe. Oh, and did I tell you the Italians had some kids up there? Some local kids—they ran wild over there—had climbed down into the Italian position, begging for food, hanging out. Ground them up, too."

"Oh shit."

"Yeah, shit. So that's why I'm in this 'nothing' job."

She was quiet for a minute. "You associate a career with the chance to get into another mess like that?"

Jim thought about it. "I guess I do. Sometimes, when I get to brooding, I refocus on what's right in front of me. A pretty day in the harbor. The pleasure of polishing my boat. A nice wine. A pretty lady. Keeping it simple, here, boss."

She nodded. "I appreciate your telling me this. It explains a lot. Now I just want to cry."

"When I think about all that, so do I, Special Agent. You better get back to bed."

She gave him a long look, then nodded and quietly left the cabin. Jim didn't know what to think, so he went back to sleep, hoping not to dream about that ravaged red hillside far away.

Went bowling last night. Not duck pins—more like fuck pins. It was really kind of funny, watching those cops doing the funky chicken trying to get away from my little surprise. Running around down there like scared rabbits. And then I talked to them on their own radio circuit—that was perfect. They still don't get it. Those are my tunnels, not their tunnels. They think they can catch me with motion detectors, and then they come up on a clear tactical radio frequency and let me listen. Keystone Kops. They ought to be making movies. And when it was all over? They just leave. I think they don't like it down there. I saw a couple of the Yard cops, and they were spending more time looking around at all that concrete than they were looking for me. I could have reached out and touched two of them once I put the lights out. Too bad I didn't have my vampire rags. Tap one of those fat bastards on the shoulder and give him a quick look and a big old friendly hiss? Would have had two moving sewage leaks.

The security guy is the one behind all this. Messing with my tag. Bringing that redhead agent down there with him. You know who I mean. The one that goes around here showing off her legs while shining that untouchable attitude. She's not even pretty, not like some of my classmates, right? No, she's a hard case. Talks tough. Hell on wheels when it comes to hassling mids, but not so good when she comes down into my part of our dear old Academy. I'm going to have to deal with her, too, I think. Word is, she's hassling the hell out of a bunch of firsties. Over that Dell thing. Well, shit. I guess they have to go through the motions, don't they? I mean, plebe does a Peter Pan, God, I love that line, and at least they have to seem like they're doing something about a mess like that. Have you seen the newspapers? Banging on about the hazing, how it's getting out of hand. Hell, that wasn't hazing. I think it was like the ultimate come-around. You know, like the TV show? Come around, plebe. Or maybe, Come on down! Damned if he didn't. And dressed for the occasion, too.

I can read the Executive Department E-mails. Did you know that? Can't read the ones from NCIS—they're encrypted, so that's that. Too hard. But I can read everything the little dant's efficient assistant is sending out, and isn't he a regular motormouth. I think my little deal here is going to work. I think someone's going down—ahem, that was a poor choice of words, I guess. I think someone's going to be blamed for what happened to Baby Brian Dell. Not the precious system, either. I think someone's going to be "responsible" in part—yes, that's the term they're using. Responsible in part, so they can point and say, There he is. Or is it, There she is? Yes, I think this is going to work. But first, I need to attend to a loose end. Someone who knows a little more than he should. Probably because someone else talked too much. People shouldn't talk so much. Either way, I'm going to up the ante somewhat. Try my hand at some electrical work, right here in Mother Bancroft. You'll know what I'm talking about when you hear about it. Yes, you will.

Meantime, I think I'll go sharpen my dress sword. Now there's a thing of beauty. It doesn't talk, doesn't make phone calls, doesn't send E-mails. It just hangs there in my closet along with my Marine dress blues. I put my gloves on before I handle it. Keeps it nice and shiny. I've got one right-hand glove that's got a dozen cuts across the thumb where I test the blade. It's not really supposed to be sharp, you know, or maybe you don't. It's just for ceremonies. But then, I know some ceremonies that aren't in the drill manual, if you catch my drift. I can shave with that thing; that's how sharp it is. Actually, I can't shave myself—a little awkward. But I can shave somebody else, and I did, just once.

Some little guy. Into occasional high-risk gymnastics. Said he wanted to fly. And so he did.

12

On Thursday morning, Jim went upstairs to the supe's office to see the commandant's schedule for the day. He wanted to back-brief him on the previous day's events. The commandant, however, had gone to Washington for the day with the superintendent. Admiral McDonald's executive assistant declined to share with Jim the purpose of the trip. Jim took the horse-holder's rebuff in stride and went to find some coffee at the mess table. Two junior officers were talking there, so he poured a cup of coffee and then joined them.

"So where are the elephants off to this morning?" he asked no one in particular. One of the JO's said he'd heard that the supe was briefing SecNav on some personnel issues. "You know, this Dell mess. And something about an NCIS agent getting beat up? Like out in town?"

Jim pretended this was all news to him and headed for his office, where he put a call in to Branner. "You hear from Midshipman Hays yet?" he asked when she picked up.

"There's a message from him," she said. "Wants a meet at twelve hundred."

"Want me there?"

"Absolutely," she said. "What's the word from the head shed?"

"Big and not so big are in D.C., briefing the SecNav on 'personnel issues'; scuttlebutt here is that it's the Dell case *and* what happened to Bagger."

"Really," she said. "Maybe I better pulse my network again; I called headquarters this morning, but nobody told me that."

"Maybe that's the message," he said. "They're getting ready to do something. Did you report what happened last night?"

"Not exactly. Left a message for Harry Chang to call me."

Jim thought for a moment. "If the séance concerns what happened to Bagger, I'm surprised you weren't pulled in."

"Probably some of our heavies from the Navy Yard *were* pulled in. Chang's out of pocket, and they wouldn't tell me where. The dant knows what we're doing, right?"

"I've been back-briefing since it started," he said. "But I can never tell what the hell the real agenda is when I talk to Robbins. We'd better catch some real deal progress at this noon meeting, or I think we're gonna get sidelined."

"Meaning they'll slap a lid on it and declare the thing solved. The Dell thing anyway. Bagger's case, they'll probably turn over to the city cops. You know, cop got clipped. Let 'em enjoy a little urban frenzy."

They were both silent for a moment. "Hey?" he said. "I enjoyed your company last night. It was nice just to talk."

"It was nice. Even without the gin rummy."

"If you want to come over again, the access code is four-three-two-one-five, as in four, three, two, one, fire."

"Four, three, two, one, fire. Got it. See you at noon."

Jim spent the next half hour on paperwork, then signed out for the Public Works Center and drove over to the power plant to meet with the utility supervisors. They pored over the system maps while Jim made a new map, this one of the grating entrances to the entire underground area. They talked about the fact that the Fort Severn diagrams were wrong, but no one seemed to get too upset about that. It was a no-go area, and that was that. Jim didn't enlighten them about the fact that the one magazine had been rigged to appear flooded.

"I've been asking about the ways *into* the underground system," he said. "What about the ways *out* of it?"

That provoked some blank stares, but then the senior engineer got the sewage-handling and transfer-system maps out. "This is a system that goes out of the underground area, but naturally, it stays sealed."

"We fervently hope," offered one of the engineers. Everyone smiled.

"What else—how about smoke evacuation in the case of an underground fire?"

"Big exhaust fans in parallel with each of the grates," the engineer said. "Depending on where the fire is, we'd try to close some fire doors to isolate it, then exhaust the oxygen supply. But the system's been added onto for so long, it's pretty porous."

"How big are the exhaust ducts?"

"Four by four, but they're filled with fan blades and vent screens. Nobody could get through one of those."

"Any other ways out?"

They all thought about it for a moment. "There's the storm drain," another engineer said, then pointed it out on the main map. "In case there was flooding, the water would flow down to the river—gravity."

"Could our guy get in or out that way?"

"Tough," the chief engineer said. "Permanent, big grating on the seawall. Submerged except at really low tide. Plus, the flaps here open only one way, and only with water pressure on the tunnel side."

Jim nodded. "So, the sewage system is completely sealed, and there's just the one storm drain? No direct connections between Bancroft Hall and the utility tunnels?"

"No, sir. Everything going from the tunnel into Bancroft is a pipe or a wireway. Nothing big enough for a human."

Jim thanked them and took his annotated maps with him. He drove back to the office, where he left the truck. Then he walked down across the Yard from the administration building, passed between Michelson and Chauvenet halls, then crossed the Ingram track field and went out onto the wide expanse of Dewey Field, right along the Severn River. If the diagrams were correct, that storm drain ought to be in the middle of the seawall bounded by Dewey Field.

He was operating under the old Sherlock Holmes principle: When all the other possibilities have been eliminated, the one staring you in the face, however improbable, has to be the answer. They had had teams on all the gratings last night. Assuming his guys hadn't been asleep at the switch, the runner hadn't used a grating. He hadn't flushed himself down a toilet, and he couldn't morph through the exhaust fans. The route through the old magazine was a possibility, but until he actually found a surface exit, he didn't know that the thing actually led to the Yard. That left the storm drain.

He walked the entire length of the Dewey Field seawall without finding it, then remembered the engineer's comment about the tides. The grating was submerged most of the time. He looked over the wall and saw that it was high tide, or very close to it. He watched the water. The streak of flotsam along the seawall seemed to be edging its way out toward the bay. Ebb tide under way? He decided to come back after the meeting with Hays. He went back to the upper end of Dewey Field and carefully paced the distance to where the storm drain should be. It supposedly ran under the walkways that sloped up to the chapel. When he reached the point where his pacing told him the drain ought to be, he looked up and saw that he was lined up with the steps between Michelson and Chauvenet. Perfect. The drain had been run so as to not penetrate either of the two academic buildings. So this was where it should be. There was a metal railing along the seawall. He got out his pocket knife and scratched an *X* in the railing at the point where he thought the seawall grate should be.

He looked around. It was close to eleven o'clock and already the first of the noontime joggers were out on Ingram. He watched for a few minutes to see if anyone appeared to be interested in what he was doing out there on the seawall. He was dressed in his usual coat and tie office outfit. Probably look like just another alumnus, he thought, recalling those thrilling days of yesteryear when he'd been a midshipman. And the program had been a whole lot tougher then, by God, sir. A whole lot tougher. He grinned and went to see if he could find a sandwich somewhere before his noon meeting.

As he was walking back up into the Yard, his cell phone chirped. It was the lady lawyer, Liz DeWinter.

"Mr. Hall," she said. "Got a minute to talk?"

"I'm on my cell," he warned.

"Yes, I know. Your chief gave me your number. This concerns a person of mutual interest."

Julie Markham, he thought. "Go ahead."

"What's your current thinking on the railroad business, Mr. Hall?"

He found an empty park bench and sat down. A group of Japanese tourists were being herded up Stribling toward Mother B. for the noon meal formation. The drum and bungle corps was thumping something martial in the central plaza, the drums echoing madly around the wings of Bancroft, creating a cacophony of rhythms. "The railroad business is still a possibility," he said. "Although I have no direct indications, I can tell you the management is less than pleased with the subject."

"My subject."

"Your subject, yes. *Uncooperative* is the term, I believe."

"I've heard a rumor, Mr. Hall. That the subject might be held back on throw-the-hats day. Until the matter is resolved. Can they do that?"

"Absolutely, counselor. Sometimes there are matters of academic probation to resolve. Sometimes health issues— whether the candidate for commissioning is still physically qualified for commissioning, for instance. Football players end up in that situation often enough."

"So they can if they want to?"

"Affirmative."

"Any progress on the underlying issue?"

"Not that I can share. But I can offer some advice."

"Shoot."

"The subject should stop screwing around." Then something else occurred to him. "You might also probe whether or not she's under some kind of pressure other than from the system. Anyone, inside or outside, another mid even."

Liz didn't answer right away. "Noted," she said finally. "I'll get in touch with the subject as soon as possible."

He looked at his watch. "Time is probably of the essence, counselor," he said, thinking of the meeting coming up in fifteen minutes. He reminded himself to tell Branner about this call.

Jim and Branner arrived together at the commandant's office right at noon. The noon meal formation was just getting under way out front. The secretary went to get Captain Rogers, then returned to show them into Rogers's office, where they found the captain and Midshipman Hays standing next to the deputy's desk.

"What do you have for us, Mr. Hays?" Branner asked.

"Nothing to report, ma'am," Hays replied, facing straight ahead and not looking directly at either of them.

"What the hell? Over," Jim said quietly.

"Sir, I spoke at length with Midshipman Markham. She insists she knows nothing about the Dell incident. She doesn't know what happened to him or why it happened. She said we could ask anybody, talk to anybody, but it wouldn't change anything."

"And that's it?" Branner said. "All this stuff about the big bad Brigade Honor Committee in the sky—she didn't *care*?"

"I'm sure she cares, ma'am," Hays said, his demeanor stiffly formal. "But she insists she's telling the truth."

"In other words: You do your damnedest; I don't care because I've nothing to hide?" Jim said.

"Yes, sir, essentially that's it."

Captain Rogers intervened. "We said at the outset that the Honor Committee had no real leverage here unless Midshipman Markham was hiding something," he said. "If she isn't, there's no case, honor or otherwise."

"I don't actually recall you saying that," Branner said. She stared at Hays. "You're telling me that you got nowhere? That even the threat of an honor investigation this close to graduation didn't make any difference to Markham?"

Hays glanced over at Rogers. "Not sure how to answer that, ma'am," Hays said.

Branner shook her head and looked at Jim. "I think we're done here, Mr. Hall," she announced. "Now we'll do it the hard way."

"What exactly does that mean, Agent Branner?" Rogers asked.

"It means I detect obstruction, Captain. I'm going to report to *my* chain of command that I smell a cover-up in progress, aided and abetted by the Academy's administration. Mr. Hall, we're outta here." She headed for the door, her face flushed with anger.

"But—but—" Rogers spluttered.

"You say graduation was planned for when, Captain?" Branner said over her shoulder. "You know the old deal when there's a homicide investigation and the cops tell the suspects, *all* the suspects, not to leave town?"

Rogers gaped at her as she led Jim through the door and out into the executive corridor. There they had to wait as the entire Brigade, all four thousand of them, filed through the side doors on their way down to the mess hall. Once the way was clear, they went through the big doors and down the steps toward Tecumseh Court, where the crowd of tourists was breaking up after watching the show. Branner's heels were clacking forcefully on the brickwork. Jim decided not to speak until they were halfway across the courtyard in front of Bancroft Hall.

"And the Oscar goes to—" he said.

"Shut up and keep walking," she said. "They're probably watching."

"And thinking about getting clean skivvies," he said with

a barely suppressed grin. "Did you see Rogers's face when you threatened to hold up graduation?"

"I did, and it made me feel just a wee bit better."

"Not that you can do anything of the sort."

"No, I can't. But they don't have to know that just yet. I need to call Harry Chang."

They turned left at the bronze bust of Chief Tamamend, the massive figurehead from the sailing ship *Delaware,* which adorned the entrance to Bancroft Hall's front court-yard. By tradition, everyone called him Tecumseh, hence Tecumseh Court. "I was really hoping that honor thing would work," she said. "But it looks like Markham's holding her ground. We're nowhere."

"Maybe, maybe not," Jim said. "I was watching Hays through all that. He wouldn't look at either one of us directly. I think I need to get to him in private, somehow. Find out what really happened."

She stopped and turned to face him. "I think they just went through the motions. Of course I was grandstanding in there, but that doesn't mean I'm not pissed. Hays very clearly implied to us that someone had something on Julie Markham. Now suddenly we get stonewalled? Bullshit."

"He may have been under orders, based on the way Captain Rogers was acting. This may be the shutdown we've been anticipating."

They reached Branner's car, which was parked illegally in one of the chapel spaces. A Yard cop car was pulling up behind it, but Jim waved him off.

"I'm going back to the office," she said. "I may have to go up to headquarters if I keep getting voice mail every time I call up there."

"You being shut out, too?"

She thought about that. "Maybe."

"Remember that meeting this morning. They might be squeezing all the local players out of the loop. Oh, and I heard from Markham's lawyer this morning." He told her what Liz had said.

"Great minds think alike, don't they?" she said. "You have my cell number?"

"Yep, got it," he said, looking at his watch. "Have to remember when it's low tide, too."

She gave him a blank look, but he just waved and continued down the sidewalk toward the administration building.

Ev called Julie on her cell phone right after lunch but got her voice mail. He asked her to call him at the end of classes that afternoon. He had done exactly what Liz had suggested yesterday afternoon when he got home. He'd taken the scull and gone out for almost two hours, until he was so tired that he wasn't sure he was going to make it back to the creek. By the time he got cleaned up and had some dinner, he felt sufficiently drained not even to want to go out of the house. He had called Liz at home and left her a message that he was just beat and going to bed early. He'd wondered for a whole three minutes if she'd be annoyed. Then he fell fast asleep and he'd almost overslept this morning.

Ahead was an afternoon seminar and then a faculty advisory board meeting. He was really anxious to hear from Julie. There were too many people moving around in her backfield: the NCIS, the Executive Department, that security officer. He wanted to warn Julie to be particularly careful, and to start communicating with Liz DeWinter. He absolutely hated not knowing what the hell was happening behind the scenes. The class bells began to ring. He groaned out loud, suddenly sick of academia.

As it turned out, it was Midshipman Hays who found Jim. Two hours later, as Jim was jogging along Dewey Field, Hays overtook him along the seawall. Jim became aware of the big shadow thumping along just behind him and turned to see who was there.

"Mr. Hall," Hays said between breaths.

"Mr. Hays," Jim replied. "This a coincidence?"

"Absolutely, sir," Hays said, looking over his shoulder. "But maybe when we get around to the far end, we could go across the footbridge, maybe take a walk in the cemetery?"

"Sounds like a plan," Jim said, and turned it up a little. Hays fell back and kept pace, about twenty feet behind him as they jogged down to Rickover Hall and then across the arched wooden bridge that crossed Dorsey Creek and took them to the athletic fields on Hospital Point. From there, they slowed to a cooldown walk and went up the hill and into the trees of the Academy cemetery. Once they were entirely out of sight of the Yard proper, Jim plopped down on an iron bench next to a massive funerary monument and toweled his face. Hays did a 360 visual check and then sat down beside him.

"Some shit happened a few nights ago," he said. "Let me tell you what it was, and then I'll tell you who it is you're probably looking for."

Jim said nothing. Hays looked around again before continuing. "The deputy dant has put a lid on the whole Dell thing. The Honor Committee was told to shove off and shut up about what you and Agent Branner brought in."

"Any explanations?"

"No, sir," Hays said. "He told us to back out and graduate. Seemed like a pretty clear message to me."

"Okay, that's useful."

"That's part of it," Hays said. "A couple of nights ago, I went back to my room from a study hall session down in Mitscher Hall. Actually, I'd been meeting with this youngster who's doing a term paper for me."

Jim nodded. The same thing had gone on when he was there: Graduating firsties, who had their hands full with finals, would pay a third-class mid to put together their senior year research paper. The firsties had to do the research and the writing, but the youngster would actually produce the formal paper.

"So. I got back to my room; my roomie's not there. I get

my uniform off, get into a B-robe, go to sit down at my desk, and I get bit."

"Bit by what?"

"By a hundred and ten volts AC. It wasn't a bad bite, because I had my rubber klacks on. But then I finally figured out that my whole desk was at line potential. The power had to be coming from my desktop PC—that was the only AC equipment on the desk."

A Yard cop car nosed along the narrow lanes of the cemetery. The cop waved at Jim, who waved back. Hays looked nervous. "Somebody had rigged this?" Jim asked.

"Affirmative. I unplugged the desktop, took a look. There was the tiniest little copper wire you ever saw, coming from the hot side of the monitor's power supply, through a hole in the case. It was married to the steel frame of the desktop with a drop of solder. Best yet, there was water on the deck on my side of the desks."

"Whoa. For a perfect ground."

"Damn straight. There were even one-inch rubber pads under the desk feet, which meant nothing happened until I touched the desk and the wet floor. One ten, straight in. And I'm not talking microvolts, either. Line voltage, line current. Just my side of the two desks. If I'd been sitting down, man, I'd have been welded to it."

"Somebody wanted *you* dead."

"Yes, sir. I think somebody did. And it wasn't my roomie. Now, let me tell you the rest of it."

"Wait a minute. Did Captain Rogers order you not to talk to me or Branner?"

"No, sir. Just said for us to 'back out.' We, the Brigade Honor Committee, are officially backed out. This is me talking here."

"Okay. The rest of it."

Hays hesitated.

"What?" Jim asked.

"I can't prove any of this," he said. "That bothers me."

"Does Julie Markham going to the electric chair bother you?"

"What?"

"That's 'What, sir?' Mr. Hays. See, the Dark Side here may shut down Branner's investigation, but they'll never shut down Branner. Or me, for that matter. And if what happened to Dell was homicide, Markham's the best suspect NCIS has. Hell, she's the only suspect NCIS has."

Hays took a deep breath and let it out slowly. He looked around the cemetery grounds again, but everyone around them was long dead.

"There's this guy," Hays said. "One of our classmates. He's also on the swim team. Calls himself 'the Shark.' Kind of a weird dude."

The Shark? The name resonated. The Shark. Holy shit, as in that tunnel tag? "This shark dude have a human name?"

"Midshipman First Class Dyle Jones Booth. The middle name's some kind of joke with him."

"Describe him."

"Big guy, freestyle swimmer. Black hair, dark, almost black eyes. Swims like a damned torpedo. Zero body friction. Totally hairless. Likes to look at you underwater as he's passing you. Has one of those no-blink looks, man. Like I said, he's out there, really weird."

"This is a Naval Academy midshipman we're talking about? A firstie?"

"Yes, sir. He was one of those special entries out of that diversity program four years back. No known parents—that's the Jones joke, and he's the first to tell you that. But this guy's smart as a whip on the engineering side. Heavy into computer geekery, too. But no real friends. Hasn't had a roommate for three years. Nobody'd stay with him. Total loner. In the Brigade and on the swim team."

"I was on the swim team," Jim said. "We were first and foremost a team. There were no lone rangers."

"This guy is. But he's unbeatable when he turns it on. Problem is, you never know when he's going to turn it on. Once he wins, he sits on the bench by himself. No high fives or anything. Goes off into some Zen Zone. He's super-fit. You wouldn't want to mess with him."

"And the Dark Side is cool with this behavior?"

"The dant's always lecturing us about results. Booth gets results. N-star for three years at the varsity level. Academic stars on his shirt, too."

"And what's this got to do with Dell?"

"Dell was a plebe in Booth's batt. The plebes are scared shitless of this guy. He doesn't run 'em so much as terrorize them. When his company O finally got on his case about it, Booth went all extreme on him. Stopped even *talking* to plebes. But he still scared them. He's a big guy and he's got that look to him. Goes down the passageway, sees a plebe, slows down, gives him the voodoo eye, plebe starts squeaking his chow call."

"Why's he still here? Why didn't the aptitude board throw him out for unsuitability a long time ago?"

"Sir?" Hays said. "You're talking way above my pay grade, okay? Guy's got a three-six cumulative QPR. He's going Marine option. Gives really good gung ho. He *sharpens* his Marine dress sword, okay? Made a plebe shove out one time over the sword, then cut a piece of paper in midair with the thing in front of the plebe. Our house Marines eat that shit right up."

It sounded to Jim like some of the Marines in Bancroft Hall needed adult supervision. "What are you going to do when you get out of here?" Jim asked.

"Surface line. Didn't have the grades for aviation or subs. Only way I got in was with the swimming, sprint ball."

Jim nodded. "Okay," he said. "What's the connection to Markham? And what's Markham got to do with what happened to Brian Dell?"

Hays looked down at the ground for a long moment before answering. "Julie and I were close for three semesters. Then it went sour. Julie took a walk on the wild side. Down at UVA at an away meet. Once that she admits to."

"With Booth."

"Yes, sir. With Dyle Booth."

"That why you two broke up?"

"Yes and no. I wanted to maintain our relationship after graduation. Julie didn't. I made a jerk of myself about it. Finally, she drops this little bomb on me. I was fucking floored. I think that was her objective."

"Julie Markham sounds like a tough young lady to me," Jim said.

Hays shook his head again. "I was in love with her. You've seen her. But after her mother died, she changed. I thought I could go with it. Didn't work."

"Other than having something to throw cold water on your romance, what's this UVA episode got to do with anything?"

"She said she told Dyle that it was all a big mistake. Dyle didn't like that. Dyle doesn't handle *no* very well."

There were other runners coming across the bridge now, but they seemed to be staying down on the athletic field.

"And?" Jim prompted.

"Julie had been mentoring Brian Dell. He wasn't her plebe or anything, but she felt sorry for the little guy."

"Whoa. That's not what she told us. She said she'd known him and a thousand of his closest friends during plebe summer detail, and then seen him around the halls of poison ivy. But otherwise, no big deal."

"Not true," Hays said. "She was helping him. His own youngster had resigned and Dell had lousy grease. The aptitude board was looking at him. You didn't know that?"

Jim thought for a moment. He had not. And Branner wouldn't have known enough to check with the aptitude board. They had just taken Julie's word for it. Shit.

"You saying what I think you're saying? That this guy Booth may have done something to Dell to get back at *Markham*?"

"Sir," Hays said, eyeing Jim warily, "all I can say for sure is that Julie wouldn't hurt Brian Dell. But Dyle Booth? That's another story. I think he's the guy did my computer up that way."

"Did you get any threats?"

"Not directly, but the last time we did swim practice together, he was giving me the shark shit. And of course he knows Julie and I were . . . well, what we were. Before he did whatever he did to her down in Charlottesville."

Jim heard the rationalization in Hays's voice. He clearly was not willing to accept the notion that whatever happened at UVA might have been entirely consensual.

"And that's all I know," Hays said. "And, like I said, I can't prove shit."

"You didn't tell this to Captain Rogers? Even after somebody tried to zap you?"

"No, sir. No proof. Plus, Julie's really sensitive about Charlottesville. Besides, today? Captain Rogers was in the transmit mode. He didn't want to hear anything from me or the other guys other than 'Aye aye, sir.' "

Jim remembered the shark tag with the WD entwined in the limbs of the stick figure. "What was Dell's first name? Brian?"

"No, sir. William was his first name. William Brian Dell."

Jim thought it over. WD. And we're back to Markham, he realized. Plus Midshipman Dyle J for Jones Booth. "I've got to discuss this with Special Agent Branner," he said. "She may want to hear this firsthand, or she may go directly to Markham."

"Sir?" Hays said, his expression tense. "Julie—Midshipman Markham—won't talk about what happened between her and Dyle Booth. Not to me, and probably not to anyone. I got the impression it was humiliating in some way."

"Not as humiliating as what happened to Brian Dell," Jim said.

Hays didn't respond.

"You're on the honor board, Mr. Hays. We both know the Academy is about to slam the lid on this incident. Maybe even as we speak. Look, Branner and I are not after Julie Markham. But if she won't talk to us, her expectations for a glorious commissioning week are going to blow up in her face. You understand what I'm saying?"

"Not exactly, sir."

"Ultimately, Mr. Hays," Jim said softly, "even if the Dark Side buries it, internally they'll want to blame somebody. This dant always has to blame somebody, right? And it's never gonna be the system's fault, is it? She won't commission."

Hays blinked but then nodded. He stared bleakly at the Severn River, where three haze gray YPs, signal flags flying, were rumbling in toward the seawall to practice mooring, pursued by a cloud of diesel exhaust. Jim prepared to get up from the bench. "You and Julie Markham still talking?"

"She's polite. As long as I keep it casual."

"Okay. If Markham won't talk to us, *we'll* question Booth. Tell her that. Ask her which version of the story she wants us to hear."

Hays frowned.

"Another thing," Jim said. "I'm telling Branner for two reasons. One is to find the truth. Second, to protect Markham."

"From?"

"From Booth, dummy. If he's the badass you say he is, once we bring him in, he may decide that Markham pointed the finger."

"But she didn't—I did."

"He can't know that, can he? So if you still value that young lady, make sure you stay in touch with her tonight, at least until you hear from either Branner or me that we have Booth. Got it?"

Hays nodded again while he massaged his calf muscles. A breeze off the river stirred the trees around them.

"There's more to this than I'm telling you," Jim said, thinking now about that shark business. "This guy could be a whole lot more dangerous than you appreciate. Does Markham's lawyer know any of this?"

"I don't know, sir. Julie's not exactly sharing right now."

"You better start. You're done exercising. Go find

Markham. Tell her that we know. Tell her we're going to confront Booth. And even if she doesn't want it, stay nearby."

"Yes, sir." Hays gulped, looking afraid. "I got it."

It was 3:30 by the time Jim got cleaned up and back to his office, where he put a call in to Branner. Voice mail. Then he called her cellphone. More voice mail. He hung up without leaving a message. Okay, Special Agent, where the hell are you? he wondered. He called her cell phone back and left a message this time for her to call him ASAP, adding that he had a line on a possible suspect in the Dell case.

He had a big decision to make. Tell the dant what he'd uncovered about a possible link connecting Markham, Dell, and this Dyle Booth, or wait to talk to Branner first. If the heavies were coming back in the cover-up mode, they'd tell him to go back to supervising parking tickets in the Yard. The dant had put him into this spider fight, and the dant could take him back out, or even take his job. A direct order from Captain Robbins was never an exercise in ambiguity. It would be a lot more difficult to back Branner off the case, unless she, too, received some unambiguous guidance from her own chain of command, who had apparently been present at the elephant conclave up in D.C. today.

His phone rang.

"You try to call me?" Branner asked.

"Yeah, both lines."

"And you didn't get me, just like Harry Chang can't get me right now unless he drives down here and clamps my wheels. I got back-channel word that they're shutting the Dell case down. SecNav decision. They're gonna rule it an accident, a DBM. Kid went up on the roof, fell off. End of story. I was on my way up to headquarters when a little bird whispered in my cell phone, so I shut off my phone and turned around. Checked voice mail and got your message."

"Right," he said. "Tommy Hays, Markham's ex-boyfriend?

He came to me with a name. We need to talk, but not on an open line."

"Well hell, detective," she said. "How about your place?"

Ev checked his voice mail when he got back to the office at 4:15. No messages from Julie or anyone else. He could understand not hearing from Julie. She might not even get back to her room until five o'clock or later, and she wouldn't be carrying her cell phone around the Yard. But he was a little worried about Liz, after basically having told her he didn't want to see her last night. He shut his office door, took a deep breath, and called her office.

"You're not mad at me, are you?" he blurted.

She laughed. "Of course not. Besides, my first ex blew into town last night for some corporate board meeting. He called me and we went out, got seriously drunk, and I think we had a grand time. Have you heard from Julie?"

He was so taken aback by what she'd said that he was about one second slow in answering. He consciously had to keep the surprise out of his voice. "Uh, no I haven't. I put a call in to her cell phone voice mail, but, um, heard nothing."

"Ev?"

"What?"

"I was kidding, Ev."

"Oh, good," he said without thinking. He heard her laughing again. Now he felt like an idiot. A teenage idiot at that.

"I'm so damned frustrated," he said. "With all this . . . *stuff* going on with Julie. Cops in Bancroft Hall. Having to pretend that either the mids or I give a shit about classes at this point in the year. The dant taking me aside to make threats."

"I did talk to Jim Hall. He confirms that they can hold up a commission. He says it's usually done with football players who can't pass the commissioning physical, but they can do it to anyone."

"Great," he groaned. "And where the hell's Julie?"

"She's got her head down. Exams are imminent. I'd suggest we leave her alone until something definitive happens. You're letting your imagination wear you down."

"That's for damned sure," he said, running his fingers through his thinning hair. "It's just that I feel I'm supposed to be doing something. Not just sitting here."

"Actually," she said, "the less you do, the safer Julie probably is. Call me tonight."

"I will. If I don't shoot myself first."

"Go row your boat again. But only half as hard this time."

It was 4:30 by the time Jim got to the marina. He saw Branner's Bronco in the marina parking lot and he pulled in next to it. Branner was sitting out in the cockpit, letting the last of the afternoon sun warm her face. She was slouched into one of the deck chairs, hands down on the chair rails and her head thrown back. Her eyes were closed. In repose, her face looked much more feminine and a lot less severe. She sat up when she felt the boat stir as he came aboard.

"So what do you figure?" he said. "If they can't call you, they can't shut you down?"

"That's an order I didn't want to hear until I talked to you. So speak to me."

He sat down and told her what Hays had told him about Dyle Booth and his own near miss with electrocution.

"Judas Priest! And this guy's a *midshipman*?" she asked, echoing his own question.

"Remember our discussion about Boy Scouts, and how this whole place operates on trust? How they assume, going in, that they're dealing with basically good guys?"

"But they must have tests," she said. "Plus, there's all this class-to-class supervision and mentoring. How can a guy like what you're describing—"

"Hays says the mids know he's weird, but he apparently goes around at full military throttle. You know the type: fills out the uniform, everything polished and spit-shined to the max, twenty-four-seven military bearing. 'Gonna be a gung ho Marine, sir, yes, *sir!*' "

A passing seagull veered away when Jim raised his voice. "But what's the connection to Dell?" she asked.

"Julie Markham. Remember, Hays is her ex-boyfriend. Apparently, they broke up because Julie Markham stepped out."

"Oh shit. With this Booth dude?"

"Apparently. Some swim team trip, an away meet. I don't have details, but the thrust of what he said was that, whatever happened, she regretted it. A lot. She subsequently shut Booth down. Booth's not pleased."

"And Dell?"

"Well, that's the interesting bit. Hays said Julie Markham kind of had Dell under her wing."

Branner's eyes narrowed. "But she said—"

"Yeah, right. Not so, according to Mr. Hays. But Hays is running scared now, after that attempt to kill him. Plus the fact that Captain Rogers told them to shut down. And graduate."

"Anybody ordered you to shut down?" she asked.

"I called in to see if the dant was back. His admin puke told me they're stuck out on Route Fifty somewhere." He looked at his watch. "They'll be back soon, though, so whatever we're going to do, like talk to Markham, we have to do it now."

"They're scared," she said. "Yesterday, they were threatening to delay Markham's commission if she didn't talk. Today, they're telling the Honor Committee they won't graduate if they *do* talk?"

"The Academy is under the SecNav's thumb. An order is an order. And I think they'll still burn Markham, just to say that they burned somebody."

She got up and stretched. Jim admired the view, then asked if she wanted a beer. She said no, but he went below to get himself one. Jupiter swore at Jim amiably for not letting him out of the cage. Jim banged the bottom of his cage, provoking more bad language.

When he came back topside, Branner was sitting down again. "How's about we call that lawyer?" she said. "Markham's not going to talk to either of us without her anyway. Get her to set up a meeting. While we still can."

"Markham probably doesn't understand that she's still in danger even if they do shut the investigation down. If not from the dant, then from Booth. Because there's more. You remember that graffiti down in the tunnels? That shark thing?"

"Yes?"

"That's what they call this Booth guy, on the swim team. Or actually, what he calls himself. The Shark."

She gave him a long, level look. "*He's* our runner? The vampire wanna-be who likes to set traps and beat people up?"

He nodded. "They ever find that missing Goth girl?"

"Not that I know of," she said, looking grim. "And he got Bagger, too, most likely."

"And tried to fry Hays. Literally, this time."

She looked across the water toward Bancroft Hall. "Man!" she said. "What kind of a monster did they let into that place?"

"A real one, if this is all true," he said quietly. "And I'm thinking that we do have a way to make Markham talk to us after all."

"How?"

"Dell was in her batt but not her company. She broke the chain of command if she was mentoring him outside his own company system. They could claim that if she hadn't interfered, whatever happened to Dell might have been avoided. Indirect responsibility, but enough to negate everything she's worked for here."

"That's pretty thin. You think they'd do that?"

"I think this commandant would. He's a surface a Navy guy. Surface guys always have to blame somebody. And remember, their system is not—repeat, *not*—at fault here."

"Much," she said, shaking her head.

"Okay, so we explain this to Markham. Now she has

everything to lose by keeping quiet. And maybe something to gain by coming clean to somebody—namely, us."

She thought for a moment. "How are we going to send for either of them if the Academy is shutting down the investigation?"

"Because so far, no one's told us that officially."

She shook her head. "I hate these frigging games."

"Then let's get moving, before they do, Markham first, then Booth. And quickly."

Ev was home, preparing to go out on the water again, when Julie finally called. "Something's happening," she said without preamble.

"Whoa, start at the beginning, Julie. What do you mean, 'Something's happening'?"

"Tommy Hays went to talk to that security officer, Mr. Hall. He told him . . . some stuff."

"What stuff?"

Julie didn't reply for a moment. He realized she had put her hand over the mouthpiece of her phone. Then she was back. "Tommy's here with me right now. We're down in Mitscher Hall, behind the mess hall. Tommy says he's going to stay close to me until he hears from Mr. Hall."

Ev shook his head. "I'm not following, Julie. What's going on?"

"Mr. Hall told Tommy that the Academy is probably going to close down the NCIS investigation, but that they're going to blame *me* for what happened to Brian—Midshipman Dell."

Ev, bewildered, dropped into a kitchen chair. "Slow down, Julie, and let's not do this on the phone. Can you get loose?"

"Dad, I think I should go to see Liz DeWinter."

Well, about goddamn time, he thought. "I heartily agree," he said. "Let me find her, tell her what's happening. She's probably still at the office. Call me back in five."

He hung up and phoned Liz, who was still in the office. Keeping the explanation very short, he asked if Julie could meet with her there. Liz said fine. Ev called Julie's cell phone and relayed the news.

"Can Tommy go with me?"

"Uh, hell, I don't know. I guess so."

"Because—oh shit, wait one, Dad." He heard the phone hit the table, and then he heard Julie say, "Yes?" He waited again while she talked to someone else. He heard what sounded like some intense conversation, then Julie came back on the cell phone.

"That was the OOD's mate. The front office says I'm to report to the commandant's office to meet with the NCIS in thirty minutes."

"Don't go," he said. "Go to Liz's office instead."

"But Dad—"

"Go to Liz's office. Then get Liz to call the dant's office and tell them you'll meet with NCIS, but only in her office. If they insist, Liz can go back there with you, but this'll give you time to talk to Liz, tell her what the hell's happening."

"Got it. I'll call you when we get there."

Ev hung up, thought about driving over to Liz's office, then went to find the scotch instead.

Jim and Branner were getting into her Bronco when her cell phone rang. She looked at Jim, who gestured for her to hand it over. He clicked it open and answered. It was Liz DeWinter.

"Mr. Hall. Did I misdial? I was looking for Agent Branner."

"Stand by one," was all he said, and then moved closer to Branner so that she could talk and he could listen in.

"Yes, Ms. DeWinter," Branner said.

"Julie Markham's on her way to my office. I understand you want to talk to her?"

"Yes, we do. But we're supposed to meet with her in Bancroft Hall. I was just going to call you."

"Sure you were. Well, look, Agent Branner, why not make this easy for everyone—you come over here to my office."

Jim nodded forcefully. "Okay," she said. "That works. Mr. Hall and I will be right over."

"Why Mr. Hall? What's he got to do with this?"

"Is Midshipman Markham still your client?" Branner asked.

"Yes, of course. She never stopped being my client. And now I hear the Academy may not let her graduate."

Jim motioned for Branner to give him the phone. "Liz?" he said. "Jim Hall. Let's not do this on the phone. We need to talk to Markham, and time is of the essence. Is she there yet?"

"No, but she's on her way over right now. Her ex-boyfriend is with her."

"Hays? Good. And may I ask a favor? Don't take any more phone calls, okay? And when Markham gets there, tell her we're coming in to talk about Dyle Booth."

"About *what*?"

"He's a mid. We think he may have killed Brian Dell."

"Whoa," Liz said. "WTF?"

"Hold that thought, and, remember, don't take any more calls. We're on our way."

Branner drove her Bronco, but Jim decided to take his truck. Both of them had turned off their cell phones to avoid inconvenient messages, but Jim had failed to turn off the police radio in his truck. The chief's voice came up on the net as they rounded State Circle and turned down toward Liz's office.

"Shit," Jim murmured, picking up the mike.

"Hey, boss, the dant's office is looking for you. And Special Agent Branner, too, apparently."

"What's the message, Chief?"

"ET call home?" Bustamente said.

"Got it, Chief, thanks. I take it the dant's back in the Yard?"

"His admin guy didn't say, but he did say the Man wants to see you, and now'd be really nice."

"Roger that," Jim said. "If anyone asks, you're still looking for me."

"Whassup?" the chief asked.

"What you don't know right now can't hurt you, Chief."

"Heard that. Standing by."

Jim thought about what to do while he waited for Branner to park. When the commandant wanted to see someone, he meant it literally, as in standing tall in his office. He suddenly didn't feel right about having asked the chief to lie for him, so he fired up his cell phone and called the commandant's office. He told them he was stuck out on Route 50, but that he'd had a message to call in. He was put on hold. He pulled in behind Branner, who came over to the window.

"I'm on disciplinary hold with the dant's office," Jim whispered after a minute had passed. Branner rolled her eyes and used her cell phone to check her voice mail.

"Mr. Hall," came the commandant's voice.

"Yes, sir," Jim replied, straightening in his seat out of habit. Branner closed her phone and leaned in to listen.

"Where is Special Agent Branner?"

"Don't know, sir," Jim said. "I've been trying to raise her myself."

"We have some new guidance in that matter you've been investigating. I won't go into details over an open line, other than to say we have a SecNav determination in the matter. Branner's people have also been informed."

"Yes, sir, copy that. Do you have new instructions for me, sir?"

"Exactly, Mr. Hall. Back out, write up a report, print a single copy, and give that to me and the source file to Pren. Tonight, if you please."

"I can do that, sir," Jim said. "I've been keeping a running file. Are there any accountability issues remaining?"

The dant hesitated. "Just one, Mr. Hall. We're going to address that via the Brigade Honor Committee. I understand you already approached the board regarding the individual in question."

"Yes, sir, but that was not productive."

"So Captain Rogers informs me. I think I can remedy that. Get me that report as soon as possible, Mr. Hall."

"Aye aye, sir," Jim said. "And that other matter? The tunnel matter?"

"We don't need any more problems on our plate just now, Mr. Hall. The SecNav made that abundantly clear. In our view, the tunnel matter should go away in two weeks, right? Thank you."

The circuit went down. A city cop appeared alongside in a cruiser and waved them out of the reserved parking spaces. Branner flashed her NCIS credentials at him and he nodded and drove off.

"Well, there it is," he said. "We've been officially backed out."

"You have," she said. "I haven't."

"No messages?"

"Lots of messages," she said. "But they all say the same thing: Call Harry Chang. No instructions, and nothing from the Academy directly."

"Then we can still go meet with Markham."

"I can. The question is, can you?"

He chewed on his lower lip. The Executive Department, at Branner's request, had summoned Markham to a meeting in Bancroft Hall. Except she wasn't going to show. Jim wondered if that fact would percolate up to the dant's office at this hour. Was the left hand talking to the right hand? If he went with Branner, he'd be disobeying a direct order, which might cost him his job. On the other hand, the Academy appeared to be ready to come down on Markham. If Markham knew the truth about the Dell incident, this was no time to sweat the small stuff. Branner was watching him carefully.

"I'll go. I think they're going to railroad Markham. Not fair."

"Unless she was indeed responsible," Branner said. "Then you're falling on your sword for nothing."

"Shit happens," he said.

She smiled at him and nodded. "Good call," she said. "Maybe there's hope for you after all."

"Up yours, Branner."

"In your dreams, cowboy."

Hey. A little bird just whispered in my ear. Actually, it was a little E-mail intercept out of the deputy dant's office. Someone's been running her mouth. And now my name's come up? The ghost of little Brian Dell getting ready to cause me trouble? I don't think so. I think I have the cure for that shit. Everyone forgetting the video? On which you are absolutely the star? Which I can have out on the World Wide Web in a New York flash?

You think that I'll just stand around if they corner me? Think I'll just break down and cry, ask for forgiveness, tell them I'm a victim, too? Bullshit. I'll take some di-rect and immediate effective action. I'll take prisoners and I'll execute their asses. I'll take the high ground and tell the whole fucking Brigade what I think of them. And then, if I have to, I'll show them all what a real man's made of when his back's to the wall. And I'll do it in front of God and everybody. And you, too.

You said you wanted to go for a ride. Nobody forced you. You said you needed a rush, some thrills to make up for your oh-so-boring, so perfectly straight life. You came on to me, remember? We had a deal. So tell me you're not going to try to stick it to me, not this late in our dark little game. Because, as we both know, I can stick it to you a whole lot worse than you can stick it to me.

Julie, baby: You bored?

They found Liz, Julie Markham, and Tommy Hays waiting for them in Liz's darkly paneled conference room. They all sat down, and then Liz began to establish some ground rules. Branner waved her off. "We have more serious issues to talk about right now. Midshipman Markham, I'm still Special Agent Branner, and I have some questions for you about Midshipman Dyle Booth."

At the mention of Booth's name, Julie Markham's face paled visibly. She looked sideways at Hays for a moment, as if to ask, How could you? Then Liz jumped in. "First, I need to know the background on all this," she said. "They just got here, and I don't know what you're talking about."

"Mr. Hays," Jim said. "Tell Ms. DeWinter and Agent Branner what you told me about Dyle Booth."

"No, don't," Julie told Hays. "Don't say anything at all. We don't have to say anything, do we, Liz?"

Liz frowned. "No, you don't, but—"

Before she could explain, Jim interrupted. "I just got off the phone with the dant. He ordered me to back out of the Dell investigation. He said that there had been a SecNav determination as to what happened to Dell."

"Then that's it, isn't it?" Julie said, trying for a confident look. "It's officially over?"

"For Dell, it was over when he hit the concrete," Branner said, producing a painful silence at the table. "But not for you, apparently."

Jim leaned forward. "I asked if there were any outstanding accountability issues. The dant said there was one, and it involved you, Midshipman Markham."

"Goddamn it, *why*?"

"You want the technical answer or the real answer?"

Julie looked again at Tommy Hays, who just shook his head in bewilderment.

"Let's hear the real answer," Liz said.

"The real answer is that a midshipman died in Bancroft Hall. Someone must be held accountable for that. The official ruling will probably be a DBM—accident. Plebe went up on the roof and fell off. Internally, they know there's more to it. Within the Academy, they're probably going to use a fig leaf, say that the system just overwhelmed a plebe.

But we know that's not the whole story, is it, Midshipman Markham?"

Julie just stared at him.

Branner leaned forward. "You told us you didn't know Dell other than as a summer plebe. But isn't it true you were secretly mentoring Brian Dell?"

Julie set her jaw and didn't answer. Hays closed his eyes, as if he was expecting to be slapped. Liz asked Julie if this was true.

"It might be," Julie said very slowly.

"*Might* be? You told *me* you didn't really know Midshipman Dell," Liz said. "Other than as a plebe among plebes."

Julie stared down at the table.

"Well, here it is, Julie," Jim said. "The dant is going to fire up the Brigade Honor Committee. Somehow, some way, they're going to pin something on you relating to what happened to Dell. If they don't know about your helping Dell, they will once a BIO starts asking questions, right? Especially if he talks to Mr. Hays here. My guess is that you won't be found directly responsible for whatever it is they're going to 'conclude' about Dell's death, but you're going to get tagged with something."

"That's not *fair*!"

"It's not fair, but it's preferable to having the system get tagged. There's always accountability, right? It's the cornerstone of their whole program. So if it can't be them, it's going to be you."

"Unless . . ." Branner began. Julie looked at her.

"For Christ's sake, Julie," Tommy Hays said. "Tell them. They think Booth may have done it. *Tell* them."

Julie got out of her chair and went to the door. It was obvious she just wanted to bolt from the room. Jim saw Branner pushing her chair back surreptitiously, but nobody else moved. Then Julie turned around to face all of them.

"I've been on the Academy swim team since plebe year," she said. "I'm a freestyler. So is Dyle. But I'm not in his league. Nobody is."

"He's a classmate?" Liz asked.

"That's right. Dyle Jones Booth. We don't compete, of course—he's on the men's team. But Dyle is . . . different. As a competitor, as a team member. He's big. He was big when he got here, and he's bulked up over the past four years. He's going Marine option. Always was. He plays the part. Tons of gung ho bullshit, but you get the sense he does it just to fool the officers."

"Are they fooled?" Jim asked.

"Yes, I think they are. I mean, the Marine officers eat that stuff right up. Dyle's loud and he's big and he's way enthusiastic about everything military—marching, drill, shooting, hand to gland, spit and polish, giving commands. All that 'Hoo-ah' noise. He's effective because you wouldn't *dream* of not doing what he says."

"Because there's always an implied threat?"

"Not implied, Mr. Hall," she said. "It's right out there. It's in his eyes. In his body language. And you get the impression he'd almost prefer it if you crossed him. Like he lives for that. 'Go ahead, punk, make my day,' that kinda deal."

"What's your connection, other than through the swim team?" Branner asked.

"Well, he's in my batt."

"He a striper?" Jim asked.

"No, sir, he's not a striper. There's something about him that I think bothered the Navy officers. He's too much. Too loud. Over-the-top. Plus, behind their backs? He scoffs at the whole striper scene. Thinks it's childish, boys ordering boys around. When he realized he'd never be one, he made like it wasn't important anyway. Goes around counting the days until he gets to go to Quantico and starts what he calls his 'real life.' "

"You think the officers are afraid of this guy?" Jim asked.

"No, sir, not exactly, but they know he's different. On the other hand, he's been a big-time medal winner for Navy in swimming, he's beyond physically fit, and he's a poster boy for the uniform. I think they're mostly anxious to graduate him and then let the Marines deal with him."

"And the plebes? How does he deal with the plebes?"

"They're scared shitless of him," she said, slipping back into her chair. Tommy Hays nodded emphatically.

"The system here is different from when you went through," she said, speaking directly to Jim. "Now they try to teach leadership from the ground up. It begins in youngster year, when every youngster is responsible for mentoring one plebe. Every second-class mid is responsible for supervising two youngsters, and the firsties supervise the whole thing in the company structure. The plebes learn to follow; the upperclassmen learn to lead, to take care of their people. It's a good system. It's a smart system. But Dyle plays outside the system."

"How so?"

"Dyle quit running the plebes, directly, about midyear. Now he menaces them. Shows up in their rooms after hours. He shadows them. Gets on a plebe and stays on him."

"Why don't the other upperclassmen call him out over this—he must be disrupting the company chain of command."

"You don't call out Dyle Booth," Hays said. Everyone looked over at him. "Nobody in his right mind would do that."

"Where's his company officer?" Jim asked.

"He's a Marine captain," Julie said. "He goes around full bore, too. He thinks Dyle Booth is superman."

"What happened between you and Booth?" Branner asked Julie.

"Dyle wanted me to go out with him. Not here, but when we went to away meets at other colleges. He said we were the best of the Navy freestylers and we ought to get together." She shivered. "When he came on to me, it brought to mind images of those Nazi super-race breeding programs." She paused for a moment. "I told him no. I told him he gave me the creeps. Besides, he knew I was seeing Tommy."

"But he persisted?" Branner asked, prodding her.

After another moment's hesitation, Julie said, "Yes." Her voice was now almost down to a whisper. "There was this one away meet, down at UVA. Tommy and I had been arguing—over the future. There was this big frat party. Believe it or not, I'd never been to one of those. They party pretty hard down there in Charlottesville. I . . . I got a little drunk."

She stopped and looked over at Tommy, as if seeking some moral support. But then she continued. "Actually, I got really drunk. Tommy hadn't gone down there, because he was still pissed off at me. But Dyle was there. He had a bunch of sorority girls hanging all over him, but he made it clear whom he wanted that night."

"Okay," Branner said brusquely. "So you had a one-night stand with supermensch. Big deal. Shit happens. What then?"

Julie blinked at the way Branner dismissed the significance of what she was saying. "Eventually, I told Tommy. He kind of went off. As he had every right to, I guess." She looked sideways at Hays, who was red-faced now, staring down at the table. "But Dyle was so triumphant. I think it was always about that—another trophy for him. He kept making comments. Every time we ran into each other, he'd have to say something embarrassing. People were talking."

Jim still wondered if they were hearing the whole story. Branner was right: A one-night hookup in your senior year ought not to be the end of the world. "Was he really trying to score again, or was he just crowing?" he asked.

"I thought it was just Dyle doing his Tarzan act, but then he got pushy, real pushy. I told him no way in hell. He kept it up. One day, I went off on him after practice. Very public scene. I said some things, the kind of things we all felt about Dyle Booth, although no one had ever come out with them before. Especially classmates. He got all quiet."

"Did he threaten you?" Branner asked.

"I started to get these E-mails," she said, running her fingers through her hair. "No name line, but they were from Dyle all right. Lots of stuff about being the Shark. They'd just appear on my screen when I'd go on-line. I couldn't do anything with my computer until I'd read them. And then they'd disappear, all by themselves. I'd try to delete them. No go. But once I clicked on them, they'd delete themselves. No path. No trace."

"What'd he say?"

"He began to tell me stuff, stuff that he'd been doing over the past year. In Bancroft. Here in Crabtown. Stuff about the Goth scene over at St. John's. Seriously weird shit. Sex parties. Some of their cult stuff. Things he called 'vampire drills.' Stuff I didn't want to hear."

"Did he talk about going into town and beating up townies?" Jim asked.

Julie nodded. "He called it 'training,' for when he got into Marine recon. He was always talking about going 'ree-con.' He said he uses the tunnels to come and go, whenever he feels like it. Says he owns them."

Jim looked over at Branner. "When did all this happen?"

"The E-mails started during dark ages—January or thereabouts. It was like I was his best friend, so he could tell me all this shit. He'd even send pictures. There was this one, where he dressed up as Dracula or something. It just bannered on my screen one night while Mel and I were retrieving some papers. It even had sound. Mel damn near fainted, it was so real, so clear . . . and so Dyle."

"You think he was getting into your room, messing with your computer?" Branner asked.

"No, I think he did it over the Brigade intranet. Dyle can make computers do anything he wants. He claims to have done shit on the faculty intranet, too. Like penetrate the faculty servers? He sent me a single history exam question once, and it was on the exam the next day." She looked at both of them. "He talked about you two. That he'd done stuff to you."

"Did he ever threaten you?" Branner asked.

"What do you mean?" Julie said, looking at Liz as if for help.

"Did he ever say that if you didn't come across, he'd do something to you? Hell-o, Julie? A threat, you know?"

Liz intervened. "Where are you going with that question?" she asked.

Branner sighed. "If this guy was threatening Midshipman Markham, she should have gone to her chain of command. Obviously, she didn't. I'm wondering why."

"Julie was a three-striper," Hays said. He saw Liz's confusion. "A striper, you know, a midshipman officer. She was a three-striper on the battalion staff. If she'd gone to the Dark Side about Dyle, she would've had to tell what happened down at UVA. That she got drunk and had sex with a classmate. Total loss of personal control. It would have destroyed her reputation in the battalion and probably in our class. Wasn't going to happen."

"From what you've told us, I'm wondering why Dyle Booth didn't tell," Branner said. "To get even for you shutting him down."

"Not his style," Julie said. "First, because that would be bilging a classmate. Not done. And second, I think he wanted to hurt me himself. The E-mails were some kind of campaign, as if he were exposing himself to me. And then he found out about Brian Dell. That I was secretly helping him. I think he decided it would be more fun to terrorize Dell than to come at me directly. And since, strictly speaking, I was outside the chain of command in helping Dell, I couldn't report Dyle for that, either."

"But surely Dell's own mentors, his youngster, the other youngster in his own company—they would have known that Booth was going after this kid."

Julie shook her head. "That was the thing. Dell's youngster resigned halfway through the year. Didn't come back after Christmas leave. He was failing three subjects, and he'd decided he hated being here. So Dell didn't have a youngster. No top cover. That was one of the reasons I took him on."

"Wouldn't somebody in his company have seen it happening?"

"Not with Dyle. He'd come in the night. Or catch Dell out on one of the athletic fields. Ambush him coming back from an E.I. you know, extra instruction, session. Sometimes Dyle just . . . appears. Plus, that company isn't one of the better ones. The youngsters in his company knew that Dell was adrift, but it meant they had one less plebe to worry about, so they let it slide. They probably were clueless about what Dyle was doing. Hell, *I* didn't know about Dyle's running him until just before . . . before Brian, you know."

"What happened?" Jim asked.

"Dell came to my room shortly before taps. Melanie was studying in the next room with some of her friends. He wanted to go topside. He was really upset. We used to talk sometimes, up on the roof. Guys go up there when they want privacy. He asked if we could meet that night, after taps. I said okay. He seemed really down, really tired. He was this little guy, you know? He looked about fourteen that night. So I said I'd meet him."

"And did you?"

"Yes. That's when he told me about Dyle. That he'd been ordered to come around to Dyle's room at all hours. That Dyle was putting shit in his E-mail account, that Dyle had penetrated his computer, erased homework assignments, shit like that. Dyle would appear after midnight sometimes, or real early in the morning. Brian said he was scared of Dyle. That Dyle was making him do stuff."

" 'Do stuff'?"

"He wouldn't say what exactly, but I got the impression that Dyle was, like, turning him out. You know, maybe sexual humiliation stuff? Like he assumed Dell was gay. You have to remember—Dyle was twice Dell's size."

"*Was* Dell gay?" Branner asked.

"I don't think so," Julie said. "More like weak. Math wizard, supposedly a high-scoring diver, but I don't know where he ever competed. He was wiry, but too small."

"Why didn't he report what was going on? Tell me this wasn't normal plebe year stuff," Jim said.

"Not at all. It's really changed, even since I've been here. It's much more structured now. That's what all the mentoring layers are about. But even so, plebes don't go to the Dark Side with complaints against the upperclass, not if they want to stay here."

Jim knew this was true. The way the system was supposed to work was that a plebe's own upperclassmen would step in if someone got out of hand. "Was he suicidal?"

"No. Just down. Felt he couldn't win. And Dyle was scaring him. He wanted to put his chit in. Resign. But not kill himself. He talked about going to another college. 'A real one,' he said."

"What did you do?"

"When I heard how bad it was getting, I told him to go back to his room and that I was going to get it stopped."

Branner had been taking notes. "How?" she asked, looking up.

"I didn't know at the time. But I had pretty much decided to go to Dell's company officer and tell him everything I knew. They had some other problems in that company that I'd heard about, so I figured they'd be in the mood to deal with an outside firstie running one of their plebes."

"And did you?"

"No," she said. "Because I ran into Dyle Booth on the way back to my room. I'd swear he knew I'd been up there with Dell. I don't know how, but Dyle gets around, especially at night. He said he'd been to my room, and then he'd come topside to find me. Anyway, I told him off. Said I was going to get this shit stopped, one way or another."

"And what did he do?"

"He went all cold. Gave me his big-deal shark look. That's what we call it on the team. That wall-eyed thing he does underwater. Told me to go ahead, knock myself out. Got real calm, like he had a plan all ready. That scared me, actually. I'd expected him to get in my face. But he backed off, said he had something to do that night out in town, and that he'd be ready to deal with the Dell problem in the morning." Julie shivered. "I had no idea then—"

"Did he actually threaten to do something to Midshipman Dell?"

Julie shook her head. "No, it was more like I could do or say anything I wanted to, but it wouldn't make any difference. To him or to Dell. I know now I should have gone right to the OOD, right then and there. But I was scared, and I didn't know what I was going to do the next morning. It never occurred to me that he'd—" She stopped, tears forming in her eyes.

Jim was about to ask another question, but he felt Branner's hand touch his arm. Wait, she was signaling. See what she says next. Jim waited for her to continue.

"I got back to my room, and Mel was already asleep. I decided just to hit my tree, regroup in the morning. Like I said, it never occurred to me that Dell was in physical danger. I figured that Dyle might run him harder, or do some physical hazing. But he'd said he was going over the wall, out into town. So I figured nothing would happen that night." She looked up at them, anguish in her eyes now. "I got that wrong, didn't I?"

Tommy Hays moved sideways in his chair and took her hand. He looked at both Jim and Branner. "Hey?" he said quietly. "This is the Naval Academy. This kind of shit, this kind of guy—this doesn't happen here. We're here to become naval officers. We all bitch and moan about the system, but we believe in it. The officers believe in it. Somehow, this evil bastard got in, and the system can't see him because they've forgotten how to look for some psycho like this."

"Julie," Liz said, "do you think Dyle Booth actually killed Brian Dell?"

"I don't know," Julie said in a very small voice. "He was big enough, and Brian was small. If he got him up on that roof, you know, by ordering him to go there, walk the ledge, something like that, he could have. Why don't you ask him?"

"That's next," Jim said. "Liz, I think you and Julie here need to go see the commandant. The supe, even. They need to hear this."

"I disagree," Liz said. "At least for the moment. You said yourself they were going to blame her for what happened to Dell. I wouldn't advise her to make it easy for them."

"I failed to take action," Julie said in a low voice. "I *am* responsible."

"Dyle Booth is responsible, Julie," Jim said. "From everything I've heard about this guy, he'd have found a way to get to Dell even if you'd gone to the OOD that night. It's not like you could have proved it."

"What are you two going to do?" Liz asked Jim.

"Mr. Hall and I are going over into the Yard and summon Mr. Booth to the front office for a little chat," Branner said.

"Good luck with that," Julie said.

"Excuse me?"

"Because he probably already knows you're looking for him. I don't know how, but that's just Dyle. I mean, there were lots of people around when the mate came down and said I had to go see NCIS. Bancroft Hall is a hive. Word gets around fast."

"We'll see about that," Branner said. "But we have other business to discuss with Mr. Booth, over and above the Dell incident."

Jim stood up, and so did Branner. "Ultimately, you'll have to go talk to them, Julie," she said.

"Why?" Liz asked.

"Because they need to hear the truth. Up to now, the administration's been playing the usual political game. Protect the Academy's image at all costs. But this is very different. We have a damned good indication of homicide here. And even if the dant still wants to run for cover, the supe won't. Admiral McDonald's not that kind of guy."

"You have an awful lot of faith in the system, Agent Branner," Julie said.

"I think Tommy here was correct," Jim said. "This system wasn't designed to spot a psychopath." He looked at his watch. "Liz, we'll call you when we get something. Right now, we need to move out."

Jim and Branner walked into the OOD's office in Bancroft Hall fifteen minutes later. Branner asked that they summon Midshipman First Class Dyle Booth to the office. The OOD said he first needed to get permission from the deputy commandant, Captain Rogers. Two minutes later, Rogers came into the OOD's office and asked them both to step into his office. Closing the door, he told them that he had orders to refer any requests from NCIS directly to the commandant.

"This is basically a continuation of what we started with the honor board," Branner said. "We have new information."

"I hear you, Special Agent," Rogers said. "But we've had a SecNav determination in the Dell case, and now the commandant has directed that NCIS activities in regard to the Dell case be suspended. Mr. Hall, we were told that you had been informed of this."

"The commandant told me to back out, yes," Jim said. "But Agent Branner here hasn't received any such instructions from her chain of command. I came along to see what was going on."

Rogers gave him a peculiar look, as if to say, Nice try, sunshine. Just then, Captain Robbins opened his door and summoned them both to come in. He told Jim to close the door and then, standing behind his desk, addressed himself to Branner.

"Special Agent Branner, what's this all about? Where have you been? Your people have been trying to contact you."

"We've been meeting with Midshipman Markham and her lawyer," Branner said. "We have new information on the Dell case."

"There is no more Dell case," the dant said firmly. "The SecNav has directed a finding of death by misadventure."

"But my investigation wasn't finished. How can anybody make a determination until the investigation is finished?"

"There are larger issues at stake here, Agent Branner," Robbins said, sitting down. "We know that Dell went off the roof and died as a result. You were directed to rule out homicide. You were directed to proceed expeditiously. I'm assuming you did that. You reported no evidence of a homicide."

"I didn't report at all," Branner said, obviously getting angry.

"Mr. Harry Chang would contradict you, I think," Robbins said. "At least he told the SecNav that no *evidence* of homicide had been uncovered."

"We weren't finished, damn it. Mr. Chang knows that."

"That's not what he said to the SecNav. He said you had no evidence."

"But there is new information," Jim said. "And we need to—"

"You, sir, need to go back to your regularly assigned duties," Robbins said. "Any taskings related to the Dell case are hereby rescinded."

They just stared at him. He put up his hands. "Look, this thing has gone on long enough. We've been beaten up in the media. Rumors and innuendo abound. Dell's parents are being torn this way and that. The Board of Visitors is asking questions. The supe and I are of the opinion that any further rooting around will only make things worse. We need to move on. The SecNav agrees."

Jim could see that Branner was about to unload with both barrels, so he tried to preempt her. "Captain Robbins, we have reason to believe that another midshipman, a firstie, was involved in what happened to Brian Dell. Maybe even had a hand in it. We can't close this case until we at least pull that string."

"*We* can and will close the case, Mr. Hall. This is no longer a matter for your concern. If Special Agent Branner has reservations, she should take them up through her own chain of command. *We* are done with this thing."

"And you're willing to let a murderer graduate from your wonderful institution?" Branner asked.

"Ms. Branner. Those are strong words. Let me ask you right here and now: Do you have a single scrap of physical evidence that someone, anyone, *murdered* Brian Dell?"

"No, but I do have evidence that a senior naval officer is obstructing me from ever getting our hands on such evidence."

The word *obstructing* hung in the air for almost fifteen seconds while Robbins and Branner glared at each other. Then he punched the intercom and told his secretary to get Mr. Harry Chang at NCIS headquarters on the line. Then he swiveled around in his chair and stared out the windows down into Tecumseh Court. Jim and Branner looked at each other. They were still standing in front of the dant's desk like a pair of truants. Then one of the lines lighted up and the secretary announced that Mr. Chang was holding on line one. Robbins, still facing away from them, reached back for the phone.

"Harry? Have you been in contact with Special Agent Branner lately?"

He waited for a reply. "No, but actually, she's right here. I've explained to her that the Dell thing is being shut down. She says that she has new information and that I'm obstructing a murder investigation. Would you like to do some calibrating?"

He listened for a few seconds, then turned around to hand the phone to Branner. "Mr. Hall, come outside with me, if you please."

Jim followed Robbins out into the secretarial area, closing the door behind him so Branner could have some privacy. No doubt Chang was going to go off on her.

"Mr. Hall, you like your job here? You want to keep it?"

Jim looked down at him. Robbins's face was controlled, but the anger was clearly visible in his eyes. The secretary tactfully got up and left the room. Jim tried to think of something really clever to say, but before he got anything out, Branner appeared in the doorway.

"Captain Robbins?" she said in a perfectly neutral tone of voice. "Mr. Chang would like a word."

Robbins gave Jim one last meaningful look and went back into his office. Branner looked at Jim and tipped her head in a "Let's go" motion. They left the office suite and went out into the Rotunda. He started to ask her what had happened, but she shook her head. They went on outside into Tecumseh Court. Night had fallen. They walked in silence down the wide worn steps, flanked by ancient bronze cannons, and continued down Buchanan Road until they reached Jim's truck. They got in and sat there in the shadows created by the streetlights. The white bulk of the superintendent's quarters, Buchanan House, gleamed in a bath of floodlights to their right.

"I am so pissed off, I can't see straight," she growled through clenched teeth.

"I got asked if I liked my job," he offered. "If that's any consolation."

She grunted.

"I was trying to think of some really cool reply just when you came to the door," he continued. "And how's Mr. Chang this evening?"

"Showing lots of teeth."

"Neat trick over a phone."

"But one he does rather well. I think he figured out I'd been playing coy with the phones this afternoon."

"Did you get to explain that we have new information on the Dell case?"

"There is no Dell case. And, no, I didn't, because I was invited to go into the receive mode right from the start."

"Know that feeling," he said. "I really did want to ask the dant what it was he was going to do to Julie Markham, but he seemed to have a locked transmitter, too."

"I can't believe they'd just fold the whole thing under a rug like this."

"Well, I don't agree with it, but I can see how the people

up in D.C. might talk themselves into it. The SecNav asking Chang, 'You have evidence of anything other than an accident?' 'Negative,' Chang replies. SecNav says, 'The security officer down there, you know, that world-famous detective? He's got some wild-ass theories, but evidence?' 'Why, no, Mr. Secretary.' 'All right, then. Wrap it up. Whole Navy's getting a black eye. Enough, awreddy.' "

"And Short Round back there going, 'Yes, sir, Mr. Secretary, we can certainly do that, sir. Right now, if you'd like, sir.' " She made a rude noise.

"Well, there is one question: Now that we've heard testimony that implicates this guy Booth in both the Dell matter *and* what's been going on down in those tunnels, what're we going to do about it?"

Branner looked over at him. "How well *do* you like your job, Mr. Hall?"

"Not well enough to cover up a murder, if that's what happened," he declared, surprising himself.

She turned fully sideways in the seat. "Sure about that? People who go standing on principle in the government usually find out where they got that expression 'slippery slope.' "

"You keep telling me it's a nothing job," he pointed out.

Branner smiled. "Tell me this: If I weren't in the picture at all, what would you do right now?"

"I'd go hunt down this kid, Booth. Look him in the eye and see if he was the guy in vampire makeup who's been screwing around with our tunnels. And if he was, I'd cuff his ass, arrest him, and haul him down to the Academy police station volleyball court for a game of Little Slugger."

"No you wouldn't," she said. "First, you're not a cop. Second, even if you were, a tune-up queers the deal for any prosecutor. Third, baseball bats went out with the KGB."

He laughed in the darkness. "What would you do?"

"Well, look. In one sense, they're all correct: We have no frigging evidence. Just the word of two frightened midshipmen. Julie Markham, who shouldn't have been messing with that plebe outside of the chain of command. And

Tommy Hays, her ex-boyfriend, who knows Booth screwed his girlfriend, and thinks the guy tried to ice him. Hell, maybe she was right: If she'd stayed out of it, his own supervisors would eventually have detected the Dyle Booth thing. As it is—"

"As it is, the kid's dead," he said. "That's all that matters now. I say we go find Booth and interrogate him."

"Say we did. He could just shine us on. Say absolutely nothing. Deny everything. Who saw him running this plebe in the dead of night? Who can prove he had any connection with Dell? The only one really pointing the finger is Julie Markham, and she's the one in trouble, not Booth."

He sighed. She was right on all counts, damn her eyes. He wasn't a cop. He had no professional training in the rights of suspects and witnesses. Booth did not have to say a frigging thing. Just then, headlights swept across their faces and they saw the supe's official Navy sedan swing into the arched driveway of Buchanan House. When it stopped, they saw the aide and the admiral get out. The two talked for a minute in the driveway, and then the admiral went inside. Jim looked at Branner.

"There's *the* Man. Wanna take a shot?" he asked.

She thought about it for a few seconds and then nodded. "Sure, why the hell not? Can't dance."

Ev got out of the shower and heard the phone ringing. It was Liz, who suggested he come down to Angelo's on the waterfront, where she was taking Julie and Tommy Hays. Resisting the urge to pelt her with questions, he said he'd be there in twenty minutes.

The restaurant was barely half full, so they had some privacy. Liz took him through the meeting with Hall and Branner while Julie and Tommy Hays sat there munching on some calamari and avoiding eye contact with Ev. When she was finished, Ev didn't know what to think, other than that he was truly upset that Julie had lied about her involvement with Dell.

"Are they going to go after this Midshipman Booth?" he asked.

"They said they were," Liz said. "But the powers that be might, in effect, protect Booth if they've decided to shut the investigation down."

"And somehow smear Julie with what happened to Dell?"

Julie started to say something, but Liz beat her to it. "The more I think about that, the more I believe we can stop it."

"How?" Julie asked. Hays, who'd reminded Julie about exams, was looking at his watch.

"Branner," Liz said. "I got the impression she wasn't going to just sit by and let that happen."

Julie was shaking her head. "That Branner woman wasn't exactly full of sympathy," she said. "Far as she's concerned, I lied to her when I said I didn't really know Brian Dell."

"Well, news flash, Julie, sounds like that's exactly what you did," Ev said. This produced a strained silence at the table, and netted him a warning look from Liz. But he plunged on. "I agree with Liz that Booth is a lot more responsible for what happened to Dell than you are. You were trying to help the poor guy; this Booth was apparently more interested in torturing him. Anyone else know you were mentoring him?"

"His roommate, maybe," Julie said. "Unless Dell kept it from him. But you know how it is with roommates."

"But NCIS knows," Hays pointed out. It was the first time Tommy had said anything about the case, and Ev nodded his acknowledgment. The waiter brought a large bowl of steaming pasta and some sauces and cheese. He put it on a lazy Susan in the middle of the table and then set out bowls. They stopped talking and attended to the food, which Ev discovered was better than he'd expected. When they were finished, Tommy excused himself, saying he had to get back for study hours. He told Julie to call him on his cell once she got back into Mother B. She said she would. He offered to chip in for dinner, but Liz waved him off. He thanked her and left.

"What should I do if they call me in when I sign back in?" Julie asked Liz. Ever since Ev had made his remark about her deception, Julie wouldn't look at him.

"Who?" Liz asked.

"The commandant. Or Captain Rogers."

"You respectfully comply. But you tell them nothing about your interaction with Dell. You tell them that, on advice of counsel, you won't discuss the Dell case. But if what Mr. Hall said is correct, I wouldn't expect any summonses."

"Unless that Branner woman sits down with the dant and spills everything," she said.

"Agent Branner has other fish to fry right now. Specifically, Midshipman Dyle Booth."

Julie glanced around the restaurant, as if half-expecting to see Booth peering in through a window. "If Dyle's gotten wind of anything, he's going to come to see me," she said.

"If you'd like," Ev said, "we can stop screwing around and go see the commandant. Or the supe. Tonight. Right now. Tell him everything that's been revealed tonight. Let him get ahold of Booth. I still think that's the way to go."

"Your lawyer disagrees most emphatically," Liz said. The waiter came and cleared away the dishes, then poured Liz and Ev some more wine. Julie took the opportunity to visit the ladies' room. Liz waited until the waiter left them alone. "Ev, what the hell are you doing?"

"She did lie, damn it. She knows better. Four years of the Academy and she *lies*? Shit. She ought to march in there, tell the whole truth, and take the consequences."

"You guys amaze me," she said, looking around to make sure Julie wasn't walking back to the table. She leaned toward him. "She's been wanting to do the same dumb thing. Look, Julie's brushing right up against a homicide investigation. Under those circumstances, you don't tell anyone *anything* until you know you're going to get something in return. A deal, a break, some consideration. In case you've forgotten, Ev, ours is an adversarial legal system."

"Legal, schmegal," he muttered, indicating with his eyes that Julie was returning. "The honor code demands it."

Liz bit her lip and did not reply. Julie slid into her chair and looked from Ev's face to Liz's. "You two look like an old married couple having an argument," she said.

"Your father's just a wee bit frustrated," Liz said, giving Ev another warning look.

"Why, because you can't do something about all this?" Julie asked Ev, her face guarded.

Joanne used to get that look, he thought. "Partly," he said. "And partly because nobody over there's behaving like they should."

Julie stared at him. He felt a tingle of fear in his belly, because she obviously understood exactly what he was saying. He could almost see her withdrawing from them. The Navy part of him was fiercely proud. The parent part was suddenly apprehensive.

Liz cleared her throat. "Julie," she said. "Your father here is having an attack of the stupids, I'm afraid. The very best thing you can do right now is nothing. Go back and get ready for exams. Keep your mouth shut, and await developments. Let's not go snatching defeat from the jaws of victory."

"No, he's not," Julie said in a low voice. She hesitated and then stood up, carefully arranging her chair at the table. "Having an attack of the stupids, I mean. Thanks for dinner, Liz. And don't worry—I'll give it a night's rest before I do or say anything." She reached under the chair, where her midshipman's hat was perched on the rungs. "You two look good together," she said, turning the hat in her hands. "I'm glad for you both. And I mean that." Then she walked out of the restaurant, her back stiff.

Ev stared at the front door after she'd closed it. The waiter zipped by and asked about coffee. They both said yes at the same time.

"Every time I think I understand Julie," Liz said, "she surprises me. You know her tones of voice—was that sarcasm?"

"No, I don't think so. But it sounded a lot like good-bye."

• • •

"Special Agent Branner and Jim Hall, security officer, to see Admiral McDonald about the Dell matter," Jim said.

The steward asked them to step in and wait in the ante-room. Two minutes later, he reappeared and asked them to follow him upstairs. He escorted them into the admiral's study, then closed the paneled doors and left. Admiral McDonald got up to greet them. His service jacket with its one big gold stripe and a smaller one just above it hung on the back of an upholstered chair. There was a half-full martini glass sitting on the side table next to his chair.

"Mr. Hall," the supe said, offering his hand. "And you are Special Agent Branner, as I recall. Please sit down. I understand this concerns the Dell matter."

"Yes, sir, it does."

"You're aware the Dell matter has been decided?"

"Yes, sir," Branner said. "But we have new information."

The admiral frowned and looked at his watch. "I can give you ten minutes. Then I have a reception to go to."

Jim launched into an explanation of why they had come to see him. The supe heard him out, asking no questions, just listening. Only once did he glance at his watch. When Jim was finished, the admiral got up and began to pace the room.

"And you feel this Midshipman Booth was involved in Dell's fall?"

"Yes, sir," Branner said. "One way or another."

"Do you have any evidence of this, other than what Markham and Hays told you?"

"Not yet, sir."

The admiral turned to face them. "So, on a factual basis, nothing has changed: You have no conclusive physical evidence of homicide. You have the unsworn testimony of two other midshipmen implicating Booth in illegal acts. But that's it?"

"We need to interview Booth," Branner said. "If he is the same individual who's been acting out in the utility tunnels, we can probably get evidence. But not if we can't even interview him."

"And the dant said no?"

"That's correct, sir. He said SecNav has spoken and that's it."

The admiral went back to his chair and stood there for a moment.

"The problem is, boys and girls, that the secretary of the entire Navy *has* spoken. Based in great part on what we've told him. And what your bosses basically corroborated, Ms. Branner. Now you're asking me to approach the throne and tell the SecNav that his findings and determinations are incorrect."

"Yes, sir. At least temporarily, until we can complete this investigation."

"Well, that's a real problem, Ms. Branner," he said, sitting back down. "Look, you probably can't appreciate this fact, but the Academy has to practice defensive siege warfare on a pretty much continuous basis. We have enemies: the liberals in Congress, budgeteers within the Defense Department, the antimilitary element of the media, the perpetual peaceniks. At one end of the spectrum, people see us holding these kids to higher standards and accuse us of being elitist. At the other end, some of our own alumni rant and rave that we're caving in to some vast feminazi conspiracy aimed at emasculating the dreaded male warrior culture once and for all."

"Sir, I—"

"Hear me out, please. When things go wrong here, as they inevitably do, the people who hate everything we stand for tend to pile on, with visible glee, I might add. And should we make accommodation, then the alumni pile on. I spend a whole lot of my time on damage control."

"I'm not sure I understand the significance of the alumni, Admiral," Jim said. "I'm an alumnus, for instance."

"I'm talking about the alumni who wear three and four stars on their shoulders. Unlike the civilian university world, Mr. Hall, our alumni sit on our promotion boards."

"So this is about turning two stars into three, Admiral?"

The admiral's face hardened. "That's a cheap shot, Mr. Hall. There are a couple hundred other officers here besides me. Being superintendent, I have to protect their careers."

"We're taking dead Brian Dell's point of view, Admiral," Branner said. "If what we've learned is true, the Academy let him down big-time."

The admiral glared at her. "That's a big *if*, Ms. Branner," he said. "And suppose you do interview this Booth and he just tells you to pound sand. What then?"

"We take him apart. We search his room. We interview his weird girlfriends over in town. We compare hair, fibers, blood, DNA, fingerprints, voiceprints, and E-mails with crime scene evidence from the muggings in town, Dell's room, Dell's body, Markham's person—in other words, we focus on a suspect and we investigate his ass."

"The problem is, you have no *evidence* to justify reopening this investigation, Agent Branner. Plus, you are just about out of time, because very soon, the vice president of the United States is going to commission the entire class, and then they will be gone."

"Not all of them, Admiral," Jim said. "There'll be football players with ruined knees, at least a couple of academic holds, maybe somebody with appendicitis. You could always add Booth to that list. Just because he graduates doesn't make him immune from military justice."

The admiral sighed and looked at his watch again.

"You know, Admiral," Branner said, "slamming the lid on this thing doesn't exactly square very well with your new ethics and morality program, does it? I mean, you're always telling the mids that the proof of the program is when people practice what they preach. I've got an idea: Why not put the question to the midshipmen? See what they'd do with it. Exams are almost here; there's a super final exam question for you."

The admiral gave her a pained look. "I've got to go. You've got to go. You have no evidence. All you have is a he says/she says finger-pointing drill. That can go on forever. At this juncture, my job is damage control. I'm sorry." He pushed a small button under the side table, and the steward appeared a moment later to show them out.

As they headed for the door, the admiral had a final question. "Mr. Hall, didn't the dant tell you to stand down from this matter? That we already had a SecNav determination?"

"Yes, sir, he did."

"Does he know you're here?"

"No, sir. He does not."

The admiral stared at him for a moment. "Correct me if I'm wrong, Mr. Hall, but didn't you come to the Academy MarDet after an incident in the Bosnia campaign? A blue on blue, where they blamed you and then found out someone else was responsible?"

"Yes, sir."

"Well, this time, I believe it *is* on you. It's been nice knowing you, Mr. Hall."

Twenty minutes later, Jim and Agent Branner sat in one of the clam bars along the city dock, having a beer and some fish and chips. They ate in silence, digesting what had just been said in Buchanan House. The clam shack was almost empty, the tourists having gone back to their hotels or into one of the local restaurants. Jim wiped oil off his mouth and hands and crumpled up the cardboard container.

"I don't each much fried food," he said, "but every once in awhile, this stuff hits the spot."

"A spot that usually stays with me forever," Branner said, patting her tummy. "So what now, Sherlock?"

"I'm conflicted, filled with self-doubt, suffering low personal esteem, and I'm probably a victim," he replied with a straight face.

She grinned. "In other words, it beats the shit out of you, does it?"

"Something like that. I know what I *want* to do, but that augurs badly for what's left of my job security."

"What job security? 'It's been nice knowing you, Mr. Hall.' You're history."

"I'm technically a civil serpent. I at least get a hearing. And I'm not sure they'd want to have any of this pop out in a civil service hearing."

"Maybe. But what they'd do in Washington is create a new position for you, then forget to budget for it. And you'd get to find a new home somewhere."

"Oh well, screw 'em if they can't take a joke. I loved it when you suggested the supe do the right thing—practice what they preach. That bit about asking the mids what *they* would do—that was medium brilliant."

"But, bottom line—"

"Even if they don't smear Julie Markham, this Dyle Booth guy gets commissioned. A Marine officer and a gentleman by act of Congress. A sadist at least, and maybe a murderer."

"There's still a chance we're wrong," she said. "The admiral kept pounding on our weak spot: zero real evidence."

An obese waiter wheezed over and removed their debris, wiping down the counter with a rag that left about as much grease as it picked up. "But they won't even let us talk to this guy," he said. "If I could just get a look at him, I think I could tell if he was the runner. I'll never forget those eyes."

She finished her beer and slid the empty bottle down the full length of the counter, where it fell off the end, landing right in the trash can. Jim knew if he tried that, the bottle would miss the can and break all over the floor.

"So now what?" Branner asked. "We just give it up for Lent?"

"You mean do what we're told for once?" He rubbed the sides of his face with both hands. He was tired, and eating all that grease had been a mistake.

She sat there looking at him as if expecting something.

An idea bloomed in his head. "Or . . ." he began.

"Or?"

"Or I could go get that tennis ball—you know, the one

our runner rolled down the tunnel that night? The one that said 'You're on'? I could go get that tennis ball, find out what room this guy Booth lives in, and put it on his desk. Then go on down to the tunnels, see what shakes out."

"Oh, I like that," she said, a nasty gleam appearing in her eye.

"I could do all that by myself, you know. My ass is already on the skids. No reason for you to burn down, too. I mean, after Bosnia, I know how to do skids."

She produced her Glock from somewhere beneath the counter and held it up for him to see. "If he did Bagger, *we're* gonna have a talk. And maybe an accident."

The waiter looked up, got wide-eyed when he saw the Glock, and backed hurriedly into the kitchen, closing the door and then the pass-through hatch.

"Put that thing away," Jim said softly, glancing at the front windows. "We need to call Liz DeWinter. See if she has Julie's cell number. See if Julie can give us Brother Dyle's room number."

Ev and Liz walked back to where Ev had parked his car. Now that it was dark, Ev had offered to give her a ride back up the hill to her house. The night was clear, with almost no sea breeze coming in from the bay. The occasional cars making the turn at King George towards the city docks seemed unusually loud. Ev thought there might be fog later. Somewhere in the distance, a church bell was tolling the hour.

"Are you mad at me?" he asked her when they got to his car.

"Little bit," she said. "I mean, I can sort of understand where you're coming from with all that honor code stuff. But a homicide investigation's the real deal."

"And the honor code isn't?"

"So, you keep telling me the Academy isn't the real world. It's a synthetic environment, where young people are trained to act like naval officers. Emphasis on the act. I think a lot of this honor code stuff is just a construct. That it doesn't translate to real life in the real Navy."

He stood by the door on the driver's side. "Actually it does," he said. "Out there in the fleet, an officer's word is his bond. Some enlisted guys might play cops and robbers with the officers and blow smoke, but an officer never lies except when he's playing Liar's Dice at the O Club bar. If they don't learn that here, they've missed the whole point."

"So you think Julie ought to, what, confess to the Honor Committee? This close to graduation? Take the chance that they might throw her out?"

"That's what she's supposed to do. The fact that she comes forward on her own hook would mitigate any punishment, as opposed to what happens if, say, Special Agent Branner goes in and drops her in the shit."

"You sound like you really are disappointed in her," Liz said. She was standing on the other side of the car, her hands on the roof.

"I'm very proud that she made it into the Academy, and also made it through."

"But?"

"But she lied. To you, to NCIS, to me. Because she was afraid, because she wanted to deflect an investigation, because she knew she hadn't really done anything to Brian Dell, who knows? She lied."

"So that's it? Four years, maximum effort, all the shit she had to take as a mid, plus the hassle of being a woman at the Academy? Losing her mother halfway through? She's wearing academic stars in an engineering program, and she's been a winner on the swim team? And you're *disappointed*?"

"As we say in the fleet, one *aw shit* can undo ten thousand *attaboys*. Of course I'm very proud of what she's accomplished. I'm also very disappointed that she lied. To her credit, I think she is, too."

Liz was shaking her head. "It's been what, almost thirty years since you got out?" she said. "And you're still locked into this honor code thing? Even if it means destroying your

own daughter's future?" Her voice rose, and Ev saw the
Marines over at the visitors' gate look up. After the New
York City atrocities, the gate guards had been much more
vigilant.

"You either believe in the concept of honor or you don't,
Liz," he said calmly. "I believed in it when I went through. I
think the mids still believe in it. It's what makes the Academy different and, at the same time, special. It's why we
should keep the place alive, all the chickenshit regs, firsties
running plebes, and plebes squaring corners not withstanding. If she joins the fleet and lies, people who will *reflexively*
depend on her word might end up dead. Remember what
business these kids are going into. It's not like being a
lawyer, where lies can be tactically necessary."

"Granted," Liz said. "But she did not kill Brian Dell, assuming someone did. That's the important thing here."

"Then Julie ought to help NCIS, not hide behind your
skirts. By the way, I think I remember this Booth. Not personally, but as a student. Fall semester."

"And is he . . . strange?"

"If he's the one I'm thinking about, yes. A little. I mean,
he's a big guy, very intense. Obviously intelligent. But he
didn't do very well in my class. It may be a reading problem."

"How the hell does someone with a reading disability
get in?"

"I pulled his admissions package when he began to slip.
As I remember, he came in under one of those special programs. Came from a pretty tough background, but he was a
championship swimmer, and he scored off the charts in math
and science. I had no idea he knew Julie, other than as a
member of the varsity swim team."

"Did you flunk him?"

"Very nearly. But I also gave him some extra instruction.
Some tutoring, if you will. He seemed to be trying, so I let
him pass."

"This night gets better and better," she said. "You tutored
the guy who may have offed Brian Dell. And he's been intimate with your daughter."

Ev shook his head. "Until tonight, I knew of no connection between Dyle and Julie, or Midshipman Dell."

"Did he ever pump you for information about Julie, especially after that weekend at UVA?"

Ev tried to remember if Dyle had ever asked him personal questions. "No, not that I can recall," he said. "We did talk about the fact that my house is nearby. He asked if I worked out, and I said, yes, and that I walked to and from work. Things like that."

Liz was quiet for a minute. "Could he have been faking the problem, in order to get close to you?" she asked.

"It's possible, I guess. Verbally, he was sharp enough. He mostly came across as a gung ho Marine officer candidate. Popped to attention when I'd come into the room, no matter what I told him. 'Sir, yes, sir' to everything. I sensed a lot of anxious energy right beneath the surface, which I attributed to his struggle with the material. He's physically imposing. He's almost my height, but bigger by half otherwise."

"How did his classmates react to him?"

"Carefully, now that I think of it. Wary, even. But I can see the Marines loving this type of guy. Hump an eighty-pound pack uphill all day and still be chanting in cadence."

One of the Marine sentries had stepped across the street to stand at the edge of the parking lot. He asked if everything was all right. Both Liz and Ev said they were fine. Then Ev had an idea. "I'm wondering if we should call the duty officer," he said. "See if we can get Julie out of Bancroft Hall for a night while NCIS finds this guy and gets a reading on him."

"You mean take her to your house? Take her home?"

"Yeah. Just until we know something more about what the hell's going on. Now that I remember Booth, I'm a little worried."

"I don't know that Julie would want to do that, not after your reaction tonight. Like you said, that sounded like good-bye."

"Well, maybe to your house, then? Would you take her in?" He looked over at the lighted outline of Bancroft Hall, which now looked faintly ominous to him. "I just don't think she should be in Bancroft tonight."

"Certainly, if she's willing to come. How would we manage it?"

"I'd get her to sign out for town liberty. She just wouldn't come back. I think we can sort out any problems with that tomorrow, once we get the commandant into it. I'm assuming NCIS is looking for Dyle right now. There's a phone in the car. Let me make a call; then you talk to her."

"Why don't I make the call and just ask her to get out of there? I don't think she'll do it if you ask her."

"That bad, huh?"

"Let's just hope Agent Branner and Mr. Hall are working on getting Dyle Booth into an interview room."

Just after 9:00 P.M., Jim entered the doors on the ground floor of the eighth wing. He went down to the basement, then walked along the corridor of darkened activity rooms until he found the elevator. He pushed the call button and waited. He was dressed in khaki slacks, a short-sleeved shirt, and black shoes. He was also wearing a dark blue Naval Academy windbreaker with the Academy logo and a dark blue ball cap with USNA stenciled on it in gold letters. From a distance, he might look like one of the company officers. As the Academy security officer, he had a right to be in Bancroft Hall, although normally he would have checked in with the watch officers in the Executive Department. As it was, he didn't intend to spend a lot of time in the eighth wing. The elevator arrived and opened. He stepped in and pressed the button for the fourth floor. The door slowly slid shut and the elderly elevator started up.

He had left Branner outside in the truck, where she could see the window of Booth's room on the fourth deck. If he actually encountered Booth, he would keep the midshipman in the room and flick the room lights on and off several times. That would be Branner's signal to come into the building and join him in Booth's room. She knew the room number.

They would then interview him and take him into custody if warranted. But he didn't expect to encounter Dyle Booth. Unable to raise the lawyer, he had called in to the battalion office and asked if he could speak to Midshipman Booth. After an interminable wait on hold, the mate came back on and said that Booth was signed out for study hall. That meant he could be anywhere in Bancroft Hall or even in an academic building. As a firstie, he would be able to go almost anywhere he wanted. But taps was approaching. He would have to be back in his room at taps, so this was the time to leave the message. Julie had said that Booth did not have a roommate, which was unusual, although not unheard of. The mate had given him the room number.

The door opened on the fourth floor and he stepped out. The corridor was empty. He could hear the familiar sounds of Mother Bancroft during study hour. Some voices were audible, as well as some music and the sounds of a shower going in the room right next to the elevator. Riding the elevator was a firstie privilege. The only other people using the elevators would be the watch officers. He hoped like hell he didn't run into the real OOD, because that would become truly awkward.

He glanced at the nearest room number and then turned left and headed toward the bay end of the building. The rooms were small and entirely uniform. Most doors were closed. The floor in the hallway was highly polished, and the place smelled of floor wax and cleaning agents. The doors to the men's bathroom were open and the pungent odor of urinal disinfectant seeped out into the corridor. A plebe came out of his room in his bathrobe, hands rigidly at his sides, eyes in the boat, squaring every corner and walking briskly down the channel, or center of the passageway. He said "Good evening, sir," as he passed the big man in the windbreaker. If he was curious about Jim, he did not show it. He was obviously trying to get to the head without running into any upperclassmen.

Jim arrived at room number 8424. Eighth wing, fourth floor, room twenty-four. The nameplate read D. BOOTH,

2002. Name and class. There was light showing through the
frosted pane in the wooden door. Jim didn't hesitate. He
knocked twice, making sure his Naval Academy ring hit the
wooden frame in two solid raps, a familiar sound in Bancroft Hall. To a plebe, it meant jump up into a brace and
prepare to sound off, because there was at least a firstie outside, or maybe even a watch officer. He pushed the door
open.

There was no one inside. It was a standard room: single-
tier bunk on either side, two desks pushed back-to-back in the
middle, an aluminum chair placed squarely in front of each
one. The beds had been made up with military precision.
There were no clothes strewn about, nor any other personal
gear adrift. No shoes, clothes, coats, notebooks—nothing.
The windows overlooked Lejeune Hall, the physical education center and home to the Marine detachment, appropriately
enough. The dark bulk of Dahlgren Hall was visible to the
right. He could see Branner's white face peering up under the
streetlights from the parking lot below. He turned off the room
lights, waited ten seconds, and turned them back on. That was
the second signal: I'm in and there's no one here. She had
wanted to come up, but he'd pointed out that if this worked,
Dyle would think it would be just Jim waiting for him. Especially if Booth asked around and was told there had been one
stranger on deck earlier, not two.

He looked around the empty room. There was a single PC
on the right-hand desk, plus a reading lamp and four text-
books. A large Marine recruiting poster hung over one of the
beds, indicating that was the one Booth used. The other bed
was tightly made up but had no pillow. The room was spot-
less and entirely squared away. He opened one closet door.
There was a full-dress Marine Corps uniform encased in dry
cleaner's plastic. It was fully rigged, right down to the
gleaming second lieutenant's bars on the shoulders. A curv-
ing sword case standing on end to the right of the uniform
contained the Mameluke dress sword. He studied the uniform, the same one he'd worn with such pride for six years.

Booth must be a really big guy. Better and better. He closed the closet door.

He was tempted to search the room, but he had no authority to do so, nor the training to do it right. In fact, he didn't really rate being in this room at all. He took the tennis ball out of his pocket and put it squarely on the keyboard of the PC. Then he had an idea. He picked it up again and went to the washbasin. He ran just enough water over the tennis ball to get it wet, but not enough to obliterate what was written on it, YOU'RE ON. Some ink ran into the sink. He smudged out the signature HMC on the basin mirror. Then he went back to the desk and tapped the keyboard. The monitor came to life, giving him a log-on screen. He typed in "You know where" and then put the damp ball back on the keyboard.

The lights had been on when he'd come in. He turned them off as he left the room. If Booth was as situationally aware as Jim expected, that would be yet another warning cue. He walked back down the corridor and pushed the button for the elevator. There were no midshipmen wandering the halls. They must really make them study these days, he thought, then remembered exams. The door opened immediately and he stepped in and pushed the button for the basement.

Three minutes later, he was back in the truck with Branner. "Anyone see you?" she asked.

"One plebe, bound for the head," he said, snapping on his seat belt. "But I don't think I registered. I doused the lights when I left, so Booth should know the moment he steps in that someone's been there."

"Now what?"

"I'm going to call the chief and see if we can get some backup on the grates. Then I propose to wait here until we see that light go back on."

"Can the chief do that?" she asked.

"He can't get extra people out. No time to plan that, and besides, the overtime wouldn't be authorized, not for this,

especially not after what the dant said earlier. But we can get
the guys who are out on Yard patrol, and maybe a truck from
over at the naval station."

"You gonna tell him we're off the books on this one?"

"The chief? Absolutely. No point in getting him in trouble. He'll probably be the security officer pretty soon."

She grunted. "You know," she said, "if Booth is really
smart, he'll chuck that ball out the window and stay home
tonight."

"Absolutely," Jim said. "But I think he'll take the challenge. Unless, of course, he tries for Julie Markham. Hopefully, she's safe in her room, with Hays under the bed
somewhere. One assumes the roommate will be cool with
that."

"Melanie Bright? From Cali*for*nia?"

"Oh. 'Ya-a,' " he replied. "Hell, they'll think it's a game.
Better let me get things set up with the chief. There's a pay
phone right over there. I need to stay off the radios right
now."

At eleven o'clock, the bells rang for plebes' lights-out. They
watched as the room lights blinked out in plebe rooms all
along the facade of the eighth wing. The chief had understood the new situation right away. Acknowledging that they
couldn't roust out off-duty people, Jim had asked him to
have the on-duty Yard cops go to all the Academy grates and
block the lower-level steel doors from the outside, beginning
now, and then for the cops on the morning shift to unlock
them when they came on duty. The chief said he'd take care
of it. He asked Jim to call him when he and Branner went
down into the tunnels. Jim gave him a general description of
Booth, and told him to alert the Yard cops to call central dis-
patch if they saw a firstie who looked like that loose in the
Yard after taps. The chief still had that radio retransmitter
set. He said he'd set it up just inside the Mahan Hall grate
entrance, and leave two radios with it for them to use. He'd
be topside, starting at midnight, with a radio tied to that fre-

quency. They knew Booth could listen to that frequency, but it was better than nothing, and Booth probably did not have jamming equipment.

"That's mighty good of you, Chief," Jim had said. "But that's getting directly involved. I mean you on the radio."

"What radio?" the chief had replied blandly.

Jim deliberately had not told the chief about the storm drain entrance on the seawall. Booth was possibly using some as-yet-unknown entrance to the old Fort Severn magazine rooms, but there was an equal chance he'd use that big storm drain tunnel. The grating he'd seen was at least five feet in diameter. Even someone Booth's size could move quickly up that big pipe and into the main utility tunnels, and it wasn't as if there would be sewage or anything truly unpleasant in the storm drain.

As they waited in the truck to see if Booth would return to his room, Jim asked Branner why she was risking her job.

"Because you need some adult supervision?" she asked.

He sighed and she laughed. "Okay," she said. "Try this. I'm the supervisor of the Naval Academy NCIS office. It's my supervisory judgment that there's new and important evidence regarding what happened to Special Agent Thompson. Nothing to do with Midshipman Dell, of course."

"Ah."

"So I'm not disobeying orders here so much as exercising initiative. About Bagger. Not Dell."

"It sounds good," he said doubtfully.

"Look," she said. "We catch Booth in the tunnels tonight, we'll have enough to open the whole thing back up, SecNav or no SecNav. Especially if I can have five minutes alone with him."

"Just by catching him down there?"

"We have the unexplained Dell death, linked by Markham to Booth. We have the missing college girl, who went into the tunnels, most probably with Booth. We have Bagger's fatal assault case, plus some other assault cases over in town, linked to some guy in vampire drag—whom *you* saw in the tunnels. We have various destruction derbies down there since you've been looking for this guy, linked to a tag with a shark logo. Booth calls *himself* 'the Shark' on the Navy swim team."

"Okay, so lots of circumstantial. But if Booth remains silent, we've got jack, right?"

She gave him a wolfish smile. "Like I said, Mr. Naval Academy Security Officer, I'm along to provide some adult supervision. By now, Booth has probably figured out that you know more than you should. And you've directly challenged him to meet you in the tunnels. If he's been watching Markham, and I think he watches pretty good, he's probably aware that she bolted out to her lawyer's office earlier today. He'll be more than prepared to meet you down there. One-on-one denotes personal combat, don't you think?"

"Absolutely. Especially to a Marine recon wanna-be."

"Okay, then. It's probably going to get interesting down there—that's more his turf than ours. What he doesn't know is that *I'm* going to be down there. You two get together, you need to talk a little trash, provoke him into some boasting. Something that I can hear. I'm the arresting officer here. That'll do it."

He just looked at her for a moment. "He won't do that unless I'm in the corner," he said.

She smiled at him. " 'Tiger, tiger, burning bright,' ". she said.

"Bleated the goat," he replied. "The one tied to the stake."

"Got any better ideas? Like you said, it's not like we have a bag full of evidence here. Tell you what: As soon as he admits doing Bagger, I'll just cap his ass, and then it'll be just us chickens testifying at an inquest about an accidental shooting. That would get the balance of justice about right."

"C'mon." He laughed. "You can't just go shooting the guy."

"Watch me. In my book, that's better than having some Communist defense lawyer get him off."

He shook his head. Wyatt Branner at the O.K. Corral. She

probably would do it, too. He glanced up. The light was on in Booth's room.

"Yo, Houston," he said, switching on the engine. "I believe we have contact."

They drove to the back of Mahan Hall and parked the truck in the Alumni Hall parking lot. The chief materialized out of the darkness as they approached the grate.

"Decided to hang around and give you these personally," he said, handing over the radios. "Plus a message—from a Mr. Harry Chang?"

Branner stepped forward. "That will be for me," she said.

"Yeah, sounded like it. Mr. Chang was in a bad mood. Says he thinks you and my boss here are up to some wild-haired shit, to use his words. Says he has it on best authority that Mr. Hall has been told to cease and desist in regards to the Dell case, and that you have been similarly so instructed. Asked me to pass that along, should I happen to see you out and about the Yard."

"And you said?"

"I said that I didn't know anything about any police operations, and if *I* didn't know anything, there weren't any. That I had no idea where either of you was, but if you were together, it was probably not business."

Jim smiled in the darkness, especially when he saw Branner's expression.

"Anyways, he also said there were some people coming down tomorrow morning from headquarters to . . . lessee, this guy used a lot of code. Oh, yeah, he said there were some people coming down to 'collate the available evidence, compile the final *official* report, and to review some recent management concepts with Special Agent Branner.' "

"Tomorrow morning?" Branner asked. "Definitely not tonight?"

"That's what the man said," the chief replied. "The retransmitter is in place in the main tunnel. I got guys physically securing all the grates from the outside. You want me to seal the one over on the Johnnie campus?"

"Can you?"

"Leave it to me. You're trying to catch this vampire runner, right?"

"Right. We think we know who he is."

"Why tonight?"

"Mr. Hall left him a little invitation," Branner said. "Plus, another mid has given us reason to believe this guy had something to do with the Dell kid's flying lesson."

"Man, oh, man. This is definitely not my father's Naval Academy."

"Chief, I need one more favor," Jim said. "Will this radio reach all the way over to the public works center?"

"Sure," the chief said. "That's a ten-watt transmitter."

"I need you to go there, tell the utility watch officer that we're in the tunnels, and listen for a code word: *lights-out.* This guy has had a couple years to put his own surveillance network up, and I think he gets electrical power for it by tapping into local lighting circuits. If I speak that code word, I need all the juice in the tunnels turned off. When I say, 'lights on,' turn it all back on, okay?"

"I can handle that," the chief said. "You going along, Special Agent?"

"Wouldn't miss it, Chief," she said, patting the bulge where the Glock lived.

"Watch out using that thing down in the tunnels, Special Agent. That's one big ricochet chamber."

"Only if I miss his criminal ass, Chief," she said with a sniff.

The chief gave her a two-finger salute and they went down the steps and through the steel door. They heard the chief lock it behind them, then brace the door with a metal bar. It was five minutes to midnight.

Ev and Liz picked Julie up in front of Dahlgren Hall. She carried a small overnight bag. She got in the backseat without a word. Tommy Hays had walked her out to the car. He waved and she waved back as Ev made a left turn and drove up the circular drive in front of the chapel.

"Any problem signing out?" he asked.

"No, sir."

Ev looked sideways at Liz, who arched her eyebrows as if to say, Told you so. He went out the Maryland Avenue gate and drove up to State Circle, where he let them out by the gate to Liz's house. He tried to think of something to say to Julie, but he couldn't come up with anything, so he told Liz he'd be at home for the rest of the evening. She nodded and took Julie through the iron gates.

As if I had anywhere else to go, he thought as he circled around the old Weems estate and headed back down in front of the St. John's College campus. There were a few students out and about among the giant old trees on the front lawns. He stopped to let two oddly dressed girls cross the street. They looked like they were going to a Halloween costume party. Okay, he thought, so Julie's pissed off at me. And at herself, because now the onus is on her to solve the honor problem. Ev wondered if the NCIS team had picked up Dyle Booth yet.

He tried to visualize Julie dating a guy like Dyle Booth but couldn't quite do it. They had nothing in common except the swimming. Julie came from a very traditional family background; Booth from the white fringes of a Baltimore ghetto. Liz might have been right: The acerbic way Dyle could verbalize things didn't square with a verbal skills problem. Had the kid been manipulating him in order to get at Julie?

Ev parked the car and got out. The night was very still now, with enough humidity in the air to give nearby lights a soft penumbra. Not quite fog yet, but soon, he thought. He went up to the darkened house and let himself in. He turned on the porch lights behind him, then turned them off. No point in porch lights—no one was coming to see him tonight. He walked down the darkened hall to the kitchen, through whose windows he could see the dock lights, which came on automatically at dusk. The furniture was all gray in the dim light. He stood at the kitchen sink and considered what he'd done this evening: alienated his daughter, and very possibly Liz as well. Could he have phrased it differently? Been more diplomatic? Explained it to Liz first, and not said anything to Julie? Yes.

He stared unseeing though the windows, knowing that it was dumb to be just standing here in the dark. He wanted to call Liz, but that wasn't on, not tonight. He found himself wondering what else he didn't know about his daughter. He turned on a light, fixed himself a snifter of scotch, and then went down to the dock to sit by the water. The highly varnished bottom of his upturned scull glistened in the dock lights.

13

At just past midnight, the main tunnel looked and sounded familiar: sterile concrete walls and ceilings, smelling faintly of ozone and steam, with the hum of electronic equipment racks and the quiet rush of steam permeating its entire length. They walked slightly uphill toward the King George Street interchange with the city utility vaults. They passed the big shark graffito, which remained unchanged. They did not speak, in deference to the possibility that Booth had the tunnels wired for sound as well as visual and electronic surveillance. The big steel doors leading out to the city tunnel were locked. Jim unlocked them and tried to pull them open. Neither of them budged.

"Okay! Chief," Jim murmured.

"Hope we don't get a fire down here tonight," Branner whispered, looking at those locked doors.

"We do, we call for help," he said, holding up his radio. He keyed the transmitter three times. There was a moment of silence, and then both of their radios clicked three times back at them. He stepped into an alcove to mask his voice.

"All the doors blocked?" he asked the chief.

"Affirmative."

They walked back toward the intersection where the Mahan Hall grate door was, checking equipment room doors and generally looking around for signs of anyone else being down there. Then they continued down the long stretch under Stribling Walk, Jim watching in front of them and Branner walking backward, keeping an eye out behind them. When they got to the dogleg turn, Jim stopped, put his fingers to his lips, and listened hard. He'd felt a change in the air pressure. Something had been opened. Then he remembered the storm drain. He pointed back up the tunnel and whispered that he was going to check the storm drain's flap doors. Booth might have figured out a way to open them from the drain side. She indicated she'd wait for him, just out of sight in the dogleg turn.

Jim yanked out his own weapon and went back up the tunnel. He walked to one side of the steel plates running down the center of the tunnel to avoid making unnecessary noise. The vestibule above the storm drain did not have any sort of door or hatch leading from the main tunnel down to the drain itself. The whole point was to have an immediate draining point for any water that got loose in the tunnels. But all the main grating access doors should be closed and locked. So what had been opened?

He got to the vestibule and the spring-loaded, sloping flap doors. He got down on his hands and knees and pushed on the center of the crack between the two metal flaps. They moved, but not easily. Putting a foot on one flap, he pushed against the hinge hard enough to expand the crack enough to get his hand into it. He could feel air streaming past his head. He ran his hand up the full length of the right-hand flap edge, but there was nothing but smooth metal. He switched his foot and tried the left-hand side.

Bingo, he thought. He felt a crude U-shaped handle bolted to the other side. So someone coming up from the river *would* have access from the main drain pipe. He was withdrawing his hand when his wrist was seized in a viselike grip and he was pulled headlong right through the two flaps. He yelled, dropping both his Glock and his radio, as his body hurtled down through the doors into a sloping circular concrete pipe. It was pitch-black in the storm drain once the spring-loaded doors snapped shut behind him, and the bottom of the pipe was slippery with ancient moss and the trickle of water that was constantly draining out of the utility tunnel complex. Whoever had grabbed him had essentially flung him down the drain, and he skidded on his backside for an unknown distance until he gathered his wits enough to spread out his arms and legs and stop himself. He immediately flipped over onto his stomach and snatched out the Maglite. He shot it up the tunnel and saw nothing at all except his gun and his radio. It felt as if the storm drain was sloping down at about a ten-degree angle. Easy enough to maintain his position, but steep enough to have slid him almost sixty feet from the doors. Whoever had grabbed him probably had gone up through the doors once Jim had opened them. Branner. He had to warn Branner.

He scampered back up the drain, staying low enough not to hit his head, and recovered the radio first. He called Branner, but the thing didn't seem to be working. He turned it over. The battery compartment had opened and the battery pack was missing. He swore and retrieved his Glock. He shone the light up and down the tunnel, looking for the cigarette pack–sized battery, and finally saw a flash of shiny metal. He recovered the battery, his hands fumbling because everything was wet. Son of a bitch had moved the doors to attract his attention, then simply pulled him into the tunnel. Strong son of a bitch, too. While Jim had been skidding down the drain, their quarry had gone through the flap doors and now was loose in the tunnel.

Hunched over beneath the flap doors, he fumbled to get the battery back into the radio, and then, realizing he was wasting time, swore again. Stuffing the radio and battery into a pocket, he pulled the flap door with the handle down into the drain. The yellow lights of the main tunnel flooded the drain. He stood up through the opening and yelled for Branner to look out, but she didn't respond. Then he realized he'd screwed up again: Branner had probably heard the commotion when he went through the flap door, but now Jim had just given away her presence to Booth, who must have heard him yell. Screw it, he thought. He hoisted himself through the flap doors, fighting with the spring hinges, which were pinching into him like aluminum mandibles. He got up and trotted down toward the Bancroft Hall end of the Stribling tunnel. When he got to the dogleg, Branner wasn't there. Now what? he wondered. He called her name, but she didn't answer. Had Booth managed to take her down? He couldn't have—she'd been waiting for him.

He pulled out the radio, dried off the battery contacts, and put the thing back together again. Where the hell was Branner? Then he had an idea. Maybe she was not answering in order to make Booth think Jim was faking it, trying to make Booth think he had backup. He put the radio up to his mouth but did not squeeze the transmit key. Then he gave a series of orders to a host of imaginary backup people. Then he did squeeze the key and said, "Lights-out." Two seconds later, when the entire tunnel went dark, he flattened himself between two equipment cabinets.

At least the radio system is working, he thought. Branner should have heard him doing his deception routine and figured it out. Booth was in the tunnel. But where? And where was Branner holed up? She should be close by. He tried to think of the layout of the tunnel walls in the vicinity of the dogleg. Around the corner was the cross tunnel that led out toward the harbor area and the old Fort Severn doors. Branner could be anywhere. Hell with it. It was time to get it on with young Mr. Booth.

Keeping his Maglite handy but off, he patted the Glock and started feeling his way in the pitch-black tunnel, heading back toward the vestibule above the storm drain. He called out Booth's name but got no answer. He called it again.

"Yo, Booth! Or is it Count Dracula-a-a? Where are you, Booth? The doors are all locked tonight, so it's just us chickens down here, Booth. And chicken seems to be the word, hey, Booth?"

He listened to the darkness, but there was nothing stirring. Some of the equipment behind all the cabinet doors was still going, but the ventilation was off and the tunnel was starting to get warm. He kept inching his way along the wall on the Annapolis side, bumping quietly into steel cabinets, wireways, and pipe nests. He called out again.

"Hey, big guy. Come on *down*. Let's have us a little chat."

His fingers itched to turn on the Maglite. He had a vision of Booth in vampire drag, hanging upside down from the tunnel ceiling, waiting to pounce. His hand remembered that powerful grip that had pulled him down into the storm drain. His knees and elbows still stung. But he'd seen nothing. He stopped to listen. Then he felt a presence in the tunnel.

Was something *there*?

He pointed the Maglite in the direction his senses were indicating and waited.

Nothing moved.

He took another sideways step and stopped again. "C'mon, Booth. We know what you did. You can't win this thing."

A voice whispered right into his left ear. "Sure I can, Hall-Man-Chu."

Jim barely suppressed the urge to jump out into the tunnel and snap the light on. The voice had been right beside his ear, but his ear was right next to a solid steel cabinet. No way could there be anyone there. It had been a chilling voice, a metallic whisper. As if someone was synthesizing it. He lifted his left hand above his ear and felt around until he encountered a tiny plastic box. There was a screen on the front of it. A speaker.

"Because, Booth, like I said, the doors are all sealed tonight. All except the storm drain, and I have people sealing the river grate as we speak. It's like Hotel California, Booth—you can come anytime you want, but you can never leave."

There came a booming sound of something heavy being shut way down the storm drain tunnel. The river grate, right on cue. But the voice spoke in his ear again. "Who wants to leave, Hall-Man-Chu? I certainly don't. I've been looking forward to this."

Jim began to perspire. Booth was speaking on the tunnel announcing system, which was a string of speakers scattered throughout the tunnels, so that the PWC could make announcements to people working down below. Shit! Was Booth in the PWC ops station? Or had he just tapped in? Yeah, that was it—he had tapped into the speaker system. And also provided it with some electrical power. Guy was good.

"So let's chat, Drac," Jim said, trying not to let his voice betray the anxiety he was feeling. If Booth could do sound, maybe he could do lights, too. And maybe even video. So Jim didn't dare turn on his flashlight. "You can talk to me or to all of us."

"You mean both of you, don't you?" whispered the speaker. "Although one of you is—what's the word?—indisposed." A nasty laugh. "So what is it you think you *know, sir,* other than that you're alone down here on *my* turf?"

Indisposed? He didn't like the sound of that. Had he taken Branner? "I know you're some kind of whack job who had something to do with Brian Dell's so-called accident, for one thing," he said. Then he moved back away from the speaker, very slowly, standing on tiptoes so as to make absolutely no sound. The darkness remained absolute. There weren't even any lights from the power panel showing in the passageway.

"*Accident*? You don't know shit. Is that what Hot Wheels is telling you? Silly girl. She has it all wrong. Oh, and I know where she is right now, too. With that pretty little lawyer. You know her? Did you know she's doing Julie's daddy these days?"

What? Jim thought as he continued to reposition himself. He felt for the radio. He had to figure out when to call for the lights, but he didn't want to do it before he knew where Booth was.

"Surprised there, Mr. Security Man, *sir*? Mr. Hall-Man-Chump? Mr. *Lame*-Man-Chump is more like it. Here's whassup: I'm going to do you and your butch buddy there, then deal with Hot Wheels. Then, who knows—maybe I'll just go radio-silent and wait to throw my hat in the air with the rest of my sterling classmates."

Jim kept moving, turning as he went, one arm held out in the darkness to keep himself from bumping into anything, the other holding the Maglite close by his hip, ready to snap it on. He thought he was moving back down toward the dog-leg turn, closer to the Fort Severn doors. Was Booth using a radio to key the speakers? If so, he could be anywhere in the tunnel complex. Or right behind him.

"No way, Booth," he said. "We've told too many people about you. Your name's already on the graduation hold list."

The voice just laughed. Jim had moved far enough away from his starting point to be between speakers now, and the voice had an echo to it. He still sensed that there was some human presence nearby, but he couldn't pinpoint it. "Not what *I've* heard, Mr. Security Officer, *sir*," Booth whispered. "The word in the third is that the Dark Side's gonna rug this one. The dant's had some guidance from on high. Accident. All an accident. Very sad, but there you are. Told those naughty mid coolies not to go up on the roof. Told 'em a million times."

"All true, Booth," Jim said, stopping in place now and listening hard. "Except Julie's given NCIS enough to reopen this thing. I personally told the supe we'd be reopening, or he could read it in the newspapers. And you know how the supe hates newspapers."

"She can't get me without getting herself," the voice said softly, as if Booth were closer. Much less of an echo. "I know her. You don't. She's complex, Julie is. And she'll never do that. Life for Julie is all about Julie, see. And without her, you and your rent-a-cop pals got jackshit. Most importantly, the Dark Side wants it over, Mr. Hall, *sir*. Even if you leak to the Annapolis crab wrapper, no one's going to give a shit. By direction."

"So where's the Goth girl, Booth? What happened to little Miss Natter? Do you happen to know? Annapolis cops are looking into that one, by the way. They won't care what the SecNav has to say."

"They don't care, period, Mr. Insecurity Officer, *sir.* It's a missing persons case. And besides, if it all goes south, I'm prepared to do the honorable thing. And the name wasn't Natter. In her world, she was Krill."

"Krill, Drill, Snapping Shrimp, for all I care," Jim said. "But we've given them your name as our best bet for the downtown Batman. See, the issue is time. Their investigation will take more time than you've got days left here. And that will give *us* time to pull the scab on Dell. You're done, shithead. Come on *down!*"

Booth didn't answer this time. Jim bumped into something on the side of the tunnel. He felt behind him and his fingers told him it was a door. It was ajar. There was a strange chemical smell coming from behind the door. He picked up the radio and called softly, "Lights on." Nothing happened.

He called again, louder this time, feeling with his fingers for the radio's power switch to make sure it was on. He heard what sounded like fading laughter coming from the speakers, then silence. The radio appeared to be working. Had the son of a bitch trashed the retransmitter? Screw it, he thought, and snapped on the Maglite.

The tunnel was empty in both directions. The concrete was strangely gray in the blue-white beam of the Maglite. There was enough humidity in the air now that he could actually see the shape of the beam. He was standing right next to the equipment room. He nudged the door open with his foot. The chemical stink was stronger. A can clinked as it rolled out of the way. Shining the light on it, he saw that it was a can of diesel engine-starter fluid. And then he saw Branner. She was slumped against a telephone switchboard cabinet. There was a swatch of duct tape plastered over her mouth, and what looked like a small sponge sticking up out of it under her nostrils. There was more duct tape wrapped around her arms and legs.

He recognized the smell: ether. Starter fluid contained ether. He looked both ways again and then stepped into the room. He bent down and snatched the tape and sponge away from her face. She groaned but did not open her eyes.

He stepped back out into the main tunnel and checked both ways with the Maglite again. Still nothing. No one lurking. He listened carefully. No one coming, either. He tried the radio again, but there was no answer. His fingers were sticky from the duct tape and stank of ether.

He felt the warm air stir, but it wasn't like the last time he'd been down, when there had been a distinct pressure change. This was different, more subtle. He keyed the radio again and saw the tiny red light come on, indicating a transmit signal. The radio was working. The signal just wasn't getting out. He could go up the tunnel and check the retransmitter, but then he'd have to leave Branner. He went back inside after sweeping his light around the tunnel one more time. He set the Maglite down on the floor and used his knife to cut away the duct tape from her arms and legs. She groaned again but still didn't open her eyes. He could smell the ether on her breath. She's going to hate life when she does wake up, he thought, the smell nauseating him.

He felt another stir of air as he checked her pulse. Booth must be big and fast to have been able to get Branner, the judo instructor. He had to get her out of here, and get her some oxygen and medical attention. That much ether, she might get chemical pneumonia. He reviewed the tunnel layout in his mind. The nearest exit grate was next to Dahlgren Hall, about 150 feet to the right, beyond the oak doors to the Fort Severn tunnels. It was at least two, maybe three hundred feet back to the Stribling Walk grating, and twice that to the interchange between the Academy and the town's utility tunnels. The ether smell was making him increasingly nauseous. He knew he was forgetting something. Okay, so he'd carry or drag her to the—What was that?

He'd heard a noise but couldn't identify it. He stopped to listen. Not a noise, exactly. A vibration. A rumble?

He hadn't heard it; he'd *felt* it. Yes, definitely. A rumble from out in the tunnel. And then another sound.

Water. Rushing water. Lots of rushing water.

Oh shit.

Booth had probably opened one of the big valves on the fire main. Or maybe on the main containing potable water. Or both. He was going to flood the tunnels big-time.

Gotta move right now, he thought, his head spinning from the ether fumes. He grabbed Branner under her arms and tried to get her up into a fireman's carry, but there wasn't enough space in the equipment room, and she was heavier than he expected. As he eased her back down onto the floor, the rumbling got louder, and he felt, rather than saw, the first rush of water out in the passageway. Felt it and smelled it. A distinct odor of chlorine filled the already-humid air. He grabbed the light and shone it out the door. The water was flowing like a big black river, already covering the entire width of the floor and rushing down toward the storm drain.

The storm drain.

Well hell, that would take care of any flooding problem. That thing was four, maybe five feet in diameter, plenty big enough to drain off whatever the pressurized lines could put out. Even as he thought that, he felt water seeping through his shoes. He looked down. There was a two-inch coaming between the equipment room and the main passageway. The water was already coming over the top of it.

The water was rising. The flap doors to the storm drain must be blocked. But how? They were spring-loaded to open when there was any pressure in the tunnel.

That U-shaped handle. If Booth had stuffed something through the crack, a piece of rebar or something similar, the doors would allow water to leak through, but they wouldn't open. And Booth could have done that while getting away, because the storm drain tunnel was some distance from where they were.

He put the Maglite under his right armpit and grabbed Branner again, straightening her out so he could pull her through the door and out into the main passageway. The water was rushing by. It had a real current now, and it was coming up over his ankles. The glow from the flashlight illuminated Branner's feet, which were making a V-shaped wake in the torrent. He checked his orientation, made sure he was going the right way, and then began to pull her through the water toward the dogleg turn. He thought about finding the source of the water, then remembered all those valves on the fire main were outside the grating doors. The *locked* grating doors. By the time he found the right one, it might be too late, the way this water was rising.

He got about twenty feet before he tripped over something and landed hard on his behind. Branner's head dropped underwater for a second and she came up spluttering. She sat up, her face white in the light, felt the water, and automatically rolled over to get to her hands and knees. Then she got a strange look on her face and began to vomit into the flood. Jim felt absolutely helpless as he watched her convulsions, even as he realized how fast the water was rising. As Branner slumped back down toward the floor, he grabbed her again and held her up.

"Wha—what happened?" she gasped. "What's all this water? Where are we?"

"Booth got you with ether," he said, getting to his knees. It was getting hard to stay in position. "Can you get up?"

She started to nod but then was racked by a bout of dry heaves as the ether worked its poisonous spell. He just held her while her entire body spasmed against him. The water was over a foot deep now.

He pulled her to her feet and put his arm around her to steady her while urging her forward. It was like walking through molasses, and the water was up to their shins.

"Booth's flooded the tunnel. We've got to get out of here."

"The radio?" she asked weakly.

"I think he got the retransmitter. I can't get a signal out. They're gonna know they have a leak down here as soon as someone looks at a water-pressure gauge." And shuts down the system before the tunnel completely floods out, he fervently hoped. And doesn't count on the storm drain to solve the problem.

He got her through the dogleg turn and then pointed her toward the Dahlgren Hall access grate. The water was knee-deep now and still rising. There was less of a current, but violent swirls knocked them from one side of the tunnel to the other. Jim tried not to think of all that electrical equipment behind the doors as they labored past them. Branner was able to move on her own finally, which meant Jim could use the Maglite again. They held on to each other as they leaned back against the current. Suddenly, they felt the current reversing, shoving them backward from their objective. Now what the hell? he thought as they both almost went down into the swirling blackness. Then the current subsided entirely. Even so, the water seemed to be rising faster now, and Jim could feel the pressure building in his ears. As they stumbled up to the grating door, he reached for his keys. Which was when he remembered that all the grating doors were blocked from the outside. Not just locked but physically blocked.

They were trapped. Unless the chief got to a door and unblocked it, that water would continue to rise until it filled the tunnels. And the chief, waiting for Jim's signal up in the PWC operations station, might not even be aware that there was a problem. And even if he did, he'd have to get to the right grate. He saw that Branner had figured it out at about the same time.

"What do we do?" she said in a shaky voice.

Holding the flashlight under his right armpit, Jim fished for the collection of tunnel keys in his pants pocket and began fumbling until he found the one that unlocked the door. The water was now above their belts. There was no more current, just that inexorable rise. Jim could feel intense pressure in his ears now. He pushed the door, but it didn't budge. Definitely blocked.

"We go back," he said. "Try another door."

"But—"

"They may have missed one. The radios don't work. They don't even know we have a problem. We can't just stand here and drown. Let's go."

Branner fished her own flashlight out of her belt and they pushed through the rising waters, heading back toward the dogleg turn. Jim tried to figure out how Booth had known to flood the tunnel, but then realized Booth must have been listening to the radio circuit and heard them confirm the doors were blocked. Big mistake to have mentioned that.

His tunnels, not ours, he reminded himself as he pushed himself through the black water. It was slow going, and he found himself pulling Branner along with him. She still wasn't 100 percent capable.

"We have another option," he said. "We get to that vestibule above the storm drain before the water gets over our heads, maybe we can force those flaps open."

"But the river grating is blocked, right?"

"Yeah, but that would dump the water. Give us time for the people in the PWC station to realize there's a problem."

"Not if it's high tide."

He thanked her for reminding him. His own brain wasn't working all that well as the humidity rose. It was getting hard to breathe. Just then, there was a loud humming sound, and the cracks around an equipment room door to their right glowed momentarily with an unearthly blue-green light. Jim felt a tingling in the water as something big shorted out in the equipment room. Branner must have felt it, too, because she swore softly. They came abreast of the Fort Severn doors as another equipment room flared briefly. This time it was more than a tingle. Up ahead were a dozen more cabinets.

"They'll know something's up with that shit going on," he said, puffing as he forced himself through the chest-high water.

"May be academic," she gasped as she tripped over something on the floor. Jim tripped, too, and they both went down into the water, losing their flashlights. They came up blowing water out of their mouths, and then Jim dove back under to get his Maglite. Hers was gone.

"Deck plates are coming up," he said.

"We're getting nowhere," she said. "You got a key for these doors?"

Jim stopped and looked apprehensively at the big oak doors. "Yeah, but we don't want to go in there. It's a damned cave-in waiting to happen."

She pushed water away from her chest in an effort to stand upright. "No choice," she said. "We're outta time. We can't get to the next door and find out it's blocked, too. Which it will be."

Another piece of electrical machinery shorted out down the passageway, and this one, sounding like a welding torch, blew vicious white sparks through the air vents and out into the passageway.

"Okay," he said, getting the keys out. He held the light under his chin as he searched for the key to the left door. Even as he was looking, he knew this wasn't a good idea. At the end of the Severn tunnel was that magazine, which was below the level of the main tunnel. Going in there would trap them like rats, unless they found the way up through that hole in the back. And he had never found out where that hole came out topside. *If* it came out topside.

"Hurry," she said, hiccupping. "I'm treading water here."

The water was up to Jim's chest as he sorted through the bundle of keys. It seemed to be taking forever. Then he remembered that these doors took the antique keys. Why hadn't he known that as soon as he began looking? The atmosphere was compressing hard and he was having trouble thinking. Oxygen mix must be off, he thought as his fingers found the big key.

He slammed it into the lock, but it didn't work. Two doors. Two keys. He'd picked the wrong one. Back to sorting keys again. He found the second one and shoved it into the lock.

"I open this thing, we're going for a ride," he said, his

brain beginning to spin from lack of oxygen. Branner said something, but he didn't hear it. The air had filled with a white mist as the rising water compressed it. He was barely aware that there were more flashing vaults on either side of them as the supposedly watertight doors gave way.

He felt himself swept down the stairs and into the ancient brick-lined tunnel in a roar of rushing water. Just before he was tumbled down the arched passageway along with Branner, some detached part of his brain noted that the air was a lot better now. Somehow, he managed to hold on to his flashlight while trying to ignore what was happening to his arms, elbows, knees, and head as the tidal wave rushed them into the tunnel. He caromed off the small cave-in he'd caused the last time down and only just managed to grab Branner as she whirled past him. They didn't stop until the wave of water came to the T junction leading down into the magazine area, and even then it was only because Jim got wedged across the intersection, with Branner plastered against him, yelling something he couldn't hear above the roar of the water. He held on to the edge of the wall with one hand and grasped Branner with the other as the water quickly filled the tunnel.

Dumb idea, dumb idea, dumb idea, his brain chanted as he watched in horror while the water just kept coming. If they were dislodged, they'd be swept down into the magazines and pinned against that ceiling until they drowned. There'd be no time to get into that hole. They were screwed, blued, and tattooed.

Branner had managed to wedge herself in place and was yanking on his arm. He turned to see what she wanted and she pointed urgently at the wooden door in front of them. The door to the cross tunnel.

"Key?" she yelled above the roar of the water, which was now swirling back up to their chests and rising fast.

He grabbed for the keys and for one horrible moment couldn't find them. Then he remembered he'd attached them to a belt reel. He reached way underwater and found the bundle dangling there. In the process, he dropped the flash-light, and this time it went down the stairs into the magazine vestibule before he could grab it. Branner saw it go. She didn't hesitate. She launched off the wall and let the water take her down into the vestibule. By this time, only a few feet of air remained near the top of the tunnel, and Jim was left in total darkness. But the current was slacking as the tunnel filled, so he could relax his grip on the wall and push across the tunnel to the door. Except he couldn't find it in the darkness. His grasping hands felt only tottering bricks, and he actually dislodged a couple of them while patting around for the oak door.

For a moment, he wondered if he'd become disoriented and was searching the wrong wall, but then he felt the smooth surface of the wood. Holding on to the key with a virtual death grip, he pushed it at the door, searching in the darkness for the lock. Now only about eight inches of air remained at the top of the arched ceiling, so he had to duck underwater to find the lock. It took him three tries, but he finally felt it. Then, amazingly, there was light as Branner surfaced alongside him, the Maglite in hand. He pointed with his chin, and they both went under, Branner pointing the light while Jim worked the key. The lock turned and the door swung open, and once again they went for a ride, but a shorter one this time, fetching up with a painful crash against yet another door at the end of the thirty-foot-long cross tunnel. This time, they managed to get to their feet as the water swelled through the open door behind them and filled the cross tunnel. When it was just about two feet from the ceiling, the current slacked off and Jim pointed to the open door.

"We need to close that before we open this one," he gasped. "That way, we won't flood the other tunnel."

Branner understood at once. They swam down to the door and pushed it shut, holding it by kicking vigorously while Jim got the key back into it and locked it. Then they took a moment to get their breath. The water was no longer rising in the cross tunnel, although they still only had about twelve inches of air. Then they heard a deep sustained rumbling from behind the door and the entire door frame began to shake, rippling the water in the cross tunnel as they stood there on tiptoe.

"It's caving in," he said, watching the ceiling now as the vibrations from the other side precipitated the ominously familiar rain of dried mortar. "We'd better move."

They half-walked, half-swam down to the other door. Jim wasn't sure whether they'd gone up the tunnel or down. In the darkness, it was hard to tell. Branner held the light while Jim put what he thought was the right key in the door. It didn't work. He tried the other key. It didn't work, either.

"What the fuck?" Branner said, pushing a hank of wet hair out of her eyes. Beyond the far door, the rumbling was tapering off, but the door itself was making noises now. Jim flashed the light down on it and they saw that it was bulging under the sudden pressure of the tunnel collapse. Jim frantically tried all the keys that fit the Fort Severn doors, but none of them worked. Righty-tighty, lefty-loosey, he reminded himself, but the lock didn't budge. Damn thing had let them into the tunnel—why didn't one of these keys work? He had never gone into the right-hand tunnel because—why? He couldn't remember. Hell, he couldn't even think. There was more water than oxygen in the air. The rain of mortar dust was turning into a spatter of old lime. Branner was looking at him expectantly. Then he had a bad thought: Maybe it had been the right-hand tunnel that had collapsed. But no—that wouldn't affect the door behind them. He shook his head in frustration and to get the sweat out of his eyes. Why was it so warm?

"Is this water rising?" he asked Branner.

"I don't think so," she said, still staring back at the other door. The whole door frame was creaking and cracking under some enormous strain. Just for the hell of it, Jim tried the ornate iron door handle, reaching underwater and pushing it hard down. To his astonishment, the door opened, allowing yet another tidal wave to sweep them off their feet and out into the right-hand magazine tunnel in a tumble of arms and legs. Branner dropped the light and the wave of water swept it down into the tunnel. But the waterfall effect was over quickly this time, as the full flood couldn't reach them. Not yet anyway, Jim thought, remembering the cross tunnel's door.

He got to his feet and chased the Maglite. He came back to where Branner was sprawled on the floor in about six inches of water.

"This is getting tiresome," she said, spitting out bits of mortar and wringing out the edges of her clothes.

"Lemme get this door closed in case the other one gives way. But as long as these doors hold, we're not going to drown."

He shone the light at the other door, which was leaking water around its seams. He closed the near door, then tried to find a key to lock it. This time, one of the keys worked. Once he had the door secured, he looked around by the beam of the Maglite. As far as he could see, this tunnel was the mirror image of the one he'd been into before. He could see the cement-block wall where the PWC people had sealed the gun pit tunnels. The anteroom to the actual magazine sloped down, just as the one on the other side had. The air was mustier and reeked of wet cement. Branner got up and came over to where he was standing, sniffing the air.

"What?" she said.

Jim shone the light up and down the tunnel area. Then he held it still. There was a mist in the air, but it wasn't water. He felt the pressure in his ears again and tried to clear them, to no avail.

"What's that mist?" Branner asked.

"Mortar dust," he said. "These tunnels are unstable. The cement between the bricks isn't really cement anymore."

"What's holding it all up, then?" she asked, lowering her voice.

"Faith, hope, and charity," he said. "And some Roman engineering. Look, on the other side, there was what looked like a way out, in the powder room. Some kind of ventilation hole. We searched topside but never found the outlet. We need to see if this magazine has the same arrangement."

"Why not go back to the main tunnel—that way, right?" she said, pointing back up toward the main tunnel complex.

"Because it's flooded to the ceiling by now, remember?"

"Oh, yeah," she said, frowning, aware now that her brain wasn't working all that well, either. "Does that mean we go *down* this tunnel?" She eyed the locked oak door behind them, remembering how the frame of the other one had been shaking. Obviously, down wasn't what she wanted to do just now.

"I think we have to take a look," he said. "By now, they have to know something's happened. All the utilities, all the electric power in Bancroft Hall's gonna be out. All sorts of shit shorted out. Phone lines dead."

"I'll buy that," she said, leaning against a wall and examining the bruises on her arms. "Except that it's almost two o'clock in the morning. But what can they do about it? And how can they get to us?"

Good questions, Jim thought. At the least, they'd have to drain the tunnel, and the main route for doing that, the storm drain, was blocked. He wondered which lucky soul would get the honor of going up the storm drain from the river and pulling that blockage loose.

"They'll realize the storm drain's blocked. Once they get that opened, the tunnels will drain themselves." All except these old fort tunnels, he realized—they were one level below the main passageways. From the sound of it, the left-hand tunnel had already caved in, and this one didn't look too great. He shone the light beam down the tunnel again and saw the same silent cement snowfall. If that bastard goes, he thought, we're buried. And they might not even know we're in here.

"Wonderful," she muttered, as if reading his thoughts. "Powder room it is."

They walked down the now-slippery brick slope. When they got to the anteroom in front of the magazine, there was at least two feet of water pooled on the floor, glimmering in the light from the flashlight. The magazine doors were identical to those on the other side. Jim sloshed through the water to one of them while Branner held the light on it. He worked the latches and pulled hard. The door resisted but then moved, and, to their astonishment, the anteroom was flooded with white light.

Inside the powder room, the floor was flooded to the same depth as in the anteroom. But that wasn't what got their attention. The room was lit by four fluorescent light fixtures mounted vertically on the wall beneath the domed ceiling. These lights were on despite the lack of electrical power throughout the rest of the system. There were six lab benches, all filled with various kinds of electronic equipment: video monitors, what looked like PCs without their cases, oscilloscopes, tools, a crude telephone switchboard, several printers, and three large wiring patch panels where wires of every description were jumbled into complex loops. On one side of the room, now almost afloat, was a single mattress, of the kind found in most midshipmen's rooms. Next to it there was a small refrigerator. A makeshift hanging bar for clothes was rigged on the opposite wall, where there were some civilian clothes, as well as what looked like the vampire costume. A trash can in one corner had pizza boxes and beer cans in about equal numbers.

"Son of a bitch," Jim murmured as he surveyed Booth's lair. "I wonder how long he's been hiding out down here."

"Two, three years anyway," Branner said. She walked over to one of the printers. "Check this out—doesn't this look like an exam?"

Jim went over and examined the printout. "Sure does. Shit, he's probably been tapping the whole Academy intranet down here. Listening to E-mails, copying admin traffic. Look at that headset—it's tied to that PBX switchboard."

"Where's he getting power for these lights?"

As they looked around, they heard the whine of an inverter. They found a stack of car batteries hooked to the inverter, which was producing the AC power for the lights.

"Pretty slick," Jim said. "Got his own power supply. This whole place looks like some mad scientist built it. Remember what that kid said about Booth—supernerd with a bad attitude?"

Branner nodded and ran her fingers through her wet hair.

"What pisses me off is that I never came over here," Jim said. "Everybody agreed that this side of the tunnel complex wouldn't be useful, because it went nowhere near Bancroft Hall. That damned door wasn't even locked. Let's look for the way out before any more of that tunnel caves in."

There were the same two square holes in the back corners of the domed ceiling at the end of the room. Each one had a small pipe running up into the hole from about two inches above the floor. But this time, there was no ladder.

"Where are we, in relation to the buildings topside?" Branner asked.

"I don't know," he said. "The maps we had were wrong about the other side, and about the Fort Severn layout in general. I never came over on this side because I was looking for a way in and out of Bancroft. We could be anywhere under Lejeune Hall, or even the field house. Or maybe even into the city. Hell, I don't know."

They heard some more noises from the tunnel complex outside. Jim went over to the steel magazine door and pulled it shut. It seemed to him that the water was a little bit deeper. Probably leaking around doors, he thought. Then they heard a loud bang from in the right-hand tunnel. They looked at each other, not saying anything. Jim was about to go back to the door for the cross tunnel to see what had happened when they heard what sounded like a small giant banging on that door.

"Cross tunnel just flooded out," he said. "Damned door didn't hold."

He opened the steel door enough to shine the flashlight outside. The hammering sound had subsided into a steady vibration, which was being transmitted by the aging masonry to every joint in the anteroom ceiling. The mist became a fog as more and more of the cement vibrated out of the cracks between the old bricks. He swung the door closed again and reset the latches. They didn't have much time before the whole thing caved in. He looked up at the ceiling of the magazine itself, but the cement covering it was smooth. Even if the anteroom caved in, this would probably hold. He hoped. He looked over at Branner, who was staring fixedly at that door. The expression on her pale face revealed that she fully understood their situation. The vibrations outside got louder.

Jim pocketed the Maglite and began pulling one of the lab benches over toward the right-hand corner of the room, underneath the closest vent hole. The fluorescent lights flickered and then steadied. He shone the Maglite beam up into the hole. He couldn't see anything at all, just blackness.

"Try the other one," he said.

They shoved a second bench under the left-hand hole. This time, he could just make out something way up in the exhaust shaft. The fluorescents flickered again and the pressure in their ears mounted. Branner looked over at the steel doors as they shifted audibly on their tracks.

"The other one had a ladder. He doesn't just drop into this room. But how the hell we're going to get up there, I do not—"

There was a crashing roar from outside the steel doors and then a wicked thump as something big hit them from the other side. One of the fluorescents fell off the wall and crashed down onto a bench in a flare of chemical light as a hundred sprays of water began blowing through the cracks around the doors, low at first and then rising fast. As the water began to swirl around their legs, Jim leaped across the room to the low rack where the inverter was mounted above the batteries and got it turned off just as the first of the batteries sputtered beneath it. The lights went out immediately, but they were no longer standing in water with an AC generator going. He sloshed back to where Branner was trying to hold the lab table in position beneath the hole.

"We'll try to hold our position here," he shouted above the rush of water as it boiled through the cracks now, flooding the space at the rate of a foot a minute. "The water'll lift us to the hole."

Branner's face was frozen in fear in the glow of the Maglite. "Then what?" she wailed.

"We pray," he shouted back as the doors, which had been built to resist pressure from inside the magazine, let go with a groan of fracturing metal and the room flooded with dizzying speed. Holding on to the thin pipe at the side of the hole, they rose with the water until their heads were bobbing directly beneath the four-foot opening in the ceiling. Stuffing the Maglite into his trousers pocket, Jim grabbed Branner and turned her around so that he could hug her from behind. The water forced them into the hole, where the air pressure rose immediately as the pocket was compressed by the flood below. Jim felt his right ear and then his left pop painfully, and heard Branner yell in pain as her ears resisted the pressure change. But then they stopped rising as the water pressure and the pressure in their air pocket reached equilibrium. Jim fished out the flashlight and switched it on. The water boiled ominously around their legs as the magazine finally flooded completely. Small bits of debris from Booth's lab surfaced around their faces. Jim shone the light straight up.

"Anything?" Branner gasped. Jim saw that her eyes were closed. She had said she didn't like confined places; this must be sheer terror for her, he thought. To his vast relief, the light revealed the bottom rungs of a ten-foot-long ladder. It was not permanently mounted to the shaft wall, but appeared to be hanging from a hook up at the top of the shaft. There was a rope coiled around a pulley at the top of the ladder. Finding the ladder was the good news, he thought. The fact that the bottom rungs were fifteen feet or more above them was the not-so-good news.

"Ladder," he said. "This is the way he got in here. Now we just have to get to it."

Branner opened her eyes and looked up. The movement

put their faces together. She looked at him and he grinned at her. "This has to be true love," he said.

She tried to laugh, but it didn't quite come off. "I'm right on the edge of screaming my head off until this all goes away," she said, her voice cracking.

"Except that it won't," he reminded her, trying to keep it light. The Maglite was beginning to give out, so he switched it off. She immediately asked him to turn it back on, which he did.

"You have no idea how scared I am right now," she said. "But I do know how to get to that ladder."

"And the answer is?"

"Chimney climb," she said. "Move to the side as much as you can, and I'll use my legs and back to go up the wall."

He'd seen the technique and understood. "Okay; if you start to fall, let me know, so I can get out of the way."

She squeezed herself sideways across the square shaft and started the maneuver. "If I start to fall, you'll know it, not that you'll have anywhere to go."

"Just a thought," he mumbled. "We'll both go down."

"What's this 'we' shit?" she said as she started up the wall, wedging her legs against the opposite wall as she slid her backside up the surface. She was already puffing in the hot, humid, compressed air.

"I think that ladder is hanging on a hook," he said, shining the light past her body. "I guess it'll hold if you grab it."

She didn't answer, putting all her remaining energy into the climb. He kept the light shining past her face and pointed at the bottom of the ladder. He noticed there was a series of hooks, with the lowest visible one right in front of his face. The shaft appeared to be thirty feet high. Booth probably climbed down the ladder, wedging himself like she was doing, and then repositioned the ladder to the next set of hooks.

Jim kept himself afloat by wedging his own legs against the far side wall. The only sounds came from Branner's exertions as she inched up the wall and the occasional thump and rumble from one of the flooded tunnels outside. He wondered if the cave-ins would show up on the surface. Not until daylight, if then. He looked up again. She was making progress, but it was slow going. The pressure in his ears was so great now that he had a headache, not to mention several points of road rash from being tumbled around in the tunnels. He wondered where Booth was. And how he'd gotten out once he released the flood. There were going to be some red faces when they got out of here. If they got out of here. He had no idea of what was up at the top of the shaft, but that ladder must lead to some kind of escape. You hope, he thought.

He shifted position to see better and to keep the fading Maglite pointed up so Branner could see her objective. Sweat was running into his eyes and he had to blink repeatedly to clear them. He tried to focus on the hook in front of his face, then realized it wasn't there.

Huh? Where'd it go?

He felt around in the water and found the hook, but it was no longer at face level. It was now at chest level. Which meant—what?

That the water was rising. That he was rising with it. There was obviously enough pressure to force the water column in the shaft to rise all the way to the top. But if the tunnel had collapsed, where was the water coming from? He couldn't think straight.

Okay, keep it simple. Linear. If she doesn't make it to the ladder, we'll just float up to the ladder. And beyond, to the top. That's the good news. But then we'd better be able to open whatever the access is, because all our air has to be leaking out of the shaft up there for the water to be able to rise behind it. Should he tell Branner? He looked up again, even as he felt the hook touch his stomach.

"How's it going?"

"About five more feet," she grunted. "This is harder than it looks."

"It looks plenty hard," he said. "Can you see what's up there?"

"No," she said. "Focusing on the ladder. How strong are these hooks?"

"They're pretty big," he said. He saw that she had stopped to catch her breath. In the silence, her breathing sounded very labored. He hoped like hell she didn't fall, because there was no way he'd be able to get out of the way, and she was ten feet above him at least. In the dimming light, he could see that she had locked her legs across the shaft and had her whole back pressed against the wall, her hands down at her sides. He couldn't see her face.

"I have good news and bad news," he said, finally, when she didn't move.

"Bad news first," she said.

"The water is rising."

"My brain isn't working in all this mug; what's that mean?"

"It means that we need to beat it to the top and the outside before it pushes all the air out of this shaft."

"Wonderful," she said after a moment. "What's the good news?"

"I lied. There isn't any good news."

"Hate it when you beat around the bush like that."

"I know."

She started her climb again, causing a small cascade of droplets to fall around him. He tried to think of something clever to say, but he couldn't. He felt for the hook. It was below his groin. Think positively, he thought. That air has to be getting out somewhere up there or the water couldn't rise. Means that the shaft must come out near or on the surface. Has to. Or why would there be a ladder hanging up there?

Unless it had been hanging there for one hundred fifty years.

He banished that thought.

"Got it," Branner announced from above. "Now what?"

"Climb the ladder," he said. "Gently."

"Gently?"

"Just climb it; see what the hell's at the top. Call for room service."

"Can you give me more light?"

"That's it, I'm afraid."

He heard her change position in the shaft, and then the creak of wood as she very slowly transferred her weight to the ladder. He didn't look up; doing so hurt the back of his neck. He could feel the hook down around his knees now, and the weight of his Glock in its holster felt like a small brick pressing against the small of his back.

More creaking from above him, and, despite the cramp in his neck, he looked up. He could see Branner's legs on the ladder as she climbed up into the gloom. The flashlight was really failing now, casting little more than a weak gray beam into the humid mist. But at least the hook appeared to be holding.

"We have a door," she said at last. He heard a rattle. "A locked door. A locked *metal* door, in fact."

He groaned. "Old or new door?" he called up to her.

"I think it's old. Can't tell with no light. Feels solid, though. Maybe iron."

He gauged the distance to the ladder. He was still eight feet or so below the ladder's lowest rungs. He was too tired and probably too big to do what she had done with that climbing maneuver.

"Is there a handle? Any kind of latches, top or bottom?"

He waited while she felt around the surface of the door. "Nothing," she said. "Not even a keyhole, at least not that I can find. Nor any hinges."

"Frame?"

Another moment. "Feels like wood. *Ow!* Yes, wood. I just got a splinter."

"What's above it?"

"Top of the shaft."

"Brickwork or cement?"

"Feels like both. A veneer of cement over bricks, maybe? Hard to tell."

He felt for the hook to gauge his progress up the shaft. He couldn't find it. "Can you tell how the air's getting out?"

"Wait," she said. He kept as still as he could while treading water so she could listen. He felt around for the hook again, but it was gone. The bottom of the ladder wasn't that far away anymore. Water was rising faster.

"I can hear some air moving, but I'm not sure where it's getting out. Feels like there are hinges at the top of this door, like it's some kind of flap, not a door? I think the air's getting out around one of these hinges."

"Can you stop it? Jam something in the crack?"

"I can try, I guess," she said, and he heard the rustle of clothing above him, then a ripping sound. He put a finger out in front of his chest and pressed it against the wall facing him, his arm floating as level as he could get it. Almost immediately, his body began to rise above the level of his arm.

"There," she said. "I ripped a sleeve off my shirt. Stuffed it in the crack. I can't hear air moving anymore."

He concentrated on the position of his arm. Had it stopped moving? He thought it had.

"Here's what I think," he said. His voice was getting hoarse in the hothouse atmosphere. "This shaft, and the other one, were pressure-release chambers in case there was a fire or explosion down in the magazine. That door probably is a flap, designed to let go under pressure and vent the chamber down below."

"How does that help us?"

"That flap door isn't going to open with a key. Can you feel around, down at the bottom of the flap? There has to be a latch plate of some kind, so Booth could get out."

She moved on the ladder. Booth had probably rigged a latch arrangement on the other side using either the original latch or a new one. He would have left it open whenever he came down here, and latched it when he wasn't down here.

"There's something on the other side. I feel rivets or bolts. Can't see which."

"Okay. Right now the water's stopped rising, I think."

"And?"

"Booth had that other shaft blocked off with a piece of sheet metal, remember? So I'm proposing to swim back down this shaft, out into the magazine, and open those big doors. That will let a wave of water in and put pressure on that flap. Then it'll—"

"Jim?"

"Wait. Then it'll push that flap out; and we can—"

"Jim!"

"What?" Why was she interrupting him? He was trying to get them out of this trap.

"That won't work," she said patiently. "There couldn't be *any* water up in this shaft if the magazine wasn't already flooded. There won't be any wave of water."

He looked up. She was a dim figure up in the haze at the top of the shaft. His mind was whirling. Of course she was right. What the hell had he been thinking? Shit. He was losing it.

"How close are you to the ladder?" she called.

"A couple of feet, but I'm not rising anymore."

"I'm going to pull this rag and let some more air out. As soon as the water lifts you to the ladder, climb up to where I am. I'll get off it and wedge in up here so we don't lose it. Maybe we can dislodge this brickwork above the top of the door. It's all crumbly, like in the rest of the tunnels."

"And then?"

"There's four feet of brickwork above the flap door. If we can make a hole, we're out. But I'll need you for that. We need brute force to get it done."

"So I'm a brute now?"

"You were a Marine, weren't you?"

He laughed, making a surreal sound in the shaft. "I'm gonna report you to the commander of political correctness down in Quantico," he said.

"Yeah, right, and she'll probably gum me to death. Can you reach the ladder yet?"

He was closer, but not quite close enough. But then he realized he could probably do what she had done, for that short a distance. He positioned himself and began to back-walk up the shaft. His clothes felt heavy as his body came out of the water. He had put the Maglite into his shirt pocket to free his hands, and it was bobbing its feeble beam everywhere.

"Got it," he said, grabbing the bottom rung of the ladder. The bottom, which had been hanging vertically, pulled out at an angle as he grabbed it, reminding him of the tower jump ladder back in the Nat.

"Okay," she said. "Let me get off it; then you climb up."

He waited while she maneuvered above him, and then she told him to come on up. He climbed the ladder, first with his arms and then with both feet and arms, showering water back down into the shaft. When he reached the top, he stopped, puffing with the exertion of breathing the warm, wet air. From this position, he was able to shine the fading beam down onto the bottom of the flap door. There were eight rivet heads out in the middle of the bottom part of the door. He kicked out at the flap. Predictably, it hurt his foot. Whatever it was, it was solid. He could hear the sound of air whistling past some obstacle above the door.

"Look above it," she said, and he raised the light. He saw the familiar sight of ancient brickwork, the mortar between the joints eroded a half inch into the joints, the bricks uneven in shape and alignment. He climbed a little higher on the ladder and felt the bricks, placing himself face-to-hip with Branner's hunched body. He pushed on the bricks. They didn't move.

"I don't know," he said wearily. "There are probably several courses there. Feels pretty solid to me."

"Pull, don't push," she said, adjusting her position. Her legs were wedged across the shaft and her head was right up at the top of it.

Jim took a deep breath and got very little out of it. The air seemed denser, more moisture than oxygen. He pulled at the most exposed brick. He couldn't be positive, but he thought it did move this time.

"We sure could use a pry bar," he said. Although not exactly an echo, his voice came right back at him. "I've got a knife, but it's much too small."

He eased himself back down the ladder two rungs to look at that latch area again and then noticed that his feet were wet. No, not wet—submerged. He pointed the light down, looked, and swore. The water had risen all the way up the ladder. As he stared, the black water rose above his ankles and onto his shins. Branner saw it, too.

"What do we do!" she wailed.

"Plug the airhole again, *quick*!"

As she reached across to stuff the sleeve back into the crack, the ladder shifted and she lost her perch against the wall. She fell clumsily past the ladder and down into the water, nearly knocking Jim right off the ladder. The rag patch disappeared. Jim swung sideways to avoid being hit and then went upside down on the ladder before he could regain his balance. While Branner thrashed around in the water below him, he scrambled back to the right side of the ladder and climbed back to face the flap door. The flashlight was barely putting out a yellow glow.

He looked down. The water seemed to be coming up faster now, and the whistling noise was louder. Branner was rising with it, hanging on to the ladder but not getting on it. In a few moments, the water would rise all the way to the top of the shaft and would snuff them out. Desperate now, he reached out from the side of the ladder and kicked the flap door with all his strength. It clanged in the darkness, but the latch, or whatever it was, held. The water was up to his hips now, and he could see Branner's face only as a gray blob just beneath his hip.

"Get underwater!" he shouted. "Take a deep breath and go deep. Do it! *Now!*"

He heard her take a huge breath and then the blob disappeared from sight. He pulled the Glock out of his waistband holster, shook it to clear any water out of the barrel, then swung aside and opened fire on the back of the latch. The noise was punishing as he emptied the gun at the back plate of the latch, which was almost submerged. Squinting his eyes and leaning as far out to one side as he could, he fired again and again, shutting his eyes each time a bullet blasted back at him or went spanging around the brickwork. Twice, he felt a lash of burning pain on his upper back, but he kept firing. The last two rounds blew water everywhere as the level came up past the back plate, and then he was squeezing on empty. He dropped the Glock and lunged again with his right leg, smashing it against the flap once, twice, three times. Branner surfaced alongside him, gasping for air. She realized what he was doing and joined in, kicking with all her might at the flap door as the water rose completely over its top. And then it let go.

In one small tidal wave, they both were swept into the hole where the flap had been, but then their hips got jammed in the ladder rungs and neither of them could get through.

"Wait, *wait!*" Jim shouted. "Let the water get out!" Even as he said it, he had to summon all his strength not to keep scrambling to get out. He grabbed the side wall to keep the flap from coming back down and cutting off their hands, and then they waited for another minute as the water subsided to a steady waterfall over the coaming of the flap. Then Jim disentangled his legs from the ladder and dropped out onto a tiled floor. He turned around and helped a trembling, white-faced Branner out. Her eyes were huge with fright and she held on to him with a desperate grip as they sank down onto the floor. There was light in the room, light that was coming from under a door. He could see a maze of pipes and valves along one wall. There was a wall of old lockers on the opposite wall.

Branner gulped down fresh air and then removed her hands, looking at them. They were darkened with something. "You're bleeding," she said. "Let me see."

"Ricochets," he said. "Doesn't feel like anything went in." He bent his head while she surveyed his upper back and arms.

"You've got three tears in your shirt; I need more light to see how deep they are." She wiped her hands off on his shirt. "Another fucking door! Where the hell are we now?"

"Out of that goddamned shaft, and that's all I care about. This is modern construction. Try the door."

The water kept coming up and over the lower sill of the flap door, which was hanging back down in position. It puddled on the floor and then ran under the room's door. He could see the flap's latch assembly in the half-light, the metal torn to pieces by the gunfire. Thank God that thing was old metal, designed to give way, he thought. Branner crawled on her hands and knees to the doorway and reached for the handle.

"If this thing's locked, I'm going to do some serious screaming," she said.

But it wasn't. She pulled it open and the room was fully illuminated by a battery-operated fire-safety light. They could see a basement corridor outside, filled with more pipes and pumping machinery. The smell of chlorine wafted through the door, and Jim began to laugh.

"What?" she said, eyeing him suspiciously, obviously suspecting hysteria. She was still down on her hands and knees, her hair hanging over her forehead.

"I know where we are," he said. "We're in the basement of Lejeune Hall. That far wall with all the pipes? That's the foundation of the swimming pool. We're down beneath the fucking swimming pool!"

She tried to pull her soaked clothes away from her body for a moment but then gave up. She looked like a drowned puppy. "After all that, you bring me to a swimming pool?" she asked.

"Can't dance," he said weakly.

An hour later, Jim and Branner were sitting on the stone wall running along the portico of the second wing of Bancroft Hall, watching the circus. The entire Yard seemed to be filled with red and blue flashing lights as emergency crews worked to remove the water from the utility tunnels. Each of the major gratings was surrounded by firemen, police, and PWC workers, most of whom were standing around and looking down into the water-filled pits that had been the grating entrances. Jim was being careful not to lean back on anything. His tattered and bloody shirt covered a mass of bandages, which in turn covered the three grazing wounds he'd received from the ricocheting rounds in the air shaft. In the light of the emergency light stands set up around the Yard grates, they could also see a knot of white uniforms up on the superintendent's front porch, where the supe, the diminutive commandant, and several Academy staff officers were conferring with the commanding officer of the Public Works Center. Directly above them, dozens of curious faces peered out of darkened windows in Bancroft Hall.

"Regular Lebanese goat grab," Jim said to Branner. She was talking quietly on her cell phone to NCIS headquarters, giving an initial report of the evening's developments. The chief's police truck swung into the road in front of the second wing. Leaving his headlights on, Bustamente got out and came up the marble steps. The lights shone right on them.

"I guess this all seemed like a good idea at the time," he observed, waving his hand at all the emergency lights strobing away in the unusually dark Yard.

"They get that river drain open?" Jim asked, trying not to move his back too much. The EMT had whistled out loud when he'd seen Jim's back for the first time.

"Yeah, I think so," the chief said, climbing to join them up on the terrace. "The PWC troops had this big circle jerk going, trying to figure out who was gonna be the lucky bastard who got to go up the drain and free the door. You know, which union, how were they gonna do it, maybe use a YP to pull a cable attached to the door out into the river, like that."

"Lemme guess: They had so many volunteers to hook up the cable, they couldn't make up their minds."

"Yeah, right. It was starting to look like the XO himself was gonna have to climb down there and do it. Problem was, the drain's several hundred feet long, and they couldn't figure out how to pull the cable all the way up the pipe without some kinda winch. You know, that shit's heavy."

"And?"

"And while they were going on about this and that, there was this big-ass boom. Came from the storm drain. Everyone there, yours truly included, jumped a half a mile. Then the water came out like some giant was down there doing the green apple two-step. That grate on the seawall? History. Went flying out into the river."

"So pretty soon, the tunnels will be pumped out."

"Yeah, although now they gotta get down there, turn off the valves that little prick opened. They got the city water shut off upstream in town, but some other damn thing is still running water down there. Biggest priority is getting power back to Mother B. here. Anyways, they got a night's work ahead of them."

"So do we, Chief," Jim said. "We've gotta find this Booth guy."

"You actually see this little shitbird?"

"Big shitbird, I'm afraid, and no, I never actually laid eyes on him tonight. He pulled me into the storm drain, and he fed Agent Branner here an ether sandwich, but no, we never actually laid eyes on the son of a bitch. But we're going to."

Branner snapped her phone shut and rejoined them. "How's the back?" she asked, eyeing the ruins of his shirt.

"Hurts," Jim admitted. "I'm gonna have to be on top for a while."

Branner flashed him one of her hundred-yard stares while the chief tried to suppress a guffaw. But then she actually grinned. He was relieved to see that she had stopped shaking. "Washington's rousting out reinforcements," she said. "Our director's suddenly eager to reopen this thing." She glanced over Jim's shoulder in the direction of the supe's quarters. "Uh-oh," she muttered. "Incoming."

Jim turned and saw the commandant and two commanders headed for them. "Should have turned your lights off, Chief," Jim said.

"Whoops. I think I better go coordinate some shit."

"Chicken," Jim said. The chief saluted the commandant as they passed on the steps and then escaped smartly in his police pickup. The portico went back into shadow as he pulled away from the curb.

"Mr. Hall. And Agent Branner," the commandant said as he reached them. "We're so glad you're safe."

The two commanders waited discreetly down at the bottom of the steps. Jim didn't recognize either of them. "Sorry about all this, sir," he said. "Things kinda got out of hand down there tonight."

"Well, I should say so, Mr. Hall," Robbins said, giving him an arch look. "The OOD told me you'd been shot? Are you all right?"

"I had to use a gun to blast the latch off the door we escaped through," Jim said. "It was in an old airshaft. There were some ricochets. Cut up my back, mostly, but apparently nothing too serious. Do you have any idea where Midshipman Booth is?"

Robbins frowned and chewed on his lower lip for a moment. "The OOD gave me a preliminary report. Midshipman Booth is not in his room, and no one knows where he is. Midshipman Markham is signed out into town and has not returned. Any thoughts?"

Jim took in the dant's expression. The usual controlled anger was gone. In its place was something else, something he couldn't read.

"Thoughts? Yes, I have some thoughts. I think this Midshipman Booth either killed Brian Dell or caused it to happen. I think he's also responsible for the beating death of a federal agent, and some other muggings that have been taking place over in Crabtown. He may also be responsible for the disappearance of a student at St. John's. And an attempt on Midshipman Hays's life. Not to mention penetrating the Academy's intranet, filching exam material, destroying government property on a grand fucking scale, and generally running wild for the past three years while nobody, nobody at all, caught on."

"And you can prove these allegations?"

Ah, Jim thought, here it comes. "We need a little time alone with Mr. Booth. And then we'd want to show you his little underground lab setup, assuming we can still reach it.

But, yes, I think we can. He as much as admitted some of this to us down in the tunnels tonight."

"To both of you?" Robbins asked.

Jim chose not to look at Branner. "I don't know how much Agent Branner heard after she'd been disabled," Jim said. "But we sure as hell didn't cause all that"—he gestured out into the Yard at all the lights—"to happen tonight. That kid tried to kill us both."

"How did you know he'd be down there tonight?" Robbins asked.

Jim wasn't about to admit that he'd challenged Booth to go down into the tunnels. "We didn't," Branner said. "But we'd learned some things at Elizabeth DeWinter's office yesterday afternoon from Midshipman Markham, some things you may not yet know. We're thinking now that Dell's death may have been aimed at Markham. That Dell may have been a pawn in a bigger, and nastier, game between Booth and Markham."

The commandant nodded thoughtfully. "And do your superiors agree with all these . . . hypotheses?" he asked her.

"NCIS believes the investigation into the Booth matter should be expanded and pursued vigorously," she said.

The commandant eyed her carefully. "I believe you received quite different directions, earlier."

"They became OBE after we'd talked to Markham. We knew that what she was telling us would change everything. So to speak."

The ghost of a smile crossed Captain Robbins's lips, but before he could say anything, Branner's cell phone chirped. She turned to answer it, said "Okay" three times, and then closed the phone. "My headquarters wants a joint conference call with me and Mr. Hall, sir. Do you mind? We need to brief them officially, while everything's still wet, as it were."

Robbins nodded. "And then, in the morning," he said, "I'd appreciate the same courtesy for me and my staff, if that won't be too much trouble."

"Not at all, sir," Branner said before Jim could get a word in edgewise. "Thank you, sir."

Robbins started to say something, then shook his head and went back down the steps. The commanders joined him and they walked around the corner of the building toward Tecumseh Court, the two officers perfectly in step with Robbins.

"WTF? Over," Jim said quietly.

"That wasn't Chang. I paged myself. We don't need to get into a 'Who shot John' discussion with little Adolf there. Time to blow this pop stand. Get some sleep."

"Time to find that goddamned Booth."

"Let them look for him. If he's still here in the Yard, he has to hide from four thousand of them, plus the officers. Let's get you back to the boat before you fall down and I have to carry you. Some more."

"I resent that, and I'm not that bad off," he said, trying not to wince when he stood up. The bandages felt like a second skin, a badly sunburned skin.

"Okay, so let's get *me* back to the boat before *I* fall down, how 'bout that?"

Jim dreamed he was locked in a room full of telephones, all of which had started to ring at once. It was an annoying dream, which got even more annoying when he picked one up and it kept ringing.

"Answer the damned thing," Branner mumbled from beneath the covers.

He felt for the bedside phone, got it off the hook, and stuck it in his ear without opening his eyes. His upper back felt like he'd been dragged down a gravel road for an hour or so.

"Hall," he croaked.

"Mr. Hall? Good morning, sir. This is Eve, the commandant's secretary? The commandant's compliments, sir, and he requests your presence in his office at zero seven-thirty."

Jim opened one eye, glared at the clock radio. Once he was able to focus, saw that it was 6:50.

"Sure, why not?" he said, and hung up before Eve could reply.

"What?" Branner said, still underneath the covers somewhere.

"I've just been given a come-around," he said. "Dant's office, zero seven-thirty. That's a half hour from now."

"Have a good time," she said. "Don't tell anybody where I am."

"Right," he said, getting up and staggering over toward the head to shuck his clothes. Mindful of all the road rash on his back, he opted for a quick front-side-only shower. "Only thing is, they've probably got Booth," he called, and grinned when he heard her swearing.

It seemed like only an hour ago that they'd collapsed on the bed fully dressed. Branner had made some noises about going to the guest cabin, but he had sensed her exhaustion and perhaps more. Within an hour, she'd awakened in the grip of a nightmare, fiercely holding on to Jim for several minutes of uncontrolled shivering and tears. He'd finally rolled her under the covers, clothes and all, and then just held her until she fell asleep.

Twenty-five minutes later, Jim and Branner drove through the gate at the visitors' center in Jim's truck and parked in one of the slots reserved for police vehicles. They walked across the Yard and entered Bancroft through the second wing's terrace doors, where they found most of the overhead lights still out after the events of the prior night. The sound of a portable generator could be heard from the courtyard between Dahlgren Hall and Bancroft.

"Sorry about all the hysterical waterworks last night," she said as they strode down the empty corridor.

"I was getting ready to do the same thing," he said, careful not to look at her. "That was too fucking close, all around."

"Still," she replied. "I'm glad you were there."

They made it to the commandant's office at 7:29. Eve beamed her approval, then frowned when she saw Branner. Jim had managed a jacket and tie, but Branner was still in the same outfit she'd worn down in the tunnels and then slept in. It had not improved with age.

"But, um, I'm afraid this appointment is for Mr. Hall," she began, eyeing Branner's rumpled clothes. Jim cut her off.

"Agent Branner needs to know when she'll be able to interview Midshipman Booth," he said.

"Midshipman Booth?" Eve said blankly. "I don't know anything about a Midshipman Booth. I'll have to consult with the commandant. If you would both please have a seat, I'll—"

"Get in here, both of you," Robbins called from inside his office. Jim followed Branner into the commandant's inner office. He did not invite them to sit down. He stood behind his desk, peering up at Jim over his reading glasses. "I think it was made clear the other day, to both of you, now that I think about it, that this matter had been resolved by a SecNav determination."

"We're talking about the Dell matter?" Jim asked.

"Yes, Mr. Hall. The Dell matter. What else would we be talking about?"

"I was assuming you wanted to know why the utility tunnel complex was wrecked last night. Why you and your office are all running on emergency generators this morning. That you'd want a fuller explanation of what happened down there, and why we were down there."

"Yes, I do. But right now, Midshipman Markham hasn't shown up for morning meal formation. She signed in very early this morning, well after the expiration of town liberty. And another firstie is also UA."

"Gosh, let me guess," Jim said. "Dyle Booth."

"Don't tell me you've misplaced him?" Branner asked.

Robbins frowned and sat down slowly. "It's most unusual. Two first-class UA. Especially this late in the year. And most out of character for Midshipman Markham."

"But not for Booth?"

"Booth's company officer reports that he is something of a loner within the company, but he's had no conduct offenses of any kind for almost three years."

"Well," Branner said, pulling up a chair and plopping down into it. "I'm tired, so I'm going to sit down. Let me fill you in on what we think we know about Midshipman First Class Dyle Booth."

"But, see here, I—"

"You want to listen, Captain. That's what you want to do right now."

Robbins opened his mouth to protest, saw the look on Branner's face, and shut it. Jim grabbed himself a chair, reversed it, and sat down, being very careful not to strain the shirt across his back. Branner was gathering her thoughts when the commandant's door burst open. It was Captain Rogers, and he was visibly agitated.

"Sir!" he shouted. "We have a possible hostage situation. Eighth wing. One mid is threatening to throw another one off the roof!"

Branner whipped around in her chair. "Is one of them a female?"

Rogers blinked, focused on Branner, and then nodded yes. The commandant was standing up behind his desk. "Call the—" He began, then stopped. "Hell's bells, who do we call? A hostage situation! What the hell's our procedure for a hostage situation?"

Jim reached across the desk and snatched up Robbins's phone. He called the chief's direct number, got him, and told him to set up a police perimeter around the eighth wing, inside and out, to contain a hostage situation, and to get some help from the Annapolis police. To his immense credit, Bustamente said they'd get right on it. By now, the commandant was really spinning up, firing a hundred questions at Rogers, who had zero answers but began to take copious notes in a little green notebook. Branner was signaling Jim that they should get out of there.

"Sir, I'm going to take charge of the police operation,"

Jim told Robbins. "I suggest you notify the FBI office in town right away, and that you clear all midshipmen and any contract personnel out of the eighth wing. The chief will call the Annapolis fire department, tell them what we have, and request an air bag and their big ladder truck."

Robbins just gaped at him, but Jim moved quickly out the office door, with Branner right behind him. They jogged down the executive corridor to the wooden partition, through the rotunda, and into the fourth wing. Midshipmen were staring at them as they ran down the passageway and turned left into the line of buildings that led back to the eighth wing.

"Has to be Booth," Branner said. "He's got Markham."

"That's my guess," replied Jim, who was puffing now, his back on fire from the jarring. "You ready for some stairs?"

"Anytime," she said, and they turned left and up into a stairwell that led to the crossover breezeway between the sixth and eighth wings. They blasted through the double doors into the third deck on the eighth wing and stopped short. There were midshipmen everywhere being herded by upperclassmen toward the breezeway. A company officer was shouting orders, which were being relayed by several firsties. Jim and Branner let the crowd sweep past them until the corridor was empty except for the Navy lieutenant and two three-striper firsties. Jim told the company officer who they were, and asked for a situation report.

"We got a call about someone on the top deck with a gun. Big guy, shaved head, wearing sweats. He was waving the gun around and threatening to shoot people down on the terrace. Then he pulled a female up by the hair and threatened to throw her off the roof."

One of the firsties interrupted. "Sir? That guy up there is Dyle Booth. He's a firstie. We don't know who the female is. She had tape across her face."

"We do," Branner said. "Is the top deck cleared out?"

"Yes, ma'am," said the other firstie. "We got everyone down here to the crossover level."

"How do you get to the roof?" Jim asked.

"There's one maintenance access stairwell," the officer said. A phone began to ring in the company office behind him. "I should get that," he said.

"Sir?" the larger of the two firsties said once the lieutenant had stepped back into his office.

"Yes?" Jim answered.

"Sir, people going topside to the roof? They go out their windows on the fourth deck. Walk the ledge."

"Wonderful," Jim said. Dozens of ways up. And down. Branner was talking on her cell phone.

The elevator doors opened and Chief Bustamente got off along with four Yard officers in tactical gear, all carrying riot guns. Jim signaled him over.

"Put one on the crossover bridge," he said. "No access into the eighth wing on this deck except for law enforcement. Have him tape the stairways, too. Nobody goes above this deck. The other three will go with us up to the fourth deck."

While Branner was talking on her phone, Jim turned to the midshipmen. He knew there weren't enough Yard cops available to set up a proper perimeter, so he'd use the mids. "Everybody's down from the fourth deck, right?"

"Yes, sir," one said. "I checked it myself. Fire procedures."

"Good man. Go through on the crossover and set up a midshipman watch there—nobody goes across except law enforcement. Same deal down on the zero deck at all the exterior doors. Nobody comes into the eighth wing except law enforcement or the fire chief. Anyone who does come in comes here to the third deck. I want a CP set up right here in this company office, and I want all firsties running this thing."

"Got it, sir," they said in unison. One headed for the crossover; the other trotted to the nearest stairwell and headed down.

"Chief, check on that ladder truck and the air bag." The chief got on his cell phone.

The company officer came back. "That was the dant's office. Wanted a sitrep. I told them you're here and taking over."

Jim explained what he'd told the mids to do. The company officer listened and then left to supervise those arrangements. Bustamente, still talking on his cell phone, went into the company office and began moving chairs. Two more of the Yard police got off the elevator, and the chief motioned them into the office to give them instructions. Branner got off the phone.

"I told Chang's office what we think we have. They're going to alert the SecNav's office. We going topside?"

"Right now," Jim said. He motioned for the Yard cops to follow. "You guys come with us, please. One of you have a radio I can use?"

One cop pulled his off his tactical belt and handed it to Jim, who called the chief and told him that they were going up to the top floor.

"Do we know exactly where the hostage is being held?" Branner asked as they went up the final flight of stairs to the top floor of the eighth wing. The fourth floor was physically the fifth floor, as the ground floor was known as the zero deck.

"All we had was that he was yelling at people down in the inner courtyard. But he could be anywhere. This wing is H-shaped, with the inner leg overlooking the rear mess hall entrance. Right about where Dell went down, actually. Shit, we need a key to that maintenance stairway."

He called the chief on the radio and asked him to locate the key. The highly polished fourth-deck hallway, with its rows of dorm rooms on either side, was silent when they got up there. Jim stationed the sergeant in a position from which he could oversee both the wing's side leg and the cross corridor.

"This guy's reported to have a weapon," he said. "If he comes down, he'll probably climb down through a window and come out of one of these rooms. Don't let him shoot you, but don't shoot him—you duck for cover into a room, close the door, and report. He comes after you into that room, deadly force authorized, but only in self-defense. Got it?"

"Yes, sir," the sergeant said. He was in his forties and had several bars on his service pin. Jim didn't need any more midshipmen killed, even in a hostage situation.

Branner had gone into one of the dorm rooms, and now she stepped back out. "I can't see any part of the roof of this segment," she reported. "I can see the cross building, and a part of the other wing's roof. But they could be anywhere."

"They said he'd been yelling at people going into the mess hall," Jim said, starting to move down the corridor. "That'll be over on the inner leg, if they're still there."

"Or they could be holed up in one of these rooms already," one of the cops pointed out. Everybody stopped.

Of course they could, Jim thought. He kicked himself mentally for not thinking of that. He ordered the other cops to spread out and start checking rooms while he and Agent Branner made a quick check of the cross wing to see if they could spot anyone up on the roof. The chief called back to report that keys to the maintenance stairs were on the way, and that the city SWAT team had been made available. He also said that the Bureau people were inbound, and that one of their hostage negotiation teams had been activated from Quantico but couldn't be on-site for another two hours. Jim asked if a perimeter had been established around the eighth wing, and the chief reported that it was in progress.

"Chief, I need somebody to get up on the seventh wing across the way, top deck, to tell me if he can spot anyone on the eighth wing's roof. We can't see directly above us."

"Roger that. The Maryland staties have a helicopter if we need it."

"I'd like to see if we can get face-to-face with this guy, before it goes Hollywood on us. Make sure you get somebody from the Academy Public Affairs office spooled up."

He put the radio back on his belt. Branner was helping the yard cops go room to room, making sure they were all empty. Jim followed them, staying out in the center of the corridor, trying to think of what else he should be doing. There was no noise other than the opening and closing of doors as the cops and Branner checked rooms, closets, and showers. When they reached the inner leg, Jim's radio squawked.

"The midshipman officer of the watch reports from wing seven that there's no one above you on the eighth wing's roof as far as he can see. But there is one room with its window wide open, all the way down at the inboard end, mess hall side. He says it looks like a shade is flapping in that window."

"Copy that," Jim said, speaking softly. "We're in the interior leg now. Stand by one." He signaled the others to stop, then pointed down at the last door on the right side. One of the cops lowered his shotgun in the direction of the door, while the other cop continued to check rooms, although he was much quieter about it now. Jim signaled to Branner to join him and stepped back around the corner into an empty room to use his radio.

"Chief, we're going to try to roust him out and talk him down. Don't have a status on the Markham girl, but you should notify her father. He's on faculty—in the bull department. What's happening down there?"

"We got more city cops coming to complete the perimeter. The ladder truck is down for maintenance, and the nearest air bag is in Baltimore. The commandant is apparently on his way up here to the CP."

"Keep him down there if at all possible," Jim said. "How about the vultures?"

"No media yet, but I've asked the MarDet to seal the gates. Can you confirm this guy has a gun?"

"Haven't seen him. But we don't think he's on the roof anymore."

"Make sure your helper bees are behind some cover when you approach that room," the chief said. "Have them stand in nearby doorways. Don't all three of you be out in the corridor."

"Hell, Chief, you'd think I never had any tactical urban warfare training in the Marnie Corpse."

"You remember any of it?"

"He pops out with a gun, I probably will. But look, we're all out of our depth here with a live hostage situation. I'm going to try to talk him down, but if it goes south, we wait for the pros, okay?"

"We could always do that now," the chief suggested. Branner shook her head forcefully.

"I'd like to try once," Jim said. "It's not like we don't know each other."

"Your call, boss. I'll brief the dant. And we're clearing everybody out of the back part of Bancroft."

"Good idea." He looked at Branner to see if she had anything to add, but she shook her head. "Okay, Chief, let's see if he's in there."

"Of course I'm in here, you dumb-fuck civilian," a voice said over the circuit. Jim nearly dropped his radio.

"What—you forget I listened to all your circuits down in the tunnels? You think I don't have this one covered, too?"

"Oka-a-y," Jim said, trying to hide his surprise. "So you know you're in a corner, Booth. What's your program in there?"

"I'm getting ready to solve my problem, that's what, Lame-Man-Chu. I've got a package all wrapped up and ready to fly."

"A package?"

"Don't play stupid, *Jim*," Booth said, aping Branner's voice with surprising accuracy. "This package has a big mouth. I'm about to fix that problem. Ask your spotter over in seven what he sees now."

Jim looked at Branner. "We need some secure comms," he whispered. "See if there's a telephone in one of these rooms. Anywhere. Call the chief, see what the guys over in wing seven can see."

Branner hurried back down the corridor, looking for a

phone. Jim went back into the other leg of the corridor and signaled the cops to follow him. He briefed them on the situation, then told them to take up stations, one in the room catty-corner from where they thought Booth was, the other in the adjacent room. Then he retired to the corridor intersection, where he saw the chief and Branner hurrying toward him. The chief motioned him out of the corridor and into a nearby room.

"SWAT team's here. This is one of their spread-spectrum multistation radiophones. Can't be intercepted. They brought a base station into the CP so we can talk on this. It's full duplex. Hit this button to talk. Everybody can hear you, and you can hear them. Lock it down, you go into broadcast mode. Listen, the TAC lieutenant recommends everybody back out, let them bring the hostage team in, and then wait for the Feebs."

The phone chirped. Jim switched it to talk. A voice from the CP relayed the fact that the spotter in the seventh wing was reporting something hanging partially out of the window, something white, looked like a mummy.

Jim acknowledged, a cold feeling in his gut. Booth had probably wrapped Markham up in one or more sheets to immobilize her, and was prepared to drop her to her death on the concrete below. He'd put the other radio down on the midshipman's desk. He heard Booth talking on it. "So, we gonna talk, *Jim*? You said you wanted to talk me down. Don't you want to know what happened to little Brian Dell?"

"Stand by, Dyle. We're trying to outwit you. Admittedly, that takes time." He turned to the others. "We can't wait," Jim told them. "I think he's going to ice the girl and then himself. We need to engage him. Chief, see if you can figure out a way to get some assets onto the roof and snag that girl somehow."

The chief stared at him. "Like what, lasso her?"

"Do *something*, Chief. Quietly, but do something. I'll try to tie him up with talk. Get a bunch of mids together and pile every fucking mattress in the building under that window. If he drops her, maybe we can save her. But let's get going."

The chief exhaled dramatically and left the room. Jim picked up the police radio and looked at Branner. "Any bright ideas?"

"I can't think of anything," she said. "He's fixating on you, so I think you're right. Talk to him. Delay him somehow. See if you can get him out into the passageway. I'm going up on the roof and see if I can get into position, pop him if he moves to open that window."

"You just going to shoot him if you see him near the window?"

"I'm going to hide and listen, but, yes, I will shoot him if it means saving Markham. This guy is whacked-out."

They could hear some sirens winding down outside, behind the building. Jim nodded and keyed the Yard police radio. "Booth?" he said. Branner slipped out the door and headed back toward the other side of the wing.

"Yes, *Jim*?"

Jim stepped out the door and started walking down toward the end room opposite where Booth was holed up. "I'm coming down the passageway. I'll go into the room opposite the one you're in, wedge the door open, and sit down so you can see me."

"Why the fuck would I want to see you, *Jim*?"

"I'm curious, Booth. I want to see if you are who you say you are. Don't worry—I don't even have a gun."

"Sure you don't. And I believe you. Of course I believe you. But I do have a gun, *Jim*. And I wouldn't mind popping you. Wasn't for you, I wouldn't have to be doing this at all."

Jim locked the talk button down on the tactical squad's radiophone and hooked it to his shirt as he passed the cop waiting behind the cracked door in the adjacent room. He kept talking as he walked. "I'll put my hands on the desk so you can see them. And yes, I want to know what happened to Dell. The official word is he jumped on his own. Nothing to do with you."

"Well, you'd be half-right, *Jim.* He did jump on his own. Where are you, exactly?"

Jim backed up to the door of the opposite room, pushed it open with his left foot, and tripped the doorstop. Holding the Yard police radio in one hand, he backed into the empty room, keeping an eye on the frosted-glass surface of the door on Booth's side of the corridor. He pulled a chair over, twisted one of the desks sideways, making lots of noise but never taking his eye off that glass partition, and sat down. Then he laid the secure radiophone down behind a book on the desk. "I'm right across the passageway, Booth," he called, using the unsecure radio. "Like I said I'd be. The door's wide open. I'm sitting in a chair. No gun. No tricks. Just want to hear your story. Check it out."

He made sure the radiophone was showing a red transmit light; then he hunched forward in the chair, watching that frosted-glass panel. Booth could just make a judgment about where Jim was sitting and try a shot, but Jim didn't think so. He was pretty sure Booth knew he was trapped and had made some decisions. What he'd want now was an audience. Someone to listen to him. What Jim had to do was occupy Booth while the Annapolis TAC guys, who could listen in on whatever dialogue he got going, tried to recover Julie from the window.

The room was hot and stuffy, and Jim fingered his collar. Nothing moved visibly behind that frosted-glass pane across the corridor. No shadows and no noises. He had to speak loudly enough that Branner and the cop across the hall could hear. He was trying to think of something to say, when the frosted pane across the hall exploded with the boom of a large-caliber pistol, blowing fragments of glass all over the corridor. Jim ducked instinctively, then looked back over the edge of the desk. Booth was finally visible through the shattered panel, sitting at a desk that had been turned sideways to face the door, just like Jim had done. What looked like a .45 auto rested on the desk, pointing casually in his direction. Behind Booth, the window was closed and the tan roller shade was pulled down all the way to the floor. Something bulged the bottom of the shade.

Jim straightened up and nudged the secure radiophone closer so the others could hear him. "Well, Mr. Booth," he said as casually as he could. "That was a dramatic way of opening the door. Guess you do have a gun. What is that, a government forty-five?"

Booth bared a mouthful of large square teeth at him, teeth that Jim remembered from the first night's encounter with the vampire in the tunnel. Booth's face was gray with fatigue, and there were dark pouches under his eyes. His head was entirely shaved, making him look bald and almost too old to be a midshipman. For a moment, Jim thought he saw the bottom of the shade move.

"So, you're here to talk me down, Mr. Security Officer?" Booth asked. His voice was raspy, and pitched higher than Jim had expected. He was wearing Marine camo trousers, highly polished combat boots, and a green T-shirt.

"Here to find out what you're so pissed off about, Mr. Booth. Here it is, almost graduation day, and you're flooding out the utility tunnels, taking people hostage, doing God knows what to plebes. Regular one-man wrecking crew. Think of what you're doing to the Academy's image."

"*Fuck* the Academy's *fucking* image!" Booth shouted. "You think I give a rat's ass about the Academy's image? Didn't give a shit about me. All these years, winning N-stars in swimming, hundred and ten percent on the PFTs, perfect conduct record since plebe year, top ten percent of my class in math and engineering, and half my fucking class crosses the street when I come down the line?"

"Maybe they know something, Mr. Booth. Or maybe they just *feel* something. I don't know. That you in the vampire getup, knocking heads out in Crabtown?"

"Fucking A. Got behind you, too, didn't I?"

Jim thought he heard something moving along the ledge outside his window. No noise, he prayed. Not a sound. "Yeah, you did. Have to admit, you've got vampire makeup down cold. So what was up with all that? You pissed off at civilians in general, or just townies?"

"Practicing for the Corps, man. Plus entertaining my pussy posse."

"Oh, yeah, the Goths; I've seen them. Coyote-ugly, most of them. Tell me you're not into all that bullshit, are you? Drinking blood? Worshiping at the altar of Death? Somehow, I can't quite feature you and Marilyn Manson on a date."

Booth laughed. "Fuck no, the only part of the Goths I was into was between their legs. They're professionally bored, so I had to play the part to get it on with them. You know, here's an Academy dude, only he's back in black. Had my pick, man. Had my pick."

"It was me, I'd have to be a little drunk, do one of those weirdos. I mean, like that whiteface shit? They always look like they're about to puke right through their nose rings."

Booth grinned, showing all those teeth again for just a second longer than necessary. It was obviously a move he'd perfected. Jim could just imagine what that would be like underwater. Then he heard another sound, above his head. He was sure of it this time. The TAC squad must be moving, trying to get a line on Julie Markham before Fuck Face there opened the window and let her drop. He wondered where Branner was, and whether or not the listeners on the radio circuit could hear Booth. He had to keep Booth's attention. "That shit in the tunnels—that was pretty impressive. How long have you been running?"

"Since youngster year, Mr. Security O. Just like I've been into the Brigade intranet since youngster year. And the faculty LAN, too. Shit, I had the exams before the head of the department. Then I found that old magazine space, got it set up for my computer lab. Dumb-ass PWC dudes were too scared to go down there. Especially after I showed up one night in the Drac rags and ran off a coupla their guys."

"They never mentioned that, although you're right—they weren't too keen on going down there. But I thought you were a supergeek. What'd you need the exams for?"

"Two reasons. One: to sell them. Oh, that surprises you?

Think there might be a little ethics problem out there in the Blue and Gold Brigade?"

"I suppose there are always some rotten apples in the barrel. What was your other reason?"

"I'm a data dink. Couldn't do bull. They told me it's a brain thing. The bull department cut me no slack. Always with the fucking essay questions. So I'd get the questions, pay some smart dude to write me up some answers, all hypothetical, and do it that way."

"And you're telling me that midshipmen are buying and selling exams?"

"Guys in trouble are. It's a little like loan-sharking—only guys in trouble come to the Shark. Shit, the rest of these dudes are so square, they'd faint dead away at the thought. Got that honor bug so far up their asses, they can't walk and fart at the same time."

"And you got Markham's father to tutor you in reading?"

Booth's expression changed slightly, with some of the arrogance draining out of it. "So what if I did?" he said. "I lusted after her sweet ass, figured it wouldn't be a bad move to get close to her old man. Find out where she went weekends. Where home was. Had a feeling about her, that maybe she wasn't the straight-arrow chick everybody thought she was."

"She told us about the UVA meet. The party."

Booth grinned, back in the driver's seat again. Jim wanted to look at his watch, but he didn't dare distract Booth.

"I won everything down there. Clean sweep. I think maybe that's why she finally came across at that UVA party. Or maybe it was the roofie I put in her drink. Don't remember. I do remember *her,* though. Hot and sweet. Did she tell you there was a video? Talk about a starring role."

"So what the hell was the big deal about Brian Dell?" Jim asked. "Seems like kind of a little guy for someone your size to be running."

"You go here?" Booth asked. He appeared to be listening. Had he heard the team on the roof? Jim shifted in his chair, which brought Booth's full concentration back to him.

"Yeah. Then I went Marine option."

"That was my plan," Booth said, cupping the barrel of the big .45 into the palm of his left hand. "Dell? Little shit got on my nerves. He was passive. No balls at all. He was just so fucking weak. Other plebes, you'd run 'em until they finally show a little defiance. But not Dell. I ordered him to wear girls' panties to his late-night come-arounds, and damned if he didn't do it. Said he got 'em out of the girls' locker rooms. Piece a shit faggot plebe. Didn't belong here."

"So, tell me: How'd he end up going off that roof? This roof, I guess," Jim said, gesturing at the window behind him. The moment he moved his hand, the .45 was pointing straight back across the hall. Booth had the reflexes of a rattlesnake.

"I think he got embarrassed, Hall-Man-Chu. Guy in panties on his knees in your room late at night? You figure it out."

"Can't feature you as a gay blade, Mr. Booth. Big strong guy like you. Going Marine option and everything."

Booth let a triumphant look spread across his face. "You ask Hot Wheels if I'm gay, man. She'll tell you, and I have the video to prove it. But Dell? Shit. Mouth's a mouth, man. What the hell did I care?"

"So you're saying he offed himself? Out of embarrassment?"

"Well, he—"

An imperious and familiar voice from out in the corridor interrupted, demanding to know what the goddamned hell was going on. Jim cringed. The dant had arrived. Booth's face lost all expression. He got up, came around the desk, pointing the .45 right at Jim's chest, and stopped just inside his doorway. Jim half-expected Branner to take him out from across the hall, but then he realized that Branner might be on the roof.

"What is the meaning of this, mister?" Robbins yelled. The big midshipman looked down at him with an expression of such contempt, Jim thought he was going to shoot the commandant right then and there. Robbins was so angry, he was starting the Dant Dance, probably not even realizing he was doing it. His fists were clenched and his face was turning purple.

"You!" Booth shouted at Jim. "Hands on top of your head. Twitch and you'll have three eyes, understood?"

"Okay, okay," Jim said hurriedly, clasping his hands on top of his head. "Let's not get all excited here. Nobody's going to do anything. Not the captain, not me." He said that to alert the TAC squad that there was a new complication. He could just see Robbins frozen in place beyond the right side of his door. Booth filled his own doorway. The kid was really big. And pissed off. He leveled the gun, trained it on the commandant, and ordered him to get on his knees. Robbins tried some more bluster, but then Booth thumbed back the hammer and Robbins gulped audibly.

"Get on your *fucking* knees, dickwad," Booth spat out.

Robbins, ashen now as he began to appreciate the danger he was in, sank to his knees, his hands held out in front of him as if he didn't know what to do with them. Jim tried to think of something to say so that the listening cops would know what was going on, but he couldn't come up with anything there, either.

"Got word you wanted to see me, your highness. So now you can see me, right? Got something to say?"

Robbins swallowed hard, cleared his throat, but nothing came out. Jim could just barely see the commandant's trembling hands. The captain was clearly terrified now.

"C'mon, Short Round," Booth taunted. "You're the big fucking deal in this building. You always have something to say. Spit it out, motherfucker!"

Robbins's mouth was working, but no words came out. Then Booth fired twice, blasting a pair of those huge slugs on either side of Robbins's knees. The bullets ricocheted off the floor, one shattering a glass door pane, the other exploding a fluorescent fixture in the ceiling. Booth stepped farther out into the corridor and fired three more rounds at the floor next to the terrified commandant. The rounds went howling down the corridor, smashing windows at the far end. The noise was deafening, and Jim felt his fingers unclasping, but he commanded them not to move, which was a good thing, because now the .45 was aimed back at him. There was a haze of gun smoke in the hallway. Robbins was prostrate on the floor. Booth was already back inside his doorway.

"Awfully quiet down there, Superman," Booth said. "Or are you too busy pissing your pants? Goddamn, man, look at that. It's a fucking lake. You really needed to water your snake, didn't you? Look at that! Get all those medals and ribbons wet, did you, *Dee*?"

Robbins, whose eyes were still closed, was making whimpering sounds down on the floor. "C'mon, Booth," Jim said. "You've had your fun. He's not part of this, is he?"

"He's probably the biggest part of this there is, *Jim*. All those ethics and morality sermons he made us sit through? That look like a stand-up guy to you, Hall?"

"Like I said, he's not part of *this*," Jim said. "This scene right here. This is about you, Mr. Booth. You're here to pay back Julie Markham, and then you're going to show us all what you're made of, right? I mean, shit, it's not like you're going anywhere, except maybe out to Leavenworth. You beat up a federal officer so bad, he died. You probably disappeared that Goth freak, Hermione whatever, the one you left behind in the tunnel that night. You personally wrecked the entire underground engineering facilities for this end of the Yard. You've cheated your way through school, made a mockery of everything this place stands for. Now you've made the dant piss his pants. You surely don't think they're gonna let you throw your hat with the rest of your class, do you?"

Jim stopped, because he saw the look spreading across Booth's face. The kid's hand was trembling ever so slightly. Jim tried to remember how many rounds that gun carried. Not that many, not like the nines everybody carried today. He also remembered that the thing was impossibly heavy, even for someone of Booth's heft. Seven rounds, that was it.

"C'mon, Mr. Booth. Send that pissant back down the hall before he craps and makes the place smell really bad."

Booth grinned at that and nodded. There was a gleam in the kid's eyes now that hadn't been there before. Drugs? Meth? Where was the SWAT team? How would he know when they had Julie? Then he realized something: They might manage to get a line on Julie, but they couldn't move her until Booth opened that window. Based on what he could see of the extended shade, she was hanging by her knees, literally.

"Get out of here, you fucking worm," Booth said, waving the gun at Robbins. "Slide on back down the passageway, the way you came. Only now you'll slide better, all wet like that. *Move* it, asswipe!"

Robbins didn't hesitate. He started to get up, but Booth aimed the gun right at his head, and the dant subsided with a squeak. He began to inch his way backward, literally leaving a trail on the polished linoleum. When he'd gone fifty feet back, he turned around, still crawling, and went on hands and knees like a frantic turtle until he disappeared around the corner.

Booth backed into his room, checking to see that the shade was still in place on the window. Then he sat down again, facing Jim.

"So you figured this deal out, huh?" he said. "That why you're here? You wanna watch?"

"I figured this has been coming for some time, Booth. That you knew you'd probably never make it out of here. I mean, after Dell, there's been too much heat. And all that shit down in the tunnels? But you nearly succeeded, you know."

"Yeah. They were gonna sweep it, weren't they? Until that NCIS bitch got in the way."

"She's pushy, I'll say that," Jim said, trying to keep it going. Then he saw a shadow flick past the tan shade behind Booth. All *right*. They were on the roof and they were doing something to retrieve Markham. "So why the hell did you even come here? You don't believe in any of this honor stuff. You hold the whole program in contempt. You came from nothing. What were you thinking?"

"A full boat to a degree and a commission. What else, man? That's what everybody here came in for."

"Not me, Booth. I believed all that stuff about duty, honor, country."

"Nobody believes that shit, *Jim*. All we have to do is watch how the Dark Side behaves. Hell, they knew the Dell thing wasn't right, but they were willing to hold sweepers on it."

Another shadow. Keep it going. "And you wanted to be a Marine?"

"Damn straight. At least the Marines are up-front about what they're all about. Shock troops. Stone killers. Kill a Commie for mommy. The light green machine. Pure. Simple. Hell, you know."

"I know you'd have never made it through Quantico, that's what I know."

"The fuck you mean? Look at me, man. I could eat all that platoon commander shit up for breakfast."

Jim realized that he was approaching the break point here. He needed to get Booth angry enough so that the guy focused exclusively on him, but without getting himself shot. The TAC team could listen to him talking, and hopefully know when to move. "Wrong, Booth, because the Corps's always on the lookout for psychos like you. For sick puppies who like to dress up and paint their faces. Who get young boys to do nasty things. They'd Section-Eight your ass in a heartbeat."

"Fuck that noise, man. Nobody here got wise. Why would they catch on now?"

"Because the Marines *are* the real deal, Booth. The grunts might fancy themselves Hollywood stone killers, but they expect their officers to have some personal standards beyond being physically fit. They'd catch on to you on the first day in the barracks. Hell, troops'd see you do that thing with your teeth and know you were bent."

"So how come I got through four years here, huh, smart guy?"

"Because they weren't looking, Booth. That's the problem when the Navy does social engineering instead of maintaining their standards. I still don't understand how a whacko like you even got in."

Booth laughed that nasty laugh again, waving the big pistol around. "Blame it on the nuns, man. They wanted to score an Academy appointment. I was the only dude in the school who could do the math at the eight hundred SAT level." He turned in his chair to check the bulge under the window shade, then turned back just as another shadow flicked across the shade.

"So what's the plan, Stan?" Booth asked. "You gonna make a scene, try to keep me from doing what I have to do?"

"Nope," Jim said. "Markham lied to us from day one. Between you and me, she shouldn't graduate, either. I assume you're gonna open the window, drop her ass on the bricks, and then do the right thing?"

"Not quite, smart guy. Julie's just window dressing, so to speak. But you know, since I've got nothing to lose, why not take *your* ass with me?"

"Because you only have one round left, Booth. Like I said, I'm not going to interfere. Although there may be SWAT snipers up on the seventh wing waiting for you to check the window shade. But me? I'm your testimonial, Booth. I'm going to be the only one knows how you stood up and did it like a man. Because otherwise, the Dark Side here is going to tell a very different story, right?"

Booth looked at him for a long moment. He had the gun pointed in Jim's general direction. He's probably counting rounds, Jim thought. At that moment, Booth twitched his right wrist and the magazine dropped out of the .45; with his left hand, he jammed a new one into the weapon so quickly that Jim almost couldn't even see it happen. He watched

Booth rack the slide back and chamber a fresh round, eject-
ing the lone remaining round into the room.

"Guess what, *Jim*?" He said. "Got lots of rounds left
now."

Jim shook his head in wonder. "I have to admit, that was
the fastest combat reload I've ever seen, Booth. You must
have been practicing." As in, Hello, TAC squad. He's back in
business.

"Betcher ass I practiced. And now," he said slowly, level-
ing the big gun at Jim again. "Now I think we'll see how
much of a man you are, Mr. See-cure-it-tee." Aiming carefully, he fired once, blasting one past Jim's right ear, so close
that he could feel it. The window behind him exploded in a
rain of glass. Jim hadn't moved, not because he was brave,
but because it had happened so fast.

"Well, that was close," Jim said, letting the listeners
know he was still alive. And now would be a great time to
make your move, guys, he thought.

Booth nodded approvingly and fired again, this time past
the other ear. More glass. Jim began to sweat. He tried to
calculate how quickly he could duck down behind the desk.
Dyle fired again, the shock wave hurting Jim's ears as the
round raised the hair on the top of his head and whacked into
the wall behind him, ricocheting around inside the plaster
after it hit the granite facade outside.

At that instant, a small dark shape crashed through the
window behind Booth, followed by another. There was a
blinding flash and a huge booming explosion, at which point
Jim submarined in his chair, dropping out of sight behind the
steel desk even as another round came howling right through
the back of the chair he'd been sitting in, knocking it over.
There was a second huge blast from the room across the way
as a second flash-bang let go, and then a third. Then a rattling noise, followed by another big blast, but this one out in
the passageway, then a howl of pain from the room where
the Yard cop had been hiding. Silence ensued, punctuated
only by noises from the roof. Jim was barely able to hear
anything except the ringing in his ears. The entire area was

full of smoke. As he very carefully peered around the corner of the desk, shapes in blue jumpsuits appeared out of the smoky gloom across the way, pointing guns at everything, including Jim. Then he thought he heard a couple of shots way down the hall, and another window's worth of glass crashed into a room. As Jim, still behind the desk, got to his feet, hands in full view, the roar of the .45 came booming down the hallway, dropping the TAC guys to the deck en masse while bullets whacked all around them.

"The roof! He's going for the roof," someone shouted, and Jim whirled, jumped over to the window, and looked outside. To his amazement, there was Booth, about ten windows down the hall, hanging by his fingertips from the fourth-deck ledge. Then he dropped like a cat, landing on the next ledge and grabbing the wall for an instant before letting go again and dropping to the next ledge. A TAC cop brushed Jim aside and leaned out to take a shot, but by then Booth had levered himself through a window on the second deck and disappeared. The TAC cop swore and made his report into a shoulder mike.

Jim brushed himself off, checked to make sure he hadn't peed his own pants, and went out into the hallway, where everyone was getting back up. It was hard to see or even breathe in all the gun smoke. Shoulder radios were chattering away everywhere. A big cop in full tactical gear, wearing a sergeant's shield, walked up to Jim.

"Nice going, Mr. Hall. You gave us all the time we needed. Got the girl. She's up on the roof with Branner."

"She okay?"

"Yes, sir, she is," the sergeant said, taking off his face mask and turning down the volume on his tactical radio. The other cops had fanned out down the passageway and were checking rooms. Jim's Yard cop came out of his room, obviously dazed, bleeding from the ears and nose. The TAC guys got him to sit down on the floor and sent for medical assistance. "One of our flash-bangs went slow fuse on us. Fucker picked it up and threw it back out the window just as we hauled the girl up onto the roof. Scared us all to death. Then he caught the next one, and apparently pitched it out here, got your guy. That's how he got away."

"No help from me," Jim said. "I was trying for China after he combed my hair with that forty-five."

"China's good," the sergeant said with a grin. "Ah, and here comes Ms. Branner now."

Jim turned, to see Branner's bottom easing backward through the window in the room where he'd been. Behind her were two TAC cops, who held a white-faced Julie Markham between them on the ledge until she, too, could climb through the window. One of the medics who had come up from the third floor took her in tow and wrapped a blanket around her. Branner turned to Jim and blew out her cheeks. "Some guys do all the work; some guys just sit and flap their jaws," she said. The cops grinned.

"Agent Branner here was the one on the end of the rope," the sergeant said. "She was the lightest one up there, so she hung out there to tie the harness on while you kept him busy."

"Thank God you guys could hear us talking."

"Yeah. And it was all recorded down in the ops van. We catch his ass, he's DA meat."

The radio squawked out a relay call from the perimeter cops. "Suspect broke the perimeter," someone yelled. "Academy cops say he's going into Lejeune Hall."

Jim looked at Branner. "He's trying for his lab access."

"No way—that's all flooded," she said.

"Not anymore—they drained it, remember?" Jim said. He turned to the TAC sergeant. "Tell them to get people into the basement, down where the swimming pool piping is. There's a storage room, where they keep the chemicals for the pool. That's where he's been getting into the tunnels."

The TAC cops got on it while Jim and Branner started trotting down the hallway. "Can he make it?" she asked.

"I don't know," he said, turning down the cross corridor, suddenly aware of his burning back again. Funny how that .45 had taken the pain away, he thought. "If the approach tunnels to the magazines did collapse, then the magazines still ought to be flooded—nowhere for the water to go, right?"

They ran down the stairs and outside, Branner flashing her badge as they raced through the perimeter of police vehicles and watching cops. When they finally got to Lejeune Hall, there were more cops milling around outside. By the time they worked their way down to the basement and found the storage room, the door was open and there were TAC squad guys poking flashlights down into the access hole. The big metal plate was still hanging askew, dimpled with bullet holes.

"Is it flooded?" Branner asked.

"Nope," one of the cops said. "Can't really see shit down there, but it doesn't look flooded. Somebody better call Public Works. They've got crews down there."

"So," a TAC cop asked no one in particular, "who's volunteering to go down there after his ass?"

Before anyone could answer, there came a deep sustained rumbling sound from beneath their feet, with the clatter of individual pieces of falling masonry echoing up from the access hole. Then it became very still. The access hole exhaled a small cloud of damp cement dust out into the storage room.

"May be a moot point," Jim said, staring at the hole. "With any luck, that right there was bye-bye, Dyle."

Just after sundown, a subdued Ev Markham was staring out into Chesapeake Bay from the fantail of the *Not Guilty*. Liz and Julie were down below, doing something in the galley, and he was sipping some scotch and reflecting on the day's events. The boat was back alongside its moorings at the Annapolis Yacht Club after a two-hour cruise out on the Severn and its estuary. Ev was very proud of the way Julie was bearing up after her ordeal at the hands of Dyle Booth. She'd been virtually uninjured, unless you counted some bad bruising around her midriff and knees from hanging out the window and a small knot on her head from the rescue exertions. He was mostly relieved that the whole thing was finally over, and that they now knew who'd been behind all the awful things happening at or around the Academy. He heard footsteps approaching out on the floating pier and swung around in his deck chair. It was the security officer, Jim Hall, and Agent Branner. He got up and unlatched the railing gate.

"Come on aboard," he said. "Liz is down below. I'll get her."

The two came up the plastic steps on the pier and walked onto *Not Guilty*'s pristine deck. Hall was wearing a gray business suit, and Branner was wearing a form-fitting blue blazer over a gray skirt. She kicked off her low-heeled leather shoes as she stepped aboard, in deference to the shining deck. They both looked tired, and Ev offered them a drink, but they both declined.

"I'd love one," Hall said, "but then I'd probably fall asleep right here on the boat. We just came by to give you and Julie a quick sitrep. She is here, isn't she?"

"Here they are now," Ev said as Liz and Julie came up the companionway and out onto the stern lounge area. Liz repeated Ev's offer of a drink, but they again politely declined. Everyone sat down. Ev noticed that Hall was being careful not to rest his back against the curved Naugahyde sofa.

"I imagine there's been some paperwork to do after all this," Liz said.

Branner smiled. "Many trees' worth," she said. "Many trees. With all those cops out there this morning, there's paperwork about the paperwork. Plus, the Bureau got into it."

"When will they want to see Julie?" Liz asked.

"With any luck, they won't," Hall replied. He told them about a three-hour meeting with the commandant earlier that afternoon, after some semblance of order had been restored in Bancroft Hall. With the exception of the room that had been flash-banged, and several bullet holes and lots of broken glass up and down the fourth-deck corridor, the actual damage had been minimal. The mids, disciplined as ever, had reoccupied their building, cleaned everything up, and returned to their routine.

"We went over the entire case with the supe and the dant during that meeting. I did the part about the tunnel runner, Branner here did the Dell case, and we jointly went over the parts where the two came together. Then we had a separate meeting with our cops, the town cops, and the Bureau people."

"So it was Booth in the tunnels?" Liz asked. Ev noticed that Julie still appeared to be distracted, as if she were mulling something over. She'd been very quiet ever since they'd picked her up at the dispensary earlier.

"Yes," Branner said. "And it was Booth terrorizing the back alleys of Annapolis with his vampire act. Mr. Hall here managed to get him to talk for the record, as it turned out, because the TAC squad always records its radiophone network anytime there's an incident."

"We've been laying low all afternoon, Mr. Hall," Ev said. "Liz suggested the boat because we could get away from any media and at least the landline telephones. We did call into Bancroft to tell them where Julie was, but no one seemed to want her back right away. Thanks to you, I assume?"

"What really happened to Brian Dell?" Liz asked.

"As best we can tell, Booth was hazing him, late at night. He made him do some bizarre things, such as wearing women's underwear, and perhaps even sexually assaulted him. Our best take on the matter is that Dell did in fact commit suicide after being humiliated one time too many. I suspect that Booth saw it happen, or even egged him on. But that's all we know, and, of course, that version came from Booth."

"So it wasn't Dell who was gay, but this Dyle Booth?"

"I think Dyle Booth was just your basic sadist, as well as being someone who hated everything the Academy stood for. He was never really accepted by his classmates, so he ended up holding the entire program in contempt. If I can indulge in a little amateur psychology, I think all this violence at the end, these increasingly outrageous acts, was an indication that he knew he'd never make it in the Corps. He wasn't homosexual. He was just very badly bent."

"But he did do this to Brian to get back at me," Julie said in a small voice, speaking for the first time. Ev wanted to reach out to her, but she had been so withdrawn all day that he'd been afraid to make the first move.

A yacht rumbled into the marina from the outer harbor and blatted its horn for a line-handler. A young man came trotting down the pier from the clubhouse. "I think he did this to Brian Dell because he could," Hall said, casting what looked to Ev like a quick warning glance at Branner. "The fact that Julie had pulled Dell under her wing probably made Dell a better target, but he was already a qualified target for the likes of Dyle Booth."

"Shit. Shit. *Shit,*" Julie muttered, shaking her head. "I should have spoken up way earlier."

"Well, you had something to lose, didn't you, Midshipman Markham?" Hall said. "He told us about the video."

"What video?" Ev asked, sitting up in his chair. Hall didn't answer, but he looked at Julie expectantly.

She took a deep breath. "After that weekend in Charlottesville, Dyle sent me a video clip over the Academy intranet. Somebody at the party had filmed everything. I guess you could say I was the star. Dyle said he'd put it on the Web unless I did what he wanted."

"When did he do this?" Branner asked softly.

"The clip came right after the UVA weekend," Julie said. "Come to think of it, that was probably where my underwear went adrift. But the threat to put it on the Web was yesterday morning. He called it my 'graduation present.' "

"Sweet," Branner said.

"Where's the video?" Ev asked.

"No one knows," Jim said. He was watching Julie's face, but she just shook her head.

"And that's how he was able to take you prisoner this morning?" Branner asked.

Julie nodded. "I stewed about it all day and all night. Especially after having to run away from Bancroft Hall last night." She flashed her father a quick look but then faced away again. "Then when I heard that something huge had happened down in the tunnels, I figured it must have to do with goddamned Dyle. I went to his room, but he wasn't there. So I waited. A long time. But he didn't come back. Thirty minutes before reveille, I gave up, went back to my room."

"And there he was?"

"And there he was. All dressed out in his jarhead costume. He put a knife to my throat, said he'd stick Mel if I made a sound. She was asleep in her rack, right there, next to us. He pulled me out into the passageway and put a pillowcase over my head and taped it. After that, I don't know where we went, but we ended up on the roof. That much, I could tell. Right as morning meal formation was going down, he started screaming crazy shit down into the court. Now I know what Hitler sounded like."

"Where's Booth now?" Liz asked.

"We think he escaped back down into the tunnels," Hall said. "The old part, the Fort Severn magazines. Way down there, under Lejeune Hall. But we also think they collapsed while he was down there. Knowing what we know about those tunnels, we suspect he's dead."

Julie just nodded. "Good," she said. "Dyle needed to be dead. Hell, I think he *wanted* to be dead."

"The final part of our meeting with the heavies was about you, Midshipman Markham," Hall said.

"Oh, I can just imagine," she said. "Four valiant years, down the tubes." She looked over at Ev. "Sorry to disappoint you, Dad. Almost made it."

Ev really wanted to get up and hold her, but Hall was shaking his head.

"Actually, I think you're going to be all right," he said. "There's maybe something you didn't know: Booth gave you a roofie that night at UVA."

Julie just stared at him.

"What's a roofie?" Ev asked.

"Rohypnol," Branner said. "The date rape drug. A taste-less, odorless, clear liquid you put in the girl's drink and she's all yours, all inhibitions gone, and, what's even better, she won't remember a thing."

"Holy shit."

"He said that? He slipped me a roofie?"

"Did you get tested afterward?" Branner asked. "Anyone do a rape kit on you? Blood test?"

Julie shook her head. "I thought it was all me, getting drunk, letting it happen. Just once, in four years, letting go, totally losing control. That was the Dyle effect. And let me tell you, I dreaded that commissioning physical exam like the end of the world."

"Well then, you had no way of knowing," Branner said. "But he told Mr. Hall here that he gave you a roofie. Put it in your drink. You never would have noticed until the next morning, when I'm sure you did notice."

Julie blushed but then nodded. "I was so damned ashamed—of myself, of Dyle, even. Everything they teach us here . . ."

"Well, like I said, I think this is going to come out all right for you," Hall said. "The commandant does not view your mentoring Dell as a serious conduct offense. And the fact that you weren't entirely forthcoming in the NCIS in-vestigation can be justified by the grotesque blackmail Booth was running. They're working on an official version of events, but your part in it is going to get sanitized. A lot."

"Why are they doing this?" Julie asked.

"Because you really didn't do anything so very wrong, Julie," Hall said. "You tried to help some poor plebe who was barely afloat, and in the process you crossed paths with a sadistic monster who had fooled the system, big-time. I think they're more than a little embarrassed about that too."

"But I lied when I said I didn't know Brian very well!" she said. "That's—"

"Understandable, given the circumstances. Before this

morning's events, Booth was already responsible for two other deaths. If it hadn't been Brian, it may well have been someone else. We think he was getting a taste for it. And what he did last night in the tunnels was absolutely homicidal."

Julie shivered. "When he hung me out that window, I thought it was all over. But then he said we'd go together when the time was right."

"Sometimes things work out," Hall said.

"So it's finished?" Ev asked. "She can graduate?"

"As best I can tell, unless she blows an exam or two."

Julie blinked and then put a hand to her mouth. "I want to go home, Dad," she said, finally facing Ev. "I think I want a big sleeping pill and twelve hours to enjoy it."

Ev stood up, more than happy to oblige. "When does she have to be back?"

"They said Sunday night, eighteen hundred," Hall said, also standing. "Agent Branner will want to get a written statement for the record, but she can do that early next week. Why don't you take her home, Prof? We're gonna secure, too. It's been a long damned night and day."

Ev gathered up his jacket and shoes, put his arm around Julie, and escorted her off the boat. He told Liz he'd call her later, and she just smiled and waved. He hoped, as they went up the pier, that the smile was a good sign. He was vastly relieved at the outcome of the meeting in Bancroft Hall and that Julie was going to graduate after all. But in ten days' time, she'd be on her way to Pensacola, and he still had no damned idea of what he was going to do then.

Jim watched them go as darkness settled on the marina, and then he and Branner got ready to leave. Branner unsuccessfully stifled a huge yawn as she went over to the railing and began putting on her shoes. Liz DeWinter came over as Markham and his daughter passed out of sight around the clubhouse building.

"Okay," she said, looking up at him. "How'd you really manage all that?"

"Manage what, counselor?" he asked innocently.

"Getting my client out of the shit. As all you boat-school types have told me repeatedly, they take that honor code very seriously over there."

"Oh, that," Jim said, teasing her just a little until he saw Branner giving him that range-finding look over Liz's shoulder. "Well, a certain captain, who shall forever go nameless, walked right into my little standoff with Booth on the fourth deck up there. Booth held this officer in somewhat low regard. He emptied a forty-five all around said individual, who was at the time attempting to find that fabled route to the Indies right through the center of the earth."

"And?"

"And he may have pissed his pants. Just a little."

"Just a little?"

"Well, perhaps more than a little. Think lake."

"Ah."

"Yes. And as he was winding himself up this afternoon to unleash the Honor Committee and the Brigade investigators and all the rest of the ethics and morality mafia, I called for a coffee break and had a private word, during which he and I reviewed certain aspects of the incident that had not yet reached the public domain."

"How you do go on, Mr. Hall," Liz said.

"He's learning," Branner said from across the deck. "Slowly, though."

"I certainly am. Anyway, in the fullness of time, you can share this insight with your erstwhile client. Maybe *after* she throws her hat in the air and swears the appropriate oath."

"And tell her what, exactly, Mr. Hall? That you blackmailed the dant into letting her go forward?"

"Call it leverage, not blackmail. Plus it seemed like the appropriate thing to do, counselor. And I guess you can tell her, 'Welcome to the real Navy, Ensign.' "

Liz started to chuckle. Jim took Branner's arm. "Come on, Special Agent. It's tree time in the city."

They drove back over to Jim's marina, which was not nearly so grand as the AYC, and then had to hunt for a parking place big enough to accommodate the pickup truck. After much backing and filling, he got the thing wedged in between two much smaller vehicles. Branner then discovered that she couldn't open her door.

"This damned thing needs tugboats," she said. "Let me ask you something: You really think Booth's dead?"

"Shit, I hope," Jim said with a yawn. "He was a resourceful bastard. I guess you'll have to get out this side."

She didn't move. "I mean, what if those tunnels didn't collapse? What if that was something else caving in down there?"

"They collapsed when we were running for our lives," he pointed out.

"So what was that noise this morning? When we were all trying to figure out how *not* to be the first one to go back down that hole?"

"Um."

"Yeah. So what was left to cave in down there?"

"Maybe we should call the PWC?" He looked at his watch: 8:15. "They must still have crews down there, restoring power, drying those cabinets out."

She rolled down her window, looked again at how close the other car was, and shook her head. "Yeah, I think we should. Just in case. Otherwise, we're assuming. I always get bit right in the ass when I make assumptions."

"Oh, is that what it takes?" Jim asked, provoking a pained look. My prospects aren't looking so good, he thought. He said, "Okay," then put a call in to the chief, who got him patched through to the PWC ops station. They, in turn, put him through to the on-scene coordinator down in the tunnels, a Lieutenant Commander Benson. Jim identified himself and briefly explained his problem. Benson, who said he was near the Fort Severn tunnel doors, told him to hold the line and he'd go take a look.

"Where would he go, if he did get out of that mess down there?" Branner asked.

"Either back into Bancroft Hall, where he could probably hide, for a little while anyway, or into town, where he could go to ground with his Goth crew."

"Yeah, but they're just college kids. They'd only hide him until the heat began to build. You said he was ready to grandstand his way into the next world. If that was the case, what else might he do?"

"My brain's failing and my back hurts like hell. What are you getting at?"

"Would he try again for Markham?"

Jim had to think about that one. The cops had enough, based on what had been captured on tape, to put him away. Not to mention the fact that Booth had fired on the TAC squad officers. But this was Dyle Booth they were talking about.

"He might," he said. "Just to show us he could. But that hole under Lejeune Hall went to the right-hand magazine. Which we know was flooded. Both those tunnels should have collapsed. I can't—Wait one. Yeah, Mr. Benson?"

Benson said they'd checked both tunnels left and right. Left was collapsed right up into the anteroom.

"And the right one?" Jim asked, a small tendril of apprehension coiling in his stomach.

"The right one was open," Benson reported. "All the way down to the right-hand magazine. Lots of muddy mortar, but the ceiling was holding, barely. The cross tunnel had collapsed, and part of the right-hand magazine had collapsed."

"Which side of the magazine collapsed, as you looked in from the door?" Jim asked, looking at Branner, who now appeared to be wide awake as she listened. Benson said he hadn't gone down there personally. Place scared him to death. But the cleanup crew's supervisor said there was apparently a ladder of some kind sticking down out of a hole in the ceiling, if that helped.

Jim sighed, thanked him, and hung up. "Right tunnel held," he announced.

"Oh shit," she said. "We'd better alert somebody. And

we'd better call Professor Markham, warn him that Booth might be loose."

"That's not a call I'd like to get right now," he said. "Why don't we go out there, tell him in person, maybe baby-sit the place for the night? Although Booth is probably long gone."

"You start driving," she said, pulling out her own phone. "I'll call my people. All that Washington help is still down here. They can notify the Feebs if they're still in town. And I guess we need to tell someone in Mother B. that their favorite psycho might still be up and running."

"And he's only had all fucking day to get his shit together," Jim said as he eased the pickup out of its parking place without removing anyone's mirrors. *"Damn it!"*

Ev took a cup of coffee and a bottle of scotch out to the dock, where there was a small picnic table and two benches. He turned on the small spots at the water end of the boathouse to attract the bugs and settled down to absorb the darkness. Julie had gone up to her room after an awkward good night at the bottom of the stairs. The night was clear and almost warm, with only a few spring mosquitoes buzzing. In another month, it won't be possible to come out here at night, he thought. The summer mosquitoes would first rip up the dock planks, take away the table and chairs, and then come back for the humans.

There were other dock lights twinkling across the still black waters of the creek, and at least one unhappy outside dog was trying to wear his owners down with a steady, incessant barking. After the past couple of days he knew he ought to be sleepy, but he wasn't, and sitting out here was preferable to staring at the ceiling in what had been his and Joanne's room. He poured some scotch into the coffee and recapped the bottle. He noticed he was drinking more these days, and enjoying it more, too.

His and Joanne's room. Well, not anymore, and that was one good thing to come out of all this. He'd found a woman to fill that gaping hole in his life, tiny as she was. The fact that she could talk about Joanne and his prior life made it even better, because if she could accept it, then maybe so could he. Liz was in so many ways a sweet woman, but there was some steel in there, too. He wondered how many other lawyers had taken a look at her and made some legally fatal underestimations. He felt a vibration along the planks of the dock.

"Is that scotch?" Julie asked, materializing out of the darkness in the penumbra of the boathouse spots. She was wearing a set of Navy sweats and white socks, and she had an empty glass in her hand.

"Didn't know you liked scotch," he said, sliding the bottle toward her as she sat down.

"Have to learn sometime," she said, pouring a half inch into her glass. "Have to do better with booze than I've done so far if I'm going to be a naval aviator." She sipped some and made a face. "Tastes like medicine," she muttered.

"In my day, a naval aviator's breakfast was officially a cigarette, a cup of coffee, and a puke."

"Now it's a Coke, a handful of Midol, and a puke, or so I'm told," she said.

"You don't have to drink to fly, you know," he said.

"On the other hand, I may want to," she replied, looking out over the black water. Something swirled out in the middle of the creek. "Man. It seems like it was just parents' weekend."

"Sweating exams?"

"Not really. This semester was a pretty light load. I could bust them all and still have the QPR I need to leave."

"Well, what'd you think of it? Your four years at the Academy?"

"As in, 'Other than that, Mrs. Lincoln, how'd you enjoy the play?'"

Ev laughed and poured them both some more scotch.

"Discounting my Dyle Booth experience," Julie continued, "it wasn't bad. In fact, it was pretty good. Solid. Long, maybe, but at least they get you out in four. Most of my high school classmates screwed off their freshman year and now they have another one to go."

"You think you have a good class?"

"Yes," she said, trying some more scotch. This time, she didn't make a face. "Better than those weak-ass babies in O-three. That's another thing my civilian friends will never have—real classmates."

He nodded. "Very true. And that's for life, too, no matter if they stay in or get out. In fact, at my twenty-fifth reunion, the most rah-rah people were all the ones who got out after five years. Apparently, there's something missing out there in civilian life, too."

There was another swirl, something fairly big, out in the creek. Tide must be in, he thought. Some big fish is here for some easy pickings.

"In a way, the Academy's so artificial," she said, settling deeper into her chair. "We have all these rules, standards, universal athletics, mostly smart people, profs who all speak clear English, and reasonably ethical people. While my high school friends got summer jobs at Burger King or smoked dope at the beach, we were going all over the world on summer cruise. And we have the next five years wired."

"But no money, to speak of."

"Yeah, but most of them won't have much either. The money difference doesn't get big until five years down the pike. Besides, none of them will get to strap on an F-eighteen Super Hornet and go blasting off a carrier. Money can't buy that."

"Assuming you make it to jets," he warned. "Not many do."

"Hell, Dad, that's assuming the dant doesn't change his mind in the next week." She was quiet for a moment, then turned to look at him. Her face was barely visible in the darkness. "I'm sorry about the lies. Charlottesville. And especially Dyle Booth."

Ev nodded in the darkness. "Just don't do that in the fleet," he said. "You'll be an officer. You can't let go like that anymore. And if anybody puts the squeeze on you, go tell your boss. It's not all Dark Side out there."

She did not reply, and he felt he'd said enough. He was suddenly glad it was dark. He wondered if it was a porpoise out there as something surfaced again, closer to the pier, just out of the dim cone of light from the spots. He could hear it blowing, but not squeaking. They came into the creek sometimes, hunting.

"I hope so," Julie said, hugging her knees to her chin. "One of the reasons I turned Tommy off was because of what happened down there at UVA. Plus, I had no one else to tell. What are you looking at?"

"I wonder if that's a porpoise out there," he said, leaning forward to listen. He got up to go investigate. Julie got up, too, following him down to the very end of the dock, where the steps were. Ev tilted one of the boathouse spots down as he reached the end of the dock, aiming it down into the water, where he saw a shimmering white face with a huge mouthful of teeth just below the surface. Julie saw it at the same time and screamed just as Dyle Booth surfaced, ten feet off the dock.

For a moment, Ev was frozen in place. He distantly heard a screen door slam next door, and then his neighbor, Jack Johnson, called out to them, asking if everything was all right. At that moment, Dyle raised an ugly black government .45 auto and pointed it at them, drooping the muzzle just enough to drain the water out of it. He was treading water effortlessly, staying just off the dock. He tilted his head in the direction of Johnson's voice. Ev understood.

"Yeah, Jack, we're okay," Ev called.

"Thought I heard a scream," Johnson said. "Is that Julie with you?" His voice carried with perfect clarity across the water. Dyle was grinning again, but that .45 never wavered. Julie seemed to be still frozen in shock.

"She got a splinter, Jack. We're okay."

"All right, Just checking. Night, Ev." The old man went back into his house. Dyle moved a little closer to the dock. He called Julie's name, and she slowly, very slowly, looked down at him.

"Thought it was over, didn't you, TC? Thought you'd dodged a bullet? You forget something, TC? You forget our little deal?"

Julie swallowed and moved closer to her father, but she didn't say anything. Ev could feel her trembling. "What the hell do you want, Mr. Booth?"

"Fuck you, *Professor,*" Booth spat back at him, ducking almost all the way back under but keeping the .45 aimed right between them. "You never gave a shit about me. Thought I was some dumb ass kid. I could see it every time I came in. And your precious little girl there. Too good for the likes of me, right, Julie? Except for that once, huh? You thought it was pretty good that night, didn't you, baby?" He slapped the water hard. "Look at me when I'm talking to you, *bitch!*"

"She wasn't thinking at all if you gave her Rohypnol, Booth. That how you get your girls? A little better living through chemistry? Couldn't get any on your own?"

"Dad, don't," Julie murmured, but it was too late, as Dyle stopped his movements in the water and settled back down until only his face and the muzzle of the gun were above water.

"Tough talk from an old has-been who's ten feet from the business end of this," he said, waggling the .45 and once again drooping the nose to make sure the barrel was dry. "You were Navy once. You do understand I can drop you both in under a second, right?"

"What the fuck do you want here, Booth?" Ev demanded again, getting angrier by the second. "They know what you did. They know what you are."

"What I am? *What* I am? And just what's that mean, Professor? You have no idea of what I am."

Ev had been trying to think of what to do, but now he just let his brain ride, his old pilot instincts kicking in. He moved ever so slightly to get closer to Julie. "What you are is a piece of shit, Booth," he said. "A highly polished turd that got by the treatment plant and into the drinking water. You're a technogeek, right, Booth? A whiz with the computers?" He moved again, not picking up his feet but just willing his body to ooze its way closer to Julie. He didn't really know what he was going to do, but he was going to do something. Almost there, arm's length. He felt his leg come up against his scull, which was lying upside down on the dock. "You know what Gee-Go means in computer talk, right, asshole?"

Booth's face tightened into a furious rictus. Those huge teeth dominated his entire face. Teeth and burning, clearly insane eyes. Ev was almost to the point of being able to touch Julie, inside of arm's length now, except the damned boat was in the way. "Gee-go, Booth. You're the personification of gee-go. G-I-G-O. Garbage in, garbage out. The academy let the barriers down and you slipped over the rim of the bowl like the stinking piece of shit you are, Booth."

"Dad, stop it," Julie wailed. "He means it."

"You tell him, TC," Booth said softly, dipping again into the black water while his other arm oared his body back into position to keep facing them directly. The boat, Ev thought. Use the boat. Booth dipped down into the water again for just an instant, and Ev backhanded Julie with all his might, a sudden blast of adrenaline pumping him so hard that he knocked her off her feet even as he bent down, grabbed the boat, and in one surprisingly smooth thrust slid it directly at the evil face in the water. Booth fired once, a huge, booming shot that slashed the air where Julie's head had been an instant before, and then, a split second before the prow of the boat hit him in the face, he fired again, and this one caught Ev in the left side of his chest, spinning him around like a dog under a bus. Ev was conscious of being down on his side, down on the edge of the dock, as Julie scrabbled on hands and knees back up the dock, screaming something at Dyle and then for someone to help them. The gun went off again, this round tearing through the decking, splitting one board into pointed fragments that lashed Ev's face and hands. Ev lifted his head to look back down into the water, but his neck muscles betrayed him and his face sank back down onto the shards of wood.

Have to get up, he told himself, must get up. He heaved again, trying hard for more air. Something wrong with my lungs. But he managed to get up on his hands and knees, turning deliberately to face the water and ladder, but then Dyle's glaring face was rising over the edge of the dock. He heard dogs barking somewhere in the background, the sounds of voices, Julie still yelling. He thought he saw lights coming on, but his eyes were focused on Dyle as he came up the ladder. One of Dyle's eyes was swollen shut and he was bleeding from his nose, where the boat's sharp prow had hit him squarely, but he was grinning that terrible grin, his open eye focused right on Ev's face. He stepped up onto the dock, out of the cone of light from the spots, his huge body gleaming, and suddenly he was bending over Ev, grabbing him by the hair and jerking him upward so he could look into Ev's eyes. Ev grunted as a huge wave of pain washed through his chest, and he heard himself making a gargling noise in his throat.

"She warned you, old man," Dyle said softly, struggling to hold Ev up so he could push the nose of the .45 under Ev's rib cage. Ev couldn't do anything except try to breathe. He was having trouble focusing his eyes, and he couldn't even look up into Dyle's grinning face because Dyle's forearm was in the way. He felt Dyle glance sideways up the pier, where Julie was still yelling for help.

"Goddamn you. We had a deal, *bitch,*" he hissed, but Ev didn't think she could hear him. He felt Dyle pull the hammer back. "Not here to do Julie, you stupid fuck, but you? You don't count, see?"

Ev felt his body sagging, and Dyle had to pull harder on his hair to keep his face up.

"Look at me," Dyle growled, and Ev tried again to focus. All he could see was a mouthful of teeth, and then he felt his fingers close around a big piece of the shattered dock planking.

"That's the Look, Pops. Hold still now, don't move— don't want to get anything on me, do we?—and then everything's gonna be all right."

Ev suddenly felt footsteps running back down the pier, and he heard Julie screaming, "No, no. What are you do- ing?" as Dyle looked over at her and grinned again. Summoning every ounce of strength he had left, Ev stabbed upward with that stiletto-sized splinter, catching Dyle in the belly and, because of the angle, driving all eighteen inches of it right up into Dyle's heart. For a terrible instant, nothing happened, and he realized he could feel Dyle's beating heart pulsing through the piece of wood. Then he felt the stub end of the .45 barrel that had been pressed to his own side fall away, and then Dyle, cross-eyed now, let out a long, wet sigh and collapsed like a huge sack of potatoes, a fountain of blood welling up out of his mouth, past all those devil teeth, until his entire weight was pressing down on top of Ev.

Goddamn, he thought. I was having enough trouble breathing without this shit. Then there were people, hands, lights, and lots of noise. He heard other voices, familiar voices, more feet pounding down the dock. He thought he heard Julie sobbing. Tried to lift his head, tried to tell her it was okay, that Booth was all done, but from the sounds of it, Julie had clearly lost it. He couldn't get himself upright because the dock was slippery with all the blood. He even thought he heard Agent Branner yelling something.

So do something, Ev, a voice in his head was saying. Take charge here. Talk to her. Call her name. Hell, call any name.

But which name? he wondered dreamily. Julie. Liz. Joanne. Branner? Branner didn't have a name, now that he thought of it. All these women around him. His own voice was echoing maddeningly in his head. You ought to call one of them, Ev. You really should. This is not time to lose control, not after everything that's happened. Just say a name. Pick one, Ev. Because if you don't, you may have to go with Booth.

"Liz," he croaked.

"Don't talk; just be still," a woman's voice was whispering in his ear, her soft, cool hands on his cheek. Amazingly, he detected a splinter in his other cheek, the cheek that was sticking to the pier. He felt the weight of Booth's body move farther sideways. "You'll be okay," she said. "The EMTs are coming. Just hang on. Stay awake. Keep breathing."

Keep breathing. Right, he thought. He tried to say something, anything, but he just couldn't get enough good air down into his lungs, where the pain was, terrible, suffocating pain now. Yet in a way, he wanted to laugh. Here was yet another woman telling him what to do. It figured. Even so, he thought he'd picked the right name. He tried it again, but nothing came out this time but a big red bubble. Then all the noise seemed to withdraw into a rush of darkening echoes. His ears filled with the sound of wind rushing through trees, a veritable roaring, and he decided, Okay, enough's enough. Just go with it.

Jim Hall and Branner sat in her Bronco in the parking lot outside the Navy and Marine Corps Memorial Stadium, listening to the echoes of the vice president's voice as he wrapped up his commencement speech. The parking lots were filled with cars and security vehicles. In a few minutes would come the three cheers and the blizzard of white midshipmen's caps going up again and again as the class of 2002 achieved its freedom.

"Eight minutes," Branner noted, looking at his watch. "I guess if you have a heart condition, you tend to cut to the chase, even when making a speech."

"As if they're listening," he said. "See all these new cars out here? They belong to the mids. Notice anything about them?"

"They're all better wheels than I drive," she said.

"No. They're all pointed nose out. You're gonna see a Le Mans start in the away direction here in about fifteen minutes."

"Why so fast?" she asked. "What are they afraid of?"

"That the Dark Side might change its mind."

There was a sustained round of applause within the stadium. Then a new voice began speaking. It was hard to make out precisely what he was saying because of the way the speakers reverberated around the stadium and the parking lots.

"I can't believe you really want to leave all this behind," Jim said. "Trade quaint Olde Annapolis for the frigging Washington Navy Yard."

"Well, it's just about as old as this burg," she said. "And looks it, too."

The band began playing some martial music, and then there was the rumble of everyone standing up for the oath of office. They listened through the open windows, waiting for the big cheers. They came a minute later. They could just see some of the hats flying through one of the walk-through arches on the side of the stadium.

"All done," Jim said. "Now it's Enswine Julie Markham. Lower than whale shit once more. One moment, a firstie. Now an officer plebe. Funny how that works."

"At least it isn't Second Lieutenant Booth," she said.

"Amen to that," he said. "And to think he swam all that way, up the river and into that creek. He knew right where to go, too."

"You'd think the Academy would have seen this coming," she said, watching the gates. "I finally got his admissions record yesterday, got his personal history."

She told Jim about Booth's background. How he'd been born and raised in a Baltimore housing project, apparently never knowing his father. His mother had come to Baltimore from West Virginia, trying to catch up with the man who got her pregnant. She ended up staying because there was little to go back to in the coal hills. She'd gone from welfare to work and back again, having two more children along the way, before getting shot and killed in a convenience store holdup when Dyle was twelve. He'd gone into the system, then was placed in a foster home, where the couple, a retired teacher and his wife, recognized Dyle's latent intelligence and got him into the Catholic school system, eighth grade right through high school. Some teacher comments alluded to a violent streak, based in part on his size, but they were collectively of the opinion that this problem had been addressed by some of the Dominican brothers in his high school. He'd demonstrated a pattern in high school of excelling in math and science, but sometimes getting *C*'s in his nontechnical classes. But the combination of mathematical ability and athletic ability had proved irresistible to the Academy.

"All in all, he turned into one scary dude," she concluded.

"He was when he was doing that vampire thing, I'll tell you that much. I can still see that face."

"Well, the professor did exactly the right thing then, didn't he?"

He shook his head and then took her hand, surreptitiously now, because people had begun to stream out of the stadium. "I'm going to miss you, Special Agent," he said.

"I was serious about coming to work for NCIS. You've impressed Harry Chang, and that's about all it would take."

"That would mean having a real job. A career. You know that's a big step for me, Special Agent."

"You know these people are going to fire your ass. What else do you have to do?"

He shrugged. "I guess I could sit on my boat a lot, harass my parrot. Cherry-pick the bars, bring young lovelies back to my yacht, ply them with charm and some really good booze, have my way with them all night. You know, the usual. I mean, hell, somebody's got to do it."

"So many girls, so little time, huh?"

"Something like that. I may even take the boat out one day. Get up one of those all-girl crews, sail topless out of the harbor, or group moon the AYC. And all because you won't tell me your first name."

She clucked sympathetically. "But maybe if you came to Washington . . . I mean, there's a marina right next to the old battleship gun factory at the Navy Yard. You get to hear gunfire most nights. You were a Marine—you must miss that. And Jupiter could curse pigeons all day long. Oh, and up there, they're called women, not girls."

"Oh. *Women.* But how do those Washington *women* feel about unemployed, non-career-motivated wharf rats? Seems to me everyone in D.C. is either on the take or on the make. Not sure Jupiter and I'd fit in."

She looked over his shoulder. "Incoming," she murmured.

He turned around and saw Julie Markham, resplendent in her graduation whites and gleaming new one-stripe shoulder boards, pushing her father's wheelchair toward the Bronco through the flood of fleeing graduates. Liz DeWinter followed behind them, barely visible in a white linen suit, white gloves, and huge floppy hat. Jim and Branner got out to meet them.

"Congratulations, Ensign Markham," Jim said. "If I were still in uniform, I'd collect that dollar."

"Our battalion master chief already got it," Julie said with a little smile. It was traditional that the first enlisted person to salute a newly commissioned officer received a silver dollar. "But thank you both. For everything."

"Second that," her father said. Jim thought he looked older and thinner, but losing a lung that way probably contributed. At least he was alive. When Liz put her hand on his shoulder, his face dropped ten years. Jim could relate to that.

"And the records are all cleaned up, right?" Jim asked. "Books closed on the Dell incident?"

Julie's face grew serious as she nodded. "Admiral McDonald didn't quite look at me when he handed over my commission, but at least he kept a smile on his face."

"You meet the new commandant?"

"Nope. And probably never will. Supes, dants, plebes, report chits, BIOs, formations—that's all in the past now. Thanks to you both. Again."

Branner shook her hand and then Ev's, nodded politely at Liz DeWinter, who gave her a cool smile in return, and then got back into the Bronco.

"I heard a story," Julie said to Jim. "That the real reason the dant closed the books on all this was because of something you said to him during that meeting. Like you had something on him."

"Stories are a dime a dozen after an incident like this one," Jim said, glancing at the professor to see what he might know. Markham's face was a polite mask. "Usually, the stories come from people who weren't there but who want to pretend they were. I think they closed the books because it was becoming too politically painful to keep them open."

Julie gave him an appraising look for a moment. All of a sudden, Jim thought, she looked very grown up indeed. "I suppose no one will ever tell the whole truth about this, will they?" she said.

"Probably not."

She didn't say anything, just looked at him expectantly.

"Welcome to the fleet, Ensign," he said. "Happy landings at Pensacola."

"I've told her that a good landing is one you can walk away from," Ev offered. "But that a great landing is one where they can use the airplane again."

Julie smiled and then they left to join the escaping hordes. There was a flurry of sirens and red lights as the vice president's motorcade eased its way through the crowd. Jim got back into the Bronco, where Branner was watching the stream of ebullient graduates, trailed by teary-eyed parents, girlfriends, and soon to be ex-girlfriends as the mids, now officers, headed out for those fabled seven seas.

"Professor Markham looks like he was shot at and missed, shit at and hit," she observed.

"Actually, shot at and hit," Jim said. "He's lucky to be alive. Forty-five can put a truck down. I'm surprised he's out of the hospital."

"Lady lawyer looked pretty spiffy," Branner said. "What there is of her."

"Hmm," he said, being very careful.

Branner turned in the front seat to look directly at Jim. She was wearing one of her short A-line skirts, which made it a dramatic turn. "You really want to know my first name?" she asked.

"Hell yes," he said, thoughts of lady lawyers long gone.

"I have a tattoo," she said, her green eyes bright. "It takes some finding, but that's where my name is."

"Finding."

"It's privately placed, as the brokers say. But first, you'd have to come up to Washington."

"Washington?" His voice almost squeaked as she did something with her hair. Every part of her seemed to move at once. "For how long, Special Agent?"

She shrugged. "Long enough to find it?"

"But, like I said, I have so much to do here in Crabtown. There's the boat. And Jupiter. Painting. Scraping. Brightwork. And, hell, just lotsa stuff. You know me—I'm the security officer. Very important, very busy."

She discovered a small snag in her stocking, just above her right knee. She licked two fingers and massaged the errant material. "Like I said, it's going to take some exploring. But if you can still read by the time you find it, well, then you'll know." She ran both hands partway up her thigh to smooth out the rest of the nylon, then pushed her skirt back into place. She cocked her head expectantly. As if he had a chance in hell.

He swallowed once and then grinned. "Oh, shucks, Branner, I might as well." He paused. Then they both said it in unison, "Can't dance."

Julie Markham stopped on the steps of the eighth wing to soak up a quiet moment of personal triumph. She had changed into civvies, and her car was packed for the trip south to Pensacola. She was finally done. Everything was out of her room. Liz had taken her father out to lunch at the Yacht Club, where Julie was supposed to join them shortly. She'd said her good-byes to Tommy, Melanie, and several of her company classmates as everyone got ready to leave Mother B. for the last time. The exodus of the class of 2002 was just about over, with the echoes of noisily promised correspondence already beginning to fade. There were even some parking spaces along the Yard's streets. Bancroft Hall overlooked the whole messy process with stony indifference. A gaggle of mokes, as the cleaning crews were called, pushed canvas-sided trash dollies toward the ground-floor entrance, hoping for some commissioning week treasures.

She could almost feel the marble facade of the eighth wing towering over her back. She'd been able to see the still-broken windows on the other side of the wing as she packed up. But all that was behind her now. Dyle. Brian Dell. Even Tommy. Poor Tommy.

Directly in front of her was Lejeune Hall, with its strange ramped entrances, which always reminded her of a castle's sally ports. Probably made the Marines feel at home. She took a deep breath. She had some unfinished business there.

She took her last bag to the car, locked it, looked around to see if anyone was watching her, and then walked over to Lejeune. She went in one of the side entrances, found the right stairwell, and went down into the basement. The familiar smell of pool chemicals hit her. How long have I been swimming competitively? she wondered. Twelve years? Seemed like forever. She could still taste those McDonald's breakfasts, shoved down her throat after predawn practices while someone's bleary-eyed mom drove her and her teammates to school. She already felt a little out of shape after not swimming for an entire week.

She walked along the narrow passageway that contained the pool piping and the racks of chemicals and chlorine bottles. The air was, as always, humid and warm, and the overhead lights were all encased in steam-tight globes. There was no one about, and her footsteps echoed quietly in the hot, wet air. The hum of machinery was almost comforting.

She reached the storage room, with its broken door. Nothing got fixed quickly at the Academy. She stopped in front of the door and listened for sounds of anyone else down in the basement, but there was only the whine of the filtration pumps. She pulled the door toward her, scraping its bottom edge over the tile. She stopped and listened again. Just to make sure. The light inside the storage room was still on. Some of the tiles were warping up off the floor, and there were hundreds of muddy footprints. Straight ahead was the three-foot square hole in the wall, with its hingeless metal plate dangling forlornly from its bullet-smashed latch. A faint smell of wet cement seemed to be welling up from the black hole. To her right, along the wall, there was a bank of empty rusted steel lockers, which had obviously not been used for a very long time. She poked her head out the partially opened door to make sure no one was coming down the passageway, then went over to the locker nearest the back of the ruined door. She hesitated and then lifted the rusted latch. The door squeaked open reluctantly on partially frozen hinges.

Inside, there was a mildewed laundry bag on the floor of the foot-square locker. She reached in, picked it up, and pushed the door shut. She took the bag over to the square hole in the back wall and pulled the strings to open it. Inside were all the elements of her Goth rig. The long black slit skirt. Those thigh-high fishnet stockings and black witch clogs. The studded dog collar. A bulging makeup kit. Fake fingernails. The fingerless gloves. The ridiculous wig. The very special video, its cassette broken and the tape pulled out in an unusable tangle.

All of it. She shivered, but now it was over. She felt bad about Dell, because she really should have anticipated how far Dyle might take it. And she felt even worse about what had happened to her father. But she'd warned her father not to provoke Dyle. He hadn't really come to do anything to her. Even that whole scene in the dorm room had been aimed at getting that security officer into the room, so Dyle could boast. The popinjay commandant showing up like that had been gravy. Fucking Dyle. He'd taken her right out to the limits again, but he wouldn't have dropped her. Not Dyle. He'd known, ever since Dell's death, that he'd never make it out of there, never make it to the Marines. The only person Dyle was going to hurt that night at her house was Dyle. But give him that: He'd been a true believer, right to the end. Death before dishonor and semper effing fi, right? He'd only come up the river to find her so she could watch him finally do it. That had been part of their deal. She had been required to watch, to witness that he was man enough.

She felt another twinge of guilt about what had happened to her father. Her games with Dyle had been her sole, burning secret, the one part of her life that no one, especially not her father, had known about. That was the reason she'd lost it on the pier when Dyle shot her father: they had a deal, all right, but the second part was that no norms were to get seriously hurt. But Dyle had gone increasingly, frighteningly out of control: first Brian Dell, then that agent, and Krill—what had he done with hapless Krill?

She took a deep breath to steady her nerves. No future in this kind of thinking. Their secret game was over. And everything that had happened, well, that had been Dyle driving the train, not her. Which made it okay. Her father was going to recover. And now he had Liz, so he was going to be all right. She had her diploma and her gold bars. As long as everything worked out, then what had gone on before was just—history, that's all. She nodded to herself and took another deep breath. Then she closed the bag and reached through the hole to drop it. She heard it hit somewhere way down below in the shaft with a muddy thump. No one would ever be going back down there. She popped her head into the hole for a moment, but there was nothing to see. Just the strong smell of old wet cement. She backed out, thinking about all that was to come, flight school, her new life as a naval officer, fast exciting men, all the new horizons, and, if she was lucky, really lucky, the feel of a hot jet in her hands and between her knees. Everything lay in front of her. And only a few tingling memories of the walking, talking chaos that had been Dyle Booth fading behind her. Every time with Dyle had been the ultimate high-wire act, especially the last time. It was positively amazing how sheer terror could make you feel alive as never before or after. She hoped the jets would be that big a rush. Everyone said they were.

She smiled one last sly smile. A roofie. As if.

"Damn you, Dyle Booth, you crazy bastard," she whispered, remembering still the way that sliver of wood had throbbed in time with Dyle's final heartbeats. "Am I going to miss your zone or what."

Then she cleared her face, reassembled her midshipman's dutiful mask, no, her ensign's dutiful mask, took a final deep breath, and left the storage room for her new life among the norms. What was done was done. Everyone, even the Dark Side, was ready to get past it. Closure: that's what everyone always wanted, right? But, hell, she thought as she climbed the stairs: everyone says those jet jocks are crazy bastards. Maybe there was hope. Maybe Dyle wasn't the first of his kind to get through here.

Author's Note

All three American military service academies reflect the societies that they exist to serve. That sometimes makes life hard for the officers who run the academies, because they strive daily for perfection in a decidedly imperfect world. To the degree they tell the truth about why they require the things they do from the cadets and midshipmen, the young men and women typically respond by doing the right thing. It's when the senior people succumb to outside pressures and relapse into that "do as I say, but not necessarily as I do," form of leadership that trouble comes. These are smart kids. Not only can they see right through that sham, but sometimes they play it back to their seniors in very interesting ways.

Mostly I've been factual about the setting, but this is as much a story set *at* the Naval Academy as it is a story *about* the Naval Academy. And because it's wholly fiction, I've taken some liberties in describing the regimen at Annapolis in order to better suit the needs of my story. That's one of the benefits of writing fiction: If you want to, or where you have to, you can just make it up. I've done some of that in this book, with the most obvious example being the timing of when Julie Markham would have been on plebe summer detail. I've also embellished the scope of the underground tunnels—a lot, in fact. The remains of the Civil War–era Fort Severn are undoubtedly submerged in the various land-filled fields that make up the Yard's waterfront, but I doubt that anyone's been down there for a long time. The degree of public access to the academy grounds since September 11, 2001, is also quite different from what I've described.

I received a great deal of generous help from all sorts of people at the Academy, and at all levels of the organization, including midshipmen. Sometimes I learned more than I wanted to know, but I've found that's not unusual when I'm researching these books. As always, I'll leave it up to the reader to speculate where the boundaries are between fact and fiction, but one thing's clear: Those boundaries rarely remain stationary when you assemble four thousand of the country's best and brightest young people and then presume to teach them something about the issues of leadership, honor, ethics, gender, and personal morality. As one of the characters observes in the book, the problem is that they learn. I'm proud to note that the Naval Academy courageously has chosen to address these issues head-on. That this sometimes has a purgative effect on tradition should not be held against the institution, the Jurassic barks of some aging alumni notwithstanding.

For the record, none of the characters in this book are intended to reflect actual people at the Academy, either currently or previously serving, and any resemblance to actual incidents or people, living or dead, is entirely coincidental.

PTD
Georgia, November 2001

Turn the page for an excerpt
from P. T. Deutermann's next book

THE FIREFLY

Coming soon in hardcover from
St. Martin's Press

Prologue

The man who calls himself Jäger Heismann awakes in the dimly lighted recovery room of the private cosmetic surgery clinic in northwest Washington, D.C. He blinks rapidly to clear his sticky eyelids and then checks his watch. Almost midnight. Fire time. He closes his eyes for a few more minutes. His brain is not quite clear yet. He hears a nurse attendant come into the room, smooth his covers, check a monitoring panel, and leave. He does a mental situational-awareness check: He's just been through the last of the eighteen procedures of his year-and-a-half ordeal, this one relatively minor. His lower face and lips are numb and feel swollen to his touch. His lungs feel heavy and there is a soporific wave lapping at the edges of his brain, but otherwise he's in no pain. He concentrates on deep breathing to disgorge the last remnants of the anesthetic. The monitor behind him beeps encouragingly.

Sometime later, he opens his eyes and checks his watch again: midnight. His head is just about clear.

He sits up and swings his legs gingerly out of the bed, then waits for his balance to stabilize. He thinks about what he's about to do and summons the adrenaline necessary for the task. There's still a slight heaviness in the bottoms of his lungs, so he does some more deep breathing, shoulders back, focusing on extending his diaphragm. The monitor's beeping noise accelerates as he comes alive, so he reaches up and hits its power button and then removes all the probes and wire patches from his skin. There's no IV. He gets up, pulls on his street clothes, still doing the deep breathing and using a towel in his mouth to suppress the sounds of a sudden coughing fit. He goes over to the closet where he stashed his small duffel bag earlier, takes out the liquid Taser gun and its fluid pack, and carefully straps it on. He retrieves his jacket and slips it on loosely over the Taser gear.

He cracks opens the door to the hallway and listens while he arms the Taser unit. He can hear the nurses cleaning up in the surgery, one door away, and the low murmur of the two doctors talking in their office, a door away in the opposite direction. The men first, he decides.

One more really deep breath. He detects the slight taste of something chemical at the back of his throat. Then he adjusts the portable tank pack and steps out into the hallway, the stubby Taser gun in hand, its fluid tube trailing around to the small of his back. He walks quietly down the hall and pushes the door to the doctors' private office fully open. They're still in their scrubs, drinking tea. The fat older Paki is dictating notes into a small machine. They both look up, surprised, although hardly alarmed. They never see the Taser in his hand. He points its boxy snout at the fat one, barely sees the charged stream arc out, and then the swarthy man is going over backward in his chair, flopping onto the carpeted floor like a pregnant fish. Heismann then turns and nails the other one, the young one, only two years out of Karachi, whose mouth is opening to protest. His whole body jumps and then pitches forward into a fetal position on the floor, one heel twitching audibly. Heismann waits a second and them hits each of them again, this time aiming directly for their exposed throats, sending them deep into a stunned stupor.

The equivalent of 400,000 volts. Nonlethal, they call it. Looks lethal to him. They're not dead—yet. He hefts the portable tank, tightens one strap, and then goes down the hall to the surgery.

Two women in green scrubs are loading the autoclave

with trays of instruments. One of them sees him and smiles. "You're up," she says brightly.

"Ya," he mumbles, and drops her with a jolt to the throat. The tray of instruments crashes to the floor. The other, eyes widening, realizes something's terribly wrong and puts out her hand defensively. Heismann fires the stream right at it and she makes a sound like a turkey as her arm snaps back into her face. She stumbles against the autoclave, then folds to the floor, arm twitching. They both end up on their faces, so he fires a second stream at each one, hitting them in the back of the neck, hearing them grunt in turn. Then he turns off the unit and pockets the Taser. Mentally smiling at the memory of the instructor's careful warning about that sequence: "Unit off, *then* pocket it. Never the other way round." He grabs some plastic gloves out of a box and puts them on.

He drags the two semiconscious doctors down to the surgery and dumps them around the operating table. Then he drags the nurses over. The younger one has one unfocused eye partially open. She can see him. She groans, but she still can't move. He begins setting up for the fire, then pauses. If they'd all been working in here, one of them would have seen the fire and tried for the fire extinguisher. Right. He drags the middle-aged nurse by her heels over to the wall near the door, where there's a fire extinguisher. He puts it near her clenched hands. Then he pulls the pin and fires it in the direction of the operating table's curtain, covering the floor and lower wall in white powder, where the arson squad should find it. He can see her fingers twitching, but she still can't move her arms. Plenty of time, although he has the feeling he's missing something about the nurses.

Leaving the one nurse by the door, he repositions the remaining "victims" on the other side of the operating table. He glances again at his watch and then sets up the oxygen system for the fire. He's especially careful with the system lineup, ganging the two green service tanks together to ensure a plentiful supply. There are two spare nitrous-oxide tanks in a separate locker with a glass front panel. These are the ones he swapped out on Sunday, and they are fakes. What looks like metal valves and pressure gauges are instead heavy-gauge plastic, which shortly will melt.

Making sure the service valves are closed, he uses his cigarette lighter to burn through the oxygen-gas supply hose where it passes right over the wall receptacle. He takes an insulated screwdriver from his little bag and chooses the autoclave's three-pronged plug as the ignition source. He pulls one of the surgical curtains back to the wall, making sure it's in contact with the autoclave's cord. Then he pulls the plug partially out of the wall and touches the hot prong and the ground prong at the same time with the blade of the tool. There's a nasty snapping noise and a brief flash of arc light, but then the breaker trips down the hall, taking some of the surgery's lights with it. Dumb design, he thinks as he extracts the lighter again.

He checks to see that the blade prong has been physically cut by the arc, then ignites the hem of the surgical curtain. This, too, he had replaced on his 2:00 A.M. visit Sunday, substituting plain nylon for the fire-resistant Nomex curtain that had been there. This material flares nicely, first scorching, then whooming into an ugly flame that quickly blackens the white ceiling tiles above it. He edges toward the door, watching the fire spread. Plenty of starting fuel in this room, with all that plastic tile ceiling, one entire wall of drapes, piles of surgical linens, the plastic laser-equipment cabinets. A dense, boiling cloud of noxious black smoke gathers rapidly along the ceiling like an angry octopus. He watches the sprinkler heads, but they do not fire. Good. Got them all. He opens the door of the locker containing the spare nitrous-oxide bottles, cracks the valves on the bottles, and then cuts on the main oxygen lines. He listens to make sure the hanging hose is hissing at full volume. Then he steps through the door and closes it behind him.

He figures he has about a minute before the flame-detector alarms go off. They're embedded in the building's security system, so he hadn't been able to cut them off. The sprinklers had been simpler—one maintenance valve. He takes one more thing out of his bag. It's a badly scorched folding steel clipboard. Inside is an equally scorched medical record, with the clinic's name and address printed on the forms. He removes the record, goes over to the water fountain on the wall, and soaks the cardboard jacket thoroughly. He puts it back into the metal clipboard and drops it into a metal record rack just outside of the surgery's door. He pats it once. He hopes it survives, because it's the key deception element—the bait, preburned to leave just the important bits legible.

He can hear the fire now, and the hallway walls are beginning to tremble. Fluorescent lights are starting to flare and dim, and the handle on the surgery door is hot to the touch. He listens at the vibrating door and smiles when he hears the familiar roar of an oxygen-fed fire. Getting really hot in there, he thinks, and it's going to get a whole lot hotter, especially when those altered nitrous-oxide bottles join the fun. The heavy plastic heads have been designed to melt through at only five hundred degrees and then release the flammable gas through a venturi nozzle that will feed the fire without exploding all at once. The bottles themselves have been designed to melt at one thousand degrees, which should happen about three to five minutes into the fire. By the time the fire department arrives, the humans in that room will have been reduced to carbonized goo. Something heavy goes down inside the burning surgery, so he grabs his bag, makes sure the doors to the office and records room are wide open, and then leaves through the clinic's back door. He walks around front, gets in his car, and drives off.

When he's two blocks away, he remembers what it was about the nurses and mutters an audible curse in German. The third nurse: the sexy brunette. Thirtysomething, the *Ammies* would call her. She hadn't been there tonight. But of course she had seen him previously, several times. She knew what he looked like *before* those Paki doctors had done their magic. And wasn't she the record keeper? He slows and pulls over in front of an apartment building, stops the car, turns out the lights, and tries to think. He should have noticed before this. And now he has a big loose end to attend to. The record keeper. *Damn!*

He sits there in the car, forcing his still-muddied brain to remember her name. Wall. Something Wall. Catherine? No. He instinctively turns his head when he hears sirens approaching up Kalorama Road. He leans sideways down into the front seat as the big engine set goes bawling by, its red and white strobes lighting up the inside of his car. The engine is pursued by a fire chief's car, its red dome light flashing. Another engine comes up the avenue a minute later. He looks at his watch. Alarm-system call, probably. But plenty of time for the gas-oxygen mix to have done its job.

But now he must make an important detour. One woman. Shouldn't be too hard, but still . . . He has her address in his computer. Sunday wasn't the first time he'd made a nocturnal visit to the clinic, courtesy of the nurses' sloppy security procedures. Just like every office he'd ever been in. Access codes written down in phone books. Keys and even spare keys on plainly visible hooks. He could go back to his apartment, look up the address, go there tonight even.

Another fire engine comes up Kalorama, preceded this time by a police car. Second alarm. Excellent. Big *hot* fire. The surgery and certainly the upstairs rooms, all fully engaged. The floor sagging. Those spare bottles puddling into nondescript slag. He waits for the fire engine to go by, checks both ways for police, and then pulls out. He goes one full block before remembering to turn his headlights back on. Damned anesthesia.

No, he decides. Not tonight. Of course he needs her dead, like the others, but he remembers the old Army maxim: If you want something bad, you'll probably get it bad.

No. He has seven weeks until *der Tag*. The big day. Plenty of time to set up one final incidental kill. He will do this correctly. Go there, do a proper reconnaissance; see precisely where she lives, get inside, see about alarms, neighbors, dogs—the usual. She doesn't know anything that can point to what's coming, and she certainly doesn't have his name. Assuming the records room and all its contents are destroyed, the only name that should survive the fire is the one planted deep in the metal record holder, along with the tantalizing but fragmentary transcript.

He brakes hard as some idiot Washington driver runs a red light and nearly broadsides him. He automatically looks to see if there's a police car, officers who might have seen the criminal, but of course there isn't one.

Because they're busy just now, he remembers with an icy smile. And soon, very soon, they'll really be busy.

* * *

Heismann, watching them argue, decided to go check out that car. Keeping low, he opened the big wooden door wide enough to slip out. Staying bent over, he went right, away from the back porch light, and then down the driveway to where her car was. He crouched beside it on the side away from the house, then crept over to the driver's side of the man's car. The engine was still making ticking noises as it cooled in the night air. It was a large four-door sedan. He checked the house, but the front windows were still dark. He looked inside the car and saw a radio handset and a small console below the dashboard. He looked through the back window and could see the radio antenna embedded in the glass, but there was another one, a stubby wire antenna sticking up out of the trunk. He slipped behind the car and checked the plate. District plate, but no sign of government decals. He examined the taillights and saw the extra lens for a white or blue strobe light.

Very well, then. Police.

He went up to the grille to confirm that, ran his fingers along the warm plastic louvers, where he found another pair of recessed strobe lights. Definitely police.

Talking to the nurse about what? Their sex life? Or that doctored medical file he'd left behind at the clinic?

If this was about the bait, what would the policeman do?

Demand that she come in, tell all she knew about the clinic, the patients, especially the patient in that record? Federal agents, now police. Weeks after the fire. Surely they did not suspect her of starting the fire. So this had to be about something else. Something that would concern the sole survivor.

It had to be the bait.

He took a deep breath of cold night air, stood up, and then began moving back to the garage. It was too soon. Much too soon. The deception plan had been designed to play out in two stages. The first was to drop an indication that a patient at the clinic, whose name was unknown, was planning to bomb the Union State speech. That had been the point of leaving the fake record behind at the scene of the fire, in such a way as to ensure that it would survive the fire. By mentioning the Union State speech, they had established the wrong target, and, more importantly, the wrong time line. As long as everyone in the night crew died in the fire, stage one would initially be all they had. But for whatever reason, this nurse had survived. His reaction to that unexpected development had been to drop the second critical piece of information into the investigation, but Mutaib had scotched that idea. Told him to kill her.

Now federal police, and even a city policeman, were talking to her all of a sudden, weeks after the fire. The nurse might inadvertently compromise the timing of the second stage of the deception, which involved getting the *Ammies* to focus on that last name in the transcript's Nazi pantheon, Heismann. They'd need a description, and Interpol, which had a file on Heismann, would give them one. The trick was that his Interpol description no longer pertained, not after a year of cosmetic surgery. At the beginning of their search, they wouldn't know that. And they would also think they had some time, because stage one had pointed them at the Union State speech.

But everything depended on their being unaware, at least for a while, that he had a totally new physical identity. With all these policemen suddenly converging on his loose end, there was now a distinct chance that this damned woman could reveal that one crucial bit of information much too soon.

Mutaib was right. And he had already failed once to do what he had promised to do.

He would have to take her now. Tonight. Direct action. No more delay.

He'd tested the car's doors, but they had been locked. A security light had been blinking out its warning on the dashboard. Besides, he'd brought no tools, other than a small flashlight, the minibinocs, and his trusty Walther. So improvise. Do something to bring the policeman out into the backyard. But what? Shoot him? No. Too drastic. The hue and cry would be tremendous. Something else. He had to disable the policeman, not kill him. Unless, of course, the policeman himself forced the issue. But the policeman wasn't the objective; it was that damned woman he needed to silence.

He scuttled back up the driveway and into the garage again, swinging the big doors almost shut behind him. Looking through the crack, he could see that they were still in the dining room, talking, faces frowning, the policeman up now, walking around, agitated, although not shouting. Not an argument, more like a serious discussion. He needed to get that man out into the backyard, away from the woman. Disable the policeman, then disable and grab the woman, take her down the hill, drown her in the creek, and stuff her body under a rock. "Disappear her," as the Argentine secret police liked to say. *Desaparecidos*. Wonderful expression, that. Those Argies were German-trained, too. By real Germans. Back when Germany commanded some respect in the world. Not like now.

He looked around the garage for something to use to set up a trap. A wire of some kind. Something that would ensnare the policeman if he came running out. He spotted the band saw. It gave him an idea.

He checked back to see where they were. They were still visible in the window and still talking. He moved to the band saw and used a bench brush to wipe off all the cobwebs. He felt the band blade—a flexible steel ribbon of serrated teeth

one-quarter of an inch wide and about two and a half feet
long. Times two: The band would be almost five feet. That
would do. He unscrewed the wing nuts that held the housing
cover and pulled it off, revealing the pulley wheels and the
tensioning latch. He rotated the latch and the band sagged
off the steel pulleys. He undid the bottom cover and removed the entire band. The teeth were still sharp and spiked
his hands, even through his gloves. He laid the band on the
workbench and searched for metal cutters, which he found
on a Peg-Board wall. He cut the band, ducking his head
when it snapped back into one flat ribbon of teeth and then
flipped like a live thing down onto the floor.

He went back to the crack and looked out. She was still
sitting there, head in hands now, while a shadow was visible
moving around the kitchen. He went back and retrieved the
glistening band, then spotted a miter box, its short, hard-
backed, fine-toothed saw gathering webs on the bench. Perfect. Now all he needed was something large to throw
through that dining room window. He looked around and
spotted the vise.

"How much money we talking about?" Cat asked from the
kitchen, where he was refilling his coffee cup.

"They paid eighty, base pay," she replied. "Plus overtime
for day work, and benefits. The bonus I reported was five
grand; the cash bonus was twenty." She was getting tired of
this. She was suddenly ready for him to leave, go see his
goddamned kid.

"Wow. And you invested all that?"

"Most of it. My broker, God bless her, pulled me out in
early 2001, and we slapped it all in grade A, six and half
percent tax-exempt munis. Everything."

"Those guys must have been making a fortune," he said.
"And you've got what—a couple hundred large working for
you, tax-free? Nice."

She had a lot more than that, but he didn't need to know.
Not now. "The IRS probably won't think so," she said. "An-

other reason I don't want to go front and center with the Treasury Department."

He sat back down at the table. "I'll tell you what, Con. I think with the right shyster, you could get immunity from all that tax shit if you were willing to lay it out, everything that was going on at that clinic. You might have to pay some back taxes, but that would be negotiable. Your info is too valuable. Foreigners getting ID changes right here in Washington? Shit. Those DHS people would go nuts for that."

"And what if they lock me up?" she said, chewing a nail. "After nine eleven, they rounded up a shitload of people, and some of them are still in jail, no charges filed, no bond, no lawyers. Hitler would feel at home here these days."

He laughed. "No way. Hitler kept it simple—just the gestapo. We've still got eighty odd law-enforcement outfits here in D.C. alone, the DHS not withstanding. It's like this Morgan guy—him and his Office of Special Investigations. That should be Bureau work."

"How's about I do an anonymous tip? Write something up, drop it into the system. Or I can give it to you—you can say you developed it from a confidential informant as part of this arson investigation."

He grunted sympathetically. "Like they wouldn't know who that was? With one person surviving the fire? C'mon, Con."

She screamed as something large crashed through the dining room window, landed on the table, and knocked her computer monitor right onto the floor, where its glass face exploded in a puff of arcing white smoke. Still frozen to her chair, she stared at the billowing curtains, stunned to see a face, a horrible face, pop up into view for a split second and then disappear. She heard Cat yell, "Hey!" and then he was running into the kitchen, trying to snag his gun out of his hip holster. She willed herself to get up, to get out of that room, trying not to step on all the glass or breathe the noxious cloud of phosphorous smoke hovering above the ruined monitor. That face—something about it. It had been all eyes and teeth, as if illuminated from below. How was that possible? She heard the back screen door open and then bang shut. And then came a strange strangling noise and then a huge thump as something—Cat?—went down in a heap on the back steps.

She snatched up the phone and dialed 911 as she backed into the living room, feeling almost naked in the light, those curtains blowing in and that ominous silence outside. The phone rang and rang and rang, but no operator picked up. Goddamned District of Columbia! She hung it up and redialed, this time getting a busy signal. She swore out loud and redialed one more time, the cord stretching all the way out now. Ringing. Then she heard footsteps coming toward the back of the house. Cat? Or that face? She was terrified to go out there, but then she remembered the derringer in her pocket. The operator came on just as she pulled the heavy little gun out of her jeans, nearly dropping the phone.

"Nine one one. What is your emergency?"

She froze again. What *was* her emergency? The footsteps were still coming, and they didn't sound like Cat's.

"Murder!" she said, blurting out the one word that ought to move their asses right along. "Help me, please." And then she dropped the phone and backed into the living room, where the lights were off, as the footsteps came up onto the back porch and she heard the screen door open slowly, then bump closed. She could just hear the 911 operator saying hello several times from the handset down on the floor. They would have caller ID, and that would give them the address. But right now, she had bigger problems, for she saw the lights in the kitchen switch off, followed by those in the dining room. Definitely not Cat.

She shuffled as quietly as she could backward across the living room carpet until she felt the couch behind her legs. Realizing she was silhouetted against the dim light coming in through the front window drapes from the street, she slipped behind an upholstered chair and squatted down. The house was silent except for the noises of the wind moving the front bushes around. She held the derringer in both hands, then remembered it wasn't cocked. The two diminutive side-by-side hammers were still down on the receiver. She heard a sound in the dining room, then another.

He was coming.

His shoes were crunching through the bits of glass from the monitor. And where the hell was Cat? She folded the derringer into her belly to mask the sound and thumbed back the two hammers. She sat fully down on the floor, her back against the wall radiator, and brought the gun up. She froze, barely breathing. Let him find me. Cat had told her the effective range of the derringer was arm's length. Okay, that's where I've got it, she thought.

She heard a small noise and what sounded like a grunt of effort, and then one of the table lamps came flying over the chair and into the front window, breaking out the glass and dropping heavily on her right shoulder. She nearly dropped the gun and had to bite her lip to keep from crying out. Where are the fucking cops? she wondered. Where is Cat? And then the man was right there, pulling the chair away, towering over her, that same face, a familiar face, something in his hand, a hammer coming down in a wicked strike at her head.

She rolled to the left, toward the hallway, aimed upward, and pulled both triggers on the derringer. Two rapid-fire blasts banged the palm of her hand and she heard him yell and stumble backward, colliding with some piece of furniture. She didn't hesitate. She scrambled away from the overturned chair, rolled into the front hall, got up, and ran as fast as she could straight out the back door, where she promptly tripped over the inert form of Cat Ballard, who groaned when she hit him. Her arms windmilling, she whacked her shoulder as she hit the railing on the back porch and slipped in something wet. She sat down abruptly on the top step, then went bumping right down the steps on her backside and hit the cold concrete of the sidewalk on all fours, her hands covered in—blood?

Cat's blood?

She heard footsteps again, this time from inside the house, thumping heavily down the front hall toward the kitchen, sounding like a drunk trying to run. She saw Cat's gun lying at the bottom of the steps and reached forward to grab it as a form filled the kitchen doorway, just inside the screen.

She raised the gun and tried to pull the trigger, but her bloody, trembling hands slipped on the butt and she dropped the gun. As she lunged to retrieve it, she heard the man laugh, and then the screen door was opening and he was silhouetted in the kitchen light, shooting at her, stars of red flame blossoming in the doorway as steel hornets slashed the air by her cheeks. She screamed and began rolling across the yard, barely conscious of bullets hammering the concrete and tearing up chunks of dead grass all around her as she kept rolling, rolling, and then she was into the cedars, Cat's bloody gun still clutched in her hand. She tumbled through the dense green branches, got up, and ran straight down the hill, bushes and branches whipping her face. She was falling forward as much as she was running, caroming off small tree trunks in the darkness, until she twisted an ankle when she finally reached flat ground. She went down with a yelp, then stopped to listen.

She got up, hopping on one leg, rubbing the throbbing ankle, trying to hush her screaming lungs, her heart pounding so hard in her ears that he *had* to be able to hear it. She listened for signs of somebody coming down the hill after her, and then she could hear sirens, so she slumped back against a tree and tried not to cry. The creek was right below her, and, even in the cold, she thought about sliding down the huge boulders into that black water, if only to get that sticky mess off her hands.

He lunged out of the darkness and tackled her, sweeping her sideways and down, grabbing for her mouth with one hand while she fought, twisted, bit, and tried to shout, but he was too strong, one iron arm encircling her chest and squeezing the breath right out of her. She thought she felt Cat's gun under her knee, but she couldn't reach it. Then he lost his balance for an instant and came lunging over the top of her, giving her one glorious free shot at his crotch, which she took, kicking out with every ounce of her strength. And then he was off of her, curling into a retching ball that went sliding down the stone banks of the creek and into the water. She patted the ground for Cat's gun, found it, and crawled to the edge of the rocks, looking down, determined now, waiting for him to surface, ready to kill him, to empty that thing at him in the water. But he didn't surface. There was only the sound of the creek, running high in winter, rushing over all the rocks. Rock Creek, that's why they called it that, she thought as her adrenaline began to crash and she slowly lowered the gun.

She heard voices shouting above her on the bluff and saw blue lights flickering through the cedars. Walking backward up the hill, she kept the gun pointed down the slope, waiting for him to show himself again. She trudged back up the slope the way she'd come, step by step, the backs of her shoes filling with bits of soft dirt and mud. When she neared the top, she stopped, out of breath, her ankle pounding, her ribs sore from grappling with her attacker. She could hear men shouting, doors banging, other vehicles arriving. Then she heard an authoritative voice shouting, "What've we got, Larry?" And another man—Larry, she guessed—answered in an excited voice: "You're not gonna believe this, Cap, but it looks like Cat's punch cut his throat and then shagged ass. That's his car, and that's her car. We need some fucking dogs back here.

She froze in the cedars. Cut his throat? Sweet Jesus! And they thought *she* did it? She started to push forward, out of the cedars, determined to clear that shit right up, but then stopped in her tracks. She didn't recognize any of those voices, and she knew most of the guys on the District Homicide squad. Could she clear this up? She felt the sticky mess on her hands, Cat's blood. She hefted Cat's gun. What would that look like to a bunch of cops who were cranking up a cop-killer frenzy out there? And the guy who'd busted into her house? Where was he?

Instinctively, she backed down the hill again, watching the bluffs this time, waiting to see if someone would come through the trees, or turn loose a pack of tracking dogs. Surely the evidence in the house would reveal—what, exactly? Two broken windows. Overturned furniture. A struggle in the living room. She thought she had hit him with the .45, but then he'd come right back after her. So there'd be bullet holes in the ceiling, right? Proof that she had—what? *They'd* had a lovers' quarrel, which had escalated into a *shooting*? The derringer was still up there, with her prints all over it.

God! She needed time to think, and also time for them to go through the house, see the evidence, put it together. She knew cops. In this situation, if one of them spotted her right now, he'd probably start shooting.

And Cat: The bastard had cut his throat? Shit, shit, *shit*! Poor Cat. And now their private thing would erupt into public view. Lynn and the kids would be dragged into a media circus when the truth came out. What had that cop Larry just called her—Cat's *punch*? These were strangers, and they *knew*?

She reached the bottom again, backed into a tree, and stopped, aware now that she was back in Injun country. Had that bastard climbed back out of the creek? Was he out there in the woods now, ahead of her, waiting for her again? She shivered, both from the cold and the memory of how he'd come out of the bushes like some blood-crazed bear. She tried to remember his face, but there hadn't really been one. She began to make her way slowly north, paralleling the creek as she went upstream as quietly as she could, keeping just out of sight of the water, conscious of the rising commotion up on the bluffs: more cars, more lights, radios on external vehicle speakers.

She needed time to think. Which meant she had to get away, at least for tonight. But she had no car, no purse, no ID, no money, and no coat. And it wasn't like she could go back to the house just now, not with dogs coming. She was reasonably at home in the woods, but she had always been afraid of dogs. Especially in packs. She squeezed her sticky fingers together. Dogs would find her, too, no sweat.

The evergreen undergrowth closed around her in the darkness, but she kept going, pushing pungent pine branches out of her face while trying to make no noise, half-expecting to see that lunging form again each time she pushed a branch aside. She held Cat's gun in her right hand, and the butt was sticking to her palm now. Peering ahead, she saw a flare of headlights through the underbrush as a car came down Tilden Road and rumbled across the stone bridge at the base of the hill before disappearing into the park.

She needed to get the hell out of here. She had to go to ground somewhere, somehow. No: She had to get a car.